Abha Dawesar

babyji

Abha Dawesar was born in 1974 in New Delhi,
India, and graduated with honors from Harvard
University. She was awarded a New York Foundation for the Arts fiction fellowship and is the
author of the novel *Miniplanner*. She lives in
New York and can be reached on her Web site
www.abhadawesar.com.

Also by Abha Dawesar

Miniplanner

babyji

babyji

a novel

Abha Dawesar

Anchor Books
A Division of Random House, Inc.
New York

AN ANCHOR BOOKS ORIGINAL, FEBRUARY 2005

Copyright © 2005 by Abha Dawesar

Library of Congress Cataloging-in-Publication Data
Dawesar, Abha.
Babyji : a novel / Abha Dawesar.
p.   cm.
ISBN 1-4000-3456-6 (pbk.)
1. Teenage girls—Fiction.   2. India—Fiction.   I. Title.
PS3554.A9423B33 2004
813'.6—dc22   2004048615

www.anchorbooks.com

Printed in the United States of America
10 9 8 7 6 5 4 3 2

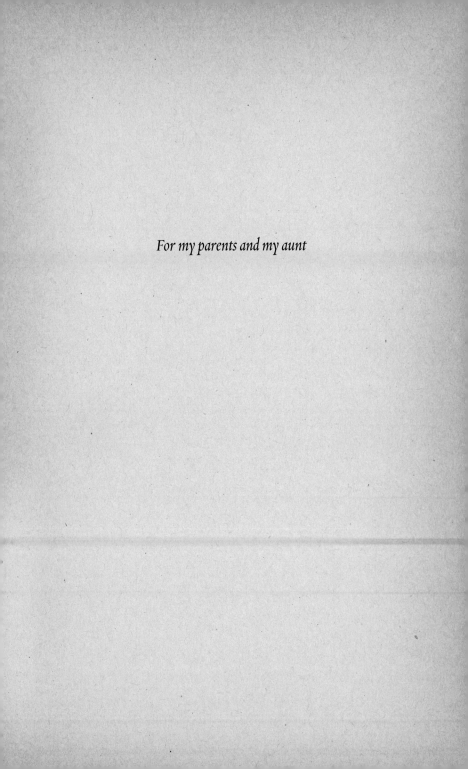

For my parents and my aunt

Contents

babyji

Unbuttoning Lady X

Delhi is a city where things happen undercover. A city where the horizon is blanketed with particulate pollution and the days are hot. A city with no romance but a lot of passion. You ask how passion without romance is possible? The same way sex without a nightlife is possible. Delhi churns slowly, secretively. What emerges is urgency.

In the Delhi I grew up in, everything happened. Married women fell in love with pubescent girls, boys climbed up sewage pipes to consort with their neighbors' wives, and students went down on their science teachers in the lab. But no one ever talked about it.

I used to be innocent, driven solely by the ambition to do something great for my country, something that involved physics. My knowledge of the facts of life was based entirely on books, and clean ones at that. I read nineteenth-century classics by George Eliot and Emily Brontë. These books never went into any details. To remedy this I decided to read Vatsyayana's *Kamasutra*. I had to do this while standing in the scooter garage, which had been converted into a storeroom. I would sneak out with a flashlight after my parents had gone to sleep. The *Kamasutra* that I force-fed myself seemed completely of another world, alien and absurd. After I read it, however, magical things started to happen. In particular, I met a woman. We first met in my school. She had come to attend the parent-teacher meeting. I was the Head Prefect.

"Where are the teachers for Class I?" she asked.

"In the Pushkin Block, ma'am," I replied.

I was susceptible at that age. I had been reading *The Citadel* by A. J. Cronin, in which the main female character was described as particularly handsome. I fancied for a moment that she was that handsome woman.

"I'll take you there, ma'am," I offered.

"What's your name?"

"Anamika," I replied.

"I like your tie," she said.

"Oh." I tugged and fiddled with my polyester number while we walked, suddenly conscious of the ridiculous figure I must cut in my school uniform of red socks and shirtsleeves. Like most schools, mine had a strict dress code. The girls wore gray box-pleated skirts. Boys up to the age of fourteen wore knickers. Everyone wore a striped red and silver tie except for the Prefects. We wore a silver and blue one.

I hated the ageism of Delhi and its antediluvian norms, which required you to address anyone older as *Uncleji* or *Auntyji* and anyone younger with diminutives. It precluded serious bonding with people older than you. I did not have the courage to ask this woman her name. She was of another generation; that sort of thing was just not done.

After I left her in front of the Pushkin Block, I felt my heart overflow with some kind of knowledge I could not immediately identify. I had imagined so many times how Newton must have felt when the apple dropped on his head and the weight of gravitational forces clicked into place. I fancied I felt that way, that a great discovery had just been made and all I had to do was write down its formula. I wished a simple object like an apple had been involved, something tangible that I could contemplate and hold, smell and bite.

I felt the urge to call her something. Something that no one else was called. A word that was not a name and that was still proportional to the immensity of the revelation unfolding within me. "India" was the first thing that slipped silently from my lips.

I hung around that part of campus so I could catch her on the way out. Eventually she emerged from the same doors that had earlier swallowed her. I pretended to look elsewhere. She came up behind me and tapped my shoulder.

"Do you like this school? I am thinking of putting my son in it," she said.

"Yes. Extracurricular activities are encouraged. We have horse riding."

"Do you know how to ride?"

"Yes, I've done it since Class II."

"I've always wanted to ride horses. But with so many extracurriculars, will you still do well on the board exams?" she asked.

"I probably will. I love to study."

"You'll do well no matter. You are obviously exceptional." She looked at the Head Prefect badge on my left breast pocket and smiled.

I shrugged. I was embarrassed but didn't want to show it.

"I have to go now. Drop by if you want to chat. Ride your bike over."

"How do you know I have a bike?"

"I've seen you bike around. I live in B-63. Come for a cold coffee on Saturday morning."

"All right."

"That's tomorrow," she said, squeezing my hand, and left.

I couldn't place her. Indians, myself included, must immediately place everyone we meet. We are a nation of taxonomists. It must be in our genes because of the caste system. There are categories for everything—educated or not, foreign car or not, *brahmin* or *banya* or what, English-speaking or not, meat-eating or not, if vegetarian then whether an eggitarian or strict, if strict then too strict to eat Western desserts with egg or not. All this in the case of women helps predict whether they might be led astray. In the case of men, whether they will misbehave with women given half a chance, take bribes, support their parents in old age, and on and on.

The system works. It is a science, thousands of years old, that has been taken to the level of a fine art. I often scorned it, but if

I had to put my hand on my heart I'd have to admit that I operated by it. It was natural for me to classify people at first sight without even being aware of it. Love happens on the edges. It happens when one can't place someone; so does hate. India was an enigma. And correspondingly rife with possibility, rich in her meanings and bountiful.

That evening was like most other Friday evenings. I went with my parents to a dinner party. The ladies all sat in one section of the living room and the gents in the other. Thanks to my age I could mill around both groups. No other kids were present. My parents often took me with them to social occasions. Over the years I'd gotten used to the company of people much older than myself.

"Do you know a good servant? Mine is going on leave for a month," lady A said.

"Mine is giving trouble," lady B chimed in.

"Servants these days, I tell you," added lady C.

I walked over to the other side where the men were discussing the India and Pakistan cricket match. I have nothing against sports, but men with thickening waists and a couple of artificial valves in their hearts discussing a five-day test match are not the most spectacular company. I went back to the women and decided to entertain myself. They were all wearing saris, their ample midriffs gathering around the folds of their waists, the shapelessness of their backs clearly visible. I visualized them minus their small, tight blouses. One of the reasons for the accuracy of the classification system is that its criteria are always spur of the moment and can be tailored to fit the occasion. Each situation generates its own classification. For example, the most obvious question to ask when you unbutton an Indian woman's blouse is whether she waxes her underarms. There are other less interesting ones, like what sort of bra she is wearing. This second question is not intrinsically uninteresting, but at that time there was just one company that made quality undergarments for women, and it made only five designs.

I was able to classify most of the women at first glance. One woman, let's call her lady X, was difficult to place. I unbuttoned her blouse several times in my head and tried imagining the two scenarios—waxed or not. Each seemed equally likely. I observed her closely for more clues.

If a woman doesn't wax her underarms, it's either because she's terribly old-fashioned, or terribly postmodern. I couldn't tell if lady X was a radical feminist. I was certain she wasn't old-fashioned. If a woman does wax her underarms she might be very hip or just middle-class in her mentality. If I could get her type down I'd know which parts of her body she depilated. Or if I knew which parts she depilated I could get her type down.

The hostess announced dinner while I was busy unbuttoning lady X. I took the general movement around the room as an opportunity to strike up a conversation with her. In a minute I discovered that she read no books, went to the beauty parlor for pedicures, and didn't work. I lost interest in her. The inquiry was complete. She did indeed wax and was predictably bourgeois.

I wondered about India, but the idea of unbuttoning her blouse filled me with such turmoil that I abandoned the half thought to the *samosas* on my plate.

Cycling on Saturday

Before leaving for India's house the next morning, I agonized about what to wear. A lot of my clothes were still young and girlie. I chose my red striped boys' shirt and jeans. I wore black boys' shoes, slapped some Old Spice on my neck from my father's toilette, and rode my bicycle over. I went at ten since she hadn't told me when to come. Nine seemed too early for a Saturday. My stomach was knotted, and my back felt very tight.

India was beautiful, and she was waiting for me. My tongue was jammed in my throat. This made polite conversation somewhat inconvenient. When she offered to make me a frothy coffee shake, I followed her into the kitchen and got ice cubes from the fridge on her orders. We took our tall glasses of cold coffee and went to the veranda in the rear of her house. I sat on the cemented ground at her feet, my shoulders leaning against the legs of her cane garden chair. I was afraid of turning around and meeting her gaze. I was embarrassed by the thoughts I had had about her the previous night. It didn't matter that I had unbuttoned all the other women's blouses; only with India was there something indecent about it.

We talked about my school and her son for a while. I had not discussed anything in this fashion with a grown-up before. My parents, their friends, and my teachers treated me like a kid, albeit a mature one. India was talking to me like I was an adult.

"Where is your son?" I asked.

"Till I can arrange for him to change schools, he's going to be with his dad."

She was divorced, and we were alone. Both facts made me unreasonably excited.

"How long can you stay?" she asked.

"About an hour," I said. I routinely went cycling for an hour on Saturday. If I stayed longer my mother would definitely ask me where I had been.

India lit a cigarette and started to smoke. I didn't know any women who smoked. I had seen women from the *jhuggis* smoke *bidis*, and once at a very snobbish party that one of my father's work contacts had invited us to, a few women had been smoking. We sat quietly while India smoked. When she was finished she threw the cigarette stub by her foot and crushed it.

"You have such thick hair," she said, running her hand through it. My hair was out of control and, according to Sheela, a girl in my class, Jimi Hendrix–like. I had to wash it every day so it wouldn't get knotted. As soon as it grew down to my shoulders, the curls would take on a life of their own, and I would have to trim it.

"Want me to put oil in your hair?" she asked.

I personally could not stand the idea of scented coconut oil dribbling down my scalp. The advertisements on TV for Parachute coconut oil were aimed at the likes of lady X. But I did not want to say no to India. Not ever and not for anything.

"We're having problems with our water supply, and I won't be able to wash it off," I said. Then without thinking I said, "But I could put oil in your hair."

"That would be lovely," she said. I realized I had made a smooth move.

We went into her bedroom. She put oil in a small steel bowl and lay down on the bed with a towel under her head. As I massaged the oil into her black tresses, she let out little ooh-aahs of pleasure. I got absorbed in her glistening skin and in the way my fingers slid easily because of the oil. After her hair had soaked up the fluid I massaged the base of her neck.

"An hour is up. I don't want you to be late. Your mother will worry," she said.

I brushed my forefinger on her neck one last time and got up. She walked me to her gate, where we stood in an uncomfortable silence. I wanted to hug her, but my heart was making embarrassing noises, and if I moved closer I was sure that she would hear them.

"I hope you'll come again," she said.

I was taken aback by her formality. I mounted my bike and put my foot on the pedal.

"Next Saturday, come early," she said, patting the steel carrier behind the seat of my bike. Without turning around I made an affirmative noise in my throat. Then I pedaled away furiously.

After I turned the corner I slowed down. I was not ready to go home. Between India's house and mine there was a vacant plot of land where a building was under construction. The workers had built *jhuggis* on one end of the site. They lived there with their children. I decided to take a shortcut and ride my bike through this stretch to avoid the main road. One section of the plot was empty. I thought I'd be able to avoid the *jhuggis* and the workers. A good three-fourths of the way through I noticed a woman squatting behind a bush, no doubt taking a pee. I got off my bike and stood still. I didn't want to ride behind her and scare her. I tried to look away but couldn't. I watched her peeing from the corner of my eye. Her sari was hitched up, and her ankles were visible.

After a few seconds the woman got up, turned around, and saw me. Her skin was dark from being exposed to the sun all day. A fiery red line of *sindhoor* adorned the parting of her hair, indicating that she was married. She stared at me, and then in an exaggerated gesture she turned, lifted her sari all the way up to her bare ass, and jiggled her backside. I thought she was trying to spite me for having stared at her, but then she turned back around, looked me in the eye, and walked away.

It was fantastic. My image of lower-class women was that they were even more conservative than educated middle-class women. First the encounter with India and now this. I had yet to turn seventeen. It seemed to me that I was on the edge of a major

breakthrough with India. Plus, a random woman had chosen to
moon me. My legs felt unsteady. I pushed my bike the rest of the
way home. I spent the day feeling restless. I thought about India
and about the other woman's dark skin and bloodred *sindhoor*.

In the evening, when I went to get air pumped into my bicycle tires, I rode past the construction site and glanced around
discreetly. She wasn't there. How could I think about a woman
living in a slum? I had been taught that the lower classes were
unclean. A lot of the women had lice in their hair. I could not
think of the *jhuggi* woman again. It was true that the lower castes
suffered and that one should be kind to them. But one helped
them from a distance. One helped them because one was of a
higher station. My mother worked as a clerk in a bank and my
father in the Ministry of Water Works. We were a middle-class
family. My parents worked hard to send me to a decent school,
but we couldn't afford a car or a trip abroad. My father went to
work on a Vespa scooter every day. He would drive with his
lunch in a large steel carrier between his feet. If the three of us
had to go out together, we always had to take an autorikshaw.
We could not act like the rich or the poor. The rich had no
morals and the poor could not have morals, they didn't even
have food. The middle classes were responsible for the moral
fiber of society. I came home feeling guilty. My mother was in
the kitchen washing rice for dinner.

"Are you all right? You seem moody," she said.

"Yes, fine. Just worried about the physics test on Monday."

I left the kitchen and went to my room. My physics textbook
was over a thousand pages. Anyone who was expected to understand differential and integral calculus and the derivation of formulae on centrifugal force should be allowed to have affairs, I
thought. A lurid image of a young man pulling up the sari of the
woman in the slum danced on the dense black text of my physics
book. I decided I would avenge myself by holding hands and
flirting with girls since Indian society was so holier-than-thou
about having boyfriends. I had never wanted a boyfriend anyway.

Soon my mother called me to dinner. At the table my father

talked endlessly about the importance of doing well in my studies. I could tell Mom was tired of hearing him lecture me every
day. I did well at school; his harangues were uncalled-for.

Changing the topic, my mother said, "A woman came here
looking for a job. Since Neeta is so unpredictable I decided I'd
hire this new woman. She said she won't take a single day off."

I liked Neeta. She smiled a lot and had long black hair. She
called me *"Choti Memsahib,"* or "little mistress."

"You didn't even give Neeta any warning. That's not right," I
said, getting emotional.

"Oh please! She's been asking for it. I like her, too, but she's
been increasingly casual about showing up."

I swallowed my dinner. I could feel tears well up in my eyes.

"This new woman will start on Monday. She'll come when
you return from school. Just supervise her closely for the first
week till we are sure about her," my mother said.

"Yes, Mom," I said as I went back to my room. I couldn't
understand myself. I didn't really care all that much for Neeta,
but I was still overwhelmed with emotion. My parents con-
trolled everything. I wished I could just go and meet India and
hang out with her in the middle of the night. I wished the
woman from the slum were at my beck and call. Images from
Hindi art movies in which the upper caste *brahmin* falls in love
with the lower caste servant and has passionate sex with her kept
whirring in my head. I wanted to fast-forward my life.

iii

The Physics of Fun

On Sunday I plunged into my books. I solved every problem at the end of the thermodynamics chapter and read my class notes from the intro to quantum mechanics chapter. On Monday I couldn't gauge if I had done well on the test, but I thought I had passed. I was so exhausted that I couldn't pay any attention to classes the rest of the day. When I got home I didn't even change from my school skirt. I unclasped my belt and tumbled onto my bed. Then I heard the bell ring. I thought it was part of my dream so I didn't move. But it kept ringing.

The woman from the slum was standing at the front door. The woman with the hitched sari. I could practically see her peeing, the memory was so vivid.

"You?" I said.

She looked at my skirt and gasped.

"I thought you were a boy," she said in Hindi. I didn't respond.

"*Didi,*" she said, addressing me as older sister even though she was clearly older.

"What?" I asked in Hindi.

"I've come to work, *Babyji,*" she replied. Was I a baby or a *Didi*? *Babyji* was such a contradiction in terms, conveying too much respect that the age of a child doesn't warrant.

"You're the new servant?" I asked, stepping aside to let her in. I was flattered she had thought me a boy.

"Yes," she said, hiding a smile and lowering her eyes. I wondered if she had followed me from the construction site, but I kept silent.

She was wearing her sari low on her hips. Her hair looked freshly washed. She sat under the sink in the kitchen where there was a water faucet and began to wash all the utensils that were piled up. I never understood why servants preferred to squat while cleaning vessels. If I ever did the dishes at home I did them standing up and using the faucet in the sink. I perched myself on a ledge in the kitchen and stared at her, my legs dangling down. Every now and then she looked directly into my eyes. When she did that I couldn't hold up to her fierce stare and would have to lower my eyes. After she was finished washing the vessels, she asked if there was anything else.

"No, I don't think so."

"I can massage your legs. They will become strong for when you cycle," she said.

"All right," I said. She had acknowledged that she had seen me cycling.

I went to my bathroom and got some lotion. Then I lay down on my stomach. I heard her rub the lotion on her hands. The sound of her hands rubbing was powerful. It was as if she were in charge or a decision were being made. My father usually rubbed his hands together when he was trying to make up his mind about which unit trusts to buy. Sleazy men in Hindi films rubbed their hands when they hatched a plot. Dr. Iyer rubbed his a second before giving you the prognosis. I was thinking all these things in my head when she lifted my skirt all the way up past my underwear, gripped my left leg firmly, and started to massage it. Involuntarily, my legs went taut. Her hands were a little rough but strong, and after a few minutes my body started to relax. The sensation of her hands taking over my flesh, kneading it, stretching it, and squeezing it was comforting. When she was done I walked her to the door and shut it behind her without saying anything.

I had always expected that something would happen in my life, something that would change it. After I'd reached puberty I

was a twinge disappointed that almost everything continued as
before. But now it seemed as if the wait were finally over. I
wasn't sure what exactly was going to happen or what it would
mean, but I was being propelled by a force no one could temper.
I was experiencing things that I was sure my friends Vidur,
Ashima, Sheela, Preeti, Deepa, Sonali, and Tina had not experienced. In fact, my momentum was such that I was almost certain
the class hoodlum, Chakra Dev, who was taller and more physically developed than any of the other boys, was soon going to be
left far behind. I was suddenly ahead of everyone. More grown-
up. I looked forward to coming home from school the next day
and the servant woman showing up. I didn't know her name. I'd
imagine the dramatic red *sindhoor* in the parting of her hair when
I thought of her.

In the evenings she would come around seven and cook dinner under my mother's instructions. While we ate she would
bring us hot *rotis* from the kitchen. I would ignore her. When we
were finished she would eat the leftovers. My mother had given
her Neeta's plate and glass.

The whole week went by with the servant massaging my legs.
She made a point of looking into my eyes without blinking. She
stared at the chasm that separated my higher birth from her
lower one and hopped right over it, even though she called me
Didi every now and then and addressed me as one would a better. At night I would lie awake, suspending the harsh reality of
being sixteen and a flimsy female with no money to my name,
and imagine that I was the man from the movies. I wanted
wealth, power, or fame, something that would help me to get the
things that the rules of the world did not permit.

On Saturday I went over to India's house again. I felt bold. I
had spent so much time thinking of myself as the man from the
movies that I felt I had already lived his experiences. I rode over
on my bike thinking myself a stud, a man of the world.

"I wasn't sure you'd come," she said, breaking into a smile.

I parked my bike in her garden and leaned forward to hug her.

It felt natural to hug her. She kissed me on the cheek and ran her hand through my hair.

Once inside the dark curtained coolness of her air-conditioned home, I was at a loss for words. She spoke in her genteel way about this and that. I was waiting for something to happen. I felt as if we were wasting time. We had an hour and we'd already let forty-five minutes slip by discussing the power cuts in the colony and the syllabus for the first graders.

I wanted to tell her I loved her. I tried to say it suddenly. But as soon as the words came to the tip of my tongue my hands shook. I excused myself and went to the bathroom. I said to the face in the mirror, Look, she's going to laugh, she'll never want to see you again, what do you know about love? You're just sixteen. She sees a kid when she sees you.

"We have a new servant," I said to her when I stepped out of the bathroom.

"You do."

"She's really sexy." I watched India's face for her reaction.

"She is," India said. Her face registered no interest.

"I guess I should go home."

When India saw me to the door she said, "Come again." It was anticlimactic.

At home the servant was stooped over the kitchen sink doing the dishes. When she did the dishes in my presence she always squatted with her sari hitched halfway up, and I could see her legs. Her legs were covered now. My mother was calling her Rani, which means queen but is often the generic term people use for servants. She was saying, "Rani, scrub the vessels thoroughly." I felt a pang of tenderness and protection toward Rani.

Rani scrubbed the dishes harder and harder. Periodically she lifted her face to make eye contact with me. Her pride and fierceness bored through me. That night I dreamt that I called her "Rani" in a soft whisper and asked her to come away with me to a place where she would no longer be a servant.

On Sunday morning, like every Sunday, my parents read the

papers and watched TV for a few hours. We got all the daily
newspapers on Sunday and some weekly newspapers and magazines as well. I read an article in the color section of the *Sunday
Mail* about how AIDS was more dangerous than any other STD.
One Indian doctor who was interviewed said it was only a matter of time before it spread to India from the West. There was a
reference in the article to Rock Hudson having AIDS. I had
never heard of him, but the article said he surrounded himself
with beautiful boys. Nothing else in the papers was as interesting as the AIDS article. I was bored. I hated watching television,
so I considered riding my bike to India's house. The previous
day had left me with a sense of failure. Being with India had felt
less intimate than it had the week before. But I couldn't convince
myself that it would feel different if I saw her again. And to fail
two times in a row would be worse, so I let it pass.

I had another physics test the next morning. My school had
introduced a Monday test system, and we had a test in one subject every Monday. The physics teacher had taken this further
and added a test every Monday. So I had history and physics this
week. History was easy. One only needed to remember facts, not
comprehend them. When the history teacher spoke I imprinted
her words directly onto my brain like newsprint and regurgi-
tated them without effort. Physics was a major pain in the rear. I
hated it. I loved it. I lay down on my stomach, propping myself
up with my elbows, and solved problems on Heisenberg's uncertainty principle. I was up to my ears in quantum mechanics. It
was bad enough to have to know that a photon was both a particle and a wave. On top of that Mr. Garg said that it was impossible to simultaneously measure the position and the momentum
of atomic particles with any accuracy. And there was a single
constant that actually quantified the combined uncertainty in
position and speed. I sat around rewriting this constant all over
my notebook with little Greek symbols on the side. If modern
science accepted duality and measured uncertainties, what difference did it make whether I was Rock Hudson chasing beautiful

boys or the village *brahmin* in love with the *shudra*'s daughter? Science had told us this century that nothing was certain. The universe was chaotic and relative; these aspects measurable. There were few hard facts on which one could base a way of living one's life. I'd always scoffed at religion as a crutch for the masses, so it wasn't even a consideration. We'd spent two thousand years only to find out that we didn't know. That moment, sprawled on my bed, changed my whole life. I was free all of a sudden. Free of the burden of knowledge and therefore of any morality that proceeds from knowledge. Only feelings counted. And sensations.

I placed my head on my physics book and daydreamt. I had fantasies about India and Rani. I mixed them up in my head till Rani was articulate and well dressed and India sensuous and earthy. If particles could be waves and waves photons then India and Rani could be each other. All sense of reality escaped me. I couldn't believe I'd been living under my parents' regime all these years without even whimpering in protest. At dinner I ate quietly and in awareness of the fact that I was different. I was free. Nothing mattered.

My parents went to sleep early. After their light was out I went to the veranda in the rear of the house, unlocked the door to the service lane, and walked over to the slum near the construction site to look for Rani. I approached the *jhuggi* quietly. I didn't want to be seen. As I neared it I heard only male voices. The area was dark except for a few kerosene lamps flickering here and there. They cast menacing shadows. Men were squatting together in small groups and laughing. Their laughs sounded sinister. They spoke in some dialect, not in pure Hindi. I could not follow them. All the women were in their oppressive six-by-six hutments, putting their litters of children to sleep. I felt unsafe. I wanted to run before someone leapt at me in the dark. I stayed in the shadows and walked quickly but cautiously so that I would not make any sound. When I was standing out on the main street again I stopped to catch my breath. I was sweating.

It was already quite late, but I decided to call on India. The streets were quiet. Her building reverberated when I rang the doorbell.

I waited at the door for five minutes before she softly asked, "Who is it?"

"Anamika."

I heard her jerk the chain on the door. India stood in front of me wrapped in a sheet.

"What's the matter? Are you all right?" she asked, touching my head.

"I'm fine. Can I come in?"

"Are you all right? What's the matter?"

"Can I come in?" I repeated. I had no idea what I'd tell her.

"Of course," she said, stepping aside to let me in. Once I was inside she made her way to her room and flicked on her bedside lamp.

I couldn't tell what she was wearing under the white sheet. Nothing, it seemed to me. She sat down carefully on her bed, making sure the sheet didn't fall off. She sat with her head and shoulders propped against the wall.

"What's the matter?" she asked again. She was sitting uncomfortably straight.

"Nothing. Can I spend the night?"

"Here?"

"Yes."

"What happened? Where are your parents?"

For a second my inner voice squeaked, You're a teenager. She thinks you're a kid. But I stifled it and thought of the equation from my physics textbook, $p(q)$ = Planck's constant and reminded myself I was free.

"My parents are at home. I want to spend the night here," I said matter-of-factly.

She was quiet for a second. I could not even hear her breathe. I held my own breath, wondering what she would say. Maybe she would laugh at me. Then she shrugged her shoulders and said, "Okay." She turned off her bedside lamp.

I kicked off my shoes and got into her bed. I was at my wit's end. I hadn't expected this to happen at all. I should have planned. I lay down far away from her and shut my eyes tightly, repeating to myself that the world was entirely uncertain. Nothing was fixed.

"What are you wearing?" I asked her.

"Nothing."

The information was too much. My body stiffened.

"Should I wear something? Does it bother you?" she asked, as if trying to comfort a child who was throwing a tantrum.

"Not at all," I lied. I was afraid of moving and accidentally touching her. There was a naked woman right beside me. There was no uncertainty about that. It was now very hot under the covers. I was wearing my jeans and my thick denim shirt.

"Do you mind if I take off my jeans?" I asked as calmly as I could.

"I don't mind."

I stumbled out of bed and got my jeans off. Then I got back into bed.

"I wish you'd tell me what's going on. This is all rather sudden," she said.

"I know."

I was feeling a little foolish. I couldn't think of anything to say. I focused again on the wave-particle duality and remembered I was free. I had nothing to lose. If my parents found out I'd be toast anyway, regardless of what I did with India. If she got angry I could just leave. It was all about an instantaneous point in time since nothing was stable. I was never going to do this again.

"Can I touch you?" I asked.

"Huh?"

I didn't think India's reaction was what you'd expect from someone who was vigorously objecting. I decided she meant yes and slid closer to her. Then I tentatively took her hand in mine and waited for her to yell and scream and throw me out of her house. She didn't. I let the palm of my hand explore hers, then her wrist, her forearm, her shoulder. Eventually she touched my hand in response. Our toes were touching now, and our calves. Then our knees and hips touched. Then I lost my powers of observation.

"Your skin is like a baby's," she said.

"Yours, too."

We must have caressed for hours. I felt as if I was living outside of my body and outside of time. At some point we drifted off to sleep and then woke up, stirring only slightly before drifting off again. I couldn't tell if she had woken up first and touched me or if I'd woken up first and touched her. My hands needed to touch her so much they moved up and down her back, her stomach, and her arms without any intervention from me.

Drifting off, I dreamt that India and I were revolving around each other as particles and then suddenly transforming into waves, tides, currents. Mr. Garg had said something about the duality that I had not noted down. He had said that if you cross a donkey and a horse you get a mule. Is a mule a donkey or a horse? It's a stupid question was his point. Something about the comment jarred in my sleeping brain. Particles weren't becoming waves and waves, particles. These were just properties of photons, and I wasn't as free as I thought. In fact, the uncertainty of Heisenberg's equation only went to prove that one could even quantify uncertainty. How could I have possibly thought that I was free and simply walked out of my house at night? I couldn't tell my parents that I was at a divorcée's house spending the night. They'd ground me on holidays. I shook India awake.

"I have to leave before my parents wake up," I said, slipping on my jeans and shirt.

"Give me one last hug," she said.

I went over and embraced her.

"I'll come after school tomorrow," I said before leaving, my heart suddenly heavy.

I shut her main door quietly and walked home. There was not

a soul in sight. I got to the service lane of my house. The door opening onto the veranda was still open. I locked it and tiptoed across the veranda. The back door of the house was open, too. I shut it behind me and went to my bedroom. The alarm clock on my table showed five. Just in the nick of time I lay down on my bed, feeling relieved. My mother woke up early every day and made me tea before going to a yoga class at the community center. Some days she would spend time gardening, even though our garden was really only a small patch of grass not much bigger than a carpet.

At school I plowed through the history and physics tests in a stupor. In physics class Mr. Garg introduced Schrödinger's thought experiment and talked at length about a cat that could be either dead or alive till one actually decided to observe it. One's observation made a difference even though it shouldn't. If there was no objective truth I could be a prima donna.

At the end of the day I got home and collapsed on my bed. I decided I'd take a nap and then go to India's. When the doorbell rang I was jolted out of my sleep. I had forgotten about Rani. She was there to do the dishes, entice me. In her long black slithery plait she had woven a string of jasmine flowers. I knew she had dressed for me. I let her in. The sense of freedom that had overtaken me the previous night evaporated. I felt constricted by my choices now. Rani was right there, fresh and beautiful. I was supposed to visit India. It all had to be done before my mother got home. Discrete human beings and exact places were involved without any uncertainty. Time was limited. I had to revisit the Heisenberg chapter with a cool mind and reinterpret it.

"I'm going to take a nap. You can tell me when you're done with the cleaning," I said.

"Are you angry with me, *Babyji?*" she asked.

"No," I replied, shutting my bedroom door behind me. I felt emotionally volatile. I had lurked around her *jhuggi* the night

before trying to find her, and now I found it hard to answer her
in more than monosyllables. I knew I was hurting her. I couldn't
help it. I couldn't, despite all my newfangled ideas about equal-
ity of the lower castes, get myself to be decent. I would never
have spoken to someone who was not a servant in that tone.
After a while I heard a knock on my door.

"I've finished the dishes. Should I go?" She sounded to me as
if she might cry.

"What's the matter?" I asked.

She stood at the entrance to my room, head bent down, mute.

"Come here," I said, pointing to the edge of my bed. Rani
always stood or squatted on the floor when she spoke to me.

"There?" she asked, pointing to the bed. She suddenly
seemed like a snail that had retreated into its shell, not at all the
defiant woman who had shaken her ass at me, transfixed me with
the bleeding red *sindhoor* on her head.

"Here," I affirmed.

She sat down on the edge of my bed, her head still bowed. I
felt awful. I put my fingers under her chin and pulled up her
face. I stroked her eyebrows. She looked up. I traced the line of
her full lips with my index finger. Her lips were slightly chapped.
I felt as if she was my responsibility and my property. I kissed
her. We were both still after that. I was shocked at what I'd just
done. I had never kissed anyone, not even India. I observed
myself from outside for a moment, my lips moving closer to hers
and touching them. I tried to formulate the uncertainty equation. And then I thought of Schrödinger's cat being dead or alive
because of the observation.

"What are you thinking?" Rani asked, smiling flirtatiously.
Her mood had lifted. I kissed her again, this time with full intention. How could I explain Schrödinger's wave function to someone who'd never been to school? My Hindi, while perfectly
fluent on a day-to-day basis, was severely limited when it came
to expressing complex thoughts.

"Nothing. You are beautiful," I said in Hindi.

She blushed. Even on her dark brown skin I could see color rise to her cheeks.

"I walked to your *jhuggi* last night. But only the men were outside," I said.

"You came to the *jhuggi*?"

"Yes. I was looking for you. I wanted to see you."

"*Didi*. Don't do that again. People of your stature should not be seen there," she said.

"Don't worry."

After Rani left I put on my shoes and rode over to India's house.

"I've been waiting. Where were you?"

"Sorry, there was some problem at home with the new servant," I mumbled.

"Your sexy servant?" There was an edge to her voice.

"Yes," I said, looking down.

"Servants these days, I tell you!"

I felt wretched for talking about Rani that way. I was a coward for letting India say things about servants in that tone. How free was I if I was so scared? India talked about servants in the same way that all other women talked about them. Maybe she was just like ladies A, B, C, and X.

"Would you like a Coke?" she asked me.

"No, thanks. My mother returns from work at five thirty, so I have to go soon."

I saw a flicker of disappointment on her face. Then she led me to her bedroom. We sat on her bed and hugged. I had still not kissed her. I wanted to now, but I had just kissed Rani. I didn't want to kiss two women on the same day. I thought it would mean I wasn't deep.

At dinner, as Rani made *rotis* for us in the kitchen, my mother asked, "How does she work?"

"She's fine," I said.

"Are you sure? Neeta asked to come back. She promises she'll come regularly now."

"Mom, the new one is fine. She's always on time and she works well."

"It didn't take you long to switch your loyalties," my mother said lightly. I shrugged my shoulders, feigning indifference.

When my parents went to sleep I slipped out of the house from the back door to the service lane. In less than ten minutes I was in India's bed, playing with her hair. I no longer needed to convince myself I was free. I felt free.

My arms brushed her side and then came to rest on her rump. Her round cheeks were like perfectly formed cantaloupe. Some girls come of age when they hit puberty. Others when they have a child. Girls like my friend Sheela when they start going to the temple. My coming of age was distinct and happened in a split second. I moved both my hands all the way down India's back and ran my palms over her cheeks. Then I grabbed both her buttocks in my hands. I squeezed them.

And came of age.

All my life I'd been taught to venerate elders. Anyone over five years older than oneself was an elder. Squeezing India's rear violated every rule of veneration. It transformed her from an elder into a sexual being, an equal. It made me an adult.

I felt overwhelmed by the sensation. I wished I could express it in words, say something to her. She was moaning softly and rubbing her smooth calves on my legs. I squeezed the flesh in my hands more firmly now. It occurred to me that I could go further. I was afraid of feeling the area between her cheeks, but eventually I let my fingers linger down the crevice where they parted till I felt a hint of hair. Her breathing got heavier. I was scandalizing myself. I was petrified. I had no idea what to do next. There was etiquette involved that I knew nothing about. I stopped.

We spent the rest of the night cradled in each other's arms, sleeping fitfully. Entire sentences from the *Kamasutra* rolled onto the screen in my dreams. The edition I had read had been in a small typescript with the painting of an ancient scroll on the book jacket. In my dreams the sentences were captions of photographs, the characters India and Rani and an upper caste *brahmin* man from some art film. I made no appearance in the dream.

When I heard the alarm go off early in the morning, I shook India awake and put my clothes on.

"I'll see you in the afternoon," I said as I hurried out.

I rushed back to my house and got into bed before my parents woke up. When my mother walked in with my morning tea to wake me up for school, I rolled across my bed and yawned.

"The way you're sprawled on that bed, one would think your husband was walking into the room. Cover yourself with a sheet!" my mother said.

I sat up and rubbed my eyes. I pouted. I took the cup of tea and wished I could share my bed and the experience of early morning tea with India.

Since I hadn't really rested much at night, the world swam in front of my eyes. I paid little attention in class. I felt superior to all my classmates. None of them, not even the rowdiest guys who brought porn magazines to school, had ever touched the naked flesh of a woman's ass. Maybe a young cousin's, but not a real woman's. I was sure of that.

"What's Planck's constant?" Mr. Garg asked the class in the physics period.

No one answered.

"Sumeet. What's Planck's constant?"

"I don't know, sir."

"Then stand up and remain standing. Vidur, do you know?"

Vidur stood up and let his head hang down. I was surprised; Vidur usually knew the answer to everything. It was too late for me to write it on a chit and pass it to him. Vidur was my closest friend at school and shared my desk, a small wooden one. We had little wooden chairs. Since two students shared a desk, most of the students had drawn a line down the middle to demarcate their surface space. If someone's pencil wandered across the line there could be a flare-up and a murderous argument during the break. Vidur and I were the only ones in our class who'd not drawn these lines. His notebook would often invade well into my space, and I'd not say a thing. Sometimes I'd put my steel pencil box, which I'd beautified with cutouts of George Michael, all the way on his side, and he would only grin in response.

"Chakra Dev," Mr. Garg bellowed.

"Sorry, sir."

"Stand up then," he commanded. Chakra Dev was the only boy in our class who shaved every day. He therefore thought he could lord it over everyone. I gloated. Not only did he not know Planck's constant, he had no Indias or Ranis waiting to see him at the end of the day. When it came down to brass tacks, it was me, not him, who was the adult.

"Those who don't know Planck's constant, stand up!!" Mr. Garg said, almost shouting.

Everyone stood up. Except me.

"Why does only Anamika know this? Where have the rest of you been?" he shrieked. Mr. Garg was very fair, and his face turned red when he lost his temper. He'd been crying himself hoarse in class explaining quantum mechanics, and no one knew a thing.

"You, Anamika?"

"The value or the meaning?" I asked, standing up.

"What?"

"Do you want the value, or do you want me to explain what it means, sir?"

"Look at them all. Why don't you explain it fully? Obviously I've done a lousy job. In fact, come here in front and explain it," he said, gesturing to the front where he was standing. I felt terribly embarrassed. I hated being singled out for anything, whether good or bad.

I decided to remain at my seat and speak. It came naturally to speak to the class after speaking in the morning assembly every day as Head Prefect. I became less aware of myself as I defined the uncertainty principle and went into details.

"Excellent. Did you all hear that? You had a test on this yesterday, and none of you knew."

Everyone was fidgeting. The students who usually did well in class were fidgeting even more. Mr. Garg was going to return our tests, and now they all feared the worst. I stood around feeling as if I didn't belong, a bespectacled girl with nothing better to do than study her physics lessons. Then I remembered it wasn't true. I turned my face away to hide the smile that came to my lips and noticed Sheela looking at me. She would obviously think I had been pleased about my academic prowess.

"Everyone sit down now and try to study like Anamika," Mr. Garg commanded.

After class my friends started teasing me. I was generally well liked, but everyone thought I was too studious. I had made a few good friends in the past two years because I had helped them with little things. When we were fifteen, Ashima had met a boy in Calcutta when she visited her father's family for the summer holidays. I had written a little poem for her that she sent him. I had asked her to describe him to me in detail, his light skin and speckled green eyes, his rosy lips and the soft blush of hair on his face. Writing the poem for her I had to love him, Jay, or I wouldn't have been able to write the poem, so I thought of him all night till I was fervently in love myself. It was successful. Since then he had been writing to her regularly.

For his mother's birthday, Vidur had wanted to give her a poem and had asked for my help. I was not able to think of anything, or to love Vidur's mother, so the next day I let him copy the poem that I had written for my mother. I didn't think there was anything wrong with this because it had already been written and my mother had already read it.

"How can you study physics when they are showing cricket on TV?" Vidur asked.

"How can you bear to watch cricket?"

Vidur wanted to join the army and was smart and well-rounded. I wanted him to think I was, too. I wanted to tell him how well-rounded India was.

"Miss Goody Two-shoes, my teacher's pet," Sheela said, com-

ing over to where Vidur and I were sitting. Usually if someone
teased me around Vidur, he would say a word or two in my
defense. Today he just grinned and then got up and walked out
of the class.

"I'm not all that good," I said.

"You may do well in exams and come first, but I have much
more fun," Sheela said.

Sheela was very popular with the boys and relatively intelligent. But she was lazy. We were not close friends, but every now
and then, when the rest of the girls in the class were mean to her,
she would confide in me.

"I saw you smirk when Mr. Garg was scolding us all," she said.

"I was smiling for another reason. It's a secret," I said. I
looked at her full pink lips and milky skin and wondered what it
would be like to kiss them.

"Don't lie. I know you were feeling superior," she said. Most
of the girls were jealous of her, but she knew I cared only about
studies and not looks and thus had no reason to give her the evil
eye.

"You have beautiful lips," I said.

She blushed.

"If you ever want to kiss, let me know," I added.

"Huh?"

"I want to have some fun, too," I said.

"Very funny," she said, looking not in the slightest bit amused.

"I'm being serious."

"You're really weird, Anamika."

I had put myself on the spot. I pretended I'd done it for effect
and laughed.

I thought about Rani on the school bus back home. I wanted to
take a nap in the afternoon with her lying beside me, but I'd
promised India I'd visit.

When Rani came to do the housework I said, "I am in a rush
today. Will you hurry up?"

"Yes, *Didi*."

It made me sick to my stomach to see that on one level I had a functional relationship with her in which she was very much my servant. Was it even possible for two people to entirely forget their status and just be human beings with each other? I had always believed it was, but now with Rani I had a real-life situation to test it with.

After she was finished cleaning she told me, "I'm done. Should I go?"

"Rani," I said, looking up at her.

"Yes, *Didi*."

"From now on I want you to treat me like an equal when we are alone. In front of other people you can behave as usual."

"I can't do that, *Babyji*. It wouldn't be right," she said, lowering her eyes.

I walked up to where she was standing at the threshold of my bedroom and ran my fingers along her lips. She reached out. A thrill shot up my spine. I pulled her into my room and flung us both on the bed. Instead of the disturbing *Kamasutra* dream where I had failed to make an entrance on the scene, I saw Rani and myself in an erotic position. I grabbed her thighs from under her sari. My hands felt the tough muscles of her legs. Her gluteus maximus was strong and toned after years of labor. She was not wearing underwear. Servants never wore underwear. I squeezed her cheeks, one with each hand. My fingers felt her heat.

I looked into her face, which was very close to mine. Her eyes were closed.

"What's the matter?" I asked, sensing some disturbance inside her.

She opened her eyes and said, "This is not right."

"Does it feel wrong?"

"No."

That was all the encouragement I needed. I went the extra few inches I had been afraid to go with India. After a while I slid my hands back down her legs and pulled down her sari.

"I have to go. But tomorrow afternoon come at two sharp," I said.

"Yes."

I closed the door behind her and brought my hands to my face. They smelt of slum, unwashed clothing, and her fluids. I went to the bathroom and washed my hands and face with soap. Then I walked over to India's. I didn't make out with her. I couldn't after I'd just been with Rani. I told her I'd try to come again at night.

"I want to make you happy," I said as I was leaving.

"You do make me happy," India said.

"No, I don't mean that way. I mean in bed."

She smiled at me and played with my hair for a second.

"You're so young, I can't believe I'm doing this," she said.

"I'm not that young," I said, closing her wrought iron gate. It was taller than I was and very fancy. I walked home feeling strangely young and strangely old at the same time.

In the evening I read my biology book and did my mathematics homework while my mom cooked eggplant for dinner. My mother had given Rani the evening off. My father played cards once a week with his colleagues from the office; it was one of those nights. He'd come home after Mom and I had eaten and watched some TV. Those were the most peaceful times. At around eight forty-five, when we were watching the news, the phone rang. I jumped up to get it.

"Can I speak to Anamika?" a girlish voice asked. It was Sheela.

"Did you mean what you said today?" she asked.

I was nervous. I could be in a lot of trouble.

"I was joking," I replied, turning to see if my mother was listening.

"You were serious. I could tell you were serious."

"No, I was pretending to be serious."

"Are you sure?"

She didn't sound like she wanted to get me into trouble at all. What if she was interested?

"Why do you ask?" I said.

"Oh! Just-Like-That," she said, her tone changing as if she was not interested in really knowing.

"No, tell me the truth," I said.

"J-L-T," she said, ending the conversation.

"Who was that?" my mother asked.

"Sheela."

"Isn't she that fair, healthy friend of yours?" my mother asked in an approving voice.

"Yes, that's her."

"You should go out less in the sun and eat more. Then you'll be like her." My mother is a typical north Indian woman who thinks women should be chubby and fair.

I didn't want her to get started. It wasn't enough that I worked hard at school and had professional ambitions. She would have been much more proud of me if I'd been lighter skinned, heavier set, and more domestically inclined. It didn't bother me as long as I was left alone. I knew I'd do better than the others, and if she really wanted one of those girls I could always bring one home. Why did my parents want me to be both this and that? Couldn't they see it was impossible for me to invest my first twenty-five years in excelling in studies and becoming a nuclear physicist if all I was expected to do for the next fifty was chop vegetables in the kitchen?

"Mom, she failed the physics test," I said.

"I never said that she was smarter than you. You're very intelligent, and I'm proud of that."

"All right, Mom, back to work," I said, getting up and going to my room. After a few minutes my father arrived. I said hello to him and went back to my room. I was waiting for them to sleep so I could slip out to India's. They didn't sleep till eleven that night. I could hear my father talking about office politics. I wanted them to wake up to the larger realities of life, to passion, love, and the fact that life was magical and dramatic. I was tired by the time they turned their lights out. I wanted to see India, but my eyes were drooping shut. I tiptoed to the living room to call her.

"I can't come tonight," I whispered as soon as she picked up. "I'll call you tomorrow," I added.

"Are you all right?" she asked.

"Yes, good night." I hung up and peeked into my parents' room to make sure they hadn't heard me. I got into bed and slept.

Utthak-Baithak

The school day began with a morning assembly, when everyone said a prayer together and sang a hymn. Someone read the main points of the news, and administrative announcements followed. As the Head Prefect I was responsible for making sure all the classes got into formation and the assembly was conducted properly. I was standing in the assembly ground when I spotted Sheela standing under a tree.

I went up to her, feeling bold in my silver and blue Head Prefect tie and badge. The difference between those in power and those not in power was most obvious during assembly.

"Why did you call me last night?" I asked Sheela.

"To find out if you meant it."

"And if I did?"

"It doesn't matter, since you didn't," she replied. She was playing with me.

"Come on, tell me," I pleaded.

"Have you ever kissed anyone, Anamika?" She had this look of superiority on her face. After all, she was the one all the guys were after. Her expression seemed to say, I know you haven't.

"Maybe," I said.

"You don't think it's wrong?" she asked.

"Wrong?"

"I mean morally."

"Oh! I don't believe in morals," I replied.

"But you're always trying to be good. You always do well in class."

"So? I enjoy studying. That hardly means I'm good."

"You mean you don't study to be good?"

"No."

"I do it only to be a good girl and make my father proud," she said.

"I do it so that I can earn a lot of money later and keep a wife," I said. Then I laughed because I didn't want her to take me seriously.

"You're strange."

The assembly ground was now full of students, and everyone was standing around. No class would ever form a line unless someone was at the microphone yelling orders. The school was enormous. It had almost six thousand students on a thirty-two-acre campus. A small forest ran around the southern and western boundaries. The assembly was held on the football field in the back where all the students and some hundred fifty teachers congregated each morning.

"Come up with me onstage while I get these people to form lines," I told Sheela.

We climbed up the steps in the front of the assembly ground.

"Class IV and V to my left, hurry up, children. Class VIII, what's taking you so long? House Prefects, please ensure all wings are in order. We're already running ten minutes late," I said. It always gave me great delight to call the students "children." It made me feel grown-up. I had been nervous to use it in the beginning when I had just become the Head Prefect, but one day I had mustered the courage to say it. No one booed at me. From then on I said it more and more often.

Within a few minutes all the students were standing in single file by class. Sheela went down to our class line before the prayer started. In the summer some children were known to faint. The school doctor had asked us to remind the children halfway through the assembly to wiggle their toes since this helped circulation. I told the girl reading the news that day to make the wiggling announcement and got off the stage. As Head Prefect I could walk around during the assembly. I needed to speak to teachers, who stood with their classes, about special events for the day. On occasion I inspected uniforms. If anyone got caught with the incorrect uniform, he or she would have to fall out of line and be punished. The standard punishment was to jog around the field.

I went to where my class stood and walked up to Sheela to do a random uniform check. I had never inspected my own section because it would be seen as very snobbish if I punished my own classmates. Even with my mild disposition toward them, I was not too popular and had to be very careful not to seem on a high horse. Today I threw a cursory glance at everyone and didn't pay any attention to boys with long nails or overgrown pinkies or those with unpolished shoes. The class goon, Chakra Dev, was wearing a green undershirt, a big no-no since the rules strictly restricted boys to wearing only white *banians* under their shirts. But I ignored him on my way to Sheela.

"Let me see your nails," I said to her.

Vidur, who was standing to her left, thought I was getting back at her for the Goody Two-shoes comment from the day before. He gave me a disapproving look. I didn't want him of all people to think I was the kind of person who held such small incidents against people.

She put both her hands forward. I touched the ends of her fingers, pretending to see how long her nails were.

"Your skirt is half an inch shorter than stipulated," I said, looking her in the eye to make sure she knew I was only half-serious.

"Should I fall out of line?" she asked, fluttering her eyes. I was alarmed by how blatantly she was flirting. What if someone noticed? But Vidur was staring at the stage.

"Yes, Sheela."

We walked to the back of the assembly ground till we were well out of earshot.

"So how should I punish you?" I asked.

"Don't make me run around the field. My skirt is high, and the guys will stare."

"You're right."

"I could kiss you," she suggested.

"No. But tell me who you've kissed," I demanded, wanting more information.

"I haven't."

"Don't lie."

"God promise I haven't," she said.

"Which god?"

"Krishna."

"He used to lie, so I don't believe you."

I could tell that I had crossed the line. I had no idea she was devout. I hadn't meant to offend her. Everyone's favorite Krishna stories were about him as a child stealing buttermilk. I liked him for stealing the clothes of girls bathing in the river.

"My uniform inspection was not complete," I said, changing the subject.

"It wasn't?"

"No. Are you wearing bloomers?"

Girls were supposed to wear white bloomers under their skirts instead of simple panties. This was because in the PT period the girls played volleyball and ran around the field like the boys, and in a coed school the parent-teacher association had decided that a girl's modesty must be protected.

"Oh! Come on, Anamika."

"Can I check?"

"Here?" she asked nervously. We were behind all the classes in the assembly ground, so unless someone actually turned around to see us they wouldn't know what was going on. The entire school was singing a hymn about Hindus and Muslims being brothers.

"Get behind that tree," I ordered.

We walked over to a short *gulmohar* tree, and I got behind her, lifted her skirt, and saw her blue panty and its wedgie. She was in serious violation of the rules. I also noticed that unlike a lot of girls who only waxed their legs below their knees, Sheela was smooth and silky all the way up. I could see the sides of her bottom, and there was gooseflesh on it. I let her skirt fall and moved around to face her again. She was red in the face.

"In view of the fact that you can't run around the field like this in a short skirt, especially without bloomers, I have to give you another punishment," I said, adjusting my glasses.

She stood looking at me, wondering what I was going to suggest. I already felt I had abused my authority.

"You have to do ten *utthak-baithaks*," I said.

There is no word in English for this particular movement. She squeezed each earlobe between her thumb and forefinger and then bent her knees, lowering herself till she was almost squatting. Then she got up, her hands still by her ears, and squatted again. I stood a few feet in front of her and watched her box-pleated gray skirt fly up and down and her thighs stretch and flex as she counted breathlessly to ten.

I was distracted in class. In between periods I would try to make my way to Sheela and talk to her. When the teacher wrote on the blackboard, I would turn around and try to catch her eye. She sat three rows behind me, so this was not an easy thing to do. The classrooms were really cramped, merely twenty by thirty feet but packed with fifty students, their desks, and their chairs. When I turned back repeatedly to look at Sheela, Vidur noticed. Eventually in history class he passed me a note asking, "What's the matter with you today?"

I liked Vidur and didn't keep secrets from him. If there was inside scoop on the school that I could not divulge to anyone, I confided in him. I trusted him to keep things to himself. For a brief moment I toyed with the idea of telling him about my recent escapades. But the poor guy was untainted and didn't even make dirty jokes like the rest of the boys. I shrugged in response to his note.

During the break we usually ate a small snack we brought from home. I made my way to Sheela. Most of us took our lunchboxes out to the playing field. Every now and then an eagle would swoop down and snatch a sandwich from someone's hands. There was also a canteen in the school, a small metal shanty where one could buy cold drinks and things to eat. It sold the best vegetable burgers for a rupee. In my twelve years at the school the cost of a Coke had gone up from two rupees to five, but the burger still cost the same. Teachers spoke badly of kids who spent too much time at the canteen. It was as if you were a good-for-nothing. Sheela was treated by someone or other at the canteen every day. I approached her before anyone else could and asked, "Can we go to the canteen?"

"Sure," she said with a smile, knowing perfectly well that I never went to the canteen.

We walked to the end of the field where it was located. A mob of young boys crowded the back. Some had been playing cricket and were sweating, their white shirts hanging out and their ties loose. The older guys had pushed their way forward and were yelling at the guy behind the counter for drinks and food. A few girls stood around wondering how to get near the counter. In that ruckus, if one wasn't aggressive one might wait for half an hour. I walked up to the mob of younger boys and tapped one on the shoulder. When he saw me he stepped aside. Everyone recognized me since I was the Head Prefect. All the younger classes were scared of me. The rowdier students who were my age and often got into trouble resented me. They could speak disparagingly of me to one another, but if they misbehaved and got yellow cards I'd often be involved, and they'd be reduced to groveling for forgiveness. The boy I had patted spoke to the older boy in front of him and said, "Let *Didi* go."

I made my way to the front and got two Cokes, two burgers, and one pineapple pastry. It was hard to balance everything. I held a Coke bottle between my elbow and waist on my right and left sides, the burgers in one hand and the pastry in the other.

Some guys were chatting with Sheela when I got back with the food.

"Anamika and I need to talk," she said, leaving them in the middle of the conversation.

She took a Coke and the paper plate with the burgers from me, slipped her arm through my arm that had been freed up, and casually led me to a more deserted spot where there were some large rocks. I didn't really know what to say to her. After the intense flapping of her skirt in the morning there was nothing more to say. We sat on a huge black rock. Its rough surface poked me through my skirt.

"I want you to answer my question about the kiss," she said.

"Yes I have," I said.

I could tell from her shock that she hadn't kissed anyone. She was popular but scared. She had believed everything the grown-ups had told her about what being good was about.

"Who?" she asked.

"No one you know."

"Is he in our class?"

"No, they are not in our class. They are older," I said.

"More than one! Two? How is it like to kiss?"

"Oh! Great," I said casually. Then I changed the topic, as if it was all a routine occurrence and asked, "Have you ever done horse riding?"

"No."

"When I get on Sugar, my favorite horse, and kick her, she gallops fast. It's fun."

"Can I try? I've never done it."

"Come with me to the riding ground one day in the PT period. I'll get you to ride. Mina always follows Sugar. If I ride Sugar and hold Mina's rein, you'll be safe."

She looked impressed. I wanted to tell her more things about myself to impress her, but I couldn't think of anything. We walked to the canteen and deposited our empty bottles in a crate.

"You don't think what you did was wrong? Especially two people?" she asked.

"Two women. But I felt close to them," I said.

She looked even more troubled.

"Only the soul matters," I declared. I didn't quite believe it myself. I couldn't imagine feeling for a boy what I felt for Rani or India. If only the soul mattered, then I would have to consider Vidur as much as I was considering Sheela. I knew him better than anyone else, and his soul was the sweetest.

We went back to class silently. I wondered if I'd bungled up by telling her. If she told anyone, my reputation would be at stake. I walked to my seat and sat down next to Vidur.

"What's this going on between you and Sheela all of a sudden?" he asked.

"Nothing," I said.

"You know, you've looked really pleased for a few days."

"I am pleased," I said.

"Why?"

"Oh, nothing! I can't tell you."

"Why not? You don't trust me?" Vidur's aggressiveness was surprising.

"I just can't tell you," I said.

Our exchange ended abruptly because our chemistry teacher, Hydrogen Sulfide, walked in. No one referred to her by name. Hydrogen Sulfide had a vile reputation. It was rumored that when her first daughter, Lata, was born, she had refused to hold or feed her. It was rumored that H_2S had said, "That dark and ugly brat can't be mine." Mercifully for Lata none of her siblings that followed were any fairer, and she had been saved from being treated any worse than the others. H_2S always wore *salwar kameezes* with the *kameez* sleeve at a three-fourths length. No matter how hot the weather was she wore *kameezes* with tight-fitting sleeves. Somebody had said that she was trying to hide burn marks that she had sustained when her husband poured a chemical on her arms. She was extremely unpopular because she'd slapped the prettiest girl in the senior class once for no reason and mumbled something about "all that hair falling on your face." Even the other teachers had said that it was because Hydrogen Sulfide was jealous of youth and beauty. The girl had gained so much sympathy after that incident that at the school farewell, when her class was graduating, she had been voted "Miss Cool."

Everyone stood up and sang out, "Good morning, ma'am" in

unison to H_2S. Then we sat down. Vidur's chemistry textbook was lying in the middle of our desk. He pulled it back to his side and looked slightly upset.

After a while, when the teacher had her back to the class, I gave Vidur a slip of paper with a smiley face. He'd usually return such notes with funny additions on the slip. This time he ignored me. By the end of class, when all my overtures had gone unreturned, I temporarily lost my sense of proportion.

When the teacher was about to leave we all got up and sang out, "Thank you, ma'am." Instead of joining the chorus I kicked Vidur sharply under the desk, pulled him roughly toward me by the elbow, and whispered in his ear, "I'm having an affair."

From behind his glasses I could see his left eye bulge out a little in shock.

"Who is he?"

"I can't talk about it. Please try to understand."

"I understand."

Our geography teacher walked in. Everyone was still standing and sang out, "Good morning, ma'am."

"We are going to learn about waterfalls today, children," Mrs. Thaityallam announced. "I want you to draw one line through your notebooks. On one side of the line write *cascade* and on the other write *waterfall*," she instructed.

There was the rustling of paper, the opening of metal pencil boxes, and the sound of pencils grazing against rulers as everyone drew the line. I wondered if any one single adult had ever looked at our syllabus. We were learning quantum mechanics in one class and being asked to draw lines in another. Mrs. T. treated us as if we were still in primary school. In the exams she wanted us to reproduce all her points in the same order as she dictated them in class. When she talked about cascades I thought of India's long black hair rolling down her back. And when she told us about waterfalls I imagined Sheela taking a dip in one, like the starlet of a Hindi movie, wearing a thin white shirt and getting soaked to the skin. Sheela had the whiteness, freshness, and complexion of a clean mountain spring.

"Anamika, why are you smiling?" Mrs. T. asked me.

"Nothing, ma'am," I said, bending my head and sneaking a look at what I had written in my notebook. I was writing what she was saying verbatim without paying any attention.

"What was I just saying?" she asked.

I got up from my seat and repeated the line I'd just written.

"Good, sit down," she said.

I sat back down, aware that my armpits had broken into a sweat. Most teachers cut me slack because of my position as Head Prefect. I was supposed to set a good example for everyone, which I sincerely did try to do, and if I slipped they preferred to overlook it rather than make a scene. But Mrs. T. made no allowances for me and in fact tried to hold me to more exacting standards specifically because I was Head Prefect.

When geography class was finally over I was exhausted. We had to sit through two more classes. I doodled on the side of my notebook. I drew maps of India and wrote India in the center. I anthropomorphized the map by adding curls on the states of Gujarat and West Bengal. I imagined India's body and the map of the country liquefying the boundaries between various states so that they could overlap. When Vidur wasn't looking I added two breasts in the bang center of the map. I was itching to go home. It had been quite a day.

In the afternoon I sat on the kitchen counter at home with my legs dangling and watched Rani do the dishes.

"People would say that I am doing wrong by my husband if they knew this, but I don't think there is anything wrong. I only want to be with you," Rani said.

She had a husband! Of course she had a husband. I had always known. No woman lives alone, especially in a slum. But I was aghast. It hadn't occurred to me. I had seen her *sindhoor* again and again and simply blocked out the truth.

"He tells me it's wrong for me to work in your house washing dishes. He says I should work on the construction site with him. All the other wives work with their husbands."

"Do you love him?" I asked. That's not what I had wanted to ask.

I wanted to know if she slept with him. The Hindi word for sleeping implied the physical act of sleeping. I didn't know the word for sex in my own language.

"I don't love him," she said.

"Do you do anything with him?" I asked. I used the tone one would for a servant. I knew she would answer then.

"You mean that sort of thing," she said, lowering her eyes.

"Yes. Does he do that sort of thing to you?" I asked slightly harshly.

"Sometimes."

"How often? Every night?"

"No, some nights," she said vaguely.

"Do you like it?"

"No."

Her response had been very quick, too quick to mask her shudder. He came to my mind, an ugly man with a pitted face and filthy hands. Laughing and taking her against her will. Lifting her sari and invading her. Groaning sharply and falling asleep. Just like in a movie I had seen on TV when my parents were away. I wanted to kill him.

"Why don't you like it?"

"Sometimes he hurts me."

"Why don't you stop him?"

"Then he beats me."

"Why don't you leave him?" I asked.

"I don't have money."

"Are you willing to do other work around the house, like washing clothes?"

"Yes, and I can sweep the floor," she said.

I was making mental notes. "Maybe you can move in here," I said.

"Here, *Babyji*?" she said.

"That way you can earn some money and save some money."

"Yes. I want my own money. That's why I asked your mother for a job."

She was finished with the dishes. I took her to my room and asked her to remove her clothes.

"All my clothes?" she asked, her eyes widening.

"All."

"And yours?" she asked, addressing me with the form one used for equals.

"I'll take mine off," I said.

I felt terribly young removing my school skirt and emptying my pockets of loose change and a pencil and sharpener.

I had never before seen a woman naked like this. With India we had been under the sheets. That was more of a tactile experience than a visual one.

Rani was thin and lissome. Thinner than I would have guessed when I saw her half covered in her sari. I could see the knob of each vertebra on her back and the length of each rib on her sides. Her shoulder blades jutted out several inches from her body. She would have looked riveting in a dress. Her hips were full, however. And her breasts were perfect.

"What kind of things do you like?" I asked. I wasn't sure she would understand what I meant. My Hindi was restricted to mundane and decidedly polite conversations.

"Have you ever enjoyed yourself with your husband?" I asked, struggling to be precise.

"He's an animal. Don't pollute yourself mentioning him. Women are not meant to enjoy."

I wished I weren't young and inexperienced. I had no idea what to do. There was no way to find out except trial and error. And the terror of making mistakes. I wished I had paid more attention to the technical details in Vatsyayana's book.

Just before my mother got home I called India to apologize for not having gone over. I studied and ate an early dinner and went to bed.

The next time we had PT I dragged Sheela to the horse riding ground.

"I wore bloomers today," she said.

"Why?"

"Doesn't your skirt fly up when you ride?"

"Yeah. I wear bloomers. But it's not because my skirt flies up. That you can handle by just tucking the skirt firmly under your legs. The bloomers ensure that the saddle doesn't pinch the inside of your thighs."

The horses were tended by Nepalese *Sherpa* boys. We called them all *Bhaiyya*.

"Sameer *Bhaiyya*, today Sheela will ride on Mina," I said.

"Has she come here before? Has she paid the fees?" he asked.

"If anyone asks, just tell them that I said she can," I told him with great authority.

He went to the water trough where the horses were drinking and led Mina and Sugar to us by the reins. Sameer *Bhaiyya* and I held Mina, and he helped Sheela up onto the horse's back. I saw his hand support Sheela's thigh and looked at him. But he wasn't paying attention to her thigh. He was worried if Sheela could handle the horse. He had one hand on Mina's rump, and in the other he held the reins. I mounted Sugar and grabbed the side of Mina's rein. He showed Sheela how to hold the reins and how to halt the horse.

"Ready?" I asked, looking at her.

She nodded.

Perspiration had broken on Sameer *Bhaiyya*'s face. He was letting a novice on a horse; her parents had not signed the forms. He had let another student take over. Usually the *Sherpas* rode with us till we knew what we were doing.

"*Bhaiyya*, don't worry," I said in Hindi.

Then we set off. Sugar was the kind of horse that broke into a trot in seconds. And Mina, stubborn when all alone, would easily follow him. I wished they'd do the same today. We rode in a big circle in the horse riding ground. Sugar and Mina trotted alongside each other. I held Mina's rein for a few circles before letting go and then turned around every few seconds to see how Sheela was doing. I could see her legs squeeze the horse tightly. She was clutching the saddle with one hand and the reins with the other.

"Don't hang on to the saddle like that. Let go. Relax and let your body move with the horse."

"I am trying."

Sugar was galloping and out of breath now, and Mina followed by his side. They both huffed and hawed and made beastly noises. Sheela let go of the saddle. We were cruising. I could see Sameer *Bhaiyya* turning in small circles at the center of our big circle so that he could keep an eye on us.

"Are you liking this?" I asked her.

"Yes, this is something else," she said.

"Good."

"You're something else, Anamika," she said.

I chuckled to myself. I felt Sugar's reins in my hands and a sense of control. If you can make twenty miles an hour on a horse and be in control, you can make a few inches a minute with a lady and be in control, I thought to myself.

The horses were sweating profusely. I slowed Sugar down, and Mina followed. Eventually they came to a stop. I jumped off Sugar and patted his head. Sameer *Bhaiyya* was all smiles.

"I'll help her," I told him as he walked toward Mina.

Sheela brought her far leg over the saddle from the front. I could see she was off balance. I lifted my hands, and she slid down, firmly encased in the circle of my hands. We patted Mina.

"Sameer *Bhaiyya*, I think we should ask Sheela to salute on the horse," I said.

"She doesn't even know how to get on and off. How will she balance herself?" he asked.

"She'll be fine."

"I'll be fine," Sheela said to him convincingly in Hindi. Then she turned to me and asked, "What do I have to do?"

"We remove the saddle, you climb on Sugar's bare back without your shoes and socks, you stand on his back, let your arms drop to your side, and then bring your right arm up in salute."

"God!"

"If I can do it, so can you," I said.

"You really think so?"

"Of course," I said.

Sameer *Bhaiyya* looked tense once more. The *Sherpa Bhaiyyas* hadn't let me do this till I had been riding for six months. But he complied. He unsaddled Sugar. It was understood that it had to be Sugar, who was the most cooperative and gentle of the horses. If Sheela went crashing down, Sugar wouldn't buck.

"Take off your shoes and socks," I said to Sheela as Sameer *Bhaiyya* unbuckled the belt from under Sugar's belly.

Her feet were small and white. They were well kept.

"First we'll just make you sit on the horse," Sameer *Bhaiyya* said to her in Hindi.

She nodded.

Without saddles, horses' backs are smooth and slippery. It was a production just getting her up there. Once she had mounted and was sitting firmly on Sugar, we told her to stand up slowly. Sameer *Bhaiyya* and I stood on either side. We supported her legs and held her hands. I realized I was touching Sheela's leg, but I was focused on getting her to balance. Her foot slipped, and she fell back on Sugar's back.

"Oow," she yelped.

"No, that's fine, just do it again. You can't get hurt. We're both here. It's not that high."

She tried again. This time she made it. The heels of her feet pressed on Sugar's spine, and her toes curled on his back. We let go but stood by her side.

"Now salute," Sameer *Bhaiyya* said with enthusiasm.

I didn't watch her palm come up against her forehead or her thumb curl inward. I looked up at her legs and saw her bloomers. They stuck to her flesh where her legs came together and seemed like transparent cellophane paper.

"Excellent," Sameer *Bhaiyya* said clapping, his shapely Nepali eyes gathering into a smile.

We helped her down, and I wondered how I had become more corrupt than twenty-year-old *Sherpas* who had grown up in the mountains.

"Thank you for taking me horse riding," Sheela said as we walked back to class.

I nodded. My mind was elsewhere, weighing the pros and cons of having one more affair, with someone my own age, a girl without a husband or a son. A girl who was neither a servant nor an elder. Someone more or less my equal.

"When you climbed that horse I looked up and saw your bloomers," I said, making up my mind on the matter.

On the way home in the bus I decided that three was the right number. With two affairs one was torn between two simple choices. There was something very linear about it. I was reading a popular book on chaos theory which said that three implied chaos. I wanted chaos because then I could create my own patterns with it. I saw the beautiful fractal diagrams in the book and could see Sheela and India and Rani inside one of those diagrams, getting smaller and smaller, the pattern repeating endlessly. I closed the book feeling sure I was doing the right thing with my life. Chaos was modern physics, it was the science for today.

All Men Are Alike

Delhi is a dark city. The evening sky sags with heavy dust. Fumes the strength of twenty cigarettes burn your lungs every day. The night air is thick—nothing can be seen. Things happen in the dark. Men are killed. Their cries of anguish go unheard. If it is winter, the mornings are covered with fog, and corpses are discovered only after the shroud lifts at ten. Women are raped in the parking lots of movie theaters, often by many men in one night. They gather their torn *duptattas* and go home to avoid public scandal. Delhi's crime, everyone complains, has gotten worse. This is not true. In Delhi nothing changes.

When I was seven there was a kidnapping scare. Children were stolen and large ransoms demanded. If the parents did not pay, then the child's ear or his little finger would arrive in a parcel a few days later. I was warned not to talk to anyone. Before long I was not allowed outside the house unless an adult family member was with me. If I complained about being locked in the house, my parents simply took me to wherever they were going. I developed a predilection for people thrice my age. For adults who were my parents' friends.

After a few years the kidnappings abated. People became less paranoid about their kids. I was allowed on my bicycle during the day. I celebrated by biking on the weekends. I never noticed that the city was polluted, turning my lungs dark, infesting my bronchial passages.

School was already an important part of my life. It became

important to my social life, too. After I decided to add Sheela to my list of lovers, I started to work toward my goal. I would use my academic reputation in conjunction with my official authority to complete my project. I decided to offer her help in mathematics and physics. It would be easy for me to make an excuse to my parents, since they knew that sometimes seniors stayed back after classes for extracurricular activities. After school hours, Sheela and I could have the classroom to ourselves.

"You'll really teach me? I can't understand a word of what Mr. Garg says in class," she said after she had found on Tuesday that she had bombed the test from the previous day, again.

"Yes. It'll help us both. I will understand things better, too."

"Okay."

"Tomorrow, then?" I asked.

"I will ask my parents and call you at home to confirm."

"Call by nine. And tell your parents that we have to practice for Sports Day."

"Right," she said, winking. As soon as someone is involved in lying because of you, your association with them takes on a slightly underworld shade of dark. Things become possible that were not possible earlier. If Sheela made excuses she would automatically feel that what was happening was wrong, and if she felt it was wrong she would do something wrong to cash in on it. Not that I thought anything was wrong. But she did. And what she thought was all that mattered.

On the bus ride home I pulled out my school diary. It had a blue plastic cover with the school motto etched on it. In the diary we would write the date and then the homework given that day. I wrote Sheela as my homework for the next day.

I also thought of Rani and India. I realized that with three lovers, I needed a set of rules to follow. It would be wrong to give one of my lovers more time than the others. As long as I saw all three of them equally, it would be fine. According to ancient myths, when Kunti had heard from Arjuna that he had brought something home, she had said simply, "Share it equally with your brothers." And Draupadi, the bride he had earned at the archery contest, came to be the wife of all five *Pandavas*. They laid down rules on how to share. They would all have her equally, and she was not to be disturbed if she was with one of them.

When I got home, Rani was squatting at the front door waiting for me.

"What's the matter? How come you're early?" I asked. She looked deathly ill.

"He beat me, little mistress," she said and burst into tears.

I stepped closer to her and slipped my arm under hers. She moaned.

"It hurts," she said.

I put my hand into my skirt pocket, took out my keys, and unlocked the door. I gingerly led her to my bedroom.

"Take off all your clothes," I said and proceeded to remove my school shoes.

Rani had stopped crying, but her eyes were still wet. She was unraveling her sari very slowly. Her *pallu* fell from her shoulder, and I saw black marks on her back. I unhooked my school skirt and let it fall to the floor. Then, stepping over it, I moved closer to Rani.

"Just stand still," I said.

She let go of the half-undraped sari and looked at me. I lifted it from the ground and proceeded to remove the rest. Then I untied her petticoat from her waist and let it fall to the floor.

Her legs were blue. There were bruises and scrapes along the entire length of her thighs. I touched one spot softly with my finger. "Ooww," she let out.

She was still wearing her blouse. I unhooked it and removed it slowly from her arms, taking care not to bend her arms too much. They had the same bruised look that her legs did. Seeing her injured skin filled me with feelings I'd never had before. Murderous and tender at the same time.

"Lie down," I said.

"There?" she asked, motioning to my bed, her face taking on the look of a servant, of one who mustn't overstep bounds.

"There," I said forcefully, in the tone used for giving orders.

She lay down. I went to my bathroom and got a bottle of anti-septic and some cotton wool. Then I sat on the edge of my bed, only half-clad myself, applying the wet swab to her wounds.

"You're not going back," I said.

"He'll kill me if I don't."

I hadn't thought before I'd spoken. It wasn't up to me to keep her in the house. Moreover, if he came for her he could cause trouble. My mother would be against risking the wrath of a violent construction worker from a site next door. The entire colony of workers would be up in arms outside our house. There would be a riot. Delhi hardly needs an excuse for a riot.

"I'll kill him," I replied.

"But *Babyji*, you are only a child," she said.

I didn't respond. Did my lover think I was a child? I felt hurt. I kept swabbing her skin.

"I didn't mean it that way, *Babyji*," she said after a little while.

"What did you mean?" I asked.

"He can hurt you, he's big, he's an animal," she said.

"Does he know you're here?"

"No, he doesn't know your house. Anyway, he's lying drunk on the floor."

"When did this happen?"

"Last night. I didn't let him touch me yesterday when he came home. After being with you I couldn't. I said I was thinking of leaving the *jhuggi* altogether and living here. He hit me and hit me when I said that. Then he went out and drank."

"What did you do?"

"The woman next door took me in and told her husband to sleep outside."

I felt a pang of jealousy that someone else had helped her first. At the same time I felt gratitude toward the woman for being there. I wanted to go to the slum and give her my pocket money savings as a reward. My head was splitting. Was I really having thoughts about paying people for goodness? So many people believed that anything could be bought. I had loathed them all my life. But now I was thinking like they did. Love had unhinged me.

"Are you okay, little mistress?" she asked, raising her head from my bed. I realized I'd been taking care of her the way she had of me earlier, when she massaged my legs. She looked comfortable on my bed. The unease from before had gone.

"I'm okay. Thank God for your neighbor. I will speak to my mother. You'll stay here."

"Little mistress, are you sure? I don't want you to take the trouble."

"I'm sure," I said confidently. But I wasn't. I would have to work on my mom from every angle. I'd have to argue for women's rights and threaten to leave home if Rani could not stay. I was certain India would keep me and even keep Rani.

I looked at her. There were deep, dark craters under her eyes.

"You're very tired."

"I didn't sleep last night."

"Sleep now."

"I have to wash the vessels."

"Don't worry about it."

Rani suddenly propped herself on her elbow and said, "Little mistress, what time is it? Your mother will be here soon."

"She won't come for another hour and a half, just sleep."

I covered her with a thin sheet and stroked her hair for a little while. When she fell asleep I kissed her forehead and tiptoed out of my room. I made my way to the kitchen and did the dishes. I imagined what would happen when my mom came back. It was one of those days when my father was going out to play cards with his colleagues. I knew I could get my mom to agree to let her spend the night, but I also knew that in the long run she'd defer to my father.

After the dishes were finished I called India. "Rani got beaten," I said.

I didn't want to call her a servant even though India had never heard me call her Rani before. The idea of asking India to keep Rani if my parents refused was terrible in some ways, but it was better that she have a roof over her head at India's than that she go back to the *jhuggi*.

"Who did it? Her husband?" she asked.

"Yes."

"Mine used to beat me, too. She should leave him." India had not told me anything about her ex-husband before.

"I hope my mother lets her stay here."

"She'll be okay. Are you coming tonight?"

I hesitated a moment. If Rani was spending the night with me, I couldn't go to India's. But I wanted her to be as well inclined toward Rani as possible, should the need arise.

"I'm going to try, but it'll be a bit risky. My father might come home late."

"Don't take the chance."

"I won't. Even if I can't make it tonight, I'll definitely come soon."

"Listen, if this maid needs a place to stay I'll take a look at her. How does she work?"

"Superbly."

"Don't worry then."

"Thanks."

I went back to the kitchen and put the kettle on to make some tea. I put two china cups on a tray, got out a packet of tea biscuits, and took everything to my room. I liked the fact that our roles were reversed, that I was suddenly no longer a brat.

When I woke Rani she jumped up and said, "What are you doing?"

"I made *chai*," I said.

She eyed the cup tentatively, since she always used the glass my mother had given her. I thought she was going to protest, but she said, "You're very kind to me."

"Eat some biscuits," I said.

"Are they good?" she asked. She had served us these biscuits many times but had never eaten one. She picked one up and ate it. Then another. And another.

"You haven't eaten since last night," I remarked.

"No."

"Why didn't you tell me earlier?"

"I was not hungry. I felt ill."

"Are you feeling better now?"

"Yes."

By the time we finished our tea it was time for my mother to return. Rani carried the cups back to the kitchen. I changed my clothes and followed her. She washed both cups and returned one to the shelf, leaving the other to drain. She wiped the vessels I had washed and put them back on the shelf. We had gone back to master-servant mode without saying a word.

Soon the bell rang.

"Sit on the veranda. I will bring her to you after I've spoken to her," I said.

"All right."

I unbolted the door from the inside to let my mother in.

"Mom, Rani's husband beat her."

"All these women put up with too much from their men."

"He beat her black and blue. If she goes back he'll kill her."

"No, he won't kill her. He'll only beat her again."

"What do you mean *only?*" I couldn't believe my mother could be so callous.

"She should leave him. She earns. If she works in a few other houses she'll have enough money." My mother had ignored the emotion in my voice and had just gone on speaking.

"We can let her stay here," I said.

"You know we can't. There's no space."

"Mom, you've always said how it would be so convenient to have a full-time servant. She'll cook even in the mornings and wash all the clothes."

"That's very well, but where will she sleep?"

"She can sleep anywhere. She'll sleep on the floor in the living room." I didn't want to be the one to suggest that Rani sleep in my room.

"You know Papa doesn't like these servant types going around the living room."

"Mom, she can sleep on the floor in my room."

"It'll disturb your studies."

"No it won't. I find it easier to study late when someone else is around."

"We can ask your father," my mother said.

"Of course he'll say no. He's a man, he won't understand."

"What's wrong with you? You have such funny ideas."

"So can I tell her she can stay the night?"

"Where is she?"

"On the veranda."

"Let me talk to her."

I followed my mother to the veranda. Rani, who had been squatting on the floor, got up.

"*Namaste, Memsahib,*" she said.

"Did he beat you badly?"

"He beat my legs. He said he would break them, and he hurt my back."

"Let me see," my mother said. Rani lifted her sari slightly to show her calf.

"Let me see properly."

She lifted her sari higher.

"Have you been to the doctor?"

"No."

My mother looked at me and said in Hindi so that Rani could understand, "We'll take her to the doctor and get her some medicine. Then we can buy some *rotis* and *sabzi* from the corner shop for dinner since there won't be time to cook. I want you both to eat and go to bed before your father comes home. I'll speak to him in the morning. It's best she stay in your room tonight. Let's see what we can do."

We trooped out of the house together. I was afraid her husband might be lurking around the house. Rani looked afraid, too.

"What's the matter?" my mother asked, looking at Rani.

"*Memsahib,* my man might come for me. This is dangerous for you."

"What rubbish! I'll call the police. He dare not raise a finger when we are around."

I had never seen this side of my mom. Our lives were fairly

sheltered, and there was no need for her to get defiant about anything.

"Which doctor should we take her to?" I asked.

There were a dozen doctors running private evening clinics in our locality. Our own, Dr. Iyer, was expensive. My parents would not have been able to afford him on a regular basis, but they got reimbursements from their jobs for medical expenses. There were several cheaper doctors, but we weren't sure who was good since a lot of quacks had set up practices.

"Dr. Iyer, of course. We know he's reliable," my mother said.

I could not help being surprised. I wondered if I had known my mother in all these years. She put up a tough exterior, but Rani's suffering had reached her.

We showed up at Dr. Iyer's clinic and waited in the waiting room. Rani made her way to the corner to squat on the floor.

"You sit on a chair when you are not well," my mother said to her in Hindi.

We had our turn after fifteen minutes. I was usually made to wait outside, but my mother did not say anything when I walked into the consultation chamber with both of them.

"Mrs. Sharma, what can I do for you?"

"My daughter will explain the full story," my mother replied, looking at me.

I felt more nervous talking to Dr. Iyer in front of my mother than I did addressing the school assembly every morning in front of six thousand children. He had known me since I was a child.

"Is she only bruised, or was there also some bleeding?"

I had noticed only grazed skin, but just to be sure I translated the question for Rani.

"No. No blood," she said in Hindi.

"In that case she doesn't need a tetanus shot. We'll give her some painkillers."

He usually gave us a prescription, and my mother and I would walk to the nearby chemist to get it filled. But today Dr. Iyer went up to the cabinet behind him and stared at the vials behind the glass, rubbing his hands. After a few seconds he opened it and got out two tubes of an antiseptic.

"Tell her to apply these to her skin. And here are some pills for the pain," he said.

"How much, Doctor?" my mother asked when we were done.

"For her? Nothing." He smiled. I'd never seen him smile that way. He had been my doctor since I was born, given me all my vaccines on my bum, even administered a glucose drip to me at home when I was dehydrated. Not once had he shed his stern exterior. My mother seemed to find nothing odd about his manner. She smiled back and said, "Thank you."

As soon as we had walked out I asked my mother, "Why didn't he charge us?"

"Everyone wants to do a good deed."

"Why did he smile like that?"

"Look at her. She looks devastating. There's nothing as moving as a beautiful woman who is suffering." My mother finished her sentence abruptly, and her face took on a look that made it clear I was not to talk for a little while. There was a tiny smile forming at the corners of her mouth.

I had become aware of the feelings of love and lust only after meeting India at the parent-teacher meeting. Since then the meaning of longing had revealed itself. Previously, reading the word in books, I had only been able to imagine it. With Rani and with India I now felt it myself. Suffering and beauty had taken on new meanings in my life. Delhi became suffused with a trembling beauty when the breeze blew or when I saw a blooming flower. Everything around me made me think of the two women I loved. I felt my heart ache to be with one or the other. If the dim yellow light in our dining room cast a shadow with a jagged edge, I could not help thinking of love. From the way my mother had just spoken about Rani, I had to wonder if she knew these feelings, too. Was it possible that my parents longed for each other? I had never noticed any indication of this before. After my life had taken off a few weeks ago I had assumed that

my lovers and I were the only people in the world who felt the
way we did.

My mother and Rani had picked up the pace and were a few
steps ahead of me. They turned onto the street where the market
was. I walked faster to catch up. We went to the *dhabawalla* to
order hot *rotis* and *dal* and *sabzi*. The *dhabawalla*'s *tandoor* oven
was facing us. It generated a lot of heat, so I turned my back on it
and faced the wall. I heard my mother pay for the order, and then
I heard India's voice say, "Pack three of the soft *rotis*, please."

I whirled around. Sure enough she was there. She saw me the
second I saw her. Even before I had seen her face, I could tell it
was her from the way her hair fell on her shoulders.

"Hi," we both said in unison. Then I turned red. What would
I tell my mother? How did I know a grown-up woman in the
colony?

But India's social graces could be counted on to save any situation. She turned to my mother and said, "You must be
Anamika's mother. I met her in school. I had gone to get admission for my son. You must be really proud that she's the Head
Prefect, so intelligent and mature."

"Yes, we're proud," my mother said, staring at me unabashedly.

Rani, who could not understand the conversation, neverthe-
less understood that it was about me. She added her two bits in
Hindi, "Little mistress is the best."

India and my mother smiled at her and then looked at each
other again.

"We just came back from the doctor. Her man beat her," my
mother said to India.

"All men are alike," India said in English, then added, "Mine
was super-educated. He went to Doon School and St. Stephen's,
and he still beat me. I left him."

I wondered how my mother would react. It was better it was
out right away that India was divorced. If my mother minded she
could end all association now, should she suspect that as a divorcée India was out to get everyone's husband.

"I think she should leave him, too," my mom said.

India took a long look at Rani. My mother looked at Rani, too, and so did I. It was dark, and the streetlights were no stronger than candles. In the flickering light of seven o'clock, Rani looked broken and beautiful. I wanted to take her away and tell them they could not like to see her broken. When she was in high spirits she was prettier.

"I'd be happy to keep her if you want me to," India said.

"We're thinking of keeping her. Anamika is very determined. I'll speak to my husband."

My mother sounded enthusiastic. It was almost as if they both wanted to be knights in shining armor. India nodded to my mother. I stared at my feet. I was afraid that if I made eye contact with India I'd catch a slightly disapproving glance at my keenness for Rani.

"Well, you can let me know. I can give you my phone number," India said.

"We should get your phone number anyway. We can have you over for dinner," my mother said warmly.

Then she looked at me and asked, "Anamika, do you have a pen? We can take . . . this lady's number." My mother looked embarrassed at having to call her "this lady."

India laughed and said, "Mrs. Sharma, if I hadn't met your daughter I wouldn't know your name either. I'm Tripta Adhikari."

"I don't have a pen, just say it," I said, looking into India's eyes.

"Will you remember?" my mother asked.

"Mom!"

"Your daughter is brilliant," India said. I wondered if she was mocking me.

"Stop," I said. I used the tone I used when I spoke to her alone. The tone of a lover. I was afraid my mother would notice. It was bad enough I had not called India "Aunty" even once during this whole episode. But my mother did not notice. We finally said bye to her and walked away.

When we got home we went to the dining room and sat down

to eat. Rani sat cross-legged on the floor and put the *rotis* on her plate. My mother and I sat at the table. We were lost in our own worlds and didn't speak much. While we were eating there was a powercut.

"Let me get some candles from the kitchen," Rani said immediately.

"Just keep sitting. We don't need any light," my mother said.

It was almost pitch black in the dining room. I wished I were sitting on the floor with Rani so that I could touch her. I slid to the end of my chair and brushed my knee against her shoulder.

"It's so peaceful even though it's hot," my mother said.

"Yes," I replied, feeling a bead of sweat trickling down my chin.

"I really liked that friend of yours, Mrs. Adhikari."

"My friend?" I wanted to protest just to keep myself in the clear.

"You're the one who knows her."

"I guess you're right. She's nice."

"When Papa goes out for cards next week we should invite her for dinner."

"Why when Papa's out?"

"I just thought it would be more fun to be all women. It is possible to be genuinely good friends only with a woman. Real friendship with men is difficult. Moreover, tongues wag if a man and woman are friends."

I grunted. On the one hand, having three of the women I loved in one room would be great, but the thought of my mother and India getting along like a house on fire made me squirm.

The phone rang. It took me a long time to make my way to it without banging into furniture, but it was still ringing when I got there.

"I thought you would never pick up," Sheela said.

The house was quiet, and her voice was loud and clear over the telephone wire. I was sure my mother could hear her. I cupped the earpiece in my hand to muffle the sound and responded softly.

"So can you stay for Sports Day practice?"

"Yes."

"Good."

"My parents want to know if the school bus will drop us back." She sounded cagey, as if her parents were listening.

"Of course it'll drop us back," I said loudly for my mother's benefit. I was not allowed to take public transportation, but if we stayed back we would have no choice. I decided both on Sheela's behalf and my own that we would take the risk of catching a DTC bus.

"See you tomorrow then," she said.

As I hung up the power came back. I blinked my eyes.

"I guess we better clear the table. I want her in your room and the two of you asleep by the time Papa gets here. I don't want to have to discuss this with him till the morning."

"Yes, Mom."

Then I said in Hindi, so that Rani could understand, too, "I'll be coming late from school tomorrow. Our Sports Day practices have started."

"Yes, *Babyji*," Rani said.

My mother turned to Rani and said, "Go and sleep in Baby's room. I'll give you one of my old saris and a blouse. First take a bath, and then wear them and go to sleep."

"Yes, *Memsahib*. Can I take a bath on the veranda?"

Just like there was no question of servants eating from plates used by people of the house, there was no question of them using the same bathrooms. We didn't have a spare servants' quarter, but the veranda had a small toilet and also a water faucet. The toilet was closed off, but the water faucet was out in the open, exposed to neighbors and the people living upstairs.

"Today you can use Baby's bathroom," my mother said. "Do you mind?" my mother asked, looking at me.

"Not at all," I said.

"Good. Show her your bathroom, and I'll lay my sari out on your bed."

I took Rani to my bathroom. I had seen *jhuggi* women clean themselves in the morning. Since they had to do it in public under a common tap, they never took off their saris.

"Since you are alone here, take off all your clothes when you bathe," I said.

"In my village we had a bathroom inside the house, so I always used to bathe naked till I got married and came here," Rani said.

I told her how to shampoo her hair and also showed her my lotion.

"All this is too fancy for me," Rani said, using the English word *fancy*. I was surprised.

After Rani had bathed and dressed, my mother came to my room.

"You are so beautiful. You'll never have trouble finding another man. They will kill one another for someone like you," my mother said to her.

"Who needs a man, *Memsahib*," Rani said, looking at me. Then she added, "When there are people like you," looking at my mom.

"Just look at her, she's so gorgeous," my mother said.

"Yes," I said, feeling a steely, possessive madness creep in on me.

"Even your friend Tripta Adhikari is quite sexy," my mother said. I was afraid my mother would uncover my secrets right then as she vocalized my own thoughts about Rani and India. She showed every sign of knowing. She had referred to India first as Mrs. Adhikari and now by her full name. It was very emphatic.

I did not say anything.

"Good, Anamika, you are turning out well," she said and patted my arm. Was she being sarcastic?

"What do you mean?"

"You have a good heart, most kids are brats. They treat their servants badly. You've shown kindness. And you're talking to grown-ups and making a good impression. I always knew you were intelligent, but you are becoming mature. I'm proud to have a daughter like you."

"Mom," I said, moving closer to her and hugging her.

She rubbed my head and then said, "Go to bed now. I'll tell Papa you are asleep."

I was sure, as I led Rani away, that my mother would find a way to keep her. She had become my accomplice in this. When a woman sets her mind to something, it happens. Rani and I bolted the door from the inside and then made a bed for her on the floor. After it was made I held her hand and brought her to my bed. I turned off the light and pulled her head to the crook of my arm where she slept until dawn.

The Queen of My Heart

had set my alarm for fifteen minutes before my mother woke up. When it went off I shook Rani awake.

"You need to get back on the floor, before my mother comes in."

She was not fully awake, but she got up and went to the floor. I unbolted the door and went to brush my teeth. My mother soon came in with my tea.

"I just spoke to Papa. He says she can stay here for a few days till we think it through."

"Thank you, Mom." I leaned forward and kissed her on the cheek. I was not physically affectionate with my parents at all, but now after India and Rani it seemed natural to touch and kiss. My mother surprised me by kissing me back.

On the school bus in the morning I felt a little starry-eyed. I had never thought of my mother as a person in her own right. As someone more than a woman who had given birth to me and catered to my needs. When I was in Class IV the art teacher had made us all draw cards for Mother's Day. I had written on mine, "Mother, you are the queen of my heart."

When I was in kindergarten I would cry all the way to school till my mother hugged me and promised to be back in the afternoon. On the way home I would tell her how much fun I'd had. The next morning when I'd cry again at parting from her she'd remind me that I really did enjoy KG, but the grief of leaving my mother would outweigh all my memories of the previous day. In the afternoons I always told her, "I won't cry tomorrow because now I've grown up." Somewhere along the line I had stopped clinging to her. The full force of my love hit me today.

I felt particularly efficient that morning. I went straight to the assembly ground and made hassling announcements over the PA system. Assembly was over and done with quickly. The kids had ten minutes to loiter before going to class. I got off the stage and made my way to where my classmates stood. Vidur, Sheela, and a few others were cracking jokes. Vidur looked at me and said, "What's up today, Captain, you've been so crisp?"

"I'm in a good mood, Vidur," I said. I refused to let his ragging get to me.

"Do tell," he said.

"Nothing, just looking forward to life," I said, stealing a glance at Sheela.

"Life is one big drag. You go to school. You get a job. You slog. You have kids. They turn around and leave you in your hour of need. You die," Vidur said.

"Life is short. Grab it and enjoy the moment. There is nothing else," I said, hoping Sheela was listening. I did not want her to have any doubts in the afternoon.

"Hear hear. Our very own Sufi philosopher," Vidur said.

"If anything I'm like Bhagwan Rajneesh," I said.

"Why? Do you believe in free love and sex?" Vidur asked.

"If there is only the moment, only four things of value remain," I said. Sheela was listening carefully, as if I were about to reveal the Truth. So I stopped.

"What four things?" she asked impatiently.

"Food, sleep, sex, and mathematics."

"That's so pretentious," Vidur said.

"It's true. They are all joys of the moment. And mathematics can be extended to mean physics or music or reading, whatever intellectual activity absorbs you," I said.

Sheela looked at Vidur to see if he thought I was right.

"You have a point there," Vidur said sagely.

"But sex?" Sheela said softly, looking at Vidur and then at me.

I didn't want to be the one convincing her. I knew it would hold more weight if Vidur made the argument. She knew I had my own agenda.

"Well, sex is the ultimate in-the-moment, you know." Vidur spoke as if he knew.

"I don't know. Do you know, Vidur?" she asked him boldly. It made me jealous that she was curious about him.

"I'm saving myself for my wife," he said, blushing.

The bell for the first period rang, and we walked to class. The morning passed uneventfully. After the break we had two periods of mathematics. Our teacher, Mrs. Pillai, was the only one who did not care whether we sat in our assigned seats. Vidur and I usually didn't change our seats, but today he asked me if Mohit could sit next to him.

"If I can sit with Sheela," I negotiated.

"But Mohit doesn't sit next to Sheela. He sits next to Ashima."

"So you do the rearranging."

"You're so difficult," Vidur grumbled.

Then he spoke to the boy who sat next to Sheela and got him to move next to Ashima. I took my pencil box, ruler, protractor, compass, and notebook and went over to Sheela's desk. Mrs. Pillai was both the least and most strict teacher we had. She never insisted that we take notes or draw lines in our notebook. She didn't care what we did as long as we knew our lessons. Whoever did badly on tests got a dressing down in public. Mrs. Pillai even cussed in public. One day someone heard her say the word "fuck" in class under her breath.

"I hate that female," Sheela said as soon as I sat next to her.

"Why? She's a good teacher."

"She's better than the rest, but she's just such an awful B."

"She's not. I've never heard her gossip."

"She thinks she's too good for us. Her attitude is so arrogant and blunt."

"At least she's not holier-than-thou like Mrs. Thaityallam, constantly making a show."

"That's true."

Mrs. Pillai walked in. We all shuffled to our feet. "Please sit down, everyone. It's just not a day when I can bear to hear you all wail, 'Good morning, ma'am' in those deathly singsong voices of yours," she said to the class.

Some children giggled. Sheela turned up her nose. Mrs. Pillai was wearing her pale yellow sari. It looked good on her. She was exceptionally fair for an Indian, especially a South Indian. I wondered if Sheela felt competitive with Mrs. Pillai because Sheela was also very fair. All the "Bride Wanted" ads in the Sunday papers sought "fair, domesticated women."

The pale lemon yellow made Mrs. Pillai look very delicate. She was the only teacher in the school with real guts. Her sternness and her fragility were a potent mix. She never minced words. One had to admire that.

I loved mathematics. Unlike physics, which gave me a headache and then managed to screw up my life by putting ideas in my head, mathematics was abstract. I always got fully absorbed in problem solving and loved the challenge. I had a vision of myself at home solving numericals in the middle of the night and Rani trying to get me into bed. I knew I'd be able to resist her if I was doing probability theory. Mathematics felt very safe. If I ever wanted to run away from temptation and shield myself from getting hurt, I'd take up mathematics. We were into the second period with Mrs. Pillai when the school messenger, who worked for the principal, knocked on our door.

"Yes, *Bahadur*?" Mrs. Pillai asked. Everyone called him by the generic name one used for Nepali and *pahari* people.

"Principal *Sahib* and Counselor Madam are calling for Anamika baby," he said. The Class IV employees of the school—like the *bahadur* and the ladies responsible for keeping the toilets clean—usually called the girls "baby" just like Rani did.

"She's hardly a baby, *Bahadur*," Mrs. Pillai said with a serious face. Then she looked at me and said, "Go. They want you."

The way she said "they want you" made me feel febrile. I was embarrassed.

"Yes," I said, getting up. I walked to the princi's office, wondering what might have happened. The school counselor and the principal were both chatting when I went in. My heart had started beating fast. I wondered if anyone could know what I had been up to.

"Ah! There you are, Anamika," the principal said, his face open and welcoming. "We were thinking it's time to have a little chat with the senior class about sex," he said.

"Sir?" I said, shocked.

"We'll get a doctor in who will speak to the children and answer questions," he elaborated.

"That's a good idea, sir," I said.

"We should have a male doctor for the boys and a female doctor for the girls, sir," the counselor said.

"But Mrs. Shah, the danger is of the boys and girls having sex together, not about learning together. Don't you think they should all be in one room? We are a progressive school. We don't want to be prudes in this matter. What do you think, Anamika?"

I imagined sitting between Sheela and Vidur when the doctor spoke about sex. I liked the idea. I could trade notes with Vidur on it. I wanted to find out what kinds of things he thought about girls. Had he ever tried to sneak a look at Sheela's panties?

"I agree, sir. If the children are going to hear about it, they should be treated like adults and allowed to sit in the same room." I had purposely used the word "children" to refer to my classmates.

"Sir, I am very strongly against this. There will be a lot of parental opposition if they find out that this will happen in a coed environment," the counselor said, looking at the princi.

"But Mrs. Shah, the school is coed."

"Sir, the children will feel very embarrassed and inhibited about asking questions."

I wondered who would ask questions. I could sit quietly in the room and observe the girls as they were told about sex. I'd know how much they had known and done by the way their pupils dilated and the corners of their mouths turned into smirks. I'd have a permanent advantage over the boys: I'd be the only one to know what made the girls blush.

"Fine, Mrs. Shah, you're the counselor. This is your domain, and I don't want to interfere. But you know what we think." He looked at me when he said "we."

The teachers and the staff had more or less treated me like a grown-up ever since they had vested me with the authority of the Head Prefect. But every time something like this happened, when an adult opposed another adult and made a show of joining forces with me, I still gloated on the inside.

"Sir, should I organize the auditorium for the activity period on Friday?" I asked.

"For the girls. The boys can have it in the field outside," Mrs. Shah said.

I went back to class to catch the tail end of Mrs. Pillai's class. I opened the door and walked in. With Mrs. Thaityallam it would have been necessary to ask, "Ma'am, can I come in?" When I was forced into niceties I got tired and felt as if I was playing a part, being something I wasn't. I took my seat next to Sheela. When Mrs. Pillai finished her sentence, she looked at me and said, "All okay?"

I nodded. Sheela gave her a dirty look.

"What's the deal?" I wrote in my notebook and pointed it to Sheela.

"She wants to have an affair with you," Sheela scribbled back.

"You're crazy. She doesn't give a fig about me. You just want to have an affair with me. That's why you're so paranoid," I wrote. When the period ended, Mrs. Pillai walked out, and several kids went to the watercooler or to the bathrooms. I slid my hand under the small wooden desk we were sitting at and squeezed Sheela's thigh. She blushed.

"I liked seeing under your skirt," I said. She blushed some more.

I got up and went to take my place next to Vidur. "Hey, don't tell anyone, but they will talk to us about sex on Friday," I said to him.

"No way!"

"The boys and girls will be separate."

"That's no fun!"

"Why did you want to sit next to Mohit?" I asked.

"Don't tell anyone," he said, dropping his voice.

"I promise I won't."

"He has a German porn magazine."

"Vidur, I thought you were different," I said.

"I am. There's no harm in seeing. It's quite disgusting."

"Can I look?"

"You'll puke."

"Do you have it?"

"Yes. I am supposed to return it to him at the end of the day. You can see it if you want."

The next period was geography. There was no question of looking at a porn magazine in Mrs. Thaityallam's class. But then we had physics. After the class test Mr. Garg was on everyone's case but mine. So I opened the magazine inside my physics textbook, put them both on the shelf under my desk, and had a good look. There was a motorbike sequence with a naked man on a bike and some women in leather bending over him. All in all there were a lot of sex pictures that were revolting. I had expected the magazine to be filled with only pretty, naked chicks. There were only a few of those. Most of them had unnaturally large breasts and waxy complexions. Rani, India, and Sheela were all far superior to them. I wished the captions were in English. I didn't know any foreign languages.

Mr. Garg had turned his back to us and was drawing on the blackboard. He was trying to describe Schrödinger's wave function yet again and was sketching a box with a cat in it. He got very involved drawing the cat. Vidur turned to look at me. I was still looking at the pictures, but I could feel his eyes on me. I felt my face get hot. Vidur looked away. I didn't want Vidur to get any funny ideas about me. I looked at him for a second, to see if I could imagine it with him. The thought made my stomach turn. There was coarse black hair on the back of his hands.

I rolled the magazine tightly and turned around to put it into my backpack. As I turned I saw Chakra Dev, the overdeveloped daily shaver, looking at me. From his eyes I could tell that he knew I had the magazine. The naked German man in the magazine suddenly had Chakra Dev's face. Or maybe Chakra Dev had his body. I felt a shudder run through my being and wanted to throw up. He smirked.

Cheapads

After the bell for the last period rang, Sheela and I went to the large field in the back of the school where the assembly was held every morning. I didn't want our friends to see us hanging around, not getting on the school bus.

After fifteen minutes in the field we returned to the empty school building and sat at a desk in the back of our classroom. I bolted the classroom door from inside just in case sweepers or Class IV employees were still around.

"Take out your textbook and let's go over the first chapter," I said.

"You're really going to teach me? I just wanted to sit around and talk."

"Let's get some work done, then we can talk as much as you want," I said.

Physics was like making love. You couldn't just plunge into it. One had to start slowly and from the beginning. Sheela had not followed even the first chapter. There was no way I could start teaching her about quantum mechanics. We sat and labored away at the introduction. I made sure she had understood last year's course and recapped everything she should know so far.

"Enough, now I'm bored," she said after an hour.

"Did you understand everything?" I asked.

"Yes," she said, nodding, but I wasn't sure.

"Good."

"Maybe I should pay you?" she said.

"Pay me? I did it because you're my friend," I said, offended. She was smiling.

"Well, how would you pay me?" I asked, warming up.

"In the currency of kisses," she said.

I shrugged my shoulders. Sheela thought this was some sort of game. I didn't want to play it like a game. I wanted the real thing, like I had with Rani and India. I wanted an affair.

"Please, I've never kissed before," she said.

"Why me?"

"Because I trust you. You won't tell anyone."

"There are others who won't tell. Vidur won't tell," I said. If I gave in easily she wouldn't appreciate it. Moreover, I wanted Sheela to love me.

"But I'm not attracted to Vidur," she argued.

I suppressed a smile.

"Well, I don't know about kissing," I said and put my index finger in the pocket of her white school shirt. The shirt was thin.

"Anamika, what are you doing?" she asked, her voice almost panic-stricken.

I looked her straight in the eye as if my finger was not connected to me.

"Look, we're either going to do it or not," I said.

"Do what?" she asked, biting her lower lip nervously.

"Everything."

"I'm not going to do that. Anyway, two women can't do it."

Then she grabbed my wrist and lifted my finger out from her breast pocket. She let go of my wrist with a jerk. My hand fell to my side.

"Right, then," I said, getting angry. What did it matter that some sixteen-year-old brat was rejecting me? I had India and Rani.

"You're angry," she said.

"Not at all," I said calmly. I wasn't going to share my true feelings with her after that. It was time to go home to someone who was waiting.

"Are you sure?"

"Yes," I said, then added, "let's get going."

We walked in silence to the front gates of the school to take a DTC home. My parents had told me I could not ride in one till I was old enough to go to college. I wasn't familiar with the bus system. I had figured we'd just queue up at the nearest bus stop and ask someone.

Delhi is the kind of city it is—slow, dead, undercover, and polluted—because it does not have decent public transportation. At any time of day one can see buses so overpacked that they practically tip over when they turn the corner. People hang from the front and rear entrances since the doors have usually fallen off. The Delhi Transportation Corporation has been a loss-making operation since its inception and complains that the majority of riders travel ticketless.

As we walked to the DTC bus stop, an uncomfortable silence smoldered between us. I felt silly and immature for having gotten upset. There were two men, of the construction worker class, waiting at the bus stop. They looked Sheela up and down. They stared at her legs. Not that many women exposed their legs to begin with, but Sheela's skirt was particularly high. I saw the leer in their eyes. My blood boiled. Sheela had taken on a completely different personality. Her face had shrunk, and she stared at the ground; she knew the guys were looking at her. I wished I was a guy and could protect her, but I was shorter, thinner, and weaker than Sheela.

"Where can we get buses to South Delhi?" I asked the guys in Hindi.

They lifted their eyes from her legs and let them settle upon me. The same lasciviousness hung heavy from their stares. I wore glasses and was relatively dark. I had short hair. I was average looking and flat-chested. I wondered what on earth they were looking at.

"Depends how south you want to go," one of the men replied with a smirk.

I gave him a dumb look and said, "We are trying to go to the

Chirag Delhi area." I didn't want to reveal exact details of which colony we were going to.

"You can take seventy-seven from here."

"Thank you," I said and turned my back to them.

"Let's go off to the side and sit," I said, whispering to Sheela. It was a relief to know she was there, that I wasn't alone with the two *cheapads* at the bus stop.

We walked a few steps and sat on a concrete projection that was part of the school's outside boundary. It reeked of urine.

"You're not used to this, are you?" Sheela said.

"Used to what?" I asked. She couldn't possibly be used to acrid stench either.

"All these men on the street hassling you," she said.

"No."

"I get followed everywhere. I used to think I was doing something wrong. But now I am used to it. I got my period five years ago. So I guess I developed faster than the rest of you."

I looked at her chest. She was fairly well-endowed. And had been for as long as I could remember. It was strange to think that Sheela had developed faster than I had in any department.

A bus was coming our way. I got up to take a look at the number. It was not ours. The two guys got on the bus. As it pulled away they yelled out of the window, "Bye, sexy."

As soon as they were gone I got up to move away from the smell. The afternoon had been a disappointment. Since the moment I had put my finger in Sheela's shirt pocket everything had gone steadily downhill. Nothing was beautiful anymore, and the exquisite, bittersweet pain of longing that I had become used to feeling several times a day eluded me altogether.

After a while we saw seventy-seven approach. It showed no signs of slowing down. Sheela and I had to wave at it frantically. I was practically standing in the middle of the road to flag it down. We had to run alongside it and climb aboard because it did not come to a full stop. The bus was packed. We could not inch our way in to buy a ticket or ask the conductor where exactly it was going. Yelling to no one in particular, I asked if the

bus was headed to South Delhi. A man said "yes" without turning around. We had to hold the railings with a lot of strength
because the bus was swaying back and forth. Every time the surface of the road was uneven we flew a few inches off the steps. I
saw Sheela's forearms pulled taut. Her hands gripped the railing
so hard that her knuckles jutted out.

A few minutes later the bus slowed a little, and three men
climbed on behind us. They pushed into us as if we didn't exist.
I couldn't see Sheela anymore. I couldn't see anyone since my
whole body including my head was pressing into the guy in front
of me. I could hardly breathe. The smell of sweat filled the bus.
My backpack was sliding off my shoulders, and I had to keep lifting my right shoulder all the way up to my ear to keep the strap
from slipping.

"Are you okay?" I shouted, hoping Sheela would hear. My
head twisted at a peculiar angle.

"Barely," I heard her shout back.

I tried to turn around to look at her. I could only turn my
head by twenty degrees or so. My body was locked in at an angle.
There were too many people around us, and my backpack made
it impossible for me to maneuver. I felt a harsh pointed thing
graze the back of my thigh. I couldn't imagine what it was. I tried
to move. Then suddenly I felt human flesh. It was a guy's hand.
My heart gave a start. I wanted to scream but my voice had
seized up. I tried to turn a little more to see if I could make eye
contact with Sheela, but I couldn't even glimpse her from the
corner of my eye.

The hand had now firmly gripped my upper thigh and was
making its way higher. I turned my feet and legs by an inch in
the tiny space I had, and the hand relaxed its grip for a second.
When I had finished turning it slipped under my skirt again, this
time making its way up the front of my thigh. I could feel my
face boiling. As the bus swerved, Sheela came back slightly into
my field of vision. Her face was buried into a small bit of space
between the metal railing and the back of a seat. Something
seemed wrong. I could see her right hand clutch her backpack so

hard that its veins were popping. My eyes traveled lower. Her skirt was all the way up, and there was a hand on her bum. I could see the man's face. No one else on the bus could have seen what was going on. His right hand was in his fly. The hand under my skirt was yanking the elastic of my underwear. It broke my trance. I let out a blood-curdling howl. The people standing right in front of us shifted. Sheela turned her face when she heard my cry, and I could see that it was wet with tears. The guy with his hand under my skirt let go. I could see the forearm of the guy who was touching Sheela. His hand was rubbing her underwear very fast. His eyes were shut, and his face was all screwed up. I let go of the railing that I had been clutching and brought my right hand down on his head with all the strength I could muster. He jerked backward and clutched at the railing. His eyes opened. He looked vicious and dirty. He was a bit off balance, so I lifted my foot a few inches off the ground and kicked it in his direction. It missed him. The guy behind me was standing with one leg on the same step as me, and my foot hit his shin. He tumbled closer to me. The other guy had now regained a firm hold on Sheela and was continuing to do what he had been doing. He gave me an ugly look, as if I'd interrupted something. I screamed "Bastard!" in English and this time managed to kick him.

I had got him on the side of his leg. It hadn't done much damage, but it threw him off-kilter again for a second. His right hand was still in his pants, but his left hand had flown off Sheela and was trying to clutch the railing. I brought my foot up to the level of his fly and kicked with all my might. Sheela had turned her face and was watching me.

The man let go of the hand railing and was swaying, his left hand having flown protectively in front of his crotch. There was no door on the bus, and he was dangerously close to the entrance. I turned around fully and pushed him as hard as I could. Sheela stared. He fell off the bus and onto the road with a scream. I saw him roll on the tar and dust.

"What did you do?" she said.

The bus slowed a little. It was too packed for the driver to have seen in the rearview mirror what was going on, but one of the passengers in the front must have seen it and told the driver. The guy who had been standing behind me jumped off when the bus slowed down. I turned to see the guys. They knew each other. The guy who had been behind me was helping up the one I had thrown off the bus. He didn't seem too hurt. No one could fall off a crawling DTC bus and get hurt. A man standing nearby congratulated me, saying, "*Shabash, Beta.*" I thought I saw a lascivious look on his face and stared back with contempt.

Sheela's tears had dried, leaving streak marks on her face.

"Are you okay?" I asked.

"It was miserable," she said.

I noticed her hands were trembling.

"Let's get off this bus right now," I said.

When the bus reached the next stop I tugged her hand and pulled her off. We were in Green Park near the market. I decided we should stop for a few minutes to recover. "Let's just stabilize ourselves a little. Let's go to Evergreen and eat something," I said.

"Thank you for saving my life," Sheela said dramatically as we walked toward the market.

"I didn't save your life. He was such a creep you should have shouted," I said.

"Men are such *behnchods*. The bus was packed, and no one said a thing when you screamed." I had never heard Sheela use mother- or sister-abuses or even the F word.

"There must have been women, too, on that bus. They didn't say a thing."

"All the women were probably being eve-teased like us," Sheela said.

"Eve-teased" was such a coy word to use. I felt enraged that Sheela was using the same term the newspapers used to describe such incidents. It made the act sound routine, acceptable.

"Sheela, that was borderline rape," I said.

"No, it was not rape," Sheela said. Her face hardened.

"Well, the next thing, his whole dirty finger would have been inside you," I said angrily.

"Stop it." She started shaking again.

"I'm sorry. I'm sorry," I said, coming closer and hugging her.

"We can't do this again. We can't go on a bus," she said.

"What are we going to do? This is where we were born, this is where we grew up. Are we not going to take public transportation to go from one part of our city to another because we're afraid of goons on a packed bus?"

"I don't want to get raped," she said.

We had reached Green Park Market. The shops were all well maintained, and there weren't too many people on the sidewalk squatting and selling goods. But there was a cobbler, around thirty years old, sitting under a tree, polishing shoes. I touched Sheela's arm to stop her from walking on.

"How much will you charge to polish these?" I asked, pointing to my school shoes.

"Two rupees," he said.

"Okay," I said, bringing my foot close to the jute bag on which he was sitting.

"Why don't you remove your shoes, *Babyji*," he said.

"No, I'll put my feet here," I said, pointing to the small wooden stand in front of him. I saw men getting their shoes polished all the time with one foot placed on the stand and the other on the ground. I was wearing a skirt, and he would probably be able to see under it. But standing like that while having a man polish my shoes made me feel like a grown-up man. My society allowed the molestation of young girls in public, but if you had money then people always bowed down to you. Sheela stood near me looking at the guy bending over my right foot and then my left, applying shoe cream and buffing the leather with a cloth.

"How many shoes do you polish a day?" I asked.

He looked up at me and said, "*Babyji*, sometimes ten, on a good day twenty."

I was searching for a mocking grin on his face, but there was none. The way he said "*Babyji*" was convincing, clean. At twenty pairs of shoes a day he was making only forty rupees. Even if he got a few shoe repair jobs he was probably making no more than fifty rupees a day tops.

"How big is your family?" I asked.

"*Babyji*, I am the only one who works. I have my mother, sister, wife, and two children."

That was less than three rupees a head. It wasn't possible, this poverty. How did he manage?

"Here, *Babyji*, your shoes are shining," he said.

Then he looked at Sheela and asked her if she wanted her shoes done. She didn't. I paid him, and we walked to Evergreen.

"How do you think they live on so little money?" I asked her.

"Very frugally," she said.

"Our national priorities are upside down. We just spent *crores* to build a stadium in Delhi that we keep lit all night long. Just the lighting costs us two *lakhs* a year," I said.

"If you want to make a change you should go into politics."

"I might," I replied.

"Physics isn't going to teach you a thing," she said.

"I think it's good to know what makes the world go round, why objects fall to the earth. If we can split atoms, understand thermodynamics, maybe we'll make electricity out of nothing, save the two *lakhs* on the lighting. Create food where there is none to be found."

"Science is not the answer to everything, Anamika. God is."

"God is a radiation," I said. I had spoken without thinking, but I liked the way it sounded. "God is just a radiation," I repeated.

She looked at me, startled. After a few steps she said, "You're brilliant."

I felt a lot older than Sheela. She was so easily impressed.

We had reached Evergreen. The restaurant extended all the way past the pedestrian path of the market to the tar road. There was proper seating inside, but one could also get *chaat* and *gol-*

gappa on the street and eat it standing. It cost less. There was a guy with a big cauldron of hot oil frying *golgappas* and *aloo tikkis* right in the middle of the pedestrian pathway. We ordered two plates of *golgappas*. The incident on the bus seemed a little more distant now. These things happened all the time. But there were millions of people worse off than we were. People to feel more sorry for. One couldn't focus on one's own problems.

The *golgappa* man was filling the small round shells with *masala* water and passing them to Sheela. She put entire *golgappas* in her mouth without any juice trickling out. When he gave them to me I found that harder to do. I wasn't allowed to eat off the street. My parents said one caught infections that way. I found the *golgappa* juice much too spicy and the pieces too big. The fluid dribbled from my lips as I tried to bite them whole. I wiped my face with the back of my hand.

"Sheela, we'll take an autorikshaw. I'll drop you off first."

"If my servant sees me coming in a three-wheeler, he'll tell my parents, and they'll scold me."

"We'll stop a little distance from your house."

"How much will a three-wheeler cost?" Sheela asked.

"I'm not sure, but I have all my pocket money. Don't worry," I said.

We hailed a three-wheeler and got in. It rattled and shook, causing us to fly an inch from our seats at every speed-breaker on the road. The driver sat on the edge of his seat, leaning precariously to one side as he coughed and spat every few seconds. Since we were fully exposed on both sides, the wind blew Sheela's hair all over her face. It made her look older, like a college girl. I found it sexy. We sat in silence. When we came near her house she gave me a kiss on the cheek and stepped out. I was surprised. I was not used to people kissing each other on the cheek. Westernized people did it, but in my family it was not usually done.

I lived only ten minutes away from Sheela. I asked the driver to stop just at the beginning of the lane that led to my house and paid him off. I could not decide if I was going to tell Rani about the bus incident. I didn't want her to think such things could happen to me. I wanted to be strong and invulnerable in her mind. Moreover, I could not tell Rani we'd stayed back to fool around.

Rani proffered me a glass of cold water when she opened the door for me.

"Are you feeling better?" I asked her, seeing the blue marks on her arms.

"*Dr. Sahib*'s medicine did magic," she said.

We had only half an hour before my mother came back home from the office.

"Rani, will you massage my legs?" I asked.

"Of course, *Babyji*, I'll do anything for you."

She looked down, suddenly shy.

I removed the belt from my school skirt, letting it fall to the floor, and flopped on my bed. Rani leaned forward to remove my shoes. I lurched back instinctively, unused to anyone touching my feet. I'd let her touch me in other places that were far less polite. They are just feet, I said to myself. The only time someone had touched my feet was when I was invited by the neighbors to a *pooja* for virgins. The lady of the house had asked me to stand in a steel plate while she washed my feet. I was eight years old then. Feet were heavy with symbolic meaning. I only touched the feet of my grandparents and the icons of some of the gods in temples. I only touched the feet of the gods I liked. Rama had thrown Sita out of his house even though she was virtuous, so I never touched the feet of his idol. But I touched Krishna's feet because even in his moments of youthful dishonesty there was a transparency. I had never touched my parents' feet.

Rani's touching my feet was a gift of love. A gift so enormous I didn't know what to do. It was also a responsibility. Women touched their husbands' feet at the end of the seven *pheras*. She was now removing my socks and rubbing my feet. I had never known what it felt like to have my feet rubbed. My entire body felt relaxed and seemed to melt. Feet were just another part of the body, the lowest part because they touched the earth, I told myself. Her fingers expertly cracked every bone on each toe. Then she kneaded my thighs. She touched me gently, feeling out all the knots in my legs. I remembered the way the man's fingernail had felt on my leg. It was sharp and had almost cut my skin. The incident came back with an intense vividness. I started to cry.

"*Babyji*, Anamikaji, *Didiji*," Rani said, unable to address me suitably.

I continued sobbing. She immediately came closer to me and pulled my head onto her lap.

"What happened to my child, tell me," she said soothingly in Hindi as she stroked my hair.

I felt a hot stream of tears roll down my cheeks. My body was quivering.

"What happened to my *jaan*, my star, my moon," she cooed.

I pulled myself up and buried my face in her blouse. She put her arm around me.

"I missed the bus and another friend did, too," I said.

"How did you come back?"

"We had to take a DTC bus back from school. On the way two dirty men climbed up and started touching us," I said. My tears were still uncontrollable, and there was as much fluid coming out of my nose as from my eyes.

"Where did they touch you?" she asked. Her voice was hard and low. It was the other side of Rani. The defiant side I rarely got to see.

I pointed to the upper parts of my thigh.

"*Kameene, haramzade, behnchod, maderchod,*" she cursed.

She was sitting upright now. She held my face in her hands and kissed my eyes.

"They didn't even spare a little child like you," she said, her voice raised.

I wasn't a child. She was sleeping with me, she was my

lover. The men were dogs, but they weren't much older than she was.

"Rani, they weren't that old, only in their twenties. They were your age."

"So what? Couldn't they see you're young, a child," she said.

My tears stopped as if a tap had just been turned shut. My head was hurting.

"I'm not a child."

I wanted to argue, but I felt as if my vocabulary had dried up.

"We are together, I am not a child," I said. I was scared as I spoke that she would stop sleeping with me now because she saw me as a child.

I felt savage all of a sudden.

"I'm not a child," I screamed and pulled myself into a sitting position. I threw her on the bed and started ripping open her blouse. She closed her eyes as if she didn't want to see me. As soon as I had finished unhooking her blouse I pulled her sari down and lifted up her petticoat. I didn't know what I was doing, but I touched her and slid my finger wherever it would slide in. She was hugging me hard. Her arms were tight, almost vice-like, around my back. In my frenzy I grabbed her foot in my hand. The sole of her foot was callused and hard. I gripped it firmly. I had an image of the two men from the bus again, but this time it did not leave me cold. It made me angry, and I started pushing into Rani more vigorously. The German guy from the porn magazine, but with Chakra Dev's face, the *brahmin* from the movies with his servant, positions from the *Kamasutra* all mixed up in my head till I could no longer think. I felt rapacious and greedy for her. These feelings drove out everything. After some time her body rocked and then went still. I stopped, a little short of breath, my back entirely slick with sweat, and remembered that I had read about this moment in books.

"Are you okay?" I asked.

She opened her eyes and smiled. She seemed like a different

person. I was at the edges of my experience again. It was like being in a room where very little is visible. Once your eyes adjust you realize some parts are still in the dark, but you can't turn the light up to see everything.

"*Memsahib* will be coming soon, I should get dressed," Rani said, getting up.

I got out of bed and removed the rest of my school uniform and put on civvies. I shut the door to my bedroom and pulled out my books. I had a Monday test in chemistry coming up. I had avoided the subject all term and was sure it would show on my report card. Writing equations was distracting. Equivalence signs between different entities made me compare the people in my life.

I thought about the afternoon with Rani. Up until now we'd been very gentle with each other, but I had turned violent today, and she'd seemed to like it. I had never seen India in that state. Would she be like Rani or different? I would only understand the true elements and equivalencies of life's chemistry if I experienced how similar and different Rani, Sheela, and India were.

My mother sent Rani to my room before dinner with some peeled almonds. Mom believed that if one soaked almonds overnight and ate them they improved one's memory. I didn't think I needed to remember any better than I did. Sometimes I couldn't sleep at night because I would remember things. Today's incident was already burnt in my mind. I asked Rani to shut the door. I fed her the almonds.

"So you still think I am a child?" I asked.

"No," she said, blushing.

"No, I'm not a child," I said, pinching her through her blouse.

"*Babyji*," she said, looking scandalized.

There were so many positions from the *Kamasutra* that were cluttering my head, I could not keep one apart from the other. I imagined posing all sorts of inappropriate questions to the doctor who would address us at school. Ma'am, what is the difference between making love and having sex? Ma'am, is it true that some ladies like violence? Ma'am, is it all right for a woman who is having her period to have sex? Ma'am, could you please tell Sheela that I am a great lover? By the time Rani returned to my room to call me to dinner, my stomach was hurting from laughing at the questions I was going to ask. I wished I could call Vidur and discuss my private thoughts with him.

At night I forgot to set my alarm. In the morning my mother brought me my bed tea. Rani was still in my bed. We both woke up to my mother's knock.

"Open," she demanded from the other side.

Rani jumped out of bed and onto the mattress on the floor. She tried to wear her blouse. We had been naked. I pulled on sweats and a T-shirt. I put my underwear under my pillow.

"Hmmm," I made a sleepy noise.

I pushed Rani into a lying down position on the floor mattress and indicated that she should just pull her sari over her without wearing it properly. I threw a sheet over her. She was terrified. I pretended like everything would be fine. Then I let my mother in.

She walked in and looked disapprovingly at Rani, whose eyes were closed. Rani had taken over all the morning tasks like bed tea and breakfast. She would also pack my father's three-tier steel carrier with lunch as well as my tiffin box.

"Mom, I'm hungry. Let's get some biscuits from the kitchen," I said. I linked my arm through hers and walked out of my bedroom. I pulled the door as far shut as I could behind me. My hands were unsteady.

"Why was the door bolted?" my mother asked.

"We saw a mouse running around last night, and I got scared," I said. It was the first thing I could think of.

"But you shut the door every day anyway. Why did you have to bolt it?"

"She bolted it to assure me the mouse couldn't come in."

"Silly child. You're such a baby sometimes."

My mother got out a jar with some tea biscuits and put them

on a plate. I heard my bedroom door open. Rani had put on her clothes with lightning speed. She joined us in the kitchen and got to work. I went back to my room and got out my school uniform. My Head Prefect badge typically filled me with a rush of importance, but today it felt childish, inconsequential.

Sex-Ed

On the school bus in the morning I opened my backpack to retrieve my school diary and felt the glossy texture of the German magazine. I had carried it home, forgetting altogether that Vidur had to return it to Mohit. Indian magazines were not printed on such thick paper, and our textbooks were like rags in comparison. I ran my hand over the magazine, feeling its cold, shiny surface. I was sitting in a window seat at the front. My stop was one of the first in the morning, and I had sat in the same seat for years. I could see the back of the bus driver's head and the somewhat empty Delhi roads. Our bus passed through two large slum colonies on the way. One was situated on the top slopes of a *gandha nalla*, where all the sewage from the neighboring colonies collected. In the morning, children from the *jhuggis* would be sitting on the main road with little mugs of water, doing their daily thing. The adults usually chose spots that were less conspicuous. I rarely looked at this ritual of mass defecation, but today all aspects of life seemed strangely distant and equal: the illustrations in the German magazine, the mathematical operations of integrals, young starlets with breasts and alabaster complexions like Sheela, characters like Lulu from the Sartre book I had just read, and *cheapads* who molested girls on the bus. Everything had suddenly collapsed like a black hole into itself, and the only word that described it all was Life.

After school assembly I found my mind drifting toward a more pleasant state, one involving the smell and saltiness of Rani's skin. I could practically feel her presence. I spent the first half of the school day dreaming about her. Vidur looked at me a few times but we didn't have a moment between classes to gossip.

"You have to return that thing. Mohit called me at home and was furious," Vidur whispered as soon as the break bell rang.

We waited for a few minutes till most people had left the class, and then I put my hand in my backpack and rolled the magazine inside the bag. I wanted to be sure the front was completely hidden before pulling it out into the open. As I was almost ready to pull it out, I saw Chakra Dev walk toward Sheela's desk. A scene from the porn came into my head, except now it featured Chakra Dev and Sheela. I felt panic mount and immediately ran to where Sheela was seated.

"Hey hey," I heard Vidur say.

It was too late. I had walked toward Sheela with the porn unrolled, its cover fully exposed. Vidur's loud "hey" had caught both Chakra Dev's and Sheela's attention. Sheela gasped. Chakra Dev had caught me red-handed. I felt shame in every vein in my body.

Vidur snatched the magazine from me and rolled it again.

"I could tell the class teacher about this," Chakra said.

"You, the biggest *cheapad* in the class," Sheela retorted.

"Watch it," he said, looking at her. Then he turned to me and said, "The Head Prefect, caught with *Playboy* magazine. Ha! It'll be a scandal."

"Don't you try to blackmail us," Sheela said as if she had been caught, too.

"What do you want?" Vidur demanded.

After a few tense seconds Chakra Dev said, "I'll let it go for your sake," and looked pointedly at Sheela. Then he turned away and stalked out of the classroom.

Vidur walked rapidly to Mohit's desk and stuffed the pornography in Mohit's satchel.

"I better warn him as soon as he gets here. Better to throw it away," Vidur said.

"I want to see it," Sheela butted in. Vidur looked at me with concern.

"You can't," I said.

"Why?" she demanded, her hands on her hips.

"It's disgusting. It's not for girls," Vidur said.

"If Anamika can see it, then so can I."

"Please, Sheela, for my sake." I didn't want her to have those images in her head.

"There will be no one worse than me if you see it," Vidur said dramatically in Hindi. A line straight from a movie, in fact from every Hindi movie ever made. Even though I barely watched films I was usually able to predict the dialogue ahead of time. The stories were all similar, and they worked, each time, just like a chemical reaction in the lab.

In the afternoon the class teacher announced that doctors would be speaking to the boys and girls about sex-ed the next day. When school let out, everyone was talking about it with great excitement but in a hush. I told people about the discussion in the princi's office, about whether it would be coed or separate. The boys were all disappointed with Mrs. Shah's position. But the girls were happy they would have a female doctor speaking just to the girls.

As soon as I got home I told Rani that I had to pick up some books from a classmate's house and left for India's. She was not expecting me, and I noticed that the dining table had not been cleared. There were two plates on the table.

"Is someone here?"

"My son is visiting. Unless he gets admission to your school he will have to stay at his father's. There's no school bus from his current school to my house," she said. She seemed worried.

"When will you find out about the admission?" I asked.

"Your primary school headmistress, Mrs. Nyaya Singh, is considering the case, " India said, looking past me. I turned around.

He walked into the room right then wearing gray knickers and a bright yellow T-shirt. He was thin and tiny. Tiny. I hadn't really visualized India as a mother. I knew that he was five years old, but he looked even younger. I smiled at him. He didn't smile. Or acknowledge my presence at all.

"Hello," I said, bending down toward him. I put out my hand to shake his.

He didn't take it.

"What is your name?" I asked.

No answer.

"Tell *Didi* your name, Jeet," India said.

Finally there was a sign of life. He looked at me perplexed.

"Are you a *Didi* or a *Bhaiyya*?" he asked. He had actually confused me for a boy! I wanted to laugh, but my mother had told me that it was important not to laugh at little children when they asked questions.

"I'm a *Didi*," I said, seriously. In the silence that followed I felt the full awareness of being a *Didi*. A *Didi* who was here to make love to his mother. A *Didi* who maybe really should have been a *Bhaiyya*. Or, rather, an *Uncle*. Nothing about my life was typical of a sixteen-year-old's. No matter what sex-ed the doctor imparted, it was already too late. I had educated myself not just about sex, but about love. A singular and powerful force that had swept aside all convention and was stronger than everyone involved. A geometrical figure with greater strength in the lines joining each point than in the points themselves. Rani, India, and I, all of us, had reached a place from which we could never come back. It was impossible for me to be less of a *Bhaiyya* and to become a real *Didi*.

"Are you sleepy, my sweetheart?" India asked, lifting her son to her lap. Her tenderness with him was no different from her tenderness with me. Was it possible that my love for her was the same as my love for my mother? I sat down on a chair at the full import of that thought.

"Come, let me take you to bed," she said, kissing him. I followed them around as India carried him to his bedroom and put him in his bed. He seemed to fall asleep in seconds. Only eleven years ago I was his age; in eleven years he would be as old as I was now. I could never imagine him having an affair with a married woman, or with any woman, or even with a girl his own age.

Even Chakra Dev must have been five years old at some point. Had he been like Jeet as a child and then just turned into a hoodlum? At what age had he changed?

India closed his bedroom door and led me by my hand to her room. She shut her door, and we sat down on her bed. She immediately reached out to kiss me. I moved away.

"What's the matter?" she asked.

"Your son is in the other room," I said.

"So?"

So? So? What was I going to say to that? I shook my head.

"It's okay. He's sleeping."

"It's not that," I said.

"Then what is it?" she asked.

"It feels wrong. He's innocent," I said.

"How do you think he was born?" she said.

Sex, I thought. You had sex with your husband. And how was I born? The same way. She was right. So what was the problem? I started laughing.

But I couldn't get myself to do anything to her of the kind I had done with Rani the previous afternoon. So I talked to her instead about the German *Playboy* and the *cheapads* on the bus. I had to edit facts so that she didn't know why I had stayed back with Sheela. When I described the molestation she hugged me like Rani had, but she didn't say I was a child.

"What are you thinking?" I asked.

"That we shouldn't have an affair anymore," she said.

"Why?" I asked.

"Because you are young and I am old. Because they molested you, but I am guilty too of the same." I knew that all this would never have come up if it hadn't been for Jeet and what I had said about him being young. I was closer to her son's age than hers.

"I seduced you," I said.

"You are barely the age of consent. This is statutory rape." Before I could protest she added, "In the eyes of the law."

"Spare me your legalities," I said as good-naturedly as I could. I was getting irritated.

We heard a whine from the other bedroom. It seemed her son had woken up. India sighed and got up to go to his room. I followed her. He was already out of bed when we opened his door. I hadn't remembered India changing his clothes before tucking him in for his nap, but he was now wearing only a long striped pajama top. He had his arms out in a Christlike pose and looked up at us and said, "Hello, World."

"Hello, World," India said.

Then he came over to me, a whole lot friendlier than he had been before his nap, and said, "Hello, World! Hello, World!"

"Hello, World," I said, my heart feeling more protectiveness than it had for anyone, ever.

"I have to go now," I said, bending down to pat his head. India and he walked me to the door, and as she closed it behind me she said, "I have to think some more."

I walked back to my house wondering if India would seriously stop our affair. The thought of not having her in my life made me feel as if there was a hole inside my stomach, so big that I didn't exist. If she withdrew herself from me I would wither away. I thought of her all the time. I imagined talking to her in my head whenever there was something I wanted to share.

That night I clutched Rani as we slept, hoping she would fill the hollow spaces that India might leave.

I got up the next morning remembering the sex-ed talk. As soon as assembly was over I got the senior girls to troop into the auditorium. A slide projector was already set up. When the counselor walked in with the doctor, I asked the girls to stand up and applaud. All the girls were sitting cross-legged on the floor on *dhurries*. Three metal office chairs were placed at the front. I invited the doctor to sit in one.

"Hello, friends, we're finally old enough to learn about the facts of life. Our esteemed doctor will answer some of our questions today. But first Mrs. Shah will introduce our chief speaker," I said. Usually I would have sat on the chair in front with the guests, but I wanted to sit next to Sheela, so I went and sat on the floor.

After the counselor's intro, the doctor stood up and fussed with the slide projector. The first slide was the word STD. "Children, I will first tell you about STDs, and then I will answer any questions you have about sex or STDs," she said. The girls sat with uniformly wooden expressions on their faces. The doctor talked a little about sexually transmitted diseases, including HIV, and opened the floor to questions. There were none.

"Children, if you have always wondered about something, this is the time to ask. We won't pass judgment on you. It's natural to wonder about sex. Don't be shy," Mrs. Shah said.

"Mrs. Shah is right," the doctor said.

A hand shot up in the back of the room. It was a girl I knew only by face.

"Yes?" the doctor said.

"Ma'am, what happens if a man and woman have sex before marriage? Why is it wrong?"

"It's not medically wrong. Our society does not accept it, that's all," the doctor said most matter-of-factly.

"Doctor, how can you say that? Everything is wrong with premarital sex," Mrs. Shah said. She was all worked up.

"Mrs. Shah, I am here to answer medical questions. The students must learn which activities are dangerous to their health and which are merely a matter of social mores."

"Young children should not be having sex, Doctor," Mrs. Shah said. I thought they were going to have a fight.

"The question was about premarital sex. How old were you when you married, Mrs. Shah?"

"Nineteen."

"All I'm saying is that if you had been an unmarried nineteen rather than a married nineteen, it would have made no difference from a medical perspective," the doctor said.

The room was silent. I finally raised my hand to ask about something I had not understood in the article on Rock Hudson.

"Yes, Anamika," Mrs. Shah said.

"Ma'am, I read in an article that men who have sex with men are more likely to get AIDS," I said. The counselor didn't look happy. I looked around at the girls. Some of them looked curious, others blank. I continued, "Ma'am, how do two men have sex?"

Mrs. Shah was looking apologetically at the doctor. But the doctor didn't seem to mind.

"Well, it's not natural for men to have sex with each other. Sex was biologically designed for procreation, and as you know, a sperm and sperm can't combine to form a zygote." She paused.

Mrs. Shah looked a little relieved by the scientific turn the discussion had taken.

"But a few men still do have sex with other men," she continued. "Such men are called homosexuals. And yes, homosexuals are more likely to be HIV positive and transmit the disease since they have a promiscuous lifestyle. Do you all know what 'promiscuous' means?"

"No, ma'am," Ashima said.

"No, ma'am," a few more girls chimed in.

"Promiscuity refers to being sexually active with multiple partners. People who sleep around are promiscuous. Anyway, the West is more promiscuous, so the possibility of transmitting the virus is higher. Homosexual men also have anal sex, and the anal area has a high concentration of virus, just like the blood and semen."

"Ma'am, what is anal sex?" Tina asked.

"Do they really need to know that, Doctor?" the counselor asked.

The doctor seemed to weigh the question in her mind for a second. Mrs. Shah was squirming. Then, as if she had made a decision, the doctor looked up at Tina.

"I think, Mrs. Shah, that they should be told everything. That's a good question. Anal sex is when there is penetration through the anus as opposed to the vagina," she said, smiling brightly.

I saw Sheela tentatively wave her arm and pull it right back down. But the doctor had caught the movement.

"Yes?" she asked, moving toward where we were sitting. She looked at Sheela.

"Ma'am, if two men can have sex, does that mean two women can have sex?" she asked.

"No, they can't," the counselor said, ignoring the doctor.

"Yes, they can, Mrs. Shah. Maybe not sex as you know it. Maybe not penetrative heterosexual intercourse," she said with an edge to her voice. What had been slight hostility between them was now overt. Mrs. Shah had long nails that were painted with bright red polish. I could just imagine her clawing the poor doctor's face.

"To answer your question," the doctor continued, shifting her attention back to Sheela, her voice smooth once more, "women are capable of giving each other sexual pleasure, but once again this will not lead to procreation."

I could not tell what the doctor's real thoughts were on the matter. She looked traditional. Her sari blouse was a modest cut, and she was wearing covered shoes instead of sandals. I tried to put her through the underarm waxing test, but the results were inconclusive.

"Any other questions, children," Mrs. Shah said hurriedly. I could tell she wanted to wrap things up, as this had gotten out of control.

Shruti from my class leapt to her feet. In her high squeaky voice she asked, "Ma'am, my servant boy often wears bangles like a girl. Is he a homosexual?"

The girls in the room giggled. I thought even Mrs. Shah was about to giggle.

"Ma'am, we have *hijras* in our locality. What are they?" another girl asked.

"It's not funny, children. There is some homosexuality in India, but since it's not easily accepted we do not see a lot of it. *Hijras* are transvestites and sometimes transsexuals. They may or may not in addition to this be homosexuals," the doctor said.

Another hand went up. This time neither Mrs. Shah nor the doctor had asked for the next question. The show was rolling. It was a girl from a nonscience section. She got up and asked, "Just because it's not accepted, does it mean it's wrong?"

The doctor smiled at the girl and said, "Very good point. That should be the next topic for the senior debate competition. Science can only observe and tell us what happens in nature. It cannot pass moral judgment. It's been observed among rats that they inbreed naturally. It's optimal for them to mate with their second cousins. Genetically, that's best. Who knows, it may be optimal for humans, too."

I turned my head around to look at the reaction of the girls. Everyone was looking at the doctor with open eyes and appreciation. Mrs. Shah looked upset and resigned. She had shrunk in her metal chair. I saw her mutter to herself. She was twisting her fingers. She was barely audible, but I was sitting in the front row and heard, "Homosexuality and incest are perversions."

"Ma'am, what's a perversion?" someone asked.

"Having sex with a dog would be an example of a perversion."

The room had gasped when she said "sex with a dog." Some of the girls were shaking their heads as if they had been made to swallow lemon juice from their nostrils. They would never look at their Snoopys and Boxers and Fluffys the same way again. It gave me unexpected and immeasurable delight to see everyone getting a jolt. I liked the doctor for forcing them to wonder about something none of them had ever questioned.

The bell for the first period went off. When I thanked the doctor I said, "I know we all want you to come back, ma'am. I am sure even the boys will benefit from listening to you."

The girls cheered. The doctor beamed. Mrs. Shah escorted the doctor out of the auditorium. The girls were in a frenzy as we headed back to class. The boys were already seated. Their session had ended first, and it seemed by the looks on their faces that it hadn't been as much fun.

I was dying for the lowdown from Vidur, but Mrs. Thaityallam walked in before I got a chance to ask him. Sheela, Vidur, and I got together in the recess.

"Shruti asked about *hijras*," Sheela said in the middle of eating her tomato sandwich.

"And the doctor talked about sex with dogs," I added.

Vidur whistled.

"What about the boys?" I asked Vidur.

"They asked about mast-oo-bration," he said.

"Who asked?" Sheela said.

"Chakra Dev."

"What did the doctor say?"

"He said it wasn't bad for health," Vidur replied.

"And?" I asked. I wanted to hear more. Vidur was turning color.

"The boys were relieved," he said.

"Were you?" Sheela asked. Her face was animated and her eyes full of curiosity. It irked me. What if it made him think she was interested in him? Vidur looked down. He didn't respond.

"How often does Chakra Dev wank?" I asked.

"How often does he what?" Vidur asked.

"Wank," I said. I had read the word in a novel by an English author.

"Does 'wank' mean that?" Vidur asked.

Sheela and he both looked at me. I nodded. Sheela looked impressed that I knew slang that Vidur didn't. Vidur dropped his voice and leaned closer. He was suddenly feeling comfortable.

"Chakra Dev says he does it seven times a day. He even does it at school in the bathroom."

Sheela gasped and then brought her hand in front of her mouth with an "ohmygod" look.

"The guy must be loaded," Vidur said.

Sheela looked perplexed. I hadn't heard that term before, either, but I didn't want them to know that I was unsure of its meaning.

The bell for the break rang. Sheela went back to her desk. Vidur got out his chemistry textbook. The classroom began to fill up, and H_2S walked in. We all stood up to wish her good morning.

As we sat down Chakra Dev walked in. I didn't want Vidur to see me looking at him. I lifted my eyes without moving my head. Chakra Dev had missed some of the hair on the top of his cheek today when he had shaved. A black sprouting was visible. He stared back at me sullenly and without blinking. His lips, his eyes, the angle of his head all conveyed such total and uninhibited disgust that I thought he might want to kill me. He looked infinitely dirtier and more dangerous than the *cheapads* on the bus.

Sagai

On Sunday evening my parents were invited to the *sagai* of my father's colleague's daughter. We were going to give her two silver bowls as an engagement gift. The *sagai* was conducted at short notice since the fiancé was in Delhi from the States. My father had come home after cards one day and told us that Mr. Dhingra had to borrow money from his wife's brother since his own unit trust shares could not be cashed till a few months later. My father had jokingly said that in bygone times, arranging a husband for one's daughter would have been easier. He had referred to the *Mahabharata*, in which Draupadi's suitors had to shoot at a target in motion while looking at its reflection.

"Mom, I have tests tomorrow. I think I should stay home," I said. I wanted to have the house to myself. I never had an opportunity to spend an evening alone with Rani.

"You know Papa doesn't like it when you don't come with us to family functions."

"The Dhingras are not family. Even Papa only knows Mr. Dhingra and not his wife and daughter. Anyway, aren't my studies more important?"

"I don't think Papa will agree, but you can ask him."

I felt small and powerless. I hated to have to ask permission. My desire to spend time alone with Rani was enormous, however, so I ate my pride and asked him.

"Papa, I have a lot of work today. Can I stay home and study?"

"We'll only go for a short while so you can come back and study."

"I'll still lose two hours. Please."

"You lose more than that for your school Sports Day practice and your cycling," he retorted.

I felt my blood rise. The school Sports Day was my priority. How could he equate it with his social engagements? I didn't have the courage to argue this point.

"Papa, I've never met them. Why should I come?" My voice came out higher than I wanted it to.

"You are my daughter, and this is a family function. People are bringing their children."

"Why does it matter what everyone else is doing? Anyway, this *sagai* is only celebrating her engagement, and all it means is that she is going to sit at home cooking for some guy in America."

I wanted to do big things with my life. Obviously the Dhingra girl was only fit to be a human washing machine. I needed to study so that I wouldn't end up like her. I felt a catch in my throat that intensified as I spoke. My body was trembling.

"That's enough, Anamika," he said dismissively.

I continued standing in front of him, mute, immobile, and unbudging.

"When you grow up and have your own job you can decide what you want to do. Now you're going to do as we tell you. Go get ready," he said. My father would always use "we" at such times, as if his decision were fully supported by my mother.

I stalked out of the room and went to my bathroom. I was a slave in my own home, a caged animal. A monkey being forced to perform on the street. My heart went out to the people in communist countries who had no freedom, the citizens of authoritarian regimes. My wishes counted for nothing.

A torrent of words gushed down my brain, words I had to keep to myself. I would not be free to say what I thought till I was on my own, drawing a salary, independent in my means. I had years to wait. I went into my bathroom and let myself cry. I turned on the water to muffle the sound. I couldn't stop.

I washed my face and then looked in the mirror. I told myself to calm down. I reasoned that they couldn't stop me for long.

And even if I was forced to act a certain way, my mind was free to think. I have lovers, I thought. Once I was an adult I could earn a lot of money and do as I pleased. I would flaunt my freedom and my wealth. Fighting for my freedom now would waste my energy; an argument would get me nowhere and might invite further curtailment of my freedom. I told myself that till I was eighteen I did not have any rights, even in the eyes of the law.

I took a deep breath and went to my room to change. There was a soft knock on the door. The door opened and Rani walked in.

"Little princess. My little prince is going to a *sagai* today," she said. Rani thought I was excited about the evening outing. She reminded me of India's son, not sure if I was a *Bhaiyya* or a *Didi*, a prince or a princess.

"I tried to get out of it, but he would not listen," I said.

"My prince will dress up and look beautiful and have fun," Rani cooed.

"I hate *sagais*, marriages, *namkarans*."

"When I was a little girl, my family went to my cousin's marriage in the next village. I'll never forget the colors, the dancing and singing."

I couldn't explain to her how much I hated my father's stuffy colleagues in their cheaply made three-piece suits and flashy gold tiepins. They were low-level bureaucrats who hadn't done well enough on the civil service exams to make the grade for the foreign service or one of the more prestigious departments of the government. Water Works was as low as it got on the list. I would have to hear everyone gossip at the *sagai*. My father's friends didn't read books. Their wives were worse. Everyone was complacent and measured success and failure by the same yardsticks—car, house, electronic goods. *Jhuggi* people like Rani thought that a government job was the epitome of power and that a government servant was a very big *Sahib*. She wouldn't understand why I adored writers and scientists, intellectuals who could only be measured by the volume of gray matter in their brains. She probably didn't even know what writers and scientists were. If you didn't have any education, could you know how knowledge itself was classified? But she did know what a doctor was. Almost everyone knew what a doctor was.

I pulled out some clothes and put them on. I knew my father would have preferred that I wear a traditional *salwar kameez*, so I wore a pair of trousers. My parents were already waiting for me in the drawing room. We all walked to the door, but I lingered a moment and gave Rani a quick kiss before catching up with my parents at the front gate. The Dhingras lived nearby, so we walked to their house.

The *sagai* was being held under a red tent that had been pitched in the park in front of their house. There was a red *dhurrie* rolled out from their house all the way across the lane to the entrance of the tent. Musicians in shiny gold *achkans* played the *shahnai* and *tabla*. The ceremony was conducted with as much splendor as a marriage since the boy and girl would soon leave for the States. To qualify for the fiancée visa Priyanka could not marry till she reached America. The boy and girl exchanged garlands, as if in a real wedding. Seeing the bride and groom take seven turns around the sacred fire was always my favorite moment in weddings, but the Dhingras said that there would be no *pheras*.

Priyanka was in the middle of the tent with her fiancé. She seemed beautiful, or at least she had been made up to seem so. One couldn't really see her too well under the kilograms of jewelry around her neck and the heavy *chunnat* on her head. The boy was in a suit and had a squint and a double chin.

As soon as we walked into the tent, Mr. Dhingra, who was standing at the entrance, shook hands with my father and said "*namaste*" to my mom. He absentmindedly patted my head.

Since my father often discussed office politics at home, I knew who his real friends were, the ones he played cards with each week. They were standing together in a circle off to one side. He made his way over to them. My mother knew the wives of his colleagues. The ladies sat on red chairs on another side of the tent, and my mother made her way over to them. I followed her. The women wore heavy gold jewelry and rich gold-embroidered saris. My mother congratulated Priyanka's mother.

"*Beta*, come with me. Let me introduce you to my niece so that you don't get bored with the grown-ups," Priyanka's mother said, her hand resting on my shoulder. She grabbed my hand in hers, and we started walking to the house. We walked past the *shahnai* player who was blowing air with all his might into the tube of the *shahnai*. Hideous laughter leaked out of the house from the drawing room, where children of assorted sizes sat in a circle. I was introduced to a pudgy, dumb-looking girl in a parrot green frock and pointy pink shoes.

"We're going to play. You can join us," the girl declared.

I didn't know how to respond; it would be insulting to refuse. From the looks of it she was the leader. She had a purse with a thin strap that hung over her shoulder.

"What class are you in?" I asked.

"Class IV," she said.

"How old are you?" I asked.

"Eleven," she said, giving me a dirty look. She was two years too old for her class.

"I have a boyfriend. Do you have a boyfriend?" she asked me. Her mouth had curled up into a mean expression. She was dumb and bratty. Lord help her, I thought.

"No," I said.

"Okay, let's all play something," she said, turning around and addressing the room full of kids. She clapped her hands. Two boys who must have been Jeet's age jumped up and down and clapped their hands after her. I couldn't imagine them walking around saying "Hello, World!" in that way that made your heart melt down all the way to your feet. There was nothing charming about these boys. It was clear to me from looking around the room that all children were not the same. I had missed the proceedings for a few seconds but heard many girls, all in pink or green frocks, clapping. A lot of them were wearing lipstick and rouge. They were all acting self-important and girlie with their little purses and their shiny hair clips. I slinked out of the room and walked back to the tent.

I gravitated toward my mother. As I neared the group I could hear them talking about their daughters and the spectacular success they had had in the arranged marriage market.

"His company has sponsored him for a green card, and she'll be able to join him as soon as he gets it because he's going to list her on the application as well," one lady said.

"I hope my second daughter does well. The elder one is in Houston. My son-in-law works for IBM. I want the second one to settle in America, too," another said.

I walked past where they sat to a set of empty chairs in a corner. I wondered if I would ever get married and have children. I tried imagining what it would be like. I could easily imagine coming home from work and Sheela opening the door to welcome me. I could also imagine having a little son like Jeet walking from room to room, picking up objects and asking questions. I would earn a lot of money, and Sheela would take care of the house. She'd press my feet when I got home. I'd be working on a top secret nuclear physics project. Or on sending Indians to Mars. I'd have girls after me, but I'd be devoted to Sheela, who would be the perfect wife. Somehow the role didn't suit Sheela much. The Sheela I was daydreaming about was not the same Sheela I knew. I imagined being married to Vidur. He'd be easy enough to pass time with. Nothing beyond that was imaginable with him, however.

Even though I had a burning ambition to be successful, I hadn't addressed exactly how I was going to go about it. What was I going to do after school? How did one become a genius?

Some men walked toward my chair and stood in a little circle not far from me. They were talking so loudly that I was forced to listen. Mr. Chawla, a self-proclaimed patriot, was arguing with the others, "So what if it's less developed? India at least is our own country. We are of this soil, this water."

"Yogi Chawla, when your son grows up you'll want him to go abroad and get the best education, too. Look at us, we don't even have twenty-four-hour water supply or electricity."

"It's our country. If we don't change it, who will?" he asked.

I knew from my father's stories that none of them had been

abroad, but they were discussing *foren* countries and gushing about incinerator technology. At least Yogi Chawla was not a hypocrite like the rest. He was my father's favorite colleague.

"Look, they're going to pass the Mandal Commission recommendations. Then what will happen? When seventy percent of the seats in colleges are reserved for scheduled castes and tribes, where will our sons go?" someone else said.

Yogi Chawla grunted. The papers had editorials about the Mandal report, and I wanted to hear his answer. A caste war was now raging, with several lower castes claiming compensation for centuries of oppression and the *brahmins* claiming reverse discrimination.

"There is no way Parliament will pass it," was all Chawla said.

A new discussion started on the India-Pakistan cricket test series. They got excited and loud as they discussed the prospects for India in the game. It was too noisy for me. I stood up from my chair and walked back toward the women. At every party I felt suspended between the clump of men and the clump of women. A perpetual fence-sitter.

"I thought you were with the children," my mother said, coming up to me.

"The oldest was eleven," I said.

"I didn't think it was necessary for you to come tonight. But you know Papa."

"Can you please try to voice your opinion next time?" I said with an edge to my voice.

"Sorry, I will," she said, touching my hand.

"It's not even quiet enough for me to think on my own here," I grumbled.

"Come, I'll talk to you," she said, taking me by the hand as we walked away from the ladies.

"This girl Priyanka hasn't done a thing. A man chose her on a four-day bride-seeking mission, and just because he's in America they think the girl has done well for herself," I said.

"You're right. You don't need to go to America to be successful." She emphasized the "you," then added, "You can be a woman and start your own company here. You can become the most successful woman in the world."

"What if I want to go to America?" I asked, suddenly feeling rebellious.

"Well, you don't need to get married to go."

"Maybe I can get a scholarship and go right after school," I said.

"You're too young to leave just yet. In fact, even if you study at IIT, we would prefer you to study in Delhi so that you can stay at home," my mother said. My parents had obviously discussed this together, but they had never discussed my future with me.

I would definitely take the IIT exam, but I wasn't really sure I wanted to be an engineer. Everyone was doing engineering. I knew I would learn a lot of things in an engineering college, but what was it really going to teach me about life, death, or love?

"Mom, how do you make small talk with these ladies?" I asked, pointing my head toward the group we had just left. They had just burst into laughter.

"People gossip because their lives are dull."

"Don't you hate it?"

"One gets used to it," she said sadly.

"I don't want to get used to it. I don't want to accept boredom or chatter. Ever."

"Don't. The world is changing. You won't have to accept anything. I was thinking maybe we should invite your friend Tripta Adhikari to dinner." There was something strained, emphatic, whenever she said India's name, as if she were rolling a ball in her mouth.

"Okay, let's call Tripta," I said.

"Good. Ask her to come on Tuesday."

"I'll call her."

"What do you think of her?" my mom asked.

"Huh?"

"She's your friend. Tell me more about her."

"She seems like a nice person," I said. I could feel my back and shoulders getting tense.

"She's divorced and sexy. Are you intrigued by her?"

"I guess so." I hadn't thought in such a cut-and-dried fashion about India, but my mother had summed it up well.

"What does she do?"

I didn't know what India did. Despite our escapades I had no idea if she worked, where she worked, or when she worked.

"I don't know her well, Mom. I don't know what she does."

My mother smiled.

"What do you talk about?"

"We just talk about school."

My father came to us. Many of his colleagues were leaving, and he was ready to go. We thanked the girl's parents, congratulated the young couple again, and left the tent.

"So that was fun, Anamika, wasn't it?" my father said on the walk back home.

"No, Papa, it wasn't."

"Don't be stubborn now. You had fun."

"Rajan, you had fun because they were your friends. The children were younger than eleven. She had no one to speak to. Really, we shouldn't force her to come with us. She has board exams coming up," my mom said.

He looked at us disbelievingly.

"Okay. As you say, but you had a good time, right?" he asked her.

"Not particularly, but I'm used to such outings."

We walked silently for a few minutes.

Then I asked, "What did Rani eat for dinner?" My voice had a tinny quality. It sounded as if it was coming from somewhere else.

"Leftovers," my mother replied.

When we got home I said a hasty good night to my parents and went to my room. Rani was asleep on her thin mattress on the stone floor. She had put my night suit on my bed. I changed into it and lay on my bed, waiting for the light in my parents' room to go off. They slept with their bedroom door open. After the house was dark I closed my door and bolted it. I whispered, "Rani." But she didn't wake up. So I took my pillow, threw it on the floor next to her, and lay down. I snuggled into her arms. She stirred and hugged me, and we fell asleep. We slept like that every night, her legs and mine coiled like braids. Sometimes we would turn our backs on each other, but I would extend my arm behind me and let my hand rest on her ass. I dreamt of the word *sagai*. It was spelled out in Hindi in lotus flowers on a large pond.

Freelance

In the morning I woke up before Rani. I listened to her steady breathing for a few minutes, then got up and went to the kitchen and put the kettle on. My parents were still asleep. Then I tiptoed to the living room and called India. Her voice was husky.

"Sorry I woke you up," I said. "My mom asked me to invite you for dinner tomorrow."

"That'll be nice," she said without hesitation.

"I have to go. I'll come over this afternoon."

She made a kissing sound to say good-bye. I hung up and went back to the kitchen to make tea. I could hear activity in my mother's room and in mine. Rani's bangles jingled as she folded the mattress and sheet.

"You're up early," my mother said, coming into the kitchen.

"Just woke up early," I said. Rani had joined us in the kitchen. She looked her best when she had just woken up. Her eyelids were still heavy with sleep and her lips slightly swollen.

"Rani, could you make some *parathas* for breakfast?" my mother asked. Rani nodded.

"I am not going to yoga today. Shall we go to your room and have *chai*?" my mother asked.

"Yes," I said. I wished I could invite Rani to join us as well. Once we were both in my room, my mother closed the door purposefully and sat on my bed. She ran her hand on the bed and said, "Wow! You already made your bed today! What's going on?"

There was a twinkle in her eye. She couldn't possibly know

that I had slept on the floor. My heart jumped, but I just reminded myself not to be too paranoid.

"Nothing," I said with a shrug.

"Are you getting tired of having Rani in your room?"

"No."

"Papa thinks you're only doing this because you feel bad for her. He thinks it will distract you from your studies."

"Mom, that's not true at all," I said.

"He said you meant to study when you got back yesterday, but instead you went to sleep because you probably found her asleep and didn't want to wake her up."

"No, I was tired. The heavy food made me sleepy."

"Sweetheart, don't get too attached to her," my mother said, cupping her palm around my face. I looked down. "She is after all just a servant," she added.

I felt my ears getting hot. I nodded. My hands started trembling. I had to place my cup of tea on the bed because I could not grip it firmly anymore. I tried to think of something to say. I reached out for my official school diary. I opened its gray blue Rexene cover and flipped through a few pages.

"Mom, we're going to have more intensive Sports Day practice. I have to stay back today." I wanted to go and see India in the afternoon.

"What should I tell Rani? She's been wanting to go to the *jhuggi* to talk to her husband."

"Her husband?" I said, my voice small.

"He's apologized a few times. He sent their neighbor's wife to say that he hasn't been drinking."

"Oh!" I said, picking up the teacup again and bringing it to my mouth to cover the nudity of my face. I held it up at a tilt and sipped only a drop. It felt like a solid substance in my throat. Rani hadn't told me anything about wanting to see her husband.

"She can go today," I said.

"I'll tell her she needn't come home till dinnertime, then."

I looked at the alarm clock on my bedside table and got up to dress. My mother left the room and closed the door behind her.

All day at school I could think of nothing but Rani going back to see her husband. I floated through my tests, as if someone else were taking them. I could take no enjoyment in Vidur's company. Or even Sheela's. On the walk to India's house that afternoon I felt anxious. Would she bring up the matter of terminating our affair? I could imagine Rani going back to the *jhuggi* and India deciding I was too young for her. Life had been too good to be true these past few weeks. I should have known it was going to end. Utopia was no stable state.

The weather was very hot and the rays of the sun so fierce that the air and the sky glinted a brilliant white. I couldn't see anything unless I shaded my eyes with my hand. I eventually had to stop under the shade of a *gulmohar* tree on the short walk to India's house and pull out a book. I chose the lightest and longest notebook in my bag, my chemistry lab register, and held it over my head as I walked the remaining distance. I remembered India's face in full detail as I neared her house. Thinking of her I felt very strong, as if I could move mountains for her, lie on train tracks, leap in front of moving trucks to save her life. I didn't feel guilty about Sheela or Rani or anything else. I loved her completely and absolutely. The feeling was so intense and certain that it astounded even me. She opened the door almost as soon as I had rung the bell.

"It's so hot, I was afraid you'd get heatstroke," she said, kissing me on the cheek.

"I almost did."

"There's been no electricity all day today. It's quite hot inside, too."

"It's so cool compared to the outside it doesn't matter. Where's Jeet?" I asked.

"He's back with his dad. Yesterday was an exception," she said. I wondered if she was sad.

"What do you do?" I asked, letting my schoolbag drop on her sofa and laying my register on the coffee table.

"What do you mean?"

"My mother asked me, and I didn't know what you did for a living."

"I'm a designer. I design layouts for advertisements and things like that," she said.

"Where do you work?"

"Here. I freelance," she said.

Freelance, I repeated to myself. It sounded so exotic. A free spirit. Freedom. I wanted to freelance. I decided I would freelance when I grew up.

She had picked up my chemistry register and flipped it open. "Orgo was my favorite," she said.

"I thought you were a designer. A freelancer." The words danced on my tongue.

"I am. But I got my master's degree in chemistry. One ends up doing things one never expected to do," she said.

I wanted to voice my doubts about our dinner the next evening, but I didn't know how to do so without bringing up Rani so I only said, "Don't tell Mom we met today."

"Let me get you some cold coffee. The mixer is not working, but I'll shake it up."

The kitchen was fairly dark. I watched her move around, open the door to her fridge, get melted ice cubes from the freezer.

"Do you still love your husband?" I asked.

"No," she said. I thought she was going to say something more, but she didn't.

"Did you ever get involved with anyone else?"

"Yes. A married man."

"Did you love him?"

"Yes. But he was married."

"When was that?"

"Two years ago."

She had poured the coffee into a tall steel glass with a lid and was shaking it.

"What's that?"

"It's to shake martinis."

I didn't want to ask her what a martini was. I'd look it up. The coffee looked almost as frothy as when it was made in a blender. She gave it to me in a tall glass and then led me by the elbow to her veranda.

"We need to talk," she said ominously. It was the moment I had been dreading. I sat on one of the cane chairs on the veranda and pulled it close to the other chair.

"Anamika, I'm not going to have an affair with you."

But we are having an affair, my mind protested.

"Why?" I whispered.

"Because you're too young. I have been thinking about this. I got carried away earlier. I'm almost your mother's age, and it's not right. I don't want to hurt you."

I sat quietly and stared at my glass of cold coffee, wondering how best to convince her to continue. I was sure she had been enjoying herself when we had been intimate.

"How do you think you'll hurt me?" I asked.

"You're young, you should be with someone who can be with you. I have a son, I have duties. I can already see that this will go nowhere. We can't be together openly. In fact, you should get involved with a boy."

"You can only hurt me if you are mean. And you can do that whether or not we are having an affair."

"I'd never be bad to you."

"Then you won't hurt me."

"You should be with someone your own age."

"Age is irrelevant," I said. I truly believed it, too.

"Don't get me wrong, I think so, too. I feel close to you. Deepak, one of my closest friends, is much younger than I am. Though not as young as you. But there is no future in this," she said.

"I don't want a future. I want now. I went to a *sagai* yesterday. I think marriage is a trap."

"It is a trap," she said.

She brought her face close to mine and looked into my eyes. I ran my index finger on her lips and then kissed them. I thought she'd back off but she didn't. After a few seconds she pulled away and said, "The only way I can have this affair is if you promise me you won't get too attached."

"I promise," I said without pausing for even a second.

"No," she said, pulling my chin to her face once more, "really promise."

"Yes. Yes. Promise," I said, thinking to myself that love and attachment were two different things.

"I don't want to feel guilty for monopolizing you. You're so young you should be free," she said. Freelance, I thought to myself.

"I am free," I said, remembering the night I had come to her house for the first time, repeating Planck's constant like a mantra in my head.

"You're so beautiful, you know," she said.

I giggled.

"What are you laughing at?"

"Me being beautiful."

"But you are."

"No I'm not. I might be brilliant," I said, "but not beautiful."

"Who told you you're not beautiful?"

"I have eyes. No one needs to tell me. Anyway, it doesn't matter since it's not of any importance to me."

It was shallow to think about one's looks. I wanted to be only a soul, an intelligent mind, a heart that was brimming with passion. I wanted to be above and beyond looks.

"I'm going to convince you that you're beautiful."

"I don't care about looks."

If I dedicated any time to my own beautification, it would negate my own view of myself as a mental being. And yet I had picked apart all of India's features in my mind piece by piece for hours. I had noticed Rani's beauty and Sheela's creamy complexion. In that sense I had not shown any of them the respect I showed myself. I didn't think of any of them as pure minds. I saw them as women. I liked their flesh. Did it detract from my love for them that I loved their bodies, not just their souls?

"What are you thinking? You're so quiet," India said.

"Nothing. My mother refers to you by name. I'm not used to it. It feels strange," I said, not wanting to talk about beauty anymore.

"You've never called me Tripta. In fact, you've never called me anything."

"I didn't want to call you by name and offend you. Anyway, I didn't know your name for a while. But I have my own name for you," I said.

"What?"

"India."

"India? Why?"

"Because when I first saw you I felt the kind of love I feel for the whole country, not just for one part. For all her contradictions, her fierceness, her beauty, her rivers, and her mountains."

She moved forward in her chair and tapped my skull. "What goes on in that little head of yours? I never thought such things when I was your age. I don't even think them now."

I drank the remainder of the coffee from my glass and crunched the little bits of ice that had not yet melted. It was so strange that someone else was thinking about me. India had ideas about me, about the kind of person I was, and I did not know to what extent they corresponded to who I really was. I remembered a theorem on congruent triangles from geometry class. Laws that declared under what conditions certain shapes were equal to other shapes. Was it possible to map human beings in the same fashion, or was it inevitable that errors would be introduced?

We were quiet for a few seconds.

"You know, I don't want to use you for sex. I don't want this to be about that," she said suddenly.

"Use me for sex?" I asked. The idea was thrilling and grown-up. It sounded like the Sartre story I had read. Could she actually reduce all of me to my body and want me? It was better than being wanted for my brains. My mind had got a lot of accolades since I had started school, but my physical being had been neglected. No one had bothered with it. Even Rani, who slept with me, was with me because she was attached to me emotionally.

"I want you to use me," I said.

Mandal

I rarely called my friends at home, but I left India's house feeling the need to talk to Sheela or Vidur. Vidur was more intelligent, so I decided to call him. A man with a very polished accent answered the phone. I thought it was Vidur's cousin, who was visiting from Bombay. He asked me my name and said, "Hold on one second, Anamika." The sound of my name from his voice box was very intimate.

"Was that your cousin?" I asked.

"No, it was my father. He came home from work early."

He had sounded rather young. Vidur was well-spoken but not that sophisticated. His father spoke English with a refined, almost British accent.

"I called to talk about something. Do you agree that people who place emphasis on looks over intelligence are shallow?" I asked.

"Of course," Vidur said.

"And it's so because when one does well in class it is a result of one's effort, whereas one is born with good looks?"

"Yes, of course," he said irritably, as if such reasoning could be taken for granted.

"But Vidur, one is born with intelligence just as one is with beauty," I said.

"But one still has to work hard to do well. Remember that genius is mostly a matter of perspiration," he said, getting exasperated.

"Wait, imagine a guy in our class who is way brighter than any of us. An Einstein. Someone with a photographic memory who never has to make any effort to learn."

"That's a more difficult case," Vidur conceded with hesitation.

"Or what if Sheela argued that she has to work hard to look pretty. That she wears cucumber face masks and washes her face with turmeric, so she deserves credit for her beauty."

"Why are boys intelligent and girls pretty in your example?" he asked.

"It can be the other way around, that's not important."

"My dad says that if I had a sister, she'd be both better looking and smarter. He says he wanted a daughter," Vidur said loudly. I could tell Vidur was saying it for his dad's benefit.

I heard his father in the distance say, "I didn't say that. I was merely trying to tell your mom that girls and boys will turn out well if you raise them well." I loved the voice, its deep timbre, and the way Vidur's father enunciated his words.

"That was my colonel speaking," Vidur said.

I knew his dad was in the army, a *fauji*, but I didn't known he was already a colonel! I knew roughly how long it took a *fauji* to get to that rank. Only a few exceptional officers could skip ahead. His dad must be a different breed. I wanted to ask Vidur how old his dad was. But I didn't.

"So what's the answer? Are Sheela and Einstein junior equally meritorious?" I asked.

"I don't know. I'll think about it."

"Why don't you ask your father?" I said.

"Why don't you ask yours?" Vidur said.

"I don't talk to my father about looks," I said.

"Okay, I'll ask mine and tell you what he says tomorrow." We hung up. The emptiness of the house hit me only after I had put down the phone. I had come in with my own keys without Rani's welcome but had been too preoccupied to notice. Now I remembered that she had gone to the *jhuggi* to meet her husband.

I took off my school uniform and hung up my tie, skirt, and belt. Then I sat on the bed and stared at the wall. The heat combined with Rani's absence made me torpid. Forty-five minutes passed like that till the doorbell rang, snapping me out of my reverie. I was wearing only my school shirt, so I had to pull on pants before I could answer the door.

"How was Sports Day rehearsal?" my mother asked as soon as I opened the door.

"There were just preliminary discussions," I said. I was sure my face was turning black with guilt. I had lied before, but this time it pinched me. And yet I couldn't openly visit India as frequently as I did because then I'd have to explain why she was so important to me. If I told my mother that I was in love with India, then she would put an end to it. The lie was a means.

"I told Mrs. Tripta Adhikari about dinner tomorrow," I said.

"She's divorced. Adhikari is probably her maiden name. You should call her Ms."

"Is Rani coming back?" I asked.

"We'll find out in the evening. Maybe she can work things out with her husband."

I shrugged indifference and went back to my room. I pulled out my chemistry assignment sheet. Our teacher had handed us all a cyclostyled sheet with ten questions. The ink from the paper rubbed off on my hands. I sat at my desk and tried to answer the questions but could not get my mind off Rani. I usually did my homework without referring to my books and notes, but I couldn't focus at all. I reached in my book bag for my chemistry lab register and realized I had left it at India's house. I'd need to pick it up or ask her to bring it discreetly when she came to dinner.

Just before dinnertime I heard the bell ring. I stopped myself from jumping up and running to the door. Rani could come and find me if she wanted. I looked at my clock. The second hand moved a full circle around the dial and then another. Then another. There was a knock on my door.

"Yes," I said. Rani came in.

"Little princess, how are you?" she asked.

"How is your man?" I asked stiffly.

She came up behind my chair and put her hands on my shoulders.

"Are you angry?" she asked.

"No." My body was shaking. I was afraid it would show if I stood up. I kept my hands tucked under my legs because they were trembling, too.

"You're angry," she said. She brought her face close to mine and smiled. She was treating me like a child, a spoiled prince.

"So what's going on?" I asked.

"He wants me to go home. He said he would never drink."

"Are you?" I asked. I knew from the way I was speaking that I sounded distant, though in fact I felt I was about to break down in her arms.

"I told him I'm not leaving you. I brought my clothes," she said, stroking my neck.

I felt light, as if relief was an antigravitational force. I embraced her.

"You want me to stay here, little princess?" she asked, flirting with her eyes.

"Yes. Definitely," I whispered.

"Come eat. *Memsahib* is calling you for dinner," Rani said.

I was quiet over dinner. I didn't want to lie about the school Sports Day again. I kept my chemistry textbook on the table and peered at it while I ate. Usually H_2S gave us hints in the lab that were not written in the textbook or were hard to find. I was hoping that if I combed the chapter something in the lesson would trigger my memory and I would remember what I had written in the lab register. I made no conversation whatsoever. If my parents said anything to me I grunted. As soon as I was finished eating I retired to my room to study.

After Rani had finished cleaning the utensils she came to my room. When she saw me reading she made her bed on the floor and lay down. I waited to call India. I read for a little longer, till my parents' light went off. Then I shut my door and whispered, "Rani." She was still awake. "Come here," I called from my bed.

"Little princess, are you sure?"

"Yes." I thought I'd chat with her for a few minutes before calling India.

She had started talking like a servant again and become mindful of her position after her visit to the *jhuggi* today. I wanted to erase her background, her past, and the stigma of consorting with a person of much lower caste. This was something I could never tell anyone, not India, not Sheela, not Vidur, not my parents, not any future lover.

As we lay together, the scent of wet mud wafted in from my window.

"It smells like rain," Rani said. I got up and looked out the window. In the dim light I could see needles of water falling.

"It's raining," I said, returning to her.

"I'm very happy," she said as she ran her fingers along my forearm. I didn't want to interrupt the moment we were sharing. I decided to call India some other time and fell asleep to the smell of the earth and of Rani.

The next morning I saw Mrs. Pillai when I stepped off the school bus. The rain had cooled Delhi, and a slight breeze was blowing. The *pallu* of Mrs. Pillai's sari fluttered and flew off her shoulder. She reached forward to grab it. I was walking a little behind her and off to her side. I saw her neck stretch out a few inches like a crane's as she set the *pallu* back on her shoulder.

"Good morning, ma'am," I said, lurching forward.

"Oh! Hi, Anamika. The weather's so pleasant."

"You're looking beautiful," I said.

"Oh!" she said.

"Ma'am, can you recommend any good books? I've been reading Sartre," I said, speaking rapidly, embarrassed by the compliment I had just paid her.

"That stuff's too negative. I'll lend you something. Remind me."

"Mrs. Pillai," Mrs. Thaityallam said, intruding upon us.

"Ma'am, I'll be off," I mumbled.

"Child, remind me," she said. As I walked away I was filled with a bittersweet sensation. She hadn't ignored me completely when Mrs. Thaityallam had interrupted, but she had called me "child."

In the school assembly that day, the boy who read the news said that the government had decided to implement the recommendations of the Mandal Commission and increase the number of reserved seats for scheduled castes in schools and colleges. This was fresh news from the morning. It shocked me. It was followed by a brief talk on the Bermuda Triangle by another student. After that the principal came up and spoke. He usually addressed the school on Monday mornings. It was unusual for him to speak midweek. He spoke about merit and the value of hard work. The teachers were not supposed to take obvious political sides, and although he didn't explicitly mention the Mandal Commission, it was obvious he was talking about it.

The princi's talk created a buzz. Students clumped together to discuss it instead of walking back to class. The teachers formed spontaneous circles and argued. Voices were raised. I made my way down to where my classmates were standing.

"The new reservations are completely wrong," Vidur was saying to everyone.

"The scheduled castes have been wronged throughout our history. We have to atone for it," Sheela was arguing with equal passion.

"The *brahmins* have exploited everyone for centuries. The *chutiyas*," Chakra Dev said, materializing from nowhere. He put his hand on Sheela's shoulder as if they were both on one team.

I was incensed by his hand. Vidur's eyes were blazing, too. Sheela shook her shoulder and glared at him. "Don't touch me, mister," she said to Chakra Dev. He walked away. We all watched him till he was a few feet away before turning back to look at one other.

"For or against?" Vidur asked, looking at me.

"Against."

"Do you know how many atrocities are committed against them even now?" Sheela demanded.

"That's a separate issue from reservations and a much bigger one," I said.

We walked back to class and went to our desks.

"Hey, Vidur, did you ask your dad my question?" I asked as we sat down.

"He says it depends on the context. Intelligence is more important than beauty if you're a scientist, but if you are a model then beauty is more important."

I couldn't make up my mind if I agreed with his answer. "But is credit for one better deserved than for the other?" I asked.

"Good morning, children," Mr. Garg said as he entered the room.

Vidur leaned close to me and said, "I'll tell you later."

Physics was infernally dull that day. The class took notes listlessly. I had read ahead and knew that I did not need to pay attention because I had followed the chapter.

When Mr. Garg was writing on the blackboard I wrote in my textbook in pencil, "What did he say?" I shoved my textbook under Vidur's nose.

He wrote on a sheet in his notebook for a long time without looking up. First I thought he was writing me an answer, but then I figured he was taking physics notes because he just kept writing. Finally he closed his notebook and pulled it beneath the level of the desk, passing it to me from underneath.

I opened it to the last page. He had written, "In real life it is unlikely that someone will be as intelligent or as beautiful as in your example. It is also unlikely that he will have a corresponding level of success. It is usually not clear whether someone has achieved success without effort, purely on the basis of native intelligence or natural beauty. Furthermore, even though beauty and intelligence are qualities one is born with and that one can enhance, the mind is the jewel of one's body because it is what makes men most different from animals. It is the mind that is the *raison d'être* of man."

I was sure that Vidur had reported everything to me more or less verbatim. I didn't know how "*raison d'être*" was pronounced. As I read the paragraph a second time I imagined his dad's voice speaking to me. I tore the paper from Vidur's notebook. I had to tear it slowly, millimeter by millimeter, to keep from being heard in class. I folded it and put it in my skirt pocket.

When class was over we stood up and sang out, "Thank you, sir." In Mrs. Pillai's class I moved to the chair next to Sheela. I didn't want her to think I was a prejudiced upper caste hypocrite whose opinions stemmed from my *brahmin* birth. It was important that she know I had thought about caste objectively and reached my conclusions through reason.

"Exploitative *brahmin*," she whispered when I took the seat beside her. She had used Chakra Dev's language to taunt me. I couldn't argue dispassionately now; I felt anger in my blood. Him of all people! How could she stand to use the words he'd used?

"How so?" I asked, trying to keep calm.

"You're for the caste system," she accused.

"No, I'm not."

"Why don't you want the backward castes to improve their lot?"

"But I do. I just don't think the Mandal policy is the best way, that's all."

"They had to carry shit on their heads," she hissed.

I knew I could easily get her to see me in a different light by telling her about Rani. But she might recoil at the idea that I was physically intimate with someone from a *jhuggi*. It would be too much the other extreme.

Mrs. Pillai walked in, and everyone got up. Before we could sing out she rolled her eyes to the ceiling, waved a hand, and said, "Please don't 'good morning' me." I wondered if India ever got irritated with Jeet and told him not to "Hello, World!" her. I smiled.

I opened my copybook and uncapped my fountain pen. Before bringing my attention to class, I leaned toward Sheela and whispered, "The Mandal recommendations are perverse. If a lower caste guy gets admission on the basis of merit, he won't count in the reserved category. Reservations are for those who won't make it on merit."

Sheela ignored me and started taking notes.

As Mrs. Pillai spoke, I stared at her long neck and the movement in the tendons of her forearms as she wrote on the blackboard. I let my mind freelance.

When everyone stood up at the end of the class, I squeezed Sheela's hand in my own. I had to go back to my seat for the next class since Mrs. Thaityallam was strict about that sort of thing. "Let's talk in the break," I said as I gathered my stuff.

"Okay," she replied, still a little cold.

When the bell rang for break the classroom cleared out. The boys went off to play, and the girls went to watch them. Chakra Dev seemed to be lingering, but he eventually went out. I took my tiffin box with my marmalade sandwich that Rani had packed and walked to Sheela's desk. The sun was beating down mercilessly, and I didn't want to go outside.

"I am sorry about what happened on the bus that day," I said. We hadn't talked about it at all. And I wasn't sure why I brought it up.

"It wasn't your fault," she said.

"But it was my idea."

"No," she said, lowering her gaze. I grabbed her chin to lift up her face. She looked straight at me. The whites of her eyes looked particularly large. I felt I was swimming in them.

"Why are you looking at me like that?" she asked after a few seconds. I tightened my grip on her chin and lowered my face till my lips touched hers. The flesh of our lower lips was in contact. We got closer for a second, and then she pulled away.

"Anamika, the door is open. Are we crazy?"

"We're alone," I said calmly.

"Look," she said, pointing to the door. Unless someone actually put his head through the doorway, he would have been unable to see us. But for anyone who chose to pop his head in, we were in plain view. I got up from the small wooden chair I had been sitting on. My legs were sweating. They had left long wet marks on the chair. I went to the door and bolted it. I was sure our seats couldn't be seen through the door's small square window.

"What will people think?" she asked.

"Whatever they want?" I tucked my skirt properly under my legs so that my thighs would not touch the chair and sat down. Our lips made full contact again. As we kissed I leaned forward till she was pressing against the wall. She exhaled deeply on the side of my neck. I could not hear my own breath at all. I slowly slid my hand under her tie and let it rest on her chest. Her breathing got heavier. I reached for the button of her white school shirt and undid it.

I felt her breathing change immediately. She gripped my hand and said, "Stop."

"Why?" I asked, moving away from her face.

"Because I don't want you to."

"But you want to kiss?" I asked aggressively.

"I like kissing," she said. My hands fell to my lap, and my shoulders dropped. She moved her face close to mine and started again. After a while the door rattled. The small bolt on the top of the door held fast, but the lower part of the door vibrated.

"God," Sheela muttered. I got up to unbolt it. It was Chakra Dev. Compulsive masturbator, I thought, as I let him in.

"*Brahmins* are *chutiyas*," he said, looking down at my shirt. I didn't respond.

"Why was the door locked?" he asked unpleasantly.

"It's none of your business," I said sharply.

"It's girl business," Sheela said to him, trying to smile. She didn't want to ruffle his feathers.

"Girls," he snorted and walked to his desk.

"Tired of playing in the field," Sheela said to him. I wondered if she was thinking about him doing his thing seven times a day. Or whether his political position on Mandal had made her suddenly interested in him. I would do anything to seduce her, but I couldn't pretend that my ideas on right and wrong were different from what they were.

"It's too hot to be outside," he said to her. He opened his pencil box and took out a folded twenty-rupee note. Then he shut the pencil box and headed back to the door. When he reached it he turned abruptly and walked back, this time to where Sheela was sitting. I was standing by the blackboard a few feet from the door, impatiently waiting for him to leave. He let his elbows rest on her desk and leaned forward till his face was close to hers, then whispered something. I saw her body press up against the wall and heard her say, "No." He turned around abruptly and walked out. On his way out he gave me an angry look. I didn't shut the door this time, but I closed it most of the way and went back to Sheela's desk.

"What did he say?" I asked.

"He asked if I wanted a Coke from the canteen."

"Tell me the truth."

"I swear," she said. She put her arm around my shoulder.

"Do you want him?" I asked.

"Such a *cheapad*, are you mad?" she said. But I wasn't convinced at all. Despite his dirty nails and coarse facial hair he was still the most grown-up boy in the class. Almost a man.

The bell rang, and the building resounded with the heavy steps of boys running in from the playing field. As the classroom filled up it got hotter and sweatier. An unpleasant smell pervaded the room. I went back to my seat next to Vidur. His forearms were dripping with muddied sweat. He pulled out his pencil box from his backpack and opened it. We all kept a six-inch ruler, a protractor, and a compass in our pencil boxes. He took out his ruler and scraped it on his forearm, as if he were wiping the excess water from a window he had just washed. His brown sweat gathered in a single line at his elbow and trickled down one edge of the ruler. He shook the ruler out and let the fluid drip to the floor. He did the same thing to his other forearm.

I watched him, repulsed but unable to peel my eyes away from the flow. He saw me watching.

"How horrid," I remarked.

He shrugged indifferently.

"Your father would disapprove," I added.

He grinned. "You don't know my father. He says men sweat, that it's just a fact of life."

Beads of new sweat had formed and were sticking to the black hairs on his arms. I couldn't imagine a grown-up Vidur, a well-built army colonel with more hair than Vidur had now.

"Well, better to wipe it off than get my books dirty," Vidur said matter-of-factly.

"Girls are nicer," I responded.

"Huh?"

"Never mind," I said.

As the day wore on I started getting excited and tense in anticipation of India's visit to our house that night for dinner. I imagined her sitting in the drawing room and eating at the dining table. Our dining table and the side tables in the living room had a sunmica finish that I didn't like. We had bright curtains with a flowery print, while I would have chosen a solid color. I wished I were living in my own house where everything was completely to my taste.

In biology class I daydreamt of the evening to come, of Rani, my mother, and India talking to one another. I imagined them at ease, laughing and filling up the room with the different scents of their bodies and the colors of their clothes. But what if they felt more at ease with one another than with me? Rani and India could even fall in love. An affair with each other would suit them so much more than an affair with me, I thought uneasily. I reverted my attention to Mrs. Ganatra and her disquisition on genetics. Four sets of genes coupling in various sequences to express either dominant or recessive traits. Was I attracted to long hair and soft skin because of a gene in my body? This was not the time or place to ask Mrs. Ganatra. There would never be a time or place to ask Mrs. Ganatra.

"I'm stressed," I announced to Vidur when the bell rang.

"My father says that only grown-ups can be stressed. When we kids get worked up we are merely nervous," he said.

"Nervous about what?"

"About doing well. About not meeting our parents' expectations." Vidur's father seemed to think that he knew everything. I wanted to meet him and show him there was a thing or two he didn't know.

At the end of the day I headed out of the school building with Sheela. "Call me if you ever want to talk," I said as we separated to go to our respective buses.

"You call me," she said. As she climbed the steps of her bus she turned around and flashed a smile. It made her look like a model in one of the shampoo ads. Women would walk away from the screen and then swirl around to show their faces to the audience. I felt as if there was glamour in my life. I knew how grown-ups must feel, the men who watched the ads and the women who walked away, throwing their heads back to smile at the men with one last look. It was a forbidden world. Rani and India had not helped me discover it. They were protective of me. Sheela was my real teacher. She didn't give in to me. She was not swayed by my youth or my intelligence or my maturity or anything else. I always had to persuade her. She was a challenge.

Self-Immolation

When I got home I found Rani washing our china. We rarely got it out of the cupboard. My mother was making a huge fuss over India. Getting out the china and having Rani put in so much effort all day made me apprehensive. I went to my room, kicked off my shoes, and removed my tie. I undid my belt and unclasped my skirt, letting it fall to the floor. Then I put on pants Rani had laid out on my bed. She had spoiled me thoroughly. My mother had always insisted I make my own bed, fold my own clothes, polish my own shoes. But I knew Rani would pick up after me. It was her way of showing love. Was this how women loved? Like slaves? Devotees? No wonder men took them for granted. My mother ran around cleaning up after my father. My aunt cleaned up after my uncle, my grandmother after my grandfather. On the one hand it outraged me. But on the other I found that being a little prince suited me. When I grew up I'd have a big harem full of women. Whenever I had a visitor I'd be able to wave my hand and say, "Oh! Don't worry, she'll do it," as I pointed to one of my brides. In turn I'd provide for them, give them gifts, and protect them.

There was a knock on my door, though it was wide open.

"*Babyji*, what will you eat for lunch?" Rani asked me.

My stomach felt small and shrunken. "Nothing," I said.

"Eat something, just a little bit," she said.

"What is there?"

"I made you some *karela*. It's my mother's special recipe."

I hated *karela*. No amount of overcooking rid the gourd of its bitterness.

"We don't like *karela*, but we'll have it since you made it," I said.

Thinking of harems and rich kings and the old polygamous order made me talk in the plural form. Rani didn't notice. She skipped to the kitchen. I followed her.

She put a small amount of the vegetable on a steel plate and gave it to me. I carried it to the dining room, expecting her to follow me, but she remained in the kitchen. I went to the phone and called India. I balanced my plate on my knees as we talked.

"It's nice to hear your voice," she said.

"I'm very stressed about tonight," I said.

"Why?"

"You won't tell my mother about us, will you?" I asked.

"Of course not."

"I left my lab register on your table."

"I saw it."

"Can you bring it?"

"I can carry my big purse. But how will I give it to you?"

"If we get an opportunity, you can pass it to me. Otherwise, take it back."

"Okay."

"Do you want to bring Jeet? I forgot to ask."

"Since I haven't heard from your school headmistress yet, he's still living with his father."

"Have you ever had an affair with a woman?" I asked. I knew very little about her past except her husband and her married lover. Somehow India seemed to be the kind of woman who had always had lovers.

"No."

"Do you think you're gay?" I asked.

"Women can't be gay," she said.

"They can't?"

"It's normal for women to fool around. It doesn't mean anything." She spoke with authority. It sounded so impersonal to reduce our involvement to a phrase like "fooling around."

"Being gay is a Western construct. Indian sexuality is a spectrum, not binary," she continued.

I had no idea what she was talking about. "Western construct" sounded even more exotic than "freelance." I had heard the word "binary" only in Mrs. Pillai's class. She had said that binary representation of numbers only involved two numbers, zero and one. And spectrum was from physics, light dispersion through a prism. But I couldn't ask India to clarify. She would think I was stupid.

We hung up, and I swallowed the remaining chunks of *karela*, trying to chew as little as possible. It wasn't bitter, but I still didn't like it. I had been taught not to waste food. I took my plate back to the kitchen where Rani was squatting, washing the dishes in tepid water. I bent down and handed her my plate, then kissed her on the forehead. Her skin was damp with sweat, making my mouth taste salty. I felt as if only Rani loved me enough not to question me. Loved me almost in a blind sort of way. The salt in her sweat made me feel that I loved her in an unquestioning way, too. I held her neck and pulled it. She stood up.

"Come to my room. Let's lie down for a second," I said.

She washed her hands, then wiped them on her sari as she followed me. I wanted to hug her and be held. We lay down. She stroked my hair and smoothed my eyebrows. I closed my eyes and fell asleep. When I awoke Rani was no longer there. I heard movements in the kitchen. I looked at my table clock. It was almost time for my mother to get home. I washed my face and called Vidur. The phone rang a few times. I was about to hang up, thinking no one was home, when his father answered. I felt as if I had been speeding on my bicycle and had to brake suddenly.

"Hello," the voice said again.

"Hello. May I speak to Vidur, please. This is Anamika," I said.

"Oh, hi, Anamika. Hang on one second. Let me see where he is." He had taken my name in a firm handshake sort of tone. I waited for Vidur to come on.

"Sorry, he seems to have stepped out. Can I give him a message?"

Completely on impulse I said, "Maybe you can help me. I was wondering what 'Western construct' means." I wanted him to know that I understood some part of it, so I continued, "I mean I know it's something constructed in the West, an idea that's Americanized or European, but . . ." I trailed off, feeling silly and self-conscious.

"Is this for a class? Vidur hasn't asked me this yet."

I had not spoken very respectfully to Colonel Mathur. I hadn't said, "How are you, uncle?" or addressed him with a formal term of respect. The word "uncle" sat in my throat like a clot of badly cooked *karela*.

"Sir, it's not for a class. But is a binary way of looking at things a Western construct?"

"What sort of things?" he asked.

"Life in general," I said vaguely.

"Yes, but specifically what aspect of life?" he pursued.

"Just everything."

"You're the one who asked Vidur that other question," he said, changing the subject.

"Yes, sir." I only called Mr. Garg and some of the PT teachers "sir."

"Vidur talks a lot about you, Anamika. He thinks you're the smartest kid in the class."

"Hardly." That word "kid" again. But it was better than Mrs. Pillai's "child."

"Well, my son usually doesn't have a very high opinion of people, so you must be pretty special," he said. I felt like worms were wiggling in my stomach. I didn't want him to think I was involved with Vidur in any way.

I heard the distant ring of a doorbell on his end of the line.

"Can you hang on a second? There's someone at the door," he said.

I wiped my hands on my pants because my palms were sweating from gripping the phone.

"Looks like he's here. Should I pass him on?" he said, coming back.

"Yes. Thank you, sir," I said.

"Anamika," he said, and then paused dramatically.

"Yes," I said, feeling nervous.

"I feel very old when you call me 'sir,'" he said and laughed a little. His laugh had a rich, resonant quality just like his voice. I let my reserve drop and asked, "Is that good or bad?"

"Vidur was right. You are pretty different for your age," he said. My heart thumped.

"Here he is," he announced. Without a parting word I was switched from father to son.

"Yes?" Vidur said, suddenly filling the earpiece with a warm kind of friendship.

"I already asked your father. But I couldn't be specific," I said.

"He told me when he opened the door. Tell me the specifics."

"My friend said that sexuality is a spectrum. That binary sexuality—that is, being either gay or not—is a purely Western construct. Vidur, please don't repeat this to your father. Please think of some other example."

"Which friend?" Vidur asked.

"India," I said without thinking.

"Who?"

"It doesn't matter," I muttered.

"Who is India?" he asked loudly.

"Shhh! I'll tell you later, Vidur. Please."

"Okay, I'll find out the answer and tell you tomorrow," he said, suddenly whispering.

I went back to my room wondering what Colonel Mathur thought of me. He had not answered the question of whether it was good or bad to feel old. He'd deftly sidestepped. I had talked on the phone to a grown-up man in his house when he was alone. It felt as if it were in flagrant violation of the constructs of Indian society. Was Indian society also constructed, or was construction simply a Western thing? Was my current state of multiple affairs something I had constructed for myself, or was it Indian style—inevitable and fated? Divorced woman, servant woman, underage woman, I was pursuing them all. An honest word or two over the phone with a man was hardly worth attention. I shrugged. It was time to pick out some clothes for dinner. Something India had not seen before.

I put on a cotton madras shirt and khaki pants. Once when my father's sister had seen me in those pants she had said, "You have a good figure."

Soon my mother arrived. Rani had already prepared four dishes, rice, and *parathas* for dinner. My mother changed from her sari to a deep rust-colored *salwar kameez* and let her hair fall on her shoulders. She rarely let her hair down. When she went to work she tied it in a severe bun, and on the weekends she oiled and braided it. It was nice to see her relaxed, but I remained nervous. If India and my mother became good friends, where would I stand? I felt guilty for thinking so jealously about them. By the time India arrived at seven I had a pounding headache behind my right eye and had popped two aspirins.

"Ms. Adhikari, welcome," my mother said formally.

"Please, call me Tripta, Mrs. Sharma."

"And you call me Narayani," my mother said warmly. They were already comfortable with each other.

They had greeted each other with a *namaste* but then grabbed each other's hand and were still holding each other. When they let go, India came closer to me and said, "Hi, Anamika."

"Hi," I said and stepped closer to give her a hug. I didn't hug a lot of people. Mom would notice. India held my shoulder and kissed me on the cheek. It could pass for a maternal gesture, but her lips were soft and her breath warm. I felt myself go red. I led her to the couch with a hand on her back. Her sari blouse was cut very low around the neckline, exposing a large area of her back and the curves of her side.

"What can I get you to drink?" I asked.

"Anything," she said, looking at my mother.

"Get us Cokes," my mother said, looking at me.

"You look so young, Narayani," India said. I was walking out of the living room, and the sound of the fan muffled their words entirely. I didn't want to leave them alone with each other, but I had no choice. I sprang to the kitchen, opened three Coke bottles on the counter as swiftly as I could, and poured them into tall glasses.

"What's the hurry, *Babyji*," Rani asked.

"Nothing," I said, putting the three glasses on the tray and walking out of the kitchen.

"Come here one second, little prince," she said flirtatiously.

"Not now," I replied without turning back. I walked softly as I reached the living room, hoping to catch a few words without them knowing I was there.

"Well, you don't look a day older than thirty," I heard India say.

"You look in your twenties yourself," my mother said.

I strained to listen some more.

"Oh! I remember that night your hair was tied up. Leaving it loose like this takes off a good ten years," India said.

I walked into the room with the drinks. They both looked at me and smiled. I placed a glass on the coffee table in front of my mother and one in front of India. My mother was sitting on the single sofa, and India was sitting in the middle of the large couch. As I placed the Coke in front of India I looked into her eyes. For a second we were in our private world.

I sat on the couch next to India with my glass in my hand. I kicked off my slippers and crossed my legs on the couch. Usually my mother would not let me sit like that in front of guests, but she was in a good mood and seemed not to notice.

After a few seconds my mother excused herself to check on things in the kitchen. I turned to watch her leave the room. After she was gone I placed a hand on India's knee.

"You're really sexy," I whispered into her ear.

"Your lab register is here," she said, pointing to the large purse at her feet.

I reached down and pulled it out. I heard my mother's footsteps dangerously close, so I shoved the register under the sofa. The distinct sound of cardboard sliding against the stone floor could be heard as my mother walked back into the room. She didn't seem to hear it because of the whirring of the fan.

"I worry about my son's admission to Anamika's school," India said with a sigh.

"I am sure they will take him. After all, it's a really special case," my mother replied. They must have already spoken about Jeet for a few minutes while I was getting Cokes because my mother seemed up-to-date on the situation.

"At least you don't have to worry about the Mandal Commission. When Anamika applies for college next year they will probably have the new reservation policy in full effect."

My mother had never before expressed doubt about my ability to get into a college of my choice. It made me wonder what would happen when the number of seats under open competition shrank to a tenth of their present number.

"There is a boy called Chakra Dev Yadav in our class. What caste is he?" I asked.

"*Yadavs* are *jaats*, no?" India said.

"They are on the Mandal list and qualify for reservations even though they have by far been the most dominant caste in Uttar Pradesh economically and politically," my mother said, getting up from her seat.

She had walked to the phone and picked up the newspaper from under the phone stand. Walking back to us she opened the paper to the editorial page and handed it to India and me, saying, "See, they are deemed backward castes."

"I hope my son gets into your school before this policy comes into effect," India said. I imagined a junior Chakra Dev gaining admission over Jeet. There was no doubt in my mind right then that Chakra Dev had been born a complete hoodlum with an antisocial gene just as I had been born with a gene that preferred Sheela's smoothness to Vidur's hairiness.

"Merit is obsolete. Only the sons and daughters of politicians and rich people get anywhere," India said, closing the paper she had been reading.

"*Memsahib*, everything is ready. Should I set the table?" Rani asked, coming into the room.

My mother nodded. Rani inclined her head and left. India looked at my mom and said, "She's one of the most dignified servants I've ever seen."

"Isn't she beautiful?" my mother said.

My mind strayed to the different responses Rani's beauty evoked in people. I already knew that Dr. Iyer was moved by her suffering. I wondered what would move Vidur's father. I wanted to know more about him and about the books he read.

"Yes. I liked that one, too," my mother said. I had no idea what they were talking about.

"His last collection of stories was my favorite," India said.

How could they be talking about books at the very moment I had been thinking about them? Could it be that thoughts were composed of electrons that flew in and out of people's heads? One of mine had jumped from my brain to my mother's or India's so that they had started talking about books just when I started thinking about them. What if they picked up on my other thoughts? I wanted to protect my mental processes, lock my ideas in a steel vault lest they escape without permission.

"What do you like to read, Anamika?" India asked, turning to me.

"I try to avoid best sellers," I said. I realized it sounded snotty as soon as I had said it.

"Why?" she asked pleasantly.

"Well, I still need to cover my bases in literature. I read most of Dostoevsky last summer."

She raised an eyebrow and said, "Heavy."

"She seems to like heavy things," my mother said.

When I was in seventh grade my mom monitored what I read and stocked my shelf with Jane Austen and George Eliot. In the past year I had borrowed as I pleased from the school library (usually from the special section marked For Staff Only). The library teacher, Mrs. Catalog, turned a blind eye to what I carried out under my arm. People made fun of her, her bespectacled seriousness and yen for order. Till I had become Head Prefect my friends had called me "Catalog Junior."

"I just read a Kundera novel about a doctor who had to become a window washer," I said.

"According to my friend Deepak who returned from the States, it's the only meritocracy," India said.

"He came back to live in India? That's rare," my mother said.

"I'll introduce him and his wife, Arni, to you. They're a young couple. They can bridge the generation gap between Anamika and us," India said to my mother, reaching out to clasp her hand.

Hearing that she felt there was a generation gap between us was like having a bucket of cold water thrown on my head. My worst fear was coming true. India had more in common with my mother than with me.

Rani walked into the room carrying our plates and glasses. I walked over to the dining table and helped her. Then we all washed our hands and sat down to dinner. My mother and I usually ate with our hands. But my mother had asked Rani to bring a spoon for India.

"No need. I eat with my hands, too," India said to Rani.

"Why don't you bring your food and join us," my mother said to Rani in Hindi. It was a big gesture. But Rani sat on the floor.

"How is your man these days?" India asked.

Rani looked at me for a split second and then replied, "Men are men. They never change."

"My man also used to hit me," India said to Rani in Hindi. When she had admitted this to us at the *dhabawalla* she had spoken in English.

Rani looked shocked.

"It's because of the way they are raised by their mothers. I won't spoil my son," India said.

"I'm glad I have a daughter," my mother said.

"I wish I were a son," I said.

India and Rani laughed. My mother frowned.

"Boys take longer to grow up," India said.

"Has it been hard to raise your son alone?" my mother asked.

"He comes to my house when there is no school or if his father can pick him up. It'll be much easier once he can transfer to Anamika's school and live with me."

"Divorce must have been difficult," my mother said.

"It was harder trying to live under the same roof," India said. My mother nodded.

"The food is delicious," India said, looking at my mother.

My mother looked at Rani and said, "Did you hear that? I told you it was good."

Few people ever complimented or thanked their servants for anything. My mother was different. I appreciated her for that. Even though she was never fully able to overcome the divisions between masters and servants, she was intrinsically fair.

"I think *Babyji* will do better than any man," Rani said suddenly.

"Yes, *Babyji* will," India said. It was strange to hear her call me *Babyji*.

They were doting on me like a child. But maybe this was how women treated their men as well, bolstering their egos. After impatiently waiting to grow up, maybe I would discover that there was no such thing as growing up, that adulthood was a myth and that men were boys. I had always had a sneaking suspicion that being a grown-up was only a matter of biological age. At the *sagai* I had felt more intelligent than my father's colleagues, and I routinely felt I was more advanced than most of the people around me. While Vidur was intelligent, I knew from the way he spoke that he didn't feel like a grown-up. Sheela still saw herself as her father's daughter. Chakra Dev was the only other person my age who was also grown-up. He carried himself like an adult. A bad adult, but an adult nonetheless.

"Please don't patronize me," I said in English as lightly as I could.

"We're not patronizing you. We're just saying what we think," India said defensively.

"What did you say, *Babyji*?" Rani asked. It was the first time she had asked me to translate something I had said to someone else in English.

"She thinks we treated her like a child," India said in Hindi. I felt as if a new link had just formed between India and Rani, something independent of me. Rani nodded and smiled at her.

We finished eating and went to wash our hands. When we got back to the living room my mother asked Rani to bring out dessert. I switched on the TV so that we could all watch the news. As I walked back to sit in the center between India and my mother, I hoped that after this evening the bond between them would not prove stronger than what they had with me.

My mother and India were staring intently at the screen. I turned to see what they were seeing. They were showing a fire and smoke and young people running around. The newscaster said that a seventeen-year-old student had set himself on fire to protest the Mandal Commission recommendations. He had been hospitalized in Safdarjang Hospital and was suffering from third-degree burns. Footage from Safdarjang Hospital and the protest demonstration outside followed.

The news shifted back to the TV studio, and the newsreader said, "His condition is critical."

"Suicide?" I asked aloud.

Politicians came on next, denouncing the self-immolation and expressing grief. I imagined Chakra Dev going up in flames, even though it was a *brahmin* boy who had protested. If anyone, it would be me doused in kerosene and burning to cinders.

Rani came in carrying dessert.

I told her about the news item as she placed the tray down on the table in front of us. She had made *kheer*.

I ate *kheer* only if each spoonful had a raisin, so my mother had asked Rani to go heavy on the raisins. I scrutinized my spoonful of white *kheer*, making sure there was a raisin.

"Rani, what's your real name?" India asked.

"Basanti," she replied. It had never occurred to me to ask Rani her real name. The enormity of my thoughtlessness shook me.

"Should I call you Basanti?" my mother asked.

I told myself I preferred Rani since it meant queen.

"Whatever you want, *Memsahib*," she said submissively.

"Would you prefer Basanti?" my mother persisted.

"Rani, Basanti, same thing," she said.

"It's a pity she's not educated," my mom said.

One of the floating thought electrons from my mother's brain jumped to mine. In a second the whole world in my head changed. There was no reason for Rani not to be educated. She could go to school now. I could teach her. We could teach her how to read and write. We could educate her enough for her to move from a servant to a worker in an office. I went dizzy with the image ten years into the future of us all sitting on a couch and Rani talking to us as an equal. If electrons could jump from their orbits and leap through quanta, there was no reason Rani could not jump from a lower caste servant to an educated and real Ms. Basanti.

"Do you want to learn to read and write?" I asked suddenly.

India's eyes met mine as if she had been thinking the same thing. The airwaves around my mother's head and mine and India's were suddenly like a busy thoroughfare, jammed with synchronous signals.

"We can teach you," my mother said.

"I think we should teach her to read and write English, not Hindi," I said.

"Maybe," India said, sounding doubtful.

"I'll study," Rani said, her voice excited.

"Will Papa agree?" I asked in English.

"He will or he won't," my mother said with a shrug. She and India looked ready to go to battle on Rani's behalf.

"Did you do Each One Teach One?" India asked. It had been a national literacy program where educational kits were distributed free of charge and each literate person was encouraged to teach an illiterate person. People tried teaching their servants. The campaign had failed to touch my family or me. But Rani was a pulsing presence in our house. The possibility of educating her seemed real.

"No. Did you?" my mother asked India.

She nodded. "It didn't work too well. We should aim for more than mere literacy. Once she knows the basics she should go to a school," she said in English.

When Rani heard the word "school," she said, "If I can go to school I promise to learn fast."

"Do you know how to write anything in Hindi?" my mother asked.

"No."

"You'll learn quickly," my mother said assuringly.

"*Memsahib*, you're a goddess," Rani said, looking at my mother. Her eyes were filmed in tears. My mother placed a hand on Rani's shoulder. My heart stopped.

"This is a fruitful evening!" India said.

"Yes, who would have thought?" my mother said.

Sitting on the couch between India and my mother and facing Rani, I felt like I was some sort of patriarch already. They were all mine. I was the luckiest person in the world. Rani got up and took away the dessert bowls. I switched off the TV. It was too late for the government to separate me from Rani just by listing her on some schedule. My *brahmin* fluids had already mixed with her low caste ones. Mandal could stuff his list of schedules up his nose.

"That was a good idea, Anamika," India said, turning to look at me.

"Yes," my mother said.

"We all thought it," I said. The thought electron called "educate Rani" had bounced from one head to another because we had been sitting so close. We were all slices of one big brain. Our thoughts and feelings were like a river that flowed from the mountains down to the plains and to the mouth of the Bay of Bengal. Much the same as India herself, her sacred geography intersecting many states and making it impossible for political language brokers and separatist movements to divide her up with any precision. It was an entirely new feeling of belonging, adventure, sharing, and being something greater than one small person. Instead of paranoia about the connecting lines that joined India to my mother and Rani, I felt all the more enriched by their connections. In the end they were all connected to me.

India got up, saying it was time for her to leave. We escorted her to the door. Rani came from the kitchen to see her off as well. India hugged my mother and lightly touched Rani's elbow. I told my mother I would see India to the outer gate. Once there I leaned forward and gave her a quick kiss on the lips.

Later that night, when Rani and I were in bed, I said, "Basanti, good night," in English.

Rani tentatively said, "Anamika, gud-naight."

"G-u-d niiight," I said slowly, phonetically.

"Good night," she said with perfect diction.

C Molecule

School the next morning was agog with news of the self-immolation. During the assembly I asked the principal if he wanted to address the students again. He declined. The boy who gave the talk for the day spoke on the production of artificial rain using airplanes for seeding clouds. When he finished, we all trooped into classes.

In a grim mood I pulled out my chemistry textbook for the first period and realized that I had forgotten to retrieve the lab register from under the sofa in the living room.

"Would you set yourself on fire for a principle?" Vidur asked me as I opened my textbook to the carbon chapter.

"No," I said sternly.

"Come on, Anamika, where's your sense of humor?"

"What's funny? People are dying."

"Hey, look, charcoal and diamond are one and the same thing," he said, pointing to the little blurb next to the chapter heading.

It made me smile.

"So, who is India?" he said.

"Just a friend," I said.

"It's not a name," he said.

"It's a nickname."

"Girl or boy?" he asked.

"Woman. Divorced. Mother of a child," I said, summing her up as my mother had.

He didn't react.

"So, did you ask your father about binary Western constructs?"

"Yes," he said, a devilish grin appearing on his face.

"And?"

"You wouldn't believe the example he came up with," Vidur said. We were interrupted by the entrance of Hydrogen Sulfide.

"Anamika," she called as soon as the class was settled.

"Yes, ma'am," I said. I was resigned to being her favorite. I was one of the few creatures of the fair sex she did not hate. It was nothing short of a curse to be Hydrogen Sulfide's chosen one.

"Write the formula for isobutyl alcohol on the board before we move on."

I got up and went to the board. I hated writing with chalk. The crumbly calcium carbonate stuck under my nails and left me feeling unclean. The chalk made a squeaking sound as it touched the blackboard. It made the roof of my mouth tickle. I wrote the formula quickly and went back to my seat. Vidur was smirking when I sat back in the chair next to him.

"Anamika, Anamika, smell my rotten eggs," he teased in a whisper.

I put my foot on his and stamped it firmly.

"Carbon, children," the teacher said and turned to the blackboard.

"I'm sorry, I'm sorry," Vidur pleaded. I lifted my foot.

"What was the example?" I wrote to Vidur in my book next to the diagram of a diamond.

"Later," he wrote beneath it.

I sat through class waiting for it to end. Everything from the self-immolating schoolboy's burnt *brahmin* body to the hardest substance known to man was made of the same damn C molecule. I was reminded of what my father had said once, "Everything is one thing. It is nothing."

I brooded. The excitement from yesterday had passed. India, Rani, Sheela's silky black hair—nothing made me feel special anymore. Life felt interminable. It was no longer clear to me where anything was going. If we all had to turn into carbon sooner or later, then why not sooner? When the class ended it no longer mattered to me what Colonel Mathur had told Vidur. We stood up for Hydrogen Sulfide to leave and sat back down. I started pulling out my book for Mrs. Pillai's class.

"So, don't you want to know?" Vidur asked.

"Tell me," I said.

"He said that a typical Western binary construct was action versus inaction."

"How so?"

"Well, Westerners think that people are either doing things or not doing things. But in reality, sometimes one can do and not do at the same time. Meditation is an example. By doing, one is. And by being, one does." Vidur spoke with his eyes shut as if he were reciting from memory.

I nodded, though I was not sure what all this meant. It sounded like what my father had said.

"My father said paradox is the essence of being Indian."

"India is the essence of being Indian," I replied.

"Huh?"

"Nothing," I mumbled under my breath.

"You mean your India?"

"Nothing, Vidur," I said, this time firmly.

"What's going on?"

Mrs. Pillai saved me by walking into class. I jumped up from my seat and sang out loudly before she could stop me, "Good morning, ma'am."

"Anamika," she said, looking in my direction and rolling her eyes to the ceiling. The class burst out laughing since no one else had got up. I turned red and sat back down.

"What's wrong with you today?" Vidur asked, leaning closer to me.

I ignored him. The thought about meditation had put me in a different mood. Life felt like a roller coaster ride. I had never been on a roller coaster, but I'd read the phrase in newspaper articles often enough. My mood changed at the end of each period. I wondered if such inconsistency and turbulence were signs of weakness or merely of age.

"Anamika, you're not listening," Mrs. Pillai said, shooting a look in my direction.

"Sorry, ma'am," I said. There was no point in denying it. I sat up straight in my chair and picked up my pen. Vidur looked at me.

She drew some Venn diagrams on the board, a null set with nothing in it, then another set Ã that was the set of all objects in the universe that were not A. A and Ã made up a complete universe, a binary universe. Everything depended on how you defined your sets. If you defined B as not A then the universe was binary. Sexuality, action, and even paradox were part of a binary universe. Or one could choose quantum physics, orbits, and energy levels that allowed for many states and uncertainties. My mind had wandered again. I came back into the orbit of mathematics. It was disloyal to think of physics in Mrs. Pillai's class. Math had the same concepts as physics. I could define my sets so that the universe was the sum of sets A, B, and C or better still 1, 2, 3, . . . n. The choices were infinite, my possibilities limitless.

When class ended Mrs. Pillai looked at me and said, "Come out a second."

I followed her out. It was a hot day, and the fans in the classroom were ineffective. We had all been sweating, but I felt my body release even more sweat. I was afraid she was going to reprimand me.

"What's the matter? You look so dreamy," she said.

"I was listening," I said.

"Something's going on, Anamika. Do you want to talk?"

"Are you happy?" I asked.

"I'm tickety boo," she said.

"Would you put your hand on your heart and say you were truly happy, would you?"

She paused a moment, then said, "I guess so." She let out a breath. "What's the matter? You're not happy?" she said after she'd recovered from her own hesitation.

"I'm fine. That's not the problem," I said.

"You're growing up. It's a tough period. You're a teenager."

I didn't want this grown-up to adolescent talk. I forced a smile so that I could end the conversation. "Thank you for checking, ma'am," I said, getting formal.

"You're welcome," she said and turned away toward the staff room. I watched her small round hips sway and her white sandals flash from under her sari as she walked. Her neck was long and her back as curved and sexy as India's. I wondered if she looked the same under her petticoat and blouse.

"Not Mrs. Pillai," I thought to myself as I went back into the classroom.

When I returned to my desk, Vidur asked me if Mrs. Pillai had scolded me.

"No."

"What's the matter with you? Will you tell me or not?" he asked.

"In the break," I said.

"I'll take you to the canteen," he said. He was the only boy with whom I had ever been to the canteen.

Over a vegetable burger and a Coke I told Vidur the absolute truth. "I can't figure it out."

"What? Binary systems or spectrums?" he asked.

"How life is to be lived, what's right and wrong, what we should want, whether our morality should be about what we want or what's set down by society," I said. I was worked up.

"We're still in school, we can't know all this just now," he said, shaking his head.

"I have to know the truth. Truth is everything," I said.

"The truth about what?"

"The truth about life and about love. The truth about truth itself." I wanted to start crying. Why couldn't someone who knew everything just sit me down and tell me? Why was it that no one knew anything? How had billions of people come and gone on this earth for thousands of years and still not figured out the answers to these questions? I would die if I didn't know soon. It was the only thing that mattered. Everything rested on it.

"Is it Wednesday?" Vidur asked. I nodded absently.

"My father has a half day. Do you want to talk to him?" He looked upset. I knew then that he truly cared for me.

"He'll think I'm crazy," I said.

"I wish I could help. But I don't think all these things. I think only some of these things. He won't think you're crazy. He likes you."

"I have to go home," I said.

"Just come back home with me. We can drop you home later in the car."

"My mother will be angry," I said.

"Call her," Vidur said. I put my hand in my skirt pocket and pulled out a one-rupee coin. There was only one pay phone in the school. It was in the main building, far away from the canteen. I asked Vidur if he would come with me. I had felt the need to lie to stay back in school on Sheela's account or to go to India's house, but I was going to tell my mother the truth about Vidur. If anything my mother should have more objection to me visiting a boy. But I felt no hesitation in asking her openly.

"Mom, it's me," I said.

"Anamika, is everything all right?"

"Yes. I'm calling because my classmate Vidur says his father has a half day and can help me with some physics problems. Can I go over to his house after school? They can drop me home."

My mother didn't respond immediately. I knew she was weighing the pros and cons.

"Are you sure it'll be okay?" she asked gravely.

"Of course. Colonel Mathur and Vidur will drop me back in the car."

"Okay. Ask them to have *chai* with us."

"Thank you, Mom."

"Rani will worry about you. Be careful."

"I will."

I felt bad for Rani, but I could appease her later. I put down the phone and gave Vidur a thumbs-up.

"That wasn't too hard. Physics problem, huh?" Vidur said.

"It *is* a physics problem. Will your dad mind?" I asked.

I had been so intent on meeting his father, it hadn't even crossed my mind that I might be intruding.

"My dad would love to meet you," Vidur assured me.

By the time we walked back to class the break was over. I hadn't had a chance to speak to Sheela at all. Because of my mood swings I had forgotten about her in Mrs. Pillai's class when I could have gone and sat next to her. Now it was the geography period, and there was no chance with Mrs. Thaityallam. I looked over in Sheela's direction as Mrs. T. walked in. She was busy pulling out her geography copybook from her satchel. Eventually Sheela looked up and caught my eye. I pouted my lips and sent her a kiss across the room. She blushed. When I turned back I noticed Chakra Dev looking. He had seen me.

"Children, draw a line on the right side of your copybooks," Mrs. Thaityallam instructed.

In between the geography and history periods I went over to Sheela and said, "I really want to spend time with you."

"My parents may be going to a big function next weekend. If they do, you can come to my house in the morning."

At the end of the day Sheela, Vidur, and I walked to the school parking lot together. I didn't want to tell Sheela I was going back to Vidur's house. I pulled her aside to chat as we got closer to where the buses were parked. I walked her to her bus and waited till she got on. Then I walked back to Vidur.

"Ready, Captain?" he asked. I nodded. We climbed on. The bus was already full, so we had to stand. Everyone was sweating, and the boys were covered in dust. Most of their shirts were untucked, and their ties hung loose. A few teachers sat in the front of the bus, wiping their foreheads and faces with the ends of their sari *pallus*. Some fanned themselves with pieces of paper. Since I was the Head Prefect everyone recognized me and knew this was not my regular bus.

"Going somewhere?" one of the teachers from the junior school asked.

"Yes, Vidur's father is going to teach us physics," I said. She looked at Vidur and then at me.

"Good," she said approvingly. Once the bus started to move it cooled a little. Vidur's house was much closer to the school than mine, so his stop came fast.

xiv

The Fauji

An army orderly in khaki shorts let us into the house and said Vidur's father was playing tennis. We got rid of our school satchels, drank some cold water, and decided to head to the club.

"*Bhaiyya* is really sweet. He's been my father's orderly since I was young," Vidur said.

"What does he do?" I asked.

"Strictly, they are supposed to help only with army tasks like polishing my father's shoes and the tires of his car. But *Bhaiyya* helps us at home, too."

"They polish car tires?"

"Yes, with boot polish. And they put silver polish on the hub-caps."

We walked along the tree-lined road of the army cantonment where Vidur lived. It was much quieter than my part of Delhi. When we arrived at the club, Vidur said something to the guard, who then let us in. Approaching the courts I saw two figures and heard the distant tok tok of the ball. As we got closer the game seemed to end. The men dried themselves with towels. They wore baseball caps to shield their faces from the sun.

"My father's on the far side," Vidur said. He cupped his mouth and yelled, "Dad!"

His father waved, gathered his duffel bag, and walked over to the edge of the court where we were standing. Vidur introduced us. We shook hands.

His tennis partner also walked over to us. "Hello, Uncle," Vidur said to the other man.

"This is Colonel Divan," Vidur's father said, introducing his tennis partner to me.

"I have to run," Colonel Divan said, even as he shook my hand.

Colonel Mathur took off his baseball cap. His hair was short and clung to his scalp.

"Give me a second," he said, letting his duffel bag slip off his shoulder. He pulled out another T-shirt and ripped off the one he was wearing, turning away from me. His muscular back was smooth and glistening with sweat just like his face and head. I looked up at a tree and whistled. It wasn't decent to look at a man's bare back like this. I felt my ears turn red.

"All right, let's go," he said, turning back around. He was instantly friendly. There was no need to explain why I was there. Walking out of the club with Vidur and his father felt very natural, as if I had done it many times before.

"I think schools will soon be shut down. There were two more self-immolations, and there's a big rally planned for tomorrow, so there may be unrest," he said.

We walked on quietly for a while. Then Colonel Mathur patted my shoulder and said, "It's nice to finally meet you, Anamika."

"Same here," I said.

At home the orderly took the duffel bag from Colonel Mathur. He and I sat on two sofas in the living room while Vidur disappeared to change. I wished I weren't wearing my childish school skirt. I felt more comfortable in pants and boys' shirts.

"I'm glad you dropped by today," he said. His words came out easily, comfortably. I doubted that Vidur had ever brought any other girl home after class.

"Actually, I wanted to talk to you, sir," I said.

"Oh, no! Not 'sir' again!"

"What should I call you?" I asked. It was bold to talk like that without introducing a term of respect in the sentence.

"Call me Adit. That's my name."

"Adit?" I said tentatively, afraid that I was going to be reprimanded for disrespecting an elder. And thrilled that this moment of adulthood had finally arrived. I didn't even call India by her name.

Vidur came back in a polo shirt, looking much better than he did in his school uniform.

"Hey, Vidur, your dad said I should call him by his name," I said. It was best he be warned before I launched into a conversation where I'd say Vidur-Adit-Adit-Vidur.

"Didn't I tell you he was the best?" Vidur said, running his hand through his dad's hair. I'd not seen that sort of camaraderie between a father and son before.

The table was set. "Shall we?" Adit said. We all got up.

Over *roti* and *sabzi* Vidur said, "Anamika is having a crisis. She's under stress."

Adit looked at me and asked, "What crisis are you having, Anamika?" He sounded like Dr. Iyer inquiring about symptoms whenever I was sick and my mother took me to him.

I immediately tore off some *roti* and put it in my mouth. The way Vidur had spoken about me made me feel silly. Both Adit and Vidur were looking at me, waiting for me to speak. I felt embarrassed and wished I could chew on the *roti* forever. I reached out for a glass of water as soon as I had swallowed the last of the *roti*.

"Anamika, try explaining all that to my father," Vidur said impatiently.

"I don't have the patience to wait while my life unravels. I need to know now what's wrong and what's right. I need to know what I should truly want." I had spoken in a great rush.

"You mean in terms of your career? Whether to become a doctor or an engineer?" Adit asked.

"Or whether to simply pursue my feelings, wherever they might take me," I said.

"Where might they take you?" he asked. Vidur helped himself to more *sabzi*.

"To the moon, to hell, to suicide, to prison," I said dramatically, unable to control myself.

"Calm down," he said.

"Sorry, Adit."

He smiled at the mention of his name. His face was clean shaven, and his teeth were white. He reached out for more *sabzi*. His forearms were strong, their veins prominent. He had very little hair on his arms, and his hands were long. The phone rang.

Vidur got up from the table and shuffled to the phone in the passage leading from the dining room to the bedrooms.

"Hello," we heard him say.

"I can't believe you're his age," Adit said, lowering his voice.

"I can't believe I'm sitting here telling you I've taken on more than I can chew," I said.

"Are you having an affair?" he asked bluntly.

"Several. I have a roving eye," I said. How could I say this to a stranger, I wondered. We were both speaking softly, furtively. At that moment it felt as if nothing in the world stood between him and me.

"Adit, I need someone to talk to. I feel as if I've never expressed my inner feelings before, and they are suddenly gushing out. I'm losing my mind," I said.

"Everything will be all right, my Lolita," he said soothingly.

"Who is Lolita?"

"You don't know the book?" he asked, chuckling.

"No."

"I'll lend it to you."

"Have you ever been in love?" I asked.

"Not recently."

I could hear Vidur's voice on the phone in the other room. The call had been for him. He was talking about cricket. His voice was excited. He seemed to have forgotten about us.

"Are you true to yourself?" I asked.

"More or less."

"Do you touch your heart every day and ask what it wants? And do as it says?"

"No. That would make life impossible," he said.

"Why?"

He touched his left hand to his heart and turned his head up to the ceiling, his eyes closed. Then he said, "I hear what it says."

"What does it say?"

"It says, Adit, watch out or you'll fall for this kid," he said, looking down from the ceiling and straight into my eyes. I felt a bolt of lightning strike the middle of my chest. I felt my face go red. I was embarrassed not to have a quick comeback.

He suddenly looked unsure of himself. "Are you all right? I'm sorry," he said.

"That's all right. I'm glad you said it if it came to your head," I said, recovering.

"My heart," he corrected.

"Even more important," I said.

"You remind me of my youth. Something I can never again have."

Hearing Vidur hang up on his friend, we both fell silent. He came back to the room all smiles and announced, "The Pakistanis were bowled out. It looks like India will win the series!"

"That's good news," Adit said, looking as happy as his son. I was astonished that intelligent men liked watching games. We finished our lunch without Vidur bringing up my problems again. Every time there was a lull in the conversation because we were all chewing, I could feel my heart thumping.

After we were done with lunch, Adit put on a record. They had a fancy music system with very large speakers. The clear and loud beat of the music amplified the uneasiness in my stomach that had been building up since Adit's comment. I excused myself to go to the toilet.

In the bathroom I washed my face and looked at myself in the mirror. My Prefect's tie was still knotted tightly. I loosened it and undid my collar button. I ran my hands through my hair and adjusted my glasses. I sat on the pot and focused for a minute on Vidur, on what would happen to him if I ever had an affair with his father. There was no question of having an affair with Adit. I stood up to look in the mirror and nodded at my decision. I felt more in control. No affair that involved me could happen without my participation.

I came back out and sat on the sofa.

"Some tea, kids?" Adit asked, looking at Vidur. Then he gave me a look that discounted his having called me a kid. We both nodded. He went to the kitchen.

"Tell me more about this India friend of yours," Vidur said when Adit was out of earshot.

"She's your father's age," I said, then added, "and really sexy." Vidur didn't respond.

His father came back to us carrying a tray with three mugs. He was still in his tennis shorts. Since I was sitting and he was standing I could look at his legs without seeming to stare. His thighs were muscular and had an even brown color with very light brown hair visible only from up close. His knees were scarred from years of knocking about. As he handed me my tea I looked up and asked, "Did you ever fight in a war?"

"Indo-Pak. 1971," he said.

"He was injured," Vidur said proudly.

"Did you get a medal?" I asked.

"True *kshatriya. Vir Chakra*," Vidur said in response. He worshipped his father.

"Dad, tell her the story," Vidur said, his eyes shining.

"There's no story, really," Adit said with a lopsided smile.

"Come on, Adit," I said.

"My battalion was posted at the border. I was in artillery and got shot in the shoulder. It was so cold that it was a few minutes before I realized what had happened. In fact it was someone else who first saw the blood that had seeped through my uniform."

"Do you have a scar?"

"He does. Show it, Dad," Vidur said.

"Do you want to see it?" Adit asked.

I nodded. He stood up and stripped off his polo shirt. I had missed the scar at the tennis court because I'd looked away. He bent his body toward me and brought his right shoulder in front of my eye. The skin there had bunched up. I raised my index finger to touch it and looked at him. He nodded. I gingerly patted the scar.

"It doesn't hurt," he said. I noticed that his few chest hairs were standing. His eyes looked unflinchingly at me. I stared back and then removed my hand. I had forgotten about Vidur for a second. So had Adit.

"Is that why you want to join the army?" I asked Vidur.

"Yes."

"We'll see about that," Adit said, putting his shirt back on.

"You don't want him to join?" I asked.

"He can if he wants to. It has its pros and cons," Adit said. I nodded.

"I'm not sure what I want to do," I said, changing the subject. It was clear they weren't agreed on Vidur's career. The atmosphere in the room had become tense.

"Vidur says you are so smart you could do anything," Adit said. Vidur seemed to suffer from this notion that I was a lot more intelligent and talented than I really was. I felt awkward and looked at my wristwatch. Time had flown. It was already four thirty.

"I told Anamika we would drive her home," Vidur said.

"Of course," Adit said. Then he looked at me and asked, "When do you have to go?"

"Now," I said.

"I'm going to wear something else. It's too hot for these pants," Vidur said and got up. I felt terribly stupid sitting in my Prefect's tie and box-pleated skirt next to a sexy athlete who'd been in a war. When the door to Vidur's bedroom shut, Adit asked me in a low voice, "So, what do you want to do with your life, little lady?"

The phrase "little lady" upset me. I wished I were India with her sophistication and low-cut sari blouses. Adit would have spoken differently to her.

"I want to be a professional playboy, Adit," I said as sweetly as I could.

"That failing?" he asked.

"Failing that I'll join the army. They take women now," I said, feeling querulous.

"Why? You know they don't let women go to war," he said.

"I know. I would do it just to go to the Academy. To exercise and have a great body," I said.

"You have a stupendous body," he said.

"I mean a rough and tough body like yours," I said, deciding to ignore his comment.

"So you like mine, too," he said with a smirk. He was not going to let me ignore him.

We were both sitting on the couch, our backs resting on its backrest. He moved forward till he was leaning with his elbows on his thighs. Then he grabbed my hand in his and held my thumb in between his thumb and forefinger, giving it a hard, almost painful squeeze before letting go.

My heart started beating fast, and in my nervousness I blurted, "There's a woman you'll like."

"Huh?" His "huh" sounded exactly like his son's.

"She's closer to your age than mine. A freelance designer. Very sexy."

"I'm not looking for an affair with someone else," he whispered.

"I'm not suggesting one. I call her India," I whispered. Talking about my life to Adit made me less nervous about him. I felt he was my friend.

"India," he repeated, nodding his head.

We heard Vidur's door open. Adit slid back on the couch, increasing the distance between us. Vidur came out in shorts and sandals and a T-shirt. His legs were covered in black hair obviously inherited from his mother's side.

"Are you ready, lion?" Adit asked his son.

"Yes, Colonel."

"Why don't you leave a note for Mom," Adit suggested.

"Oh, yes!" Vidur said. He went out of the living room to the passageway where the phone was kept. The house was so quiet I could hear the sound of pencil on paper.

"My wife comes home around six. She works at American Express," Adit said.

I felt blood rush to my face when I heard him say "my wife." My mouth felt dry. I was sure Adit could read my face. I called out to Vidur in an unnaturally high voice as if he were far away.

"Yes?" he said. I ran in his direction and stood next to him.

"My mother wanted you to have *chai* with us," I said.

"After tea," he added on his note. I looked at the scrap of white notepaper. I could distinguish Vidur's handwriting from thousands. I'd sat next to him in class for years. But we wrote with a ballpoint pen in our ruled notebooks. The lead pencil on blank white paper was like a sketch. It looked like it had sounded—hurried, artistic. It was like a Band-Aid on my chest. I was relieved he was there.

We came back to the living room. Vidur put the note on the dining table under the fruit bowl with a few overripe bananas and some *chickoos*.

"Ready, kids?" Adit asked in a neutral voice. He didn't look at me. We trooped out of the house and onto the driveway.

Vidur's father backed the car out as Vidur and I opened the gate.

"You know, my mother thinks I have a crush on you," Vidur said.

"Do you?" I asked, looking Vidur in the face.

"No! You're my best friend!" Vidur said.

"I was just teasing, Vidur," I said. It felt great to have a best friend. I knew he wasn't one to use the term lightly.

Vidur opened the car door for me and slid into the backseat himself. I was embarrassed about Vidur and Adit coming to my house. Our sofas with their patterned upholstery and shiny wooden finish were very different from Adit's living room with its music system. Vidur's father was modern, and while my parents were probably from the same income bracket, his life had exposed him to travel and war. Military life was glamorous compared to the lives of civil servants.

My mother was already home when we arrived. To my surprise she held out her hand to greet Adit. I had never seen her shake hands with a man before. She'd usually fold her hands and say "*namaste*" to my father's colleagues.

Vidur shook her hand, too, and said, "Hello, ma'am."

We all sat in the living room. Adit was sitting in the same spot where India had sat.

"Would you like some *chai* or coffee, *Colonel Sahib*?" my mother asked.

Adit beamed. It was obvious he liked to be called that.

"We'll have what you're having," he said.

I was painfully aware of his thick muscular legs and his khaki shorts. He seemed indecently exposed. What if my mother noticed? I wanted to cover him.

"Mom, I'll take care of it," I said in order to escape.

"Rani's in the kitchen. Be nice to her. She was crying when I got here."

"Why?" I was concerned something had happened.

"She was worried to death about you."

I went to the kitchen. Rani had heard us come in. She was already setting a tray with cups and saucers. I grabbed her waist from behind and squeezed it. She smiled at me.

"I'm sorry you were worried," I said.

"It's all right. I am glad you are fine."

"Why were you so upset?"

"I thought something had happened to you. I remembered what had happened the last time you took the bus," she said, her eyes opened wide.

"I'm here," I whispered in her ear.

"When you bring *chai* and biscuits for everyone, bring some for yourself, too. I want you to meet my friend Vidur and his father."

"What will I say to big people?" she asked. She widened her eyes again, this time flirtatiously.

"You'll talk like you did last night with the lady," I said, leaving the kitchen.

Rani followed me out a few minutes later carrying a large

steel tray with four cups and saucers, a teapot, milk, sugar, and a plate of biscuits. She hadn't got any tea for herself. Through the tight half sleeves of her sari blouse I could see her arms straining and bulging. Her arms were lean. Her biceps looked like little mice. Her *pallu* was drawn over her head and covered a little of her face. But seven inches of flat flesh showed between her sari and her blouse. Her belly button was visible. As she bent down to place the tray on a side table, her *pallu* slid down, exposing her tight sari blouse. She quickly pulled it back on her shoulder. Adit stared at her for a second before lifting his eyes. I was glad Adit had noticed Rani, her beauty. I wanted to show her off even if he didn't know she was mine.

I said to her loudly in Hindi, "Why don't you place it down and bring your *chai*?"

My mother noticed Rani and broke her conversation to look at her.

"Yes, Rani, why don't you join us?" she said, smiling.

Adit looked at Rani again. She was so beautiful it was impossible not to feel direct and intense pleasure looking at her. After putting our trays down she went out of the room. Her sari *pallu* blew in the air behind her as she disappeared through the door.

"We're going to teach her English," I said, looking at Adit.

"That's nice," he said almost automatically. There was something patronizing in his tone. I felt like a child reciting my New Year's resolutions to an adult. I got angry with myself and with him.

The phone rang just then, and I got up to get it. It was India.

"I can hear voices," she said.

"My classmate Vidur and his dad, Adit, are here." I felt really grown-up using Adit's name. I wanted my mom to overhear me calling Adit by his name. I wanted to officialize our friendship.

"Is he nice? You've not mentioned Vidur before," she said.

"Vidur's great. He's my best friend," I said, hoping Vidur was listening.

"Can I talk to your mom?"

"What about?" I asked, feeling suspicious. I wished I'd been able to stop myself from asking.

"I want to thank her for dinner," India said. She sounded a little irritated.

"I'll call her," I said, upset at her irritation. My voice had shrunk.

"Before you go, Anamika," she said, pausing dramatically.

"Yes?" I asked. I felt she was going to break up with me.

"Will you call me later? I miss you," she said. I was taken aback by her change of tone. Moreover, she had come for dinner just the previous night.

"I'll call you when I can speak," I whispered. There was no way I could leave the house and go away at night with Rani sleeping in my room.

"Tripta wants to talk to you," I said to my mother.

"Ah!" my mother said, excusing herself. She smiled as she took the phone.

I sat next to Vidur and said in a low voice, as if I didn't want Adit to hear, "That's India."

Vidur nodded knowingly. He liked that I had shared it with him. Adit stared at the curtains on the French windows of our living room, a somewhat blank expression on his face. I was feeling unreasonable and illogical. I had become upset at him for having a wife and for having grown distant. If I wanted to be his friend I needed to be pleasant. I felt immature.

My mother ended her conversation with India. As soon as I heard her say "bye" I had a tremendous urge to shock her. I wasn't sure she had heard me say Adit's name the first time.

"Adit," I said.

"Yes?" he said, looking at me.

My mother, who was walking toward the sofa, stopped for a second. She wasn't even calling him Mr. So & So or Col. So & So. She was going all out and calling him *Colonel Sahib*. She looked in his direction to see if he had taken offence at me.

"Have you read any books by Kundera?" I asked.

"No. Have you?" Adit asked as if it were a competition. He seemed to think I was asking him questions to show how much I knew.

"Is that your question to everybody?" my mother said with sudden irritation as she took her seat again. I could tell she was flustered by this new development, these adults I was friendly with and books I talked about. The air in the room had changed. I was upset with India and Adit, and they were both upset with me. My mother getting angry felt like the last straw. I thought of Sheela's invitation to visit her house this weekend. It felt like the only thing to look forward to.

Rani came back into the living room and sat down on the floor a little distance from us. She placed her cup of tea on the floor next to her.

"I don't know how she reads that stuff," my mother said as if apologizing for my tastes.

Adit was still looking listlessly at the curtain.

"What sort of books does he write?" Vidur asked, coming to everyone's rescue.

"He's a Czech exile. There are overtones of magical realism in his work," I said.

Vidur nodded, easily impressed by my words. He was more interested in what I was reading than either my mother or Adit. Adit came back from his drifting, flashed me a fake smile, and said, "Interesting." His behavior had changed so much from earlier in the afternoon when he had touched his heart. He had become insufferably patronizing. I felt angry. I wanted to cause him a great amount of pain.

"Well, *Colonel Sahib*, you must have lived all over India in your days in the army. Which place have you enjoyed the most?" my mother asked.

"Ladakh and Kanyakumari. The tips of our country are the most dramatic. I couldn't go to Ladakh now. My body is too old for the thin air up there."

"I am sure you keep in good shape, *Colonel Sahib*," my mother said. I thought of Adit's muscular thighs, and the image of the Old Spice model from the TV commercials came to my head. They showed a close-up of his legs as he windsurfed, his quads sinewy and flexing. I drifted.

"She's a power woman. She works for American Express," Adit was saying.

"And do you want to join the army like your father or join a bank like your mother?" my mother asked Vidur.

"I want to join the army, ma'am," Vidur said.

"That's good, *Colonel Sahib*. He wants to walk in your foot-steps," my mother said.

"I don't think it's good at all," Adit said sharply.

Alarmed by his reaction, my mother immediately said, "Ana-mika has no focus."

"But Aunty, she comes first in class. You shouldn't worry," Vidur said in my defense.

My mother looked at me, and then at Vidur, and said, "What about all the competitive exams? She hasn't been preparing for them."

"Mom, I want to do physics," I said.

"What sort of career is there in physics?" my mother said to the room in general.

I stole a glance at Rani. She was looking at all of us as we spoke. Adit took a quick look at her as well. From where we were sitting, the afternoon sun bounced off of her face, making it glow and look dark and shiny at the same time.

"She can do research at the National Center for Science or go to the U.S.," Adit said.

We were done with our cups of tea. Adit and Vidur got up to leave. My mother shook hands with Adit again and said, "Thanks for helping Anamika with her physics."

My heart nearly stopped. Vidur and I had forgotten to tell him the excuse we'd used. Vidur cleared his throat loudly. Adit was quick on the uptake and said, "Mrs. Sharma, you're wel-come. She's a pleasure. Very brilliant girl you've got." Then he stepped closer to me and ran his hand through my hair in what seemed a fatherly gesture, but when his hand reached the back of my head he pinched it at the spot where it always felt tense to me. Only Rani noticed. She would rub my neck there whenever she gave me a massage.

After they were gone I pulled out my books to study.

My mother walked into the room with my almonds and asked casually, "So, how come you called *Colonel Sahib* by his name?"

I immediately felt defensive. Before I could think of what I was saying I blurted out, "So, how come you shook hands with him instead of saying *namaste*?"

My mother looked at me quizzically. Then she said, "It's not that odd to shake hands."

"You've never shaken hands with a man," I said.

"What are you trying to say?"

"Nothing. Nothing." I felt a huge dread fill my heart. I could feel I was sinking into an argument that was illogical. It was one thing to feel entirely illogical inside myself, but exposing my lack of rationality by talking this way was another matter.

"What's wrong with you, Anamika?" my mother asked. She enunciated my name. She only did that when she was about to get angry. I took a deep breath.

"I called him by his name because he told me to. He said 'sir' made him feel old."

My mother dropped the conversation and left the room, muttering, "Adolescence. Everything about you has changed in the past month."

I was incensed.

XV

Papa

I sought refuge in my physics book over dinner. I read about Einstein's general and special theories of relativity while putting spoonfuls of *rajma chawal* in my mouth. My mother had to periodically remind me to eat. To concentrate I had to read the same sentences over a few times. At nine I took my dinner plate to the living room and joined my parents to watch the news. A third boy had burnt himself.

"I don't know what's wrong with these kids," my mother said.

"They're doing it for a cause," my father said.

"Oh, Rajan! Come on. One doesn't set oneself on fire because of some parliamentary bill."

"Some people have strong principles," my father persisted.

I felt like he was trying to challenge me, accusing me of not having the same staunch moral values as the kids who were burning. I was a *brahmin*. I thought the reservation policy was wrong. Why wasn't I protesting? Putting my life on the line? Why wasn't *he* for that matter, I wanted to ask.

"Principles my foot," I said. "They are immature and reckless teenagers. Everyone's doing it out of some kind of herd instinct. They need to throw out the government, not burn themselves. That's not rational behavior. It's self-centered and ridiculous to set yourself on fire."

"They believe in it. That's how nonviolence works. That's how Mahatma Gandhi brought us independence. One harms oneself in protest."

"Please. That's a lot of shit," I said.

"Anamika!" my father shouted, getting up from his seat.

I looked at him without any apology. I said, "What?"

"How dare you talk like that?"

"To call a spade a spade," I said.

He looked at my mother and said, "What's wrong with this girl? She's too big for her boots."

"Rajan, please sit down. She's got growing pains."

Then my mother looked at me and said, "Apologize, *Beta*."

"What for?" I said.

"You shouldn't speak to your father like that."

"I didn't say anything about him. I just said his argument was no good." I did not look in my father's direction when I spoke.

"Still, that's no way to speak," my mother said firmly.

I put more *rajma chawal* in my mouth so that it was full.

"Say sorry," my mother persisted.

I looked at my father. He was glowering. It gave me a lot of courage.

"Should I say sorry even when I'm not sorry?" I said in an even voice.

My mother glued her eyes on mine and stared fiercely, trying to convey that she didn't want me to push this thing. I was sure my father would explode. I relented.

"I'm sorry," I said halfheartedly.

"No, you're not," he said with some bitterness.

I shrugged, not wanting to prolong the torture anymore. Rani must have been watching us from the passageway. She walked into the drawing room and asked my mother for further instructions. I finished the last spoonful of food on my plate and went back to my room.

I sat at my desk. It was so hot that it was difficult to keep my forearms on the desk without its surface getting sticky with my sweat. My fan was utterly ineffective even though it was turned to the highest setting on the dial, whirring away at five. As I deciphered the important things my physics book was telling me, I momentarily forgot about the humidity. The sound of the ceiling fan brought a rhythm to my insides. My emotions slid away from me.

It turned out that even though I was going to grow old and die, I could have a twin who could sit in a satellite moving at the speed of light who would not grow old at the same rate. It suddenly made perfect sense that some moments passed by quickly and others slowly. It also made sense that my brain, which I was sure did travel as fast as light, could go back and forth in time. It could travel at various speeds and make things happen inside its universe in a way that my physical body with all its mass could not. I envied Gandhiji, his fasting and low mass, his ability to eat a few almonds a day and survive. Lightness meant swiftness. It meant longevity, the closest thing to immortality.

I knew there was no practical application of this, but the idea alone was enough to make me want to keep on living; maybe even just to find a way to translate this theoretical physics into a more practical one. Turning into carbon for the sake of some political drama everyone would forget in a few months was entirely out of the question.

The notion of time being relative was even more liberating than the uncertainty principle. It did not play out on a human scale. It was for the scale of galaxies. But it didn't matter. Along one relative coordinate I was young. Immature. An adolescent. My fight with my father made no sense. My emotions for Adit even less so. I had all sorts of hormones cruising through my body at top speed that made me act impulsively. I got up from my desk to go apologize to my father.

My chair creaked as it scraped on the stone mosaic floor. The lights went out, and the whirring fan slowed down, then stopped. Everything was dark. No light filtered in from the street outside; there was a blackout in the colony. I shuffled slowly to my bedroom door, groping my way around as my eyes adjusted. The heat and humidity were oppressive now. My armpits were wet.

"Stay there, Anamika, I'll get a candle," my mother called from somewhere in the house.

"*Babyji*," Rani said.

I hoped no one had heard her. It was like a sigh, a lover's whisper. I responded with a whine of sorts.

My mom had lit a candle and was walking down the passage-way toward my room.

"It's okay, Mom, I'll sit in the living room. I can't really study like this. It's way too hot."

She turned around, and we both walked to the living room. The candle was making me even hotter. My cotton shirt was clinging to my skin, and my body felt slimy. We heard the sound of bare feet on the floor. Rani had followed us. I could see the shape of my father in front of the TV where I had left him.

"It's so hot," I complained, easing myself onto the couch. Rani grabbed a newspaper from a pile on the coffee table and positioned herself by the couch. She started fanning me.

My father turned toward us for a second. My mother wiped her face with her sari *pallu*. My eyes had adjusted to the light. I could tell Papa was looking at Rani fanning me, but I could not see the expression on his face. The room felt very still, the rustle of the newspaper in front of my face filling its void.

"You're lucky. She's very devoted to you," he said.

I didn't know how to respond. Did this mean he knew?

"Yes. She really cares for you. She loves you," my mother said.

I was afraid they were going to confront me. I was sure Rani and I had been careful and they had not seen anything, but my heart was jumping with fear. The rustle of the newspaper in Rani's hands grew louder and louder. I wanted her to stop.

"It's okay, Rani," I said to her in Hindi. I didn't want my parents to say anything more to me.

"No, *Babyji*, you'll sweat." It was odd enough that she was fanning me and not my mother, but talking to me that preciously was dangerous. Had she forgotten my parents were there?

"I wish someone were fanning me right now," my father said.

He didn't usually speak in a flippant tone like that. He was trying to suggest that my mom fan him. She was tying her hair in a tighter bun to keep it from the back of her neck.

"I wish someone were fanning me right now," she said.

I laughed, thrilled that she had given it back to him. My father laughed, too. He had been pulling her leg. I loved him.

"Papa, I'm sorry about what I said earlier," I said. It came out easily.

"It's okay. I'm sorry, too," he said.

I had never had such an exchange with my father. My mother had given in to me on many occasions, but an apology from my father was totally new.

The phone rang. It was a loud piercing ring that reverberated through the house. I jumped from the sofa and ran to get it, knocking my shin into something sharp on the way. I hadn't expected Sheela to confirm so soon that her parents were going to the function.

"It's Adit." My heart was doing sixty miles an hour now. Faster than my bicycle or my horse, Sugar. I pressed both my hands to the earpiece so that my parents wouldn't hear. I was silent.

"Is this a good time to talk?" he asked softly.

"No."

"I just had to call you. It profoundly affected me to meet you today."

"Really?" I was so happy to hear him that I was no longer angry with him.

"Is someone there?" he demanded.

I strained to see my parents in the dark. Rani was fanning my mother now. I didn't know what I could say to him without arousing the suspicion of my parents. It was probably easiest to pretend it was Vidur calling about homework.

"Vidur, I don't know the answer to that sum," I said.

"Sorry, Anamika, I shouldn't do this. When is usually a good time to call?"

"The third," I said.

"I'll call you at three tomorrow afternoon, okay?"

I put the phone down and walked slowly back to the couch, my knees weak. I needed a cohesive story for my parents. In which order had I said "really" and "yes" and "no"?

"How is Vidur?" my mother asked.

"Fine," I said. Rani was still fanning my mom. I wondered if she would fan me now instead.

"Fan *Babyji*," my mother said to her, as if in answer.

She stepped over to near where I was and started fanning me again.

"You women have it good," my father said lightly. He was right. I felt smug.

"When we have no electricity, how come the phone still works?" my mother asked.

"The dial tone and electricity are carried on a wire from the central office in DESU, which has its own generator," I replied.

"Did they teach you that in school?" my father asked.

"No," I replied.

"What do they teach you in school?" my father asked.

"Wave-particle theory, uncertainty, human biology, probability theory, geologic formations, the structure of molecules."

"Do you have any questions about anything?" my father asked.

I had a lot of questions. And it occurred to me for the first time to ask my father instead of asking Adit or Mrs. Pillai or India.

"How does one know what is good and bad? Is it set down from nature?" I asked.

"What subject do you need to know that for? Don't you want to be an engineer?"

"I need to know it for my life, Papa," I said.

"God tells us what is good and bad. Society and customs tell us."

"But our customs are different depending on caste, and what is good and bad cannot differ with caste," I argued. I was sure that it was far more permissible for Chakra Dev, with his backward caste *yadav* badge, to get away with a whole lot more than for me with my *brahmin* one.

"What's good for the goose does not have to be good for the gander. The ancient books like *The Gita* and *The Upanishads* tell us our duty, and doing our duty is good."

"Even if they were right when they were written, how do we know they are right today?"

"They are eternal," he stated flatly.

"Girls didn't go to school then. But they do now. The world has changed," I argued.

"Rajan, she's right. Women weren't meant to have careers and simultaneously raise kids. It's a different world. There are no easy answers for how we should be living our lives," my mother said. Hearing my mother speak made me realize that for my mother this whole discussion was not just about my future and me. It was about her having a job and a kid and managing a house.

"But *jaanu*, her question was about how we get our standards of morality and duty. I am not talking about other things," my father said.

"But what about happiness?" my mother said quietly.

"*Jaanu*, are you unhappy?" my father asked even more quietly.

"No, Rajan. But I wonder, with so much of duty to this and that, where is the place to live a joyful life?" She sounded tired.

"But the stages of life prescribed in the ancient books answer our need for knowledge, for love, for doing good to others, and for renunciation."

"You really think there is one single path to happiness when there are so many different types of people?" my mother asked.

"You like tea, and I like coffee. I want to be a physicist, and Vidur wants to join the army. I don't want to get married, and mom did. How can the same formula make us all happy?" I asked.

"What do you mean you don't want to get married?" my father said.

"She's too young to want to be married. Don't say anything," my mother said to him.

"At your age I didn't want to get married, either. I wanted to ride a motorcycle across the Australian outback," my father said. I knew that my mother had forbidden my father from riding a motorcycle when they got married. He had sold his secondhand Rajdoot and bought a Vespa. But my father had never talked about wanting adventure before.

The lights in the room flickered and came on. The ceiling fan started to whir again. The fridge hummed. Power was back.

"Thank God," my mother said. The light in the room seemed very harsh. My mother's face was covered with sweat. Rani's head was still covered by her sari *pallu* the way it usually was, but she had perspired so much that her hair was stuck to the *pallu*. My legs were feeling sticky, but Rani's fanning had kept my face dry. I said "thank you" to her in English.

"Back to work," I announced and got up.

In my room I poked through my school satchel and decided to attack the gargantuan homework assignment Mrs. Pillai had given us. I thought of Mrs. Pillai with her hips swaying on her way out of class. I closed my eyes and imagined my lips on hers. It was not hard to imagine at all. Was it wrong? It broke all the rules of the student stage of existence described in the scriptures. A student was a *brahmachari*, celibate and chaste by definition. On the other hand, if good and bad were to be measured, as Papa said, on the basis of whether they furthered the goal of the student life, then having an affair with Mrs. Pillai could only further my mathematical skills. I would study much harder because I would not want to disappoint her. I was thinking of nothing but having affairs twenty-four hours a day. It was insane. I opened my book and stared at the Fibonacci sequence.

When Rani walked into my room after finishing up her work for the night, I was surprised to see that over an hour had passed. I had plowed through most of my homework without losing my concentration between the folds of women's saris. She came to where I was studying and ran her hand through my hair. I closed my book.

"What does one say in English when someone says 'thank you'?" she asked me.

"Welcome," I said.

"Welcome," she repeated.

"Good," I said.

"Meaning?" she asked.

"*Accha*," I said.

"I want to learn the alphabet," she said.

"I'll write down two letters for you tomorrow before leaving for class. There are twenty-six letters. You'll know the alphabet in thirteen days," I said.

"Write four. I'll do it in half the time."

We lay on my bed hugging silently. I remembered that I had promised to call India when she had phoned in the afternoon during Adit and Vidur's visit.

"I forgot I have something important to do," I said to Rani, extricating myself from her embrace. I tiptoed to the living room and called India.

"I've been longing for you. Longing so much," she said. I felt guilty.

"It's impossible to come at night. Rani sleeps in my room," I said.

"I don't want you to take a chance. I don't want anybody to know about us."

Hearing her speak drew me into her orbit. I could have listened to her speak for hours. I wished I could go over immediately.

"What are we going to do?" I asked.

"I'll think of something. Now go back, and don't let Rani suspect anything," India said.

I went back to my room and lay down again beside Rani. Something had changed. I could only think of India now. I wished it didn't take me so much time to shift from one to the other. I wished I were as quick as an electron jumping from phase to phase. Rani was quiet. The silence frightened me. I unhooked the front of her blouse.

"No, *Babyji*," she said, putting her hands on mine to stop me.

"Why not?"

"You should sleep."

Restricted access to Rani was unacceptable. The idea that she could say no to me was downright inflammatory. I pulled her hands down to her sides and pinned her wrists to the bed. Her lips were unresponsive, like inanimate pillows.

"What's the matter?" I said.

"It's wrong. You should marry a boy like Vidur *baba*. You have your life ahead of you. I'm unlucky to have a brute for a husband," she said. I could tell she had been thinking about it all evening. In a way I was relieved that it was not the phone call or my having left the bed that had caused her to refuse me, but her own thoughts.

"Vidur is just a child," I said.

"But he'll grow up. At this age all boys are children."

"Look, there's nothing wrong. I want you," I said. I couldn't sustain a serious conversation about marrying Vidur.

"No, *Babyji*, I don't want you to do this," she said. I wondered if she actually didn't want it. But I knew that if I shifted back and commanded her as a servant I could have her. I wanted to tell her it gave me pleasure, but I didn't know the word for pleasure in Hindi. I said instead that it made me happy. From the little light in the room I could see her smile weakly.

Then instead of thinking of the Hindi movie villain, I just did everything that I thought he would do. Although she didn't stop me, I felt that some part of her was resisting me. But then there was a distinct moment when she yielded. I felt one with her and eventually fell into a deep dreamless sleep that was interrupted only by the sound of the alarm clock going off. Rani hugged me with a whimper, and I felt her body stretch itself awake. Her smile was beautiful, her happiness uncensored. If she had had doubts in the night they were gone now. I felt blessed to have her.

As I put on my school uniform I wrote *A, B, C,* and *D* on four index cards and left them with a pencil and copybook for her to practice with. When she came to my room to give me my tiffin box I pronounced each letter to her and made her repeat it. We did it twice before I left for school.

Hulla Gulla

When I arrived at school there were armed security guards all over campus. They looked at the students, especially the tall boys, with some hostility. They stopped kids who were carrying anything more than schoolbags and inspected their belongings. They had been called in to stop any untoward incidents related to Mandal. Clusters of students and teachers spoke to one another in whispers. There was an atmosphere of mutiny everywhere. The *bahadur* from the principal's office found me as I was walking toward the Pushkin Block.

"*Babyji*, the principal *Sahib* has called you."

I went to the principal's office.

"Anamika, the milieu is very uncertain. We plan to continue classes for as long as possible," the princi said to me, then paused dramatically.

"But?" I said, raising an eyebrow.

"But Delhi Administration might declare that all schools should close. We will be powerless then. I want to discuss how we can ensure the students are organized in that event."

"We should make sure there's a list with phone numbers of all the students and teachers of each class. The subject teachers should also give a four-week study plan to the kids," I said.

"Four weeks! Our Head Prefect is a pessimist!" he said.

"One never knows. I remember the curfew in 1984 went on longer than we thought."

I tried looking for Vidur and Sheela after I spoke to the princi, but it was impossible to find them in the bedlam. In the assembly ground I made announcements over the PA system, continually asking classes to line up, but they fell on deaf ears. Instead of lending an air of order to the campus, the military guards had had the opposite effect.

"What is this *hulla gulla*?" the princi asked me as he came up onstage.

I shrugged.

"Tell everyone to get into line," he said.

Stretching my authority to its limits, I started addressing the class teachers over the PA system. "Mrs. Thaityallam, please get IX E to line up," I said. Technically it was the responsibility of the teachers to make sure that students formed into lines. The Head Prefect was meant only to assist the teachers. But it was a real joy pointing out to Mrs. T., the biggest stickler for duty and decorum, that she needed to get on with her job. I thought she'd be furious with me, but she gave me a hasty glance when she heard her name and rounded up her kids.

By the time we gathered for assembly we were fifteen minutes behind schedule. We sang Schiller's *Ode to Joy*, and then a small child only a little older than Jeet read the news. He was terribly nervous at having to speak in front of the school and swallowed up a lot of words in his haste to finish reading. His thin legs shook under his gray shorts. When he walked back I patted his head.

The school talk was given by a girl in the senior class, who spoke about the mother goddess figure in the Harappan civilization. I thought of India every time she said "mother goddess."

"I'll speak when she's done," the princi said to me while she read.

"Do you want me to announce you, sir?" I asked.

"It's a good idea. Everyone is falling asleep right now," he said.

The girl spoke in a monotone. When she finished, it took a second for the school to realize that her talk was over and to begin clapping. I walked up to the microphone and said, "Everyone must have noticed all the security guards swarming our campus. I am sure you want to know what's happening. The principal is going to address us."

He walked up to me and said, "Stay here. Don't go back."

I stood next to him, staring at the six thousand children in neat formation, while his voice boomed across the assembly ground. No one was fidgeting anymore.

"If we have to close down the school, we should be prepared. In the zero period all the teachers will make lists with the phone numbers of the entire class and photocopy and distribute them. We don't want the coverage of the syllabus to suffer if we are forced to close. Is that clear?"

There was no response.

"Is that clear?" his voice resounded again.

"Yes, sir," the kids said in chorus.

"And Classes X and XII, you should realize that the board exam will be held regardless of whether we are able to cover your syllabus in class. So make sure you study." After a pause he continued, "The army has lent us these guards to prevent self-immolation. We don't want anyone to get hurt. Is anyone going to set themselves on fire?"

There was no response from the assembly.

"Is anyone going to set themselves on fire? Answer me," he thundered.

"No, sir," everyone sang.

After his talk, a sort of sobriety descended. Even the rowdier students walked directly back to their classes. I walked past Mr. Garg, who had his lips pursed together.

"Good morning, sir," I said.

"Oh, Anamika!" he said absently. Then he turned to look at me. "Yes, sir?"

"You are one of my best students. If the school shuts down, I don't want you to suffer."

I wasn't sure exactly what to say. I didn't think he was trying to pay me a compliment.

"If you want, I can come to your house and give you tuition," he said.

I was touched. Even if he intended to charge money for the tuition, it was incredible that he should go beyond the call of duty to teach me just because I was a good student.

"Thank you, sir," I said. My heart filled with gratitude. I had never given a second thought to Mr. Garg outside of the classroom. I felt as if I had tasted something beautiful and pure. His offer was so unselfish it made me believe in things I had long stopped believing in. I wished he were leading the country. I went back to my classroom feeling idealistic and full of hope.

Our class teacher, Mrs. Ganatra, who also taught us biology, passed out a sheet of paper on which to write our phone numbers. She told us to call her if we had questions.

"Don't worry about disturbing me. I go to sleep around eleven and get up early."

"Thank you, ma'am," Vidur said. A few other kids sang after him.

When the sheet came to our desk I looked at the list while Vidur was putting down his phone number. Chakra Dev had already written his, and so had Sheela. Chakra Dev's number was several down from Sheela's. I wondered if he'd seen it and noted it.

Mrs. Ganatra asked us to take out our textbooks and told us which chapters were most important and which questions we should try to answer from each chapter in the next few weeks. The main section on human biology was left to us. I had personally been looking forward to it for months (it had drawings of the male and female organs). Vidur and I had opened the book together at the beginning of the term and gleefully looked at the index—"Chapter IV, Section III: Gonads." It seemed now that the pleasure of watching everyone squirm in embarrassment was going to be lost. I was disappointed. On the other hand, if I didn't have to come to school I could devote a lot of time to both India and Rani. I could spend the days with India in her house and the nights in mine with Rani. Once in a while I might even be able to bike over to Sheela's.

The period ended by the time Mrs. Ganatra had made us mark up our books. Vidur leaned over to me and said, "If schools really close, you can come over to study. My father will teach us."

I felt my ears get hot and felt guilty when he mentioned his father.

"I'll come if he can teach chemistry. I hate it."

"Oh, yeah! He's great at it. He knows all about chemical reactions," he said, his eyes dancing. But Vidur was always playful, and one couldn't tell how much he really knew when he said things.

The next period was Mrs. Pillai's. She walked into class with her eyebrows furrowed. It was unusual to see her hassled.

"Kids, I am so sorry about this. You're going to suffer the most because you have board exams." Everyone pulled out their textbooks and stared back at her.

She turned her back to the class and picked up a piece of chalk. Most of the teachers had long nails, and when they wrote on the board I would imagine the chalk getting under their fingernails. It made me shiver. But Mrs. Pillai had slender fingers and well-clipped nails. She wrote her phone number and underlined it. She turned around to face us again.

"I know that nobody here cares two hoots about mathematics. But if anyone has a question I want you people to call me at home."

Copybooks opened, pages turned, and everyone took down the number.

"If anyone here wants to get extra classes from me, all you have to do is call. I might have classes at home if there are enough people who can come. Otherwise if you are near enough I will come by Vespa. I don't want anyone who is interested in working hard to suffer. Got it?"

"Thank you, ma'am. We appreciate it," I said. I wanted to say it before Vidur did.

"I'm glad someone appreciates it. Look at all of you. I'm more concerned than you are about your boards." She extended her hand toward the class and made a sweeping gesture that took everyone in from the window side to the wall side.

"Thanks," Chakra Dev said in an inappropriate tone. I

whirled around to see his face. He was half smiling and half
sneering. I didn't want Mrs. Pillai to go to his house and teach
him. He probably wanked off thinking of her.

I looked back at Mrs. Pillai. She was busy writing a list of chapter, section, and question numbers on the blackboard. Everyone
was copying them down. I couldn't imagine her navigating Delhi's
chaotic traffic on a Vespa, her sari fluttering about her and her face
encased in a helmet. It was thrilling that she rode a scooter. It was
rare for a woman, a sign of independence. Her light cotton sari was
starched to a crisp. Even though it was wrapped around her many
times, the outline of her petticoat underneath was visible. The sari
pallu fell off her shoulder as she wrote on the board. The weather
was very hot, and she was wearing a sleeveless *choli*. I could see the
round shiny knobs of her shoulder bone. My pulse raced.

After she finished writing on the board she faced the class
again. Her *pallu* was still slightly off her shoulder, revealing her
collarbone and the full length of her neck. My mouth watered
the way it did when I was hungry. Vidur looked up and stared at
her as well. I rubbed my face on the sleeve of my shirt so that I
could turn to see Chakra Dev. He was staring at some point
under her face, possibly her bosom. I turned back, and under the
pallu one could make out the shape of her breasts. I wondered if
she had sex with her husband and how she looked under her
clothes. After class finished and Mrs. Pillai left the room, I
turned to Vidur and asked, "Do you think she's sexy?"

Vidur maintained a disinterested look and said, "She is attractive." This was a big admission. He would never admit to anything more, even if he thought so.

Chakra Dev was hovering around and heard us. He came over
to our desk and leaned across it, his dirty elbows digging into my
school diary. I glared and pulled it out from under him. Ignoring
me, he addressed Vidur. "I spent the whole period thinking what
it would be like to fuck her."

"You shouldn't talk like that about a teacher," Vidur said, his
pupils dilating.

"Oh! Come on, be a man!" Chakra Dev said.

"Can you please move from here?" I said in an even voice. I hated his intrusion. I hated the fact that because he was a guy he was free to think as he wished and could dare to express himself.

"You're such a bitch," Chakra muttered. He pulled his weight back and stood up.

"What did you say?" Vidur said sharply.

"She is such a bitch," Chakra Dev spat out loudly. Some other people in the class turned to see who was talking.

Before I knew what was happening, Vidur had shoved the desk in Chakra Dev's direction and jumped over me to where he was standing. Vidur held him tight by the collar as if he were going to strangle him.

The sounds of desks scraping across the floor pierced the room as Ashu and Satnam cleared a path to Chakra Dev, following Vidur's lead. I had not seen Vidur get angry before. A vein on his temple was pulsing. He was thin and not very tall. Chakra Dev towered over him, but right now Chakra looked scared of Vidur, whose knee was poised to give Chakra a kick in the pants.

"Fucking asshole," Vidur hissed.

Satnam and Ashu had grabbed Chakra's elbows and were twisting them behind his back.

Chakra Dev winced.

"What did you say again?" Vidur asked.

"Sorry," Chakra Dev muttered.

"Say it again," Ashu said.

Vidur yanked Chakra Dev by the head and said, "Say it to her."

"I'm sorry, Anamika," he said, not sounding the least bit remorseful. I wanted to give him a sharp kick in his stomach.

"Don't ever talk like that about Mrs. Pillai again," I said angrily. Ashu and Satnam tightened the twist on his elbows.

"I won't," he whined.

"She's as old as your mother," I said to Chakra.

"Sorry," he said again, this time with real remorse. There was sweat on the sides of his cheek where his coarse hair was sprouting. He was definitely hurting.

"Let him go," I said to them.

Vidur brought his hand down from Chakra Dev's collar. Satnam and Ashu let their hold go with some reluctance. They
had enjoyed their power. Neither boy was very big. Chakra Dev
could have totaled all of them individually, but all three were too
much for him. He went back to his seat without looking at me.

Everyone in class had stood around watching the spectacle.
Vidur pushed the desks back to where they had been. Sheela
came to our desk and spoke to me.

"Are you okay? What did he say?" she asked.

"Oh! He just called me a B," I said.

"Why?"

"I told him to get off my desk because he said he wanted to
fuck Mrs. Pillai." I wanted to hear myself say the words "fuck
Mrs. Pillai."

"Is he crazy? She's a B," Sheela said emphatically.

"Stop it," I said.

"You like her, don't you?" Sheela said.

"She's a great teacher. Who else has offered to give us all
tuition?"

"Please. It's all for show," Sheela said.

"If there's one thing about Mrs. Pillai that even you have to
admit, it's that she doesn't do anything for show."

Vidur, who must have been listening to our conversation,
said, "Anamika is right."

Hydrogen Sulfide walked in just then, ten minutes late, and
put an end to the group discussion. In her typically dour manner
she told us what to focus on from the next three chapters. Then
she wrote her phone number on the board and said, "That's my
number."

After Hydrogen Sulfide's class we had recess. I went up to
Sheela's desk.

"Am I still invited to your house when your parents are
gone?" I asked, flirting.

"Only if you stop Mrs. Pillai-ing all the time. Mrs. Pillai this
and Mrs. Pillai that," she said, crinkling her nose and sticking
out her tongue.

I shrugged. The faces she was making made my desire for her evaporate. I said I had urgent work to do and left the classroom, leaving Sheela to Vidur. I went to the block where the junior school was located and went to the headmistress's office. The recess for the junior school was an hour earlier than ours, so the kids were in their classrooms and the building was calm. Mrs. Nyaya Singh was sitting alone in her office.

"Ma'am, may I come in?" I asked.

"Anamika, what a surprise! I don't think you've been here since you left Class V."

"Ma'am, I'm sorry to disturb you," I said. The headmistress had always liked me. When I was in the junior school I had won the annual trophy for the best All Rounder of the Year, and the head-mistress continued to tell the kids even now that the Head Prefect was an All Rounder. I knew that during the height of school intrigue, when Prefects were to be named, Mrs. Nyaya Singh had recommended me. She had said that I was the unanimous nomi-nation of all the teachers in the primary school. Mrs. Pillai had told me this. She and Mrs. Singh took the same school bus.

"What brings you here?" Mrs. Singh asked me.

"Ma'am, I know a divorced lady with a son. She has a lot of problems because her son goes to a school near the father's house. She is hoping to move him here so that he can live with her."

"I remember this case. It's Mrs. Adhikari, isn't it?"

"Yes, ma'am."

"*Beta*, the problem is that we can give midterm admission only in exceptional cases."

"But ma'am, it is exceptional. You could consider this case on humanitarian grounds," I said.

"I can look into it again," she said.

"Ma'am, the mother is suffering," I said, practically pleading now.

"For your sake I'll look again, *Beta*. Ask her to call me next week."

"Thank you, ma'am."

"Have you decided what you are doing after school?" she asked me.

"I will take the IIT exam, ma'am. I am sure I will get in," I said without flinching. A less-than-perfect answer now and Jeet's chances would be jeopardized.

"Excellent! Good luck, child."

"Thank you, ma'am," I said again and walked back to my class from the Primary Wing.

Vidur was sitting all alone in the classroom eating his tiffin.

"What's the matter?" I asked.

"Where did you disappear?"

"Just had some work," I said.

"I wanted to talk to you about Chakra Dev," he said, looking perturbed.

"Thank you for what you did. You didn't need to," I said.

He went red and brushed his hand past his face as if it was nothing.

"I think he likes Sheela," Vidur said.

"Why do you say that?"

"He asked her to go to the canteen."

"Did she?" I asked.

"Of course not," he said.

"Where is she?"

"She went with Ashima."

"So what's the problem?" I asked.

"He has her phone number now. I think he can't be trusted," Vidur said.

"That crossed my mind, too," I said.

Vidur shook his head as if it was a shame. I looked at him. His face looked funny.

"Vidur, do you have a crush on Sheela?" I asked suddenly. It hadn't occurred to me before.

He didn't make eye contact with me but said, "No. No." He denied it too much.

I bent my knees a little so that I could look him in the face and said, "Please tell me the truth, Vidur. You like her, don't you?"

He looked down at the desk and then looked up at me and said, "Please don't tell her."

This was a problem. I wished it had been someone else he liked. There were other attractive girls in the class. I didn't want to think of what could happen now.

"I won't tell her," I said, sighing.

We went to get a drink at the watercooler. A couple of young boys stood around. Only one of the several taps on the cooler was working, and the pressure was very low. I had to keep my head bent for a few minutes to get a proper drink. Vidur drank after I was done. The bell rang, and a herd of boys approached us, bringing dust from the PT field. Before anyone reached the watercoolers, Vidur and I finished and walked out of the alcove where the watercoolers were located. At the same time, from behind us, Vidur and I heard a tremendous explosion. I whirled around.

A massive firecracker the size of a grapefruit, orange and green in color, had gone off two feet away from me. The boys who had thundered in from the playing field immediately backed off. Vidur looked sharply down the corridors and went running in one direction. The firecracker had burnt fully. I shrugged and walked up to it, kicking it into a corner. Seeing that it had been spent, the boys jostled one another and formed a huge queue in front of the watercoolers.

I saw Vidur walk back, his hands clutching the necks of two boys. He was dragging them with tremendous force. I remembered the day of the investiture ceremony for the Prefects. I had been dead certain that Vidur would be made a Prefect, but though twenty boys and girls were chosen, he was not one of them. The teachers had made a huge mistake.

"It was these two," Vidur said, shoving them under my face. He let go of their necks and gave them each a wallop on the head. They brought their shoulders up instinctively and bent their necks. I raised my hand a little to stop him from whacking them again.

"We didn't do it," one of them whined.

"They were the only ones hanging around when we were drinking water," Vidur said.

"Who lit it?" I asked. I hadn't noticed anyone hanging around.

"We didn't," they both said. I had no evidence whatsoever. Even if they had been hanging around, there was no proof they lit the bomb. I stared at their faces to see if I could pick up any signs. I looked them up and down to see if they were in correct uniform. A small piece of paper the same color as the firecracker was stuck to the shoe of one of the boys.

I shouted toward the entrance of the watercooler alcove, "Someone hand me the burnt firecracker."

A few seconds later a boy came with what little remained of the firecracker. It was wet and covered in dirt, since the floor of the watercooler area was always slimy. I didn't want to touch it.

"Hold it," I said to one of the boys. He held out his hand and took it.

Word about the incident seemed to have spread. Kids popped their heads out of classrooms. Before it disintegrated into a real street show I decided to take the kids to the princi. They seemed to me to be entirely guilty.

"Look, I am taking you to the princi's office. You can tell him what happened," I said.

The boy with the telltale evidence of the firecracker on his shoe spoke. He pointed to the other boy and said, "It was Sanju's idea."

"What were you trying to do?" I asked, looking at Sanju.

"I . . . I . . . I . . . *Didi* . . . I just wanted to see what would happen," he stammered.

"What class are you in, Sanju?" I asked.

"Class . . . Class VI, *Didi*," he said.

"Do you realize someone could have gotten hurt?"

"Yes, *Didi*, I'm sorry," he sniveled.

"What's your name?"

"Digvijay."

"The two of you come with me," I said.

"Should I come with you?" Vidur asked. I shook my head.

"Sorry, *Didi*, please don't take us to the princi," Digvijay whined.

"It was your plan, and you're the ones who're shaking," I said.

"Sorry, *Didi*," Sanju whined again.

"Kids, come along," I said.

"Pl . . ." Sanju began again.

"Shut up," I said.

We walked down the flight of stairs to the ground floor. Sanju dragged his feet while Digvijay glared at the floor. As we neared the princi's office, Digvijay said quietly, "*Didi*, please, I already have two yellow cards. My parents will beat me."

"If you already have two yellow cards, you know that a third one means you'll get suspended," I said, stopping and turning around to look at him. "How did you get the other two?"

"The first time I hit a boy with a motorcycle chain. He had to get stitches. And the second time I stole money from Mrs. Divan's purse."

"Why did you do this today? Don't you ever think of the consequences?"

"Sanju has one yellow card, too," he muttered.

The red light in front of the princi's office was lit, which meant that he was busy. *Bahadur* opened the door and came out of the office.

"Who's inside?" I asked.

"PT teachers," *Bahadur* said.

"Tell him it's urgent," I said.

Bahadur disappeared into the office again and then opened the door for us to go in. The teachers were in an animated discussion with the princi. He held his hand up, asking me to wait.

"But you see, sir, he's been doing this with the students for years," one teacher said.

"Our school's reputation is at stake," Mrs. Rishi said. She was the only lady PT teacher. She usually taught volleyball and had a rough voice, the voice of paper being torn. All the male teachers flirted with her.

"Does he threaten the parents, or does he merely ask and inform?" the princi asked.

"He threatens them," two of the teachers said simultaneously.

"Well, let's see what Anamika says," the princi said. The teachers who had not noticed me all turned around.

"What, sir?" I asked.

"Has Mr. Bala ever solicited your parents to join his insurance scheme?"

"Yes," I said.

"Did they buy it?"

"No, sir."

"Did he say anything?"

"No, sir."

"And you?" the princi asked, looking at Sanju.

"No, sir. I didn't do anything," Sanju whined. He wasn't listening. His legs and hands were shaking.

"What's the matter with you, boy?" one of the PT teachers said to Sanju.

"Sorry, sir," Sanju whined.

"What happened, Anamika?" the princi asked me.

I told him.

"And you, weren't you the motorcycle chain boy?" the princi asked Digvijay, who stood motionless with his head hung down.

"Do you think there's any reason to be lenient with them?" the princi asked me.

"No. The contrary," I said.

"I'll suspend him. There's no point having such bad elements around. And we'll give Sanju a yellow card," the princi said.

I nodded.

"I didn't do it," Digvijay said.

"We didn't want to hurt you, *Didi*," Sanju bleated.

"Did someone ask you to do this?" I asked Digvijay.

"No, *Didi*," Sanju said.

"Shut up," the princi said to Sanju.

"Answer Anamika *Didi*," the princi said to Digvijay.

"I'll tell the truth if you don't suspend me," he said, still looking down. I couldn't believe he had the gall to negotiate like this with the princi. The PT teachers in the room gasped.

"I'll break your feet," one of the male PT teachers barked.

The principal gestured with his hand for everyone to stay cool.

"Just tell us what happened," the princi said soothingly.

"A senior asked me to plant the bomb when *Didi* was there. But I was late," Digvijay said.

"We decided on purpose to light it a few seconds late. It had a long thread, so we knew it wouldn't go off immediately and hurt you, *Didi*," Sanju said. He was now crying.

"Who asked you to do this?" I asked.

"I can't tell you," he said simply.

The princi was looking at me, and from behind I could feel the eyes of the PT teachers boring into my back. I felt ashamed at having been responsible for such commotion in the school. I knew the only way to shake it off was to come up with a situation where I was clean, where it was clear to everybody that I had not incited the action.

"Just nod your head if you cannot tell me," I said.

Digvijay looked up for the first time. Sanju continued to sob. The princi waited.

"Was it Chakra Dev Yadav?" I asked.

"It was him," Sanju said, howling afresh. Digvijay nodded.

"He'll kill us. He knows real *goondas*. They even have guns," Digvijay said, all worked up.

"Who is this goon?" the principal demanded.

"Sir, can I speak to you alone?" I asked. I wanted to tell the principal the whole story from earlier today, but I didn't want to use the F and B words in front of the kids or the PT teachers. He nodded and asked one of the PT teachers to take the two kids to the field and make them run a hundred laps while he decided their fates.

Once we were alone I told him what had happened earlier in my classroom. I related the story using Chakra Dev's exact words about Mrs. Pillai and me.

"Your classmates are thinking about intercourse with their teachers while your school counselor thinks a joint sex-ed class is a scandal," he remarked, laughing.

"I know. There is a huge generation gap," I said.

"I can suspend Chakra Dev today," he said.

"Sir, he'll stop short of nothing," I said, standing extremely straight. I wanted the princi to think I was stating a fact but that I was not scared.

"All the more reason to suspend him right away."

"Can I talk to him? I'll tell him we know. That you know," I said.

"So he can really harm you?"

"Sir, please trust me. I can get an apology out of him in writing by tomorrow morning," I said confidently. He was silent. I knew he would think that letting Chakra Dev go scot free would be like getting bullied by him. He was not a weak man. My chances of having my way were very slim.

"I think I can persuade him to really change his ways," I added. Then I said, "If I don't succeed you can always punish him, sir."

"Do you realize that you are now taking responsibility not just for your own well-being but for that of your classmates who were involved in the fracas earlier?"

"Yes, sir. If the bomb had not been aimed at me personally, I wouldn't even suggest this option," I replied without batting an eye.

"He has less than twenty-four hours. I expect him to come up to me at the school assembly with a letter signed by him and his father," the principal said.

"Yes, sir, don't worry," I assured him.

When I got back to class, Mrs. T. was talking about the difference between a plateau and a mesa. I had to stand at the door and request permission to enter.

"Where were you, Anamika?" she asked instead of saying yes.

"With the princi. There was a problem," I said.

"Okay, *Beta*."

As I walked to my desk I noticed Chakra Dev writing with his right hand, but his left hand was in his pant pocket. It was a strange way to sit. I was sure he was fondling himself. Taking out my notebook I noticed Vidur had already filled a sheet with differences between plateaus and mesas. I opened my pencil box and looked at the George Michael pictures for a second before starting to write what Mrs. T. was dictating.

When the bell rang Mrs. T. said, "I'm going to speak till the next teacher comes in. We have a lot to cover for the syllabus."

I decided I would wait till school was over before speaking to Chakra Dev. I was nervous about the talk I was supposed to have and unsure whether to approach him in a soft, decent way or as a figure of authority. Either could backfire easily.

At the end of the day the *bahadur* from the school office came to our classroom and handed us cyclostyled sheets of the class list. Sure enough Sheela, Vidur, Chakra Dev, and I were all listed. I decided then that it was better to call him at home, this way I'd have the option of speaking to his father at the same time.

xvii

Backward Caste

When I returned home that day I told Rani about what happened in class. I usually didn't tell her about my school life, but my mother had told her I was the Head Prefect. I mentioned Chakra Dev. I told her I had to call him. I wanted to ask her how to deal with him.

"Such people are dark. They don't change," she said. "A scorpion is a scorpion."

I was sitting on my bed recounting the story when the phone rang. My body was so relaxed I didn't feel like getting up.

"Will you answer?" I asked Rani.

She asked me if I was sure. We had not let her answer calls for us so far. But I didn't see the harm. Everyone who called could speak Hindi anyway.

She got up and walked quickly to where the phone was.

"Haloo," she said.

After a few seconds I heard her say in Hindi, "And you?"

Then she put her hand on the mouthpiece the way my mother and I always did.

"It's yesterday's *Colonel Sahib* for you," she announced.

"You forgot I was going to call," he said as soon as I greeted him.

"I have other things on my mind," I said. I wanted to say something grown-up.

"You're going to be difficult, I see," he returned.

"You see nothing over these VSNL phone lines."

"Well, I'm saying I'd like to be able to see you," he said.

I wanted to tease him, play hard to get. It was very different from the kind of immediate and serious feeling I had about India or Rani. I was always eager, serious, and ready to please them. This was lighter, more fun.

"Why? Because I'm a nubile young maiden?" I asked.

"What's the matter, Anamika? You're not taking me seriously."

"Come on, Adit, you're my friend's father. What am I supposed to do?" I said. Now I was afraid I was talking too much. Not keeping myself in check.

"We're not going to do anything. I just want to meet you," he said in a soothing voice.

"You think anyone will understand why we are meeting? My parents won't. Your son won't. Your wife certainly won't. We'll have to hide it. Anything clandestine is tantamount to an affair."

"With your 'tantamount' you're sounding like an *Indian Express* editorial," he chuckled.

"Stop making fun of me."

"We need to be secretive because our society is screwed up, but we both know we're not doing anything wrong."

"I'm already conducting three liaisons. That's more conceal-ment than I can take," I said. The word "liaisons" rolled off my tongue easily even though I had never used it before. As I said the words I saw myself walk through the gray portal called ado-lescence and into adulthood.

I visualized myself in a wedding, but instead of a groom leading me through seven circles around a sacred fire, there was a single chalk line. I crossed it three times. The first time Rani held my hand as I lifted one foot over the line, then the other. The second time India held my hand, and the third time Adit held my hand.

"I think you need to talk to someone with experience about these things. You could get badly hurt." Adit's voice had gotten more serious. "Don't ask me why or how I suddenly care about you. It has a force of its own," he continued.

"How are we going to meet?" I asked.

"I could meet you after school. I could come to your house," he suggested.

"You can't come to my house. We have a full-time servant," I said. I enunciated the word "servant" as if it were a whole sentence, a universe.

"A beautiful one at that," he said.

"Yes. Yes. Yes."

"I'm sure we can give her something to keep her quiet," he said.

I couldn't take it anymore. The charade and double life made me feel unclean.

"I'm sleeping with her," I said quietly.

"You're what?"

"You heard me," I said. He paused for what seemed like a long time.

"This is just a phase. It will pass," he said, his voice settling into a plush tone, like he knew more about life than I did. I could see him sink into his sofa while he spoke to me, his face relaxing, a knowledge greater than mine enveloping him.

"What the hell do you know?" I said, ready to explode.

"I think everyone goes through this experimental phase," he said patronizingly.

"Oh yeah? So how many orderlies have you slept with?"

"I'm not attracted to men," he said peacefully, not willing to pick a quarrel.

"Me neither," I said harshly.

"You'll eventually want the real stuff," he said with great confidence. I hated him and no longer felt close to him. I didn't see the point in talking anymore. I didn't respond.

Eventually he said, "Call me tomorrow."

"You can call me," I said.

"I will. And take my number down, too," he said.

He gave me his work number, and then we hung up. When I placed the handset down I decided to call Chakra Dev. After having talked to Adit I felt confident of managing a phone call with him. I went back to my room to get the cyclostyled sheet from my bag. Rani was sitting on the floor by my bed, staring at the alphabet. Without even knowing what was going on, Rani knew everything.

"What's the matter?" I asked.

"Nothing," she said, looking down at her feet.

"Tell me, Rani," I said, my voice changing immediately to the commanding employer's tone.

"*Babyji*, it's not my business, but I did not like the *Sahib* that day when he came here. Vidur *baba*, your friend, is very nice. But you should be careful of *Sahib*," she said.

"Careful in what way?"

"Just careful."

"Tell me the truth. What do you mean?"

"Just the way he looked at you once or twice."

"He did not look at me in any way. He looked at you," I said.

"I know these things. You're still young. Innocent."

"You're only seven years older than me, Rani. You're innocent, too," I said, laughing.

"Yes, *Babyji*, but where I'm from you learn these things at a very young age."

"So you think he desires me?" I said bluntly.

She looked a little taken aback by my coarse words. My Hindi was limited.

"Yes. I think he desires you," she said.

"I am going to speak to Chakra Dev," I said.

"I still say you shouldn't," she said.

"I have to or else he won't be allowed back to school for three weeks," I said, retrieving the sheet.

"I'll bring you some tea in the phone room. You'll need it," she said.

I had to dial Chakra Dev's number twice because my finger slipped on the dial the first time.

"Hello," he answered. His voice sounded less crude over the phone.

"It's Anamika," I said.

There was no response. He was waiting for me to make my move.

"How are you?" I asked.

"It's none of your business," he said, sounding entirely displeased at having heard my voice.

"Listen, we know about the bomb," I said, getting straight to the point. Further pleasantries seemed pointless.

No response.

"By 'we,' I mean the principal and I," I said, mustering all my authority.

"You can't prove anything," he challenged.

"The princi decided to suspend you. I stopped him," I said.

"Oh! How kind of you!" he said sarcastically. He didn't believe me.

"Those two boys confessed once the teachers confronted them," I said.

"I don't know what you're talking about."

"Shut up and listen," I said. There was silence. "I know you hate me, but I told the principal you wouldn't do it again. There's no reason to involve anyone else from the school in your personal hatred for me."

"What makes you think you are so important?"

"The fact that you had someone try to injure me with a bomb," I said.

"Just because you are Head Prefect, you think you can boss me around?"

"I'm not bossing you around. But it's only because I am Head Prefect that the princi let you go on my request. He agreed to give you twenty-four hours."

"What do you want?" he growled.

"A letter of apology signed by your father," I said.

"Fuck off, Miss High and Mighty."

"You'll really get into trouble, and I'm not going to help you again," I threatened.

"Who needs your help?"

"Fine. Be impervious to all warnings. I tried my best," I said.

"You and your big words. I liked the sound of the bomb. Shame it didn't get you. All the other *brahmin chutiyas* are burning. I want to fuck you burning *brahmin chutiyas*," he spat.

His words cut through me. I knew then that he really meant it. Chakra Dev wanted to be mad for the sake of being mad.

I hung up on him.

Rani had placed the tea beside me and was sitting on the floor, sipping from her own cup. I shook my head.

"I told you not to try," she said in Hindi. It looked as if she had followed the conversation entirely based on the tone of my voice.

In the evening I decided to be bold and go to India's house with my mother's full knowledge.

On the way I replayed my conversations with Adit and Chakra Dev. Despite my irritation I wanted to meet Adit, and despite Chakra Dev's hatred I wished he had wanted to change. India welcomed me so warmly at her door that my heart soared to the heavens, happy, free.

"I want to talk to you, but naked, in bed," I said, leading her confidently by the hand. The sensation of having a lover was no longer new.

"How did you get away?" she asked.

"I told my mother I had to speak to you about Jeet's admission," I said.

Once in her bedroom I turned off the light. We could see nothing. My heart started thumping. I fumbled with her sari, taking care not to unwind it till I removed the safety pin holding the pleats at the navel. I could no longer remember the things I had wanted to talk about. In a tremendous rush, we made our way to her bed. The round orbs of her *fesses* fit into my palms, familiar, fleshy, and mine. When we made love the second time I gripped both her feet in my hands and interlocked my fingers with her toes.

I walked home late, feeling lighter than a helium balloon, realizing only when I rang our bell that I had failed to tell India to call the headmistress next week. My impotency as Head Prefect in the matter of Chakra Dev had stopped bothering me. The principal could suspend him. It would teach the boy a lesson.

On the news at nine the headlines showed footage of another boy going up in flames. The self-immolations seemed like a forest fire, spreading rapidly and recklessly. I sat in front of the TV and yelled out to my mother to join. The boy had done it in front of news cameras, with the policemen unable to stop him. He had screamed "I'm a *brahmin*" over and over again as he burnt. The newsreader said all schools had been closed indefinitely. I let out a hoot of joy and danced around the room. My mother looked at me in shock.

"It's such sad news, how can you jump like that?"

I stopped. I felt stupid. The phone rang.

"Did you hear?" Sheela said excitedly on the other end.

"Yes."

"I'll be alone tomorrow morning. Do you want to come over?" she asked.

I was excited by her directness. But I didn't want to show it on the phone to my mother or to Sheela.

"Let me take your address. I can ride my bike," I said matter-of-factly in a low voice.

As soon as I had hung up, the phone rang again. This time it was Vidur.

"I know school is closed," I said as soon as I heard his voice.

"Dad wanted me to ask you if you wanted to come tomorrow afternoon. He'll teach us."

"How will I come there? It's far."

"He said he can pick you up on his way back from work. He needs to use up his casual leave so he is taking half a day off."

I agreed and hung up. I couldn't believe Adit was getting Vidur to do the dirty work. I told my mother I was going to see Sheela and meet Vidur. The phone rang again as I was talking to my mother. This time it was India.

"I forgot to tell you to call the headmistress, Mrs. Nyaya Singh," I said.

"You talked to her about Jeet?"

"I told her it was a humanitarian issue," I said.

"I'm the humanitarian issue," she said, then added, "I can still feel you in the pit of my stomach. I found your hair on my pillow."

I was holding my breath.

"I want you to fuck me again," she said. That word, loaded

with all the power of Sartre and self-immolation, German porn and Mrs. Pillai.

"Oh!" I whispered. Desire, acute and powerful, wrenched my guts.

"It's unbearable not to be with you, Anamika."

"I can come early tomorrow morning, but then I have to meet classmates," I said.

"Come as early as you like," she said.

"School's closed, so I'm free," I said, the unreasonable urge to dance around the room overtaking me once more, my voice running away to the rhythm of freedom.

"Do you think we can go away for a few days?" she proposed.

"Where?"

"I'll think of something and ask your mother. I want to sleep and wake up with you."

In bed at night with Rani I told her not to worry about *Colonel Sahib*. I said that Adit was honorable, like a father, though in fact he was not fully honorable.

"Do you remember the alphabet?" I asked.

She moved away from me and turned on a lamp. She showed me the copybook where I had written four letters. She had practiced on page after page, her writing getting progressively smaller and more assured. One page had other letters, in running hand. I could barely tell what was written since the handwriting was so wobbly. I made out the words "lonely" and "love" and "pain."

"What is this?" I asked.

Rani smiled flirtatiously and said in Hindi, "You tell me, *Babyji*."

"Where did you see this?" I asked, feeling hot in the face.

"First tell me what's written," she said.

"Just *raat*," I said, using the Hindi word for night.

"Only that?" she asked.

"Rani, where did you get this from?" I asked.

She reached out to my desk and gave me my chemistry register.

"It was under the sofa," she said, using the English word "sofa."

I flipped it open to the last page. Sure enough, in circular, very schoolgirlish handwriting, were some fifteen lines about nights with me and those without me, about parts of her body and her mind, about longing for me. I felt progressively hotter and guiltier as I read them. I could see Rani was watching. I wondered if she could tell that the handwriting on the last page was different from that in the front of the book. India's handwriting was a shock. It seemed like that of someone younger than Vidur and more orderly and morally pure than Sheela. I had promised India not to get too attached to her. I should have asked her to promise me the same.

"All of that can't just say night," Rani said, putting her hand on the page.

"No, they are instructions for some studies," I mumbled. To occupy her with something else I wrote some more letters in her notebook. Teaching English without the use of the Hindi script was strange. I had to tell her not just *e* for egg but also that an egg was an *anda* and that *g* stood for ghost which was a *bhooth* and that she shouldn't worry yet about the letters *o*, *s*, or *t* since we would get to them later. Teaching her to read and write in Hindi would have been more practical, but I did not remember the order of the alphabet in Hindi anymore. I had no memory of how I had learned the alphabet or learned to read.

In the morning I tore out the page from Rani's notebook on which she had written India's words as well as the sheet in my chemistry register that India had filled. After reading the sheet a few times so that I would remember her words forever, I tore both pages. It almost broke my heart.

xviii

Death

When I met India in the morning for our cold coffees, I told her everything that had happened at school and canvassed her opinion on Chakra Dev. In the bright light of the morning there was no longer the same urgency to make love. The night felt much sexier.

"I think Rani is right. You should leave him alone," she opined.

"As it stands, I have. The princi will suspend him when school reopens. I think of him as raw energy. It could be channeled either way," I said.

"He's already gone wrong. This isn't chemistry with its reversible reactions," she said. I wondered what she would have said if it were Jeet instead of Chakra Dev. Would she stop trying to improve her son because she thought it was too late?

Before I left, India told me that she might arrange for us to get a ride with her friends Deepak and Arni to a hill station where a friend had a cottage. I wasn't sure my parents would give me permission. India told me to leave that to her.

I went back home to pick up my bicycle and rode to Sheela's house. A male servant opened the door for me as soon as I rang Sheela's bell. Sheela smiled at him a lot and called him *Bhaiyya*. She took me up to her bedroom on the second floor. I shut her door.

"No, leave it open."

"What do you mean?"

"*Bhaiyya* will get suspicious," she said.

I resigned myself to having a tame study session, a bitter and certain disappointment welling up within me. I sat on her bed and pulled out my physics book.

"I want to do mathematics today," she said.

I reached for the textbook and opened it to the probability chapter. She reached for her stereo and put on a tape. It was Terence Trent D'Arby singing "If You All Get to Heaven."

"How will we study with all this noise?"

"I can't concentrate without music," she said, smiling. Her smile was right out of a TV commercial. I wondered if it was practiced.

I tried to drown out the noise and focus on probability. But she didn't let me work. She started touching my furrowed eyebrows with her finger. She whispered, "Sooo serious."

"Stop making fun of me."

"I'm not making fun. You look so cute deep in thought. So scholarly."

I felt like an utter fool. The coolest girl from class was calling me studious. I didn't want to be cute. I wanted to be sexy. I felt humiliated and ashamed.

"Do you understand anything about probability?" I asked, ignoring her.

Instead of answering me, she got up and started dancing to the music, the door to her bedroom still wide open. I worried that the servant would see her and get ideas. Her body moved in a smooth liquid motion as if she had done this all her life. She twisted her index finger and called me to her. I stood up. She held my hips and swayed. I was acutely uncomfortable and asked her again, "Do you understand probability?"

"The probability of you having fun is zero," she said, laughing. Then she squeezed my cheek between her thumb and forefinger as if I were a child. This pissed me off. I went back to her bed and looked at the textbook. I pulled out my big practice register and tried to do a sum. I felt overwhelmed and kept reading the question again and again. A small voice told me it was a good thing that Sheela wanted to dance with me, but the rest of me was unable to rise to the occasion.

Just then the servant walked in carrying a tray with two glasses of lime juice. I looked at Sheela, wondering if she would keep dancing. She did. He looked at her, placed the tray on her desk, and left. I couldn't believe she was so comfortable with him. There was something overtly sexual about Western dancing. I associated it with hippies, free sex, and loose morals. I wondered if she was having an affair with him. I went to her stereo and turned it off.

"What's the matter?"

"There's *nimbu pani* here. Plus, I want to know something."

"What?"

"Are you sleeping with him?"

"Who, Ramu *Bhaiyya*? Are you mad? He's worked with us since I was little."

I was quiet. I had thought that because Sheela was religious she would be very Indian in her outlook. Seeing her sway to American music made me wonder if I really knew her at all.

"What's the matter, Anamika? You look really unhappy. Didn't you want to see me?" she asked simply. I patted her bed where I was sitting, and she came and sat next to me.

"I'm sorry. I don't like dancing."

"But you're such a flirt," she said.

"I don't know how to dance."

"Don't you dance at weddings?"

I shook my head.

"Come, I'll teach you," she said.

She got up and pulled me to her. I suddenly became aware of the soft skin of her palm and wanted to learn how to dance. She turned on her stereo again and pulled me close. I raised a finger to ask her to hold on a minute. I closed the door and bolted it.

"What will he think? I never close my door."

"He'll think less than he thinks when he sees you dancing like that," I said. Her breasts were too ripe and her mouth too fleshy for her to act like a child.

She moved her hip close to mine. Our faces were close, and my glasses kept touching her cheek. She pulled them off and put them on her desk. I let myself sway along with her. My feet were barely moving, and my hand was under her T-shirt.

I kissed her.

"Do you like the smell of Old Spice?" I whispered.

She kissed me back, but her lips were closed. I pushed my tongue forward.

"No. I don't want to do that."

Her resistance made me try it again and again. Eventually she sighed and parted her lips a little. I fiddled with the clasp that I could feel under my hand.

"Stop, Anamika, you're making me uncomfortable."

I remembered the way she was dancing when her servant had got the drinks. After that display it seemed unlikely that my pass at her could make her uncomfortable. I persisted. She pushed my hands down from under her shirt and stepped back.

"Stop!"

She seemed angry, so I stopped and picked up the glass of *nimbu pani* and began to drink it. She picked up her glass as well. We both sat down on the bed and didn't talk. I put my hand inside her T-shirt again, this time from the front. She pushed it down, looking irritated. I lay down on the bed and dangled my legs off the side. My mind wandered to the rape scene in the *The Fountainhead*, when Howard Roark rapes Dominique without any exchange of words, and their love affair begins. Chakra Dev would do that, too, I thought, though he was no Howard Roark. I got up carefully and put my *nimbu pani* back on the table. I replaced Sheela's, too.

"I thought you liked me," I said.

"I do."

"Then why are you so resistant?"

"You're moving too quickly."

I lay back down on the bed. This time she put her face on my shoulder and played with my hair. My hands found their way back under her T-shirt. She didn't stop me. After a while I yanked off her T-shirt. Her bra was tight fitting and showed her ample cleavage. The skin on her chest was very fair in comparison to her face and arms. I had never seen such white flesh in my life except in foreign movies. I started unzipping her jeans.

"Stop," she said, putting her hand on mine.

"I'm not going to stop. I want you."

"You have to," she said softly. I felt she was resisting me only for the sake of resisting me.

"No," I hissed.

I pinned her down on her bed and held her hands above her head. I kissed her face and neck. She closed her eyes and smiled. I held her two hands in one of mine and unzipped her jeans.

"Please don't do that," she said in a panic.

"Shh," I said as I tried to pull them past her thighs. I pulled her underwear down, too.

"Anamika, please stop," she whispered urgently.

If she really didn't want me to she could scream or move away or kick me. "You're beautiful," I said as I slid my hand between her thighs where her bloomers should have been. She closed her eyes again, but this time I couldn't tell if she was enjoying it or not. I pushed with my finger. I wasn't slow, the way I had been with India and Rani. I was afraid if I was too gentle she would use it to move away. I used all the force I could muster.

She let out a howl. "Stop, it hurts."

I pulled back and said, "I just fucked you." There was blood on my finger.

She opened her eyes and looked at me as if I was sick. Then very quietly she said, "Get out of my house."

I was hurt. I hadn't meant it in a bad way. I got up and put on my glasses and collected my practice register and book bag. I wanted to talk to her.

She had got up from the bed and pulled on her jeans and her shirt.

"Why did you do that?" she asked.

"I wanted to be inside," I said.

"I don't understand you. You can be so gentle sometimes, and then at other times you're like those *cheapads* on the bus."

"I'm sorry," I mumbled. I didn't know how to respond. I wished I could say something to make her feel better and think differently of me.

She stood in the middle of her room with her arms across her chest as if she were guarding herself. I gathered everything and walked toward her door.

"I'll see you later," I said, unbolting the door. Then I left the room without looking back and descended the stairs almost in a run, the bloody finger in my pocket. The *Bhaiyya* looked out from the kitchen when I was at the bottom of the steps. I ignored him and made my way out the front door.

I unlocked my bicycle and mounted it. As I pedaled my agitation ebbed away. I thought about what had happened. I wasn't culpable for rape. I had just pushed her into doing something faster than she had wanted to.

There was a lock on the door when I got home. I had to fumble for my key and let myself in. Rani had probably gone to the market to buy vegetables. In the beginning when she had moved in with us my mother had not wanted to give her the key. But now she had her own key. I washed my face and then went through my satchel, removing the mathematica and replacing it with my chemistry textbook for studying at Vidur's house. I was no longer excited about seeing Adit. I didn't feel like a Sartre *femme* or *homme* but like human detritus. I was gauche, a quasi-rapist, a rake no better than the *cheapads* on the bus. Maybe I was being too harsh on myself, but even with the maximum benefit of doubt I was a bumbling sixteen-year-old with grand delusions about being a philanderer.

As these thoughts were whirling in my head, the bell rang. I opened the door for Adit and offered him a glass of water. He followed me into the kitchen. I filled a glass with water from the fridge and handed it to him. He drank it in one swig and handed it back to me.

"Do you want more?"

"No."

I put the glass in the sink. He remained standing in the kitchen.

"Let's go," I said.

"Anamika," he said, the sound waves gathering weight as they vibrated alone in the air.

"Yes?" I said after nothing followed the pause.

"Will you give me a hug?"

I kept standing where I was standing and said nothing. He came closer to me. For a brief second I saw his eyes, the way they were looking at me. He came even closer and squeezed me tightly. I felt relief, as if a huge charge I had been carrying inside my body had just been dissipated, grounded like electricity.

"Don't worry, I won't take advantage of you. I just needed to hug you."

The word "advantage" made me blush. I stood still as his arms squeezed me tighter and tighter.

"That feels a lot better," he said as he slowly let go of me.

I remembered Sheela again. Even a man would have behaved better than I had.

"I raped a girl today," I said.

"That's impossible," he said. I couldn't argue. I felt drained and leaned against the kitchen counter. He touched the tip of my nose with his finger.

"We'll talk about it on the way. I am sure it's not as bad as you think," he said.

"I have to get my things," I said.

"Wait," he said and led me back to the living room where he had put his briefcase.

"I brought you the book." I looked at the cover, a drawing of a young girl. The word "Lolita" looked like lollipop.

"Thanks," I said.

"Let's go," he said.

I gathered my things, and we went to his car. As we drove off I saw Rani walking toward the house in the side mirror of his car. I rolled down the window and waved to her. She waved back.

"Tell me about this girl," he said matter-of-factly as he drove.

"She's a classmate. I went to her house. I forced myself on her."

"What exactly did you do?"

"Entered, plunged, pierced," I said dramatically. I couldn't believe myself. A few minutes ago I had felt embarrassed simply hearing him use the word "advantage." The state of my being was entirely capricious. I felt like a test tube filled with chemicals, danger written all over it.

"She let you do this?" he asked.

"No. She told me to stop, but I didn't."

"I don't think that's rape. I'm not saying it was a nice thing to do, but it wasn't rape."

"You just want me to feel better. It was disgusting," I said.

"You're so young," he said.

I was feeling young. But after a while I said, "I always thought it was intelligence that counted more than age."

"It does. That's why I don't feel bad pursuing you."

My heart started up embarrassingly. As Adit drove I looked out the window. The AC was on, so I had rolled my window back up. It was nice not to have to breathe the outside air. Each time a truck or bus got ahead of us, it spewed dark smoke.

"Adit, I don't want Vidur to know anything about our friendship."

"Of course not. That's out of the question," he said immediately.

"Do you feel guilty?"

"There's nothing to feel guilty about. Thinking about you makes life a pleasure."

From his lips the word "pleasure" had more illicit overtones than the F word when Chakra Dev said it.

"I was very excited about seeing you today," I said.

"I was, too. Now if only I didn't want you, it would be perfect," he said.

I let the remark pass. Adit wanted me? My heart started beating fast again. I didn't want him to talk about it, but I was a little
drawn to the idea at the same time.

"The problem with being a man is that you think with your
little head sometimes," he said.

My friend's father referring to his anatomy like this. *Tauba!
Tauba!* I felt even my internal organs turn red. My ears were
burning. I wished I could get out of the car. I looked out the window again. We were already in the cantonment. There was less
traffic and more large, green trees. More space.

When we arrived at Adit's house, Vidur was out on the porch.
I waved to him and jumped out of the car as soon as we were
parked. Two glasses of *nimbu pani* were waiting for us inside.
The house was at least ten degrees cooler than the car. We all
sat in the low wicker chairs in the living room. Adit stretched
his legs out in front of him. They were very long. It struck me
how tall he was. Maybe even six feet tall. When I was a very
little girl I had always wanted to marry a very tall man.
My legs were stumpy. How could someone as suave as Adit
want me?

"So, kids, what do you want to study?" Adit asked us, looking
from me to Vidur.

"Organic chemistry," I said.

"Ethylene, methylene, hydrocarbon derivatives," Vidur sang.

"All right, children, take out your notebooks. And don't mind
my rotten egg smell," Adit said in a high falsetto, imitating
Hydrogen Sulfide. Obviously Vidur had told him in detail about
our teachers.

Adit explained concepts to us first in plain English, then with
some formulas, and finally with real numerical examples from
the book. Vidur paid more attention than he ever had in class.
And even I stopped thinking of everything else. We studied for
an hour, after which the orderly made us some tea and brought
out Britannia Digestive biscuits.

"Vidur told me about the incidents at school yesterday," Adit said.

"Yes, the politicians could never have guessed that Mandal would cause such an uproar," Vidur said.

"Chakra Dev almost got suspended," I said to Vidur.

"What are you talking about?" Vidur asked. I told Adit and Vidur everything that had happened in the princi's office and about my phone call later.

"If they implement Mandal, only Chakra Dev will get admission to an engineering college, even if he is suspended from school. No wonder there is such a brain drain. The brightest doctors and engineers are all in the U.K. or the U.S.," Adit said.

"Delhi University has thirty-five thousand applicants for fifteen hundred seats. If ninety percent of those seats get reserved for scheduled castes, I won't make it," Vidur said. "We're *kshatriyas*," he added. I looked at Adit. He was still doing his *dharma*, working as his ancestors had done. My father on the other hand, though a *brahmin*, was now a paper-pusher, a bureaucrat.

"Even you may barely scrape through," Adit added, looking at me with a sidelong glance.

"I certainly won't," I said, laughing.

"Get out kids, get out. Go to America or Australia," Adit said in a spirited voice. I could imagine him using the same tone to tell soldiers to go to battle.

My father's colleagues at the *sagai* professed great patriotism, but someone like Adit, who had actually taken a bullet wound for his country, wanted his kid to get out.

After the lesson Adit and Vidur dropped me off but didn't stay for *chai*. The day had left me exhausted. I had met India and Sheela and Adit, all in one day. I had also done something I was deeply ashamed of. Adit had not understood the full extent of my shame. While I could talk to him openly, I didn't feel he was as sensitive as India or Rani, who seemed to understand my heart better. But I couldn't confess to them about Sheela. They saw me as their lover, not a *cheapad* on the loose.

I opened my English textbook and read a lesson to calm myself down. Usually I read English lessons only once, in class, when everyone read them together. I had never studied for an English exam. I reread a story by Ray Bradbury that described the life of a prehistoric dinosaur-like animal who lived on the ocean floor. It was the only one of its species to survive. When he heard the low bellowing sound of a lighthouse, he thought it was a female from his species calling, so he came up to the surface of the ocean. He did this year after year on a particular date. Then it got too much and he destroyed the lighthouse, lashing at the bricks with his tail. The story was lonely. It was the opposite of my own in some ways because I had many people in my life. But deep down it was my story, too. I had split myself like an atom into many electrons and neutrons. Each subatomic particle danced with a different person and led its own life. But all of me, the whole me, did not exist for anyone but myself. On a day like today I was so alone that I didn't feel whole, even from within.

At dinner my parents and I watched the news. There had been no incidents of self-immolation that day, but a large number of college students had gathered in Delhi for a rally and sat cross-legged on the Ring Road in protest. I watched the TV set feeling entirely dead.

"You look rather upset today," my father said.

"Yes, *Beta*, what happened? Is everything okay?" my mother asked.

"I'm fine. Just tired," I said, retiring to my room. I turned off my lights before Rani joined me. When she came in I whispered to her to lie down beside me. She hugged me and fell asleep. As soon as I heard her light snoring I reflected on what had happened with Sheela. I tried to think of a single thing half as bad that I had done in my life. There was nothing that even came close. I remembered things that I had not thought about for many years. Memories that remained vivid even though they had been upstaged by the torrent of daily life, a life lived increasingly in the moment and at a faster and faster rate. It seemed that the past few months were more condensed and had more data points than entire years from before.

I remembered how I had been ashamed of Delhi, of India, in 1984. The state machinery, politicians, police, and mobs, Hindus and Muslims, all joined hands to set fire to the Sikhs as the son of the recently assassinated prime minister was sworn in. He was inheriting the prime minister's position like a fiefdom, mocking the independence that the freedom fighters had fought for, mocking democracy. After a few days the army was called in, and shoot-at-sight orders were enforced, but only after every Sikh house had been pillaged and Sikh men burnt alive, chopped, and even skewered. Stepping out of the house one could see all of Delhi smoldering, black smoke rising from everywhere. I thought of all the people who were Hindu and Muslim who had done this. I wanted to drown in shame. The guilt corroded my bones.

Feelings of shame at being a Hindu in 1984 mixed with feelings of shame at having forced myself on Sheela. I hadn't slept a wink by the time my mother woke up and Rani went to the kitchen to make our morning tea.

"You still look upset, *Beta*. Why won't you tell me what's wrong?" my mother asked, bringing my cup of tea to my bed.

"I was thinking of the Sikhs and of 1984."

"Why? Is it because the schools are closed?" My mother placed my tea by my side.

"No. What's the point? What's the point of living?" I asked.

"Let's talk to Papa," she said. She held out her hand to lead me out of bed.

I followed her to their room with my cup. My father was sitting in bed reading the paper. He told us about another self-immolation incident.

"Papa, it's better than 1984," I said.

"Don't look back at blood that has been spilled. India has survived so much violence: Partition, the British, Tamurlane,

Ghazni. It will survive this, too. History repeats itself and is full of violence. It is in our nature."

It was in our nature. Not just the nature of the Hindus and the Muslims but my own nature and Chakra Dev's, too. We all had this terrible beast inside. I wanted to tell my parents about Chakra Dev and Sheela. Maybe my father would understand.

"I really don't see the point in living if it's all going to keep repeating," I said.

"*Beta*, don't talk like this. We love you," my mother said.

I shook my head and left the room. I got back into bed and buried my head under the pillow. I thought about dying. It seemed like the rational thing to kill myself. I thought of my parents. I knew I couldn't do it as long as they were alive. I thought of Rani needing me. I couldn't do it if someone needed me or loved me. Love was the only thing in my life. Everything else had already proven itself hollow and meaningless.

I felt someone come and sit on my bed, and then the weight of another body on mine. My mother whispered urgently in my ear, "Please look at me, Anamika. Don't cry."

"I'm not crying, Mom. I love you," I said, looking up. She had brought my tea back.

"It's stone cold. Do you want me to make you another cup?"

"No," I said, taking it from her.

I tried to study during the day, but after lunch I felt very tired and slept for a little while. When I woke up I found Rani sitting on the edge of my bed, stroking my head. I had no idea how long she had been there. My sadness had rubbed off on her. She wasn't able to lift my spirits. Before my mother came home I called India.

"I hate my life, I'm sad," I said.

"What happened?"

"I don't know. I wish we could go away. I'll die here."

"Let me fix something and call you back," she said.

At dinner my parents were very gentle. We didn't speak much.

At night I returned to the Sheela problem. A day had passed since the event, more than twenty-four hours. And time always gave a fresh perspective. I tried not to think of my behavior as high or low but just as something Sheela had not wanted. I had to call and apologize. Pushing your finger into someone against their will was no way of getting into a woman's pants. I had to be more elegant when I had my way with girls.

Kasauli

Delhi felt as if it had been wrapped in a thick layer of heat. The air was a milky, translucent color, like the cover of a Chinese dumpling. Within minutes of having a bath I would be covered with tiny droplets of sweat. No matter how many times I washed my face with my astringent soap and wiped it dry, I could never quite get it to be completely dry. Rani's face looked constantly shiny. So, too, my parents' and mine. We all looked like villains in a Hindi movie. I even felt like one. I had learned that if I moved very slowly after my bath I would sweat less, so I gave both my mind and my body over to the lassitude. I walked at a snail's pace to the dining room for breakfast and returned equally slowly to my desk. During the day, while my parents were out, Rani would splash water on the veranda outside my window so that some cool air could blow into my room. But the air was static, and this mostly did not help. I liked watching the six inches of exposed skin between Rani's sari and her blouse when she carried the bucket out to the veranda. Her muscles would tense in strange places. She would place the bucket outside and pour water mugful by mugful on the veranda floor. She tipped the mug at different angles so that the water would wet every corner of the veranda. Watching Rani in motion was like listening to one's favorite song. It was like watching India's hair uncoil from a bun or seeing a photograph of the sun rising over the Ganges in Benares. It was beautiful and sacred. I wanted my life to be filled with these moments. It was the closest I could come to finding an end that was justifiable.

My mother worried about me. She worried that I had no appetite and that I was sleeping very little and working too hard. She worried that I hadn't spoken about my friends or been interested in meeting them for days. She knew that I was in the doldrums. Hence it was that when India called to ask my mother if I could go to the hills with her, my mother took it upon herself to convince my father that the break would do me good.

"It's just a few days. Her studies won't suffer, and she might cheer up," she said over dinner.

"How well do you know Mrs. Adhikari?" my father asked.

"I trust her completely to take care of Anamika," my mother said.

I ate my dinner quietly, trying to keep my expressions neutral.

"How safe is it for just the two of them to go to a hill station?" he asked.

"A young couple will drive them to Kasauli. Tripta thinks that Anamika will love their company. And she said Deepak is a karate black belt. They'll be safe," my mother said.

I decided it best not to argue on my own behalf and excused myself after dinner. My mother must have talked to my father again, because by the morning he had yielded. India's friend was away, and we'd have the cottage in Kasauli to ourselves. Deepak and his wife would stay in a nearby cottage. The hills were cooler, the air cleaner. Everyone agreed it would be good for me. With the state of political unrest escalating in Delhi, it was unlikely that schools would reopen anytime soon.

I packed the large tennis bag my mother had given me with jeans and shirts, toothbrush, and *Lolita*. Rani ironed everything that I chose to take. She even ironed my cotton panties and white socks. Neither of us spoke much. I gave her no excuse for going away. If she knew of my relationship with India, she did not say anything. She had sensed for a few nights now that I was sad, and she worried no less about me than my mother did.

As she went about ironing my things, Rani said, "*Babyji*, I dreamt that the rains had finally come and it was cool. I was making *pakoras* for you as you did your work, watching the rain.

The weather was really good. When you come back maybe the rains will be here."

I knew that Rani would miss me more than I would miss her. For me the excitement of seeing a new place, of drinking *chai* in the hills on cool misty mornings, outweighed everything else. One day maybe I'd be able to go on a holiday with her.

My mother and Rani dropped me off at India's house on Saturday afternoon. Deepak and Arni were already there. My mother seemed to like the young couple instantly. I did, too. Deepak looked freshly scrubbed and almost scholarly. His wife was petite and wore tight blue jeans. She had a nose ring. India looked terribly dignified. Despite the heat she was wearing a South Indian cotton sari with a temple border and *butta* work on the *pallu*. The sari was a soothing straw color.

"Don't worry about Anamika," India said to my mother.

"I'm not worried, Tripta. I am sure it will be good for her to have a break with you."

I went with Deepak to load my bag into his car. He had already placed India's small blue suitcase in a corner of his trunk. He put my duffel bag on top of his suitcase. It had all sorts of travel stickers on it. I read one that said Florence and another that said Rio. When we were ready to leave my mother gave me a hug and kissed me on the cheek. Rani and I could not really say good-bye properly. I squeezed her forearm tightly, and she grabbed my wrist and squeezed it. "*Babyji*, take care of yourself," she said.

"It's only a few days, Rani," I said to her.

The drive to Kasauli was six hours long. Arni and Deepak both called India "Aunty" when they addressed her. Arni was only twenty-one, the same age as Rani. Deepak was a couple of years older. They looked good together. The weather in the plains was very hot, and the car did not have an AC. Deepak said he had ordered a new car with an AC, but it was not going to be delivered for another three months. We had to leave the windows open during the drive and breathe the black exhaust fumes of the trucks on the highway. After a couple of hours we were in cleaner air. My glasses protected my eyes, but India's were watering. Though India and I were both sitting in the backseat, it was difficult to touch or be expressive. Deepak used his rearview mirror quite a lot, and I could see him looking at us now and then. Arni would sometimes touch Deepak behind his neck and rub it while he drove.

Deepak told us we would pass Kurukshetra on the way to Kasauli. I didn't know it still existed. I could not imagine the great battle between the Pandavas and the Kauravas taking place amidst its brick-and-mortar flats. Even less could I imagine Krishna revealing to Arjuna his full and terrible splendor as the Lord of the Universe on Kurukshetra's dusty plain. Deepak was whistling in the car as he drove us at top speed past the place where all Hindu philosophy had sprouted. Time soiled every-thing, even the birthplace of the *Bhagavad Gita* itself.

After a while I started reading my book. It was easy to get into Humbert Humbert's head. I instinctively knew what he was say-ing about nymphets, their barely budding breasts and their long forelimbs. I imagined Sheela as the young nymphet, and I thought of myself as the rough and sexy man who liked her. I decided that Nabokov was my kindred spirit.

I must have been chuckling a lot to myself as I read because Deepak asked me what I was reading. "*Lolita*," I told him.

"Aunty, isn't she too young to read *Lolita*?"

"Deepak, have you become the moral police?" India said.

"But she's still in school," he argued.

"Tripta, tell them I'm a sixty-year-old man," I said.

"Deepak, Anamika is more grown-up than you were at her age."

The drive got progressively steeper. I had thought that the high hill slopes would offer spectacular views, but the valley was full of clouds. As we drove higher it got cooler. The winding ascent into the Shimla hills made me nauseous, and I prayed for the car to stop. When Deepak finally said, "We've arrived," I did not feel pleasure at the majesty of the imperial red brick bungalow, a leftover from the days of the Raj, with its sloping roof tiles, or at the immensity of its garden. I just felt relief that we were now still.

Arni and Deepak were staying a bit farther up, in the center of town on the Upper Mall Road. They arranged to meet us the next day and drove off.

India's friend who owned the bungalow had left the keys with the servant who lived on the premises. The house was large and opulent, with high ceilings and a big veranda that opened onto a garden. A fresh breeze was blowing. The servant told us he had dinner ready. He was a short man in his late fifties. He spoke a strange Hindi. We washed up and dined, then retired to the bedroom. The temperature was very agreeable. There was no need for us to turn on the fan.

India sat on the bed while I rummaged through my bag for my nightclothes. She watched me pull out my stuff as she spoke.

"So, why did you call yourself a sixty-year-old man?"

"Because I identify with him, the old lech. Not the nymphets," I said.

"Do you like to lech at nymphets?" she asked.

I wished I could tell her about Sheela, unburden myself of what I had done.

"Never looked at anyone younger than myself," I said.

"I, on the other hand, am clearly leching at a nymphet," she said with a wry smile.

"Does it bother you?" I asked. I wanted her to think of me as a mature, dependable, solid man. A Hindi film hero except with more intelligence, wisdom, and good sense, which those machos lacked. Only Girish Karnad portrayed intellectual men in films, and he was hardly a hero type.

"No, it doesn't bother me. You're very grown-up," she said. "But we are in an unconventional relationship, you must admit. We can't be open as a couple at all."

It hadn't occurred to me that she thought of us as a couple. It sounded very serious.

"Do you understand me?" she asked.

"That we are a couple?" I felt I had only just learned the etiquette of lovemaking, and now I was already moving on to my next lesson. For the first time I felt she was older.

"I didn't mean 'couple' in that sense. I don't expect anything from you."

"Pleasure. You should expect pleasure," I said flippantly. I imagined I was Adit or Humbert Humbert as I said it. A grown man with a sense of lightness. But I had a gnawing feeling that growing up was not just a mental thing. One's experiences counted, too, and I had few.

I took my shorts and T-shirt to the bathroom to change. When I got back India had slid under the covers. Her clothes were piled on top of her suitcase. I felt foolish and young for having worn my nightclothes. In French books the girls just removed their clothes before getting into bed. I made my way to the end of the room to turn off the light.

"No! Don't. I want to see your face," she said.

I walked back to the bed and climbed in. I felt slightly self-conscious. I had not felt like this with Rani. In fact I hadn't felt this way with India before, either. I removed my clothes in a hurry so that she couldn't stare at me for too long. Then she pulled me close to her. Her arms and legs and belly were deliciously warm. As soon as my skin touched hers I felt I had arrived someplace after a long journey. India's embrace was so well placed, my whole body savored it. Every part of her, from the tips of her toes to her forehead, was seeking its counterpart in me. For the rest of the night we did not speak much. There was no need.

I woke up in the morning and checked my watch. It was only six. Birds were chirping. In Delhi the only sounds I could hear apart from the traffic and the milkman were the barks of stray dogs. I looked at India. She was still asleep, the thin bedsheet covering her only up to the middle of her stomach. Her brown bosom was entirely exposed to the ceiling. She looked like a painting. Life was at the tip of my fingers. All the questions I had asked myself about the meaning of life, the future, success—everything was answered. Beauty was all that mattered.

I stared at India for a while, then slowly wriggled toward the edge of the bed so that I wouldn't wake her up. I was almost at the edge when she turned a little and murmured, "Don't leave me."

"I thought you were asleep," I whispered, not wanting to stir her further.

She reached out for my hand. With a surprising grip for someone still half asleep, she pulled me back to her and embraced me. The same embrace from the previous night. Total. Kindling a flame on the entire surface of my skin.

We lay on our backs, watching the morning light filter in through gaps in the white curtains. I moved a few inches away from India and took in the view again. Her body was low and flat on the bed, her stomach concave, her breasts reaching up to the ceiling. As a child I had never thought that this world of adulthood would be accessible to me. I stretched out my right arm and placed it on India's chest, in the middle, where her heart was. I felt she belonged to me; not the person I had known and loved, but her body. I could touch it as I pleased, place my palm carelessly over it.

Until now my moves in bed had been somewhat premeditated. I would move slowly and carefully, following various instructions that my brain had filed away. In more heated moments the words from the *Kamasutra* were my guide, and I would constantly ask myself how the other person felt when I touched this way and that. But in Kasauli that morning, as my hand slid down the front of India's body and the side of her thigh, I did not think of her at all. She was mine to touch, like a doll, a toy. Her eyes were closed, her lips were slightly apart.

"Your fingertips feel as if someone is running a feather over my body," she said.

We heard some doors in the house open, and I could hear the rubber *chappals* of the servant as he fussed about in the kitchen.

"Will you open my suitcase and give me my nightie?"

I pulled on my shorts and T-shirt and went over to her blue suitcase. India's saris were neatly folded on one side, her blouses and petticoats stacked on the other. A long flimsy nightie with lace around the neck was rolled up on the side. I passed it to her. She propped herself on the bed without sitting up fully.

The servant knocked and announced that he had our bed tea. I let him in. Along with two steaming cups he brought us a plate of biscuits and four buttered toasts. India asked him if we could get more toast. A warm buttery smell filled the room. We placed the tray between us on the bed. I slid under the covers again, feeling so happy I could have died then without a single regret.

India started speaking about Deepak. She said she had known his mother for many years, and that Deepak had become her friend when he was my age. I wanted to ask her if he had been her lover as well. As she spoke of him she got very animated, and I started feeling jealous. I became more and more convinced that he had been her lover and that we were in Kasauli so that she could be near him.

"Why did you want me to meet him?" I asked.

"He's traveled everywhere, he's successful, and he's got a big heart. Most of all, Deepak is a brilliant man," she said. I felt a spasm of pain in my stomach because of the way she said "brilliant" and "man." I felt she was trying to tell me the two ways in which I was different from him. I got up from the bed and went to the bathroom; I wanted to shut the door and be unwatched. I stared in the mirror and imagined a whole series of events. Deepak and Arni would pick us up at night, and we would go to some small place in the hills for dinner. It would be deserted and dark at the restaurant, and brigands would hold up the restaurant owner. Deepak would run and hide, but single-handedly I would beat all the dacoits and capture them. I would save India and Arni from danger. Later, Deepak would come cowering out from under the table, exposed for the cowardly, pathetic guy that he was.

I had been in the bathroom for some time and began to wonder if India missed me. I pulled down the cover of the toilet seat and sat on it. It was unlikely we'd be attacked by dacoits. And Deepak, apart from being taller and stronger than I was, was a karate black belt. It might be easier to ask Deepak questions about particle physics and confound him. If he knew the subject, I could ask him about the real-life applications of the wave-particle duality and stump him. I seriously doubted he was creative enough to extend the duality from photons and waves to Arni and India. And if he didn't know quantum mechanics he'd look like a fool anyway. India had to know I was more brilliant. Nothing short of exposing the lowest, meekest, stupidest, most idiotic side of Deepak would suffice.

I wondered if India had forgotten about me altogether or was busy thinking about Deepak. I went back to the bedroom.

"I thought you were never going to come out," she said.

I grunted.

"Is everything all right?" she asked, her forehead scrunched up.

I nodded and sat on the far edge of the bed. I didn't want her to know that I felt small and insecure. I didn't want to be anywhere near her. She didn't care for me. I was a fool for having come all this way to entertain this woman who probably saw me only as a simple source of sex because her lover had married someone his own age. I wanted the holiday to end so that I could go back to my house. I wanted to leave her and that wretched Deepak to feel good about each other.

"Anamika, come here," India said softly. She tapped my pillow as she spoke. She had asked so quietly and gently that I went and sat beside her. I sat stiffly. She put her hand on mine. I felt my muscles and even my bones shrink.

"Anamika, please talk to me. Please," she said. I looked at her dumbly, unable to open my mouth. The muscles of my face had begun to twitch. I quickly lost all control of them.

"Oh, God!" she exclaimed, looking at me. Everything looked a little fuzzy to me, like a television program with bad reception. She pulled me close. She ran her hand though my hair and tugged at it. My body eased.

"What's the matter? Please talk to me," she said softly into my ear.

Her skin was warm, and her hug made me feel better. She put her hand under my shirt and touched my back. I felt that her hands and her touch were telling me the real truth about her feelings for me. Looking back, my reaction to the Deepak comment seemed foolish. After a few more minutes I felt almost normal, and my body started behaving as usual. My hands reached for her back, my face for hers.

"What happened then?" she asked after a while.

"Nothing," I said, reflecting on how my immaturity had led me astray. I had felt small and rejected, but now, since she had reassured me of her feelings, I felt fine. Pat pat pat like little slabs of butter on a plate. Explanations for everything that ever happened within a human being. Thinking about it made me feel so common I couldn't stand myself. I was like everyone else. One more photon exactly like billions of other photons exhibiting all predictable photonlike behavior.

"Tell me," she pleaded again.

"Some chemicals shot into me," I said.

"Chemicals? What sort of chemicals?"

"Jealousy chemicals," I said, feeling ridiculous.

She was silent for a moment and then said, "You were jealous of Deepak?"

I nodded.

"I don't like him that way. And I think you're as brilliant as he is," she said, drawing me close. She kissed my forehead and my lips and squeezed me tightly in her arms. I was embarrassed we were actually talking about this.

"You do believe me, don't you?" she asked.

"Hmm," I grunted, wanting to drop it.

She pulled my face away from hers and watched it closely.

"You have to believe me. I am in love with you," she said.

My heart constricted. I felt as if my body existed in only the few square inches in the center of my chest where it was almost painful. No one had ever said that to me. India was in love with me!

I looked directly into her eyes and saw that it was true. Like the advertisement in which the Kawasaki Bajaj motorcycle zooms from zero to eighty in just six seconds, so my heart zoomed. My chest stopped hurting; my heart was now floating in outer space. The world was beautiful and bathed in sunlight. From far above my heart I saw that the little hills of Kasauli and our cottage were ablaze. Illuminated. Blessed. Singled out.

I spread my arms to encircle her till my elbows were firmly against the back of her rib cage. I wanted to fuse myself with her. I wanted to bite into her like an apple and then eat her, digest her, absorb her into my bloodstream, my hemoglobin, my ESR.

"What are you thinking?" she asked.

"I don't know what to do. It's a problem. I can't have you."

"But I am yours," she said simply.

"I know, I know, but, I mean, I want to possess you like an apple," I said.

"An apple?" she burst out laughing. I didn't know how to explain what I meant. I didn't appreciate that someone who belonged to me could just laugh at what I had said. It was not permissible. It was against the rules.

I rolled over forcefully so that she was on her back and I was on top. Then I bit her cheek as if I were biting an apple. It held none of the satisfaction I had imagined. I needed to bite her and swallow. I bit her round shoulders as if they were apples, then her stomach and her knees, her toes and her back, the round lobes of her bottom. I bit them harder than everything else because they were the roundest and most applelike. But she squealed, so I stopped. I noticed that my biting had caused her to start breathing heavily, so I replaced my teeth with my lips. I gathered different parts of her flesh between my lips and kissed her all over, in the opposite order in which I had bitten. In her breathless moans and her cries of pleasure I owned her more than I owned myself and was immersed in her more than I had ever been immersed in my own self. Me, I had not yet discovered. I was an unknown quantity, a constantly unraveling mystery. But India was absolutely and completely known both carnally and otherwise. I rolled off of her with the sweet exhaustion of a man who has just hunted his dinner animal.

Dum Maro Dum

Kasauli was the greenest place I had ever seen. Bushes with exotic flowers were to be found everywhere. On a walk with India I saw pine trees for the first time. We had dallied all morning in bed, and while that had felt like a novelty, the walk reminded me that there was a world outside our bubble. She grabbed my hand in hers and swung it back and forth quite naturally. The jealous fit from earlier in the day seemed like a bout of hay fever, a crash cold, a sneeze that had left no trace.

After we got home I took a shower and waited for India to dress. I wore my jeans and my checked yellow shirt for dinner with Arni and Deepak. I had a beige anorak with me. I pulled that out, too. It had all sorts of buttons and loops on the sleeves that made it look outdoorsy. When I had imagined the scene with ruffians earlier, I had imagined wearing the anorak.

India appeared after a while in a backless blouse; I could see the small of her back and the bones of her spine. Her mustard and green sari was tied low on her hip. I wanted to tell her it was inappropriate and that she should change, but what would she think of me? I could just see Adit sipping a glass of smooth scotch and talking with her, both of them at ease. It was best to say nothing.

As soon as we greeted Deepak and Arni at our door, Deepak was "Auntying" India everywhere and running his hand along her back. Arni stood around smiling as though this were perfectly acceptable and even suggested that India sit in the front seat of the car. Much to my relief, India declined.

We got into the backseat. The sun was setting, and the sky was full of colors I had never seen. When I stopped looking out the window and saw Deepak's head bobbing in front of me, I remembered the attack of jealousy I had felt. I caught the reflection of his glasses in the rearview mirror now and then and resented that he had suddenly become important in my life while I barely registered in his.

We went to a restaurant that was part of a small resort development near Kasauli. A few honeymooners and some families were seated in the garden. I gave India's hand a squeeze as we were ushered to our table. When the waiter came around to ask what we'd like to drink, they all ordered beers. I felt ashamed of my age. The waiter looked at me. India looked at me, too.

"Would you like some beer?" she asked.

I nodded.

"Four beers for the table," she ordered coolly. Deepak and Arni looked alarmed.

I didn't want any beer. Vidur had said he had tasted his dad's drink once and it was bitter and awful. What if I hated the taste or lost control of my senses? On the other hand I needed to save face. My sipping a beer would put Deepak back in his place. I had to do it.

"Aunty, I know Anamika's very mature, but are you sure we should take this risk? I mean, her parents aren't here, and she's definitely too young," Arni said.

I looked at Deepak sitting back a little in his seat, pleased that Arni was handling this.

"Rubbish. It's perfectly fine," India said, dismissing them both with one look.

"As you say, Aunty," Deepak said. I could tell he was waiting for me to get my drink and act like an ass. I wouldn't give him the satisfaction. I would sip it slowly and stay in control. My mind was powerful and would not be a slave to my body.

"India's first brewery was established in the Shimla hills," India said to us.

"I think it's still running. They'll serve us local beer," Deepak said.

The waiter came to our table and handed us menus. At the bottom after all the food listings was the selection of drinks. It said "Beer, Rs. 180." My mother had given me Rs. 350 for the whole trip. She had put it in a small handkerchief and had asked me to keep it pinned to the inside of my pocket.

"Always keep it on your person," my mother had said.

"What should we eat?" India asked the table at large, rubbing her palms together.

I looked at the menu again. The dishes were either chicken and lamb or *sabzis* and *dal*. Even the *rajma* cost Rs. 80. What had my parents been thinking when they gave me Rs. 350 for four days? We hardly ever went out to eat, but they knew what prices were like. I would have to ask India to cover me and promise to pay her back as soon as we returned. I was sure she wouldn't mind.

The waiter brought a large bottle of beer and poured it equally into our four glasses. I immediately divided the Rs. 180 by four and felt better.

"Should we share a *dal* and two *sabzis* among the four of us?" India suggested, looking at Deepak. He nodded. India ordered for the table.

Deepak raised his glass of beer and said, "Cheers."

India and Arni grabbed theirs. I picked up mine. They all clinked their glasses. I did the same. Then I looked at them to make sure they were not watching me and hardened my face as I had my first sip. Even though I had prepared for the worst, my lips curled as the bitter fluid washed over my tongue. It was horrible. I couldn't believe people drank it.

Deepak started talking about his new job. He had just moved to a computer training firm from a company that made consumer electronics. He said his salary had increased by Rs. 8000. I began to feel impatient for the day when I would earn my own living. I never wanted to look at the cost of a plate of *rajma* and be affected by it. It was petty to have to think about money, and the only way to avoid it was to have a lot. Arni said she had quit her job when they married because Deepak made enough for both of them. I couldn't understand how a modern girl who wore tight jeans simply sat at home and lived off her husband. No wonder she had to put up with Deepak touching India everywhere. I decided I did not respect her.

I looked at the beer in my glass and took a large gulp. Then I immediately had a spoonful of *dal* to change the taste in my mouth. Then I had another large gulp of beer.

"So, are you drunk yet?" Deepak asked.

"Of course not," I said. The words slid sluggishly from my tongue.

"Don't give her a hard time. You know you had your first drink at her age," India said.

"And were you were responsible for it, Aunty?" Arni asked, looking at India.

"Of course she was. Corrupter of youth," Deepak said. I remembered how I had arrived at Sheela's house in my red shirt and assaulted her. I was a corrupter of youth, too, I thought, smiling to myself.

Dinner was over before I knew it. When the waiter brought the bill, India waved Deepak aside and put some money in the folder. I felt as if I were seeing the table from a considerable distance. Deepak and Arni seemed to have shrunk a tiny bit. Everything was very pleasant. I smiled. My lover is settling the bill, I thought to myself. I couldn't remember why I had felt anxious about that. Or about anything else.

Deepak drove us back. My mind drifted. Photons jumped from one state to another, and the words "quantum mechanics" undulated like a flag between the photons. Large wads of cash floated around along with a whimsical cat that played dead or alive. I knew I wasn't drunk because I remembered everything I had said at the table. When we got back to the cottage I tripped on the way to the door but quickly regained my balance. After we had seen Arni and Deepak off and gone back to our room, India said, "Maybe I should not have let you drink, though you did handle it rather well."

It was so damn patronizing of her to tell me she shouldn't have "let me" drink. As if she were my supervisor. I brushed my teeth with a great deal of irritation. After finishing up I went straight to bed and lay down without waiting for her. She joined me after a few minutes.

"What are you thinking about?" she asked as she pulled the covers over herself.

"How quantum physics applies to life," I said curtly.

"Tell me about it."

"Wave, particle, wave, particle. One falls in and out of love as if one is jumping over a skipping rope," I said.

"Are you in or out at the moment?" India asked.

I thought her question was very clever. I was out when I had started talking about it. But talking to her about love made me love her.

She slid closer to me.

"One can never know one's position with any certainty," I said.

Her coming closer had made me very hot.

"What do you want right now? Or don't you know that with any certainty?" she asked.

"I want to collapse my wave function into you," I said.

In immediate response, India moved closer, the pores of her skin filling the field of my vision. Her murmurs of pleasure when I pulled at her hair and the heat of her body close to mine saturated my sense organs, as the big world of the Sivalik Himalayas around Kasauli tunneled into a world of minutiae. That was my last thought before I was swallowed into the dark hole that is the playing field of love, where two becomes one.

Our life in Kasauli felt as if it had a rhythm. Though we had been there just over twenty-four hours, we had our bed teas and took a walk the next day as if we had been residents of Kasauli forever. I didn't feel like a tourist at all. I had expected the act of going away to a hill station to be an adventure. I was surprised by the sense of leisure and relaxation that pervaded instead.

India had invited Deepak and Arni over to our cottage for dinner. I did not feel paranoid about Deepak as I had the previous day. Kasauli had filled me with peace.

Deepak greeted me by saying, "Aunty was telling us about the boy in your school who got the juniors to plant the bomb." He was sitting by himself on a chair. India and Arni were on the large couch. I sat down beside him on another chair.

"Yes, I persuaded the princi not to give him a yellow card, saying I would get Chakra Dev to apologize. But I called him and it didn't work," I said.

"What will you do now?" Arni asked.

"It doesn't look like you have much choice in the matter," Deepak said, looking at me.

"I could try calling and speaking to his father," I said.

Deepak frowned. "He won't like that. It's insulting for a young man to have his father involved."

"Firstly, he's left me with no choice. Secondly, it'll be worse for Chakra Dev if he is suspended," I said.

"You're right. I had some problems in school with a friend who got into bad company. I eventually talked to his parents about it," Deepak said.

"What happened after that?" I asked.

"Rahul stopped talking to me. And then a year ago he called me and actually thanked me. He said that if his parents hadn't interfered he really would have ruined himself. He was a smack addict. He had even started stealing from home."

"I think Chakra Dev's rowdy exterior hides something else. Something hidden even to himself," I said.

"You could be right. After all, even the best people have a dark side. Why not the reverse?" Deepak said.

"I think you're taking on more responsibility than you should," India said.

"Aunty, you said she's the Head Prefect. If she doesn't take responsibility, who will?" Arni asked.

"If you've already made up your mind, then you should find his weak point, strike him when it's exposed," Deepak said.

"He's totally insensitive. He has the hide of an elephant," I said.

Deepak chuckled. "Why is it that rogues like him get all the sympathy? Girls are willing to put themselves through so much trouble for *goondas*."

India patted my hand as she got up and walked over to the stereo system. She popped a tape in and said, "Let's have some fun."

Then she turned her head a little and asked Deepak, "Do you have the stuff?"

From his jacket pocket he fished out a small parcel made of newspaper. He unrolled it and laid it on the coffee table. There was green stuff and some rolls of paper. I had a sinking feeling in my stomach. India knelt down by the table and rolled some of the green stuff into the paper. Runa Laila was singing "Dum Maro Dum" in her sultry, immoral voice. I was panic-stricken. Deepak knelt beside India and made a roll as well. He lit it and passed it to Arni, who took a puff.

"Will Anamika have one?" Deepak asked India.

"Ask her," India said to him.

"No! Really, Aunty, that's too much," Arni said in a high voice.

"Why not?" Deepak asked Arni, and added, "We were just talking this morning about how grown-up Anamika is. This is just weed."

"It's really up to her," India said, shrugging her shoulders.

"Smoking a joint with friends in Kasauli. Ah! This is life," India said, taking a long puff and exhaling. Smoke rose from her head as she threw her neck back. Despite all my negative feelings, this image of India was entirely beautiful. I knew I would never forget it.

Deepak had rolled another one by now and offered it to me. A part of me said that if I loved India I'd puff what she was puffing, eat what she was eating, and sleep when she slept. A small, reasonable voice in my head told me I was insane. I closed my eyes and imagined my mother talking to me. I felt as if I were being tested. The love of my parents, my education, every moral lesson I had learned was being challenged. I had lost the previous night when I had had the beer with them.

"No, thanks. I'll pass," I said to Deepak politely.

"Hey, it's cool. Have one, there's no problem. She was just being a prude," Deepak said to me, pointing to Arni.

"I don't feel like it," I said. My mouth dried up a little. I was afraid he might insist.

"Let her be," India said, getting up. She turned up the music a little. Deepak got up as well. They both started dancing. I felt embarrassed for India. Was she losing control of her senses? She held Deepak's hand in her own. With her free hand she smoked her joint. After a few minutes she let go of his hand, looked at me, and said, "Come dance with me."

Deepak had a beatific look on his face. Even Arni seemed a lot more mellow than usual.

"No, thanks," I said.

She swayed her hips and walked to where I was sitting. It seemed vulgar. I tried to think I was a real stud, and she was my courtesan. I was Humbert Humbert, and she was my Lolita. I remembered the way Sheela had danced. India's movements were like the slow-moving Ganges, a Ganges overflowing with thick cream. Sheela's had been lighter, like a milk shake.

She grabbed my hand and pulled me up. Arni and Deepak would see my rigid movements and laugh at me. But making a fuss was going to call even more attention to myself. So I pretended I was at ease. I swayed my hips and pursed my lips.

The servant interrupted us and said he'd made a batch of *rotis*. We went to the rectangular table and served ourselves. The discussion tapered a little. All three of them were beaming, their minds elsewhere. When the servant moved around, refilling our glasses, I felt as if he were my connection to civilization. India seemed very happy, but I couldn't relate to her. All emotions seemed illusory. Maybe the times I had felt in love with her it was a trick. Maybe Sheela had felt no connection to me when I had tried seducing her.

"Balbir was cool," Deepak said. India nodded.

A few seconds later Arni said, "I like Pranav."

I wondered for a moment if Chakra Dev would be as peaceful as they were if he were smoking with them. In class he always had a combative energy, but I had no doubt he would succumb to the influence of the joint.

Light *ghazals* played in the background. "I'm tired. I'm going to sleep," I said.

"Night, kiddo. Come back if you can't fall asleep," Deepak said.

India sent me a flying kiss. I couldn't manage even a smile back. I waved weakly and left. I threw myself on the bed and thought about my parents. I wanted to go back to Delhi; I couldn't love India anymore. I knew with absolute certainty only about my mother. My sense of being attached to her was not an illusion. With anyone else in the world there was no such guarantee. I wished I could remember the day I was born, the day the umbilical cord still connected me to her. Swimming in a vast amniotic sea, I knew I would never feel alone or on the outside. One could not be more inside.

There were rustling sounds in the living room.

"Can I take you home now, my angel," I heard Deepak say.

"You can take me anywhere. I'm yours forever," Arni said.

"For . . . e . . . ver," Deepak sang out after her.

I looked at the small table clock in the dim light and noticed it was around one. I didn't let on that I was awake when India closed the front door behind them and came back to our room. As she brushed her teeth in the bathroom I bitterly thought that no one was mine, not even tonight, leave alone forever.

At the crack of dawn I got out of bed and picked up *Lolita*. I sat in the big chair on the veranda. My mind got entirely absorbed in a drive across the United States with a dirty old man who understood me. A man I understood equally well. We were both made of the same element in the periodic table, a licentious element. I forgot all about India for a while, and in forgetting I found respite from my small emotions, my petty biology.

When the servant opened the gate by the garden, I waved to him and asked him to get me some *chai* and toast. Along with my breakfast tray, he brought me an English newspaper.

"Since the big *Memsahib* is sleeping, I thought you might want more to read," he said to me in Hindi, laying it down on my lap. He had not talked to me directly since we'd arrived.

I looked idly at the crossword for a while. There was a half-page ad titled "Just Say No," sponsored by the antidrug committee. There were tiny photographs of teens all over it. They needed to aim their ads at the likes of India and Deepak, not at kids.

I thought of Sheela. I knew she would never take drugs. I desperately wanted to be with her, to tell her how much I appreciated her purity. My heart felt heavy that Sheela would never forgive me for the way I had behaved, but I had to try. I tiptoed into the bedroom and got myself a ballpoint pen and notepad.

I stared at the ruled pages of the notepad, trying to decide what to write. Forgive me, I am sorry, I beseech you, Let me atone—all sounded common. I thought of re-creating every moment of that fateful afternoon so that she could see it from my point of view. But then she would think I was not sorry at all or that I was shirking responsibility.

I glanced at several square photographs from an advertisement in the color section of the paper. A girl from Central India glowed from the page, reminding me of Rani. An elephant in lush green grass made me want to walk barefoot. A stone temple on a beach stirred an immense longing for India's past, her kings, queens, and golden epochs. In bold text at the bottom was written "India, my India." It effused all the warmth and allure one associated with India. I felt it with every fiber of my being.

I sank back into my chair and rested my head in my hands. The notepad that said "Dear Sheela" was staring at me. My throat felt tight, as if a nut had lodged itself in my esophagus. I wished it would melt away. I couldn't bear the pressure and needed to write something, anything, to let it out. In the end I wrote to Sheela about Kasauli, about India and my mother. I didn't distinguish clearly between India, my motherland, and India, my lover. I could not distinguish between my motherland and my mother. I talked about making love to the country and achieving a mystical communion with the land, its riverbeds and plateaus.

I looked at the Department of Tourism ad again. It elicited everything I had ever learned about India in history class. The mother goddess figure of the ancient Harappan civilization, the conquest of India by the Moghuls, the mutiny of 1857, the massacre General Dyer committed at Jallianwallah Bagh, and the Partition. She had been plundered and violated and had bled a thousand times, but her visage was still beautiful. Tears started welling up in my eyes.

I imagined India, the woman, as just as great a mystery as the land. When I finally signed the letter to Sheela after eight pages, I had not said anything about that afternoon or my own monstrosity. I had also glossed over India herself, the drugs she had taken at night.

I read my letter over and over, not wanting to part with it. I saw myself as I had never seen myself before—as a concrete, distinct person with a set of thoughts and feelings, all of which were contained in the sheets of paper in my hand. Sending this to Sheela meant sending myself to her. My soul was not an intangible entity that was reincarnating from one life to another. My soul was right there on paper in my own handwriting. My soul was this letter.

I held the letter, letting the whorls of my fingertips soak up the sensation of the paper.

"*Babyji*, would you like something more to eat?" the servant asked from across the garden.

"Do you have something for this?" I asked, showing him the folded letter.

"I'll check."

"Wait, do you also have better paper, as big as this but white?" I asked, deciding to transcribe the letter so that I would have a copy.

"Should be some at home. Let me look," he said.

In a few minutes he was back with foolscap paper and a large manila envelope. I settled down to rewrite the letter. I was careful not to make any changes, even when I was tempted to improve some of the sentences. It was important that Sheela get everything exactly as I had written it down.

Once I had completed the letter I became impatient to send it. I asked the servant where the post office was. I was sure that mail in the hills was slow, especially if one used a letterbox.

"*Babyji*, I can go and post it now," he offered.

"No, please just tell me where it is," I asked him, not wanting to let it out of my sight till the postal clerk had stamped it.

"I'll take you there if you want," he said.

I asked him to wait and went back to the bedroom to put on my shoes. There was no way to lock all the doors of the house without locking India in. I decided to leave the veranda door unlocked since Kasauli seemed safe enough.

The post office was up a steep hill. I had trouble keeping up with the servant. He held the envelope in his hand and eventually had to hold my hand to help me climb. If Rani had married a man like him instead of the drunkard, she would never have come to me.

When I returned home, India was still asleep. I resumed reading my book. I was into the last ten pages when I sensed movement in the bedroom.

"Where are you?" India asked in the slow syllables of someone waking up.

"Here," I called from the veranda.

"Come to me," she said.

"I'm reading," I said. She should have said "please," I thought, feeling irritated.

"You won't come here because you are reading?" she said incredulously.

I didn't respond. After a few seconds she whined, "You don't love me anymore."

Her statement rang chillingly true. How was it possible that I could have loved her completely and then just stopped? Did it mean I'd never loved her? Maybe I'd made a mistake from the beginning. It was more comforting to think I was wrong about it from the start than to think that my heart could have felt one thing with total surety and then the opposite with just as much surety.

"What's with you this morning?" she asked from the room when I hadn't responded.

A switch in me flicked again. I got up from the large chair, dropping *Lolita*, and went inside. In the time it took me to walk the five steps from the veranda to the bedroom, I knew I needed to love her. It was just too insane and dangerous to think of love as something that could vaporize so quickly. I sat on the bed beside her and said, as much to myself as to her, "Of course I love you, that's absurd."

After a few minutes of silence, which I was afraid to interrupt for fear of saying something offensive, I said, "I want to call my mother." I felt a desperate need for some sort of reassurance.

"I was going to suggest that you do. You haven't called her since we got here. She's probably worried," India replied.

"What will we do today?" I asked. I hoped the day would be filled with Kasauli. I needed physical activity and the outside world to stop me from feeling sorry for myself.

"I'm calling Deepak so we can go for a drive," she said.

I nodded and strode up to the phone in the living room to call my mother.

"Oh! Anamika, how are you? I am missing you so much," she said.

"I'm missing you. I'm missing you very much," I said. I couldn't suppress a sob.

"What's the matter? Are you all right? Is Tripta fine?" she asked.

"I'm fine. Talking to you just made me a little emotional," I said, sobbing a little more.

"Oh! My child, come back soon then," she said.

"Yes, we'll probably leave tomorrow," I said, gaining control of the rasps of emotion running through me. My face and eyes were wet when I hung up.

India had put on her nightie and come into the living room. She had heard me on the phone and came close to hug me. I recoiled from her before I had time to realize what I was doing. I had acted as if she were some sort of untouchable.

"You're acting weird today. If you want to end it just say so," she said grimly. She looked hurt.

"I can't believe you do drugs," I said accusingly.

"We just did weed," she said.

"Drugs make you lose control of yourself and ruin you."

"I see no harm in taking a puff once in a blue moon. It puts me in a good mood," she said.

"It's a false sense of happiness. It's not real," I argued.

"There are chemical reactions associated with most natural moods. Drugs just vary the chemical balance in the body to alter your mood," she said.

"I don't think every experience can be reduced to chemicals," I said.

"When I started breast-feeding my son it used to arouse me. Then I read that oxytocin is released in the body when one is lactating, and that it's perfectly normal to feel that way," India said.

Was she that pathological? Attributing anger or happiness to chemicals was one thing, but a mother-child relationship was sacred. Did India feel everything only because a few ounces of liquid were squirting in some part of her body?

"It makes me sad that you have such a mechanical view of life," I said.

"Not mechanical, chemical. There is a difference. Why do you think we are attracted to each other anyway? It's chemistry," she said.

I shrugged and went to the bathroom with my towel. After I got ready I waited on the veranda and looked indifferently at the landscape that had filled me with such delight earlier. Had some strange morning chemicals made me appreciate its beauty? I was sad that everything had changed. India's degree in chemistry, which had made her seem so modern and sexy earlier, was now causing all these problems. The world lacked luster as a large laboratory.

Deepak and Arni arrived in a supercheerful mood. The servant had packed us a big basket with fruits, sandwiches, and water. The drive in the hills was soothing. There was no traffic on the road. The beauty of the hills and the hum of Deepak's car lulled me into another world.

"What do we live for?" I asked no one in particular when we were on our way.

"A good beer. Some R & R at the end of the day," Deepak quipped.

"What's R & R?" I asked.

"Rest and Relaxation," Arni said.

"In other words, sex," Deepak said.

"You mean drugs," I said.

"No, I mean sex," Deepak said emphatically.

"You mean sex with Arni," India said, suddenly laughing.

Arni blushed.

"I'm not allowed anything else," Deepak said good-humoredly.

"You were allowed enough in your past. All that travel— Brazil, Argentina, Norway, Italy. Should I start counting," Arni said.

I knew the capitals of these countries. When Arni mentioned them I could imagine their rough locations on the globe, their major relief features, and the bodies of water near them. But I had never imagined their women. If Rani, Sheela, and India differed so much, I could not even imagine what people on other continents were like. I felt in sudden awe of Deepak.

We stopped at a pleasant spot to eat. After we ate our sandwiches, Arni and India brought out a game of cards. Deepak announced he was going for a walk. I said I would go with him— it would be my opportunity to ask him questions about sex. I was most interested in knowing about French women. Were they all like Sartre's Lulu? Arni and India didn't even look up from their game of cards.

Deepak and I walked at the same pace, our right and left feet hitting the ground at the same time. It was like marching in the school Sports Day. I liked him more and more with each step we took.

"How many years have you worked?" I asked him.

"Just three."

"And before that?"

"I was in America studying."

"Did you like it?" I asked.

"It wasn't all easy. I had to wash dishes," he said.

"I thought people had dishwashers."

"I mean other people's dishes. I worked part-time for one year at a catering company. I didn't tell my parents about it," he said, looking at me.

"Are you a *brahmin*?" I asked.

"Yes. My family is very strictly vegetarian. We don't even eat garlic or onion. Touching anyone else's dirty plate is out of the question. I had to scrape meat off the dishes," he said.

I imagined a plateful of remnants, stinking of bones and meat. Other than occasionally washing the plates of immediate family members, I'd never touched dirty plates with my hands. My parents were extremely finicky about that sort of thing. If nonvegetarians invited us to their house for dinner, we were careful not to let the serving spoons for the meat touch the vegetarian dishes.

"How horrible! Didn't you suffer? And how come you drink?" I asked.

"Drinking is different. There are no dead animals involved. Watching my friends eat meat was never easy, but touching that stuff was awful . . ." he trailed off.

"I don't want to have to do that," I said.

"After you do something like that, you realize you can do anything to survive. There is no shame in any work that you do. Within three years of washing a plate I got a job, earning more than the seniormost person in the IAS," he said.

He was probably earning more than my father did. Still, the idea of having to clean meat-polluted dishes was very demeaning. Only cleaning the toilet was worse.

"How did you do so well?" I asked.

"As soon as I graduated from the one-year master's program in engineering, I joined a great MBA program, graduated, traveled for a few months, and found a job," he said.

"Why didn't you tell anyone about the catering job?" I asked.

"My parents wouldn't understand. They would feel really bad, as if I had been forced into doing something because of dire circumstances. You know how it is."

I nodded. "Did you have a steady girlfriend there?" I asked.

"Yes, she was from Poland. She had left when it was still an Eastern Bloc country. She took evening classes at a community college and got a degree. In the daytime she was a housekeeper."

"Is it different to sleep with a foreigner than with an Indian?" I asked.

"It was my first experience. I really loved her. She had a much harder life than I did. It made me realize that my life in India had been very sheltered."

"But was *it* different?" I was hesitant to use the word "sex."

"She was different. I think every person is different," Deepak said.

"Why didn't you marry her?"

"I wanted to come back to India. She wouldn't have fit in here. It wouldn't have worked."

"How many girls was Arni going to count in the car?"

He chuckled. "I wanted to live my life in real freedom for a while before marrying. I traveled," he said.

"Did you go to France?" I asked.

"No. I almost made it, but I met an Italian woman and decided to spend a few extra weeks in Florence."

We had sat down on a large rock and were staring at a radio tower on a hill in the distance. The breeze was cool even though the sun was shining.

"So do you think R & R is what really counts?"

"No. I was just kidding. One has to travel and see the world to decide what's important. In the end I decided that freedom is important, but it's not everything. I need India for my soul."

"I want to travel like you," I said. I needed India for my soul, too, I thought.

"You should. You're the perfect age. You would soak up new experiences like a sponge. Your world would just explode with choices. You have to do it," he said, grabbing my elbow. Then he reached into his back pocket and took out a business card. He handed it to me. It said "Managing Director."

"Call me anytime you want to talk," he said. I could tell he really meant it.

"Why did you do drugs last night?" I asked.

"Just to loosen up. I had a tough few weeks," he said, looking at me.

"Isn't it just an escape?"

"I guess I needed an escape. I don't do it often. I don't see the harm in escaping now and then. It makes life more liveable. Maybe you'll try it one day," he said.

"I'm never going to do drugs," I said.

"Anamika, the important thing is to make something of yourself. What you do on the side, whether it's sex or drugs or eating or training for the marathon, that's on the side, that's your business." He put his hand on my shoulder when he spoke.

"I really want to make something of myself," I said, turning to face him.

"Yes. You must establish yourself before you get married," he said.

I wanted to remind him that his wife had decided to just sit home and do nothing after marrying him. But I didn't want to be like Arni anyway. "Why did you marry Arni?" I asked.

"Traveling alone made me realize I had no single person to share all those experiences in my life with. I wanted someone who would be my partner in the real sense of that word."

"Do you share everything with Arni?" I asked.

"Almost everything. I will always be a separate person, but

marriage is about finding a common base, some place to call home. Some place to come back to when you are tired of fighting your battles out in the world," he said.

I thought of Rani when he spoke of home. I had left for this holiday with India without thinking much of Rani. I knew Rani would be there when I returned. I didn't need to work hard to keep her. I was exploiting her just like all the Madames X, Y, and Z exploited their servants.

When we returned, Arni and India had just ended their game of cards and were talking.

"I miss Jeet. He's with his father now, but as soon as we go back he will spend ten days with me. Ten uninterrupted days," India was saying.

"Oh, Aunty!" Arni said, reaching out for India's hand.

When India saw us approaching, she said, "Ah! They are back, let's go."

We gathered our basket and walked to Deepak's car. I took the key from his hand and opened the trunk so he could put the basket in. After he slammed it shut he put his hand on my head and said, "I like you." There was something paternal about the gesture. Adit and India, who were almost three times my age, were full of lust toward me, but this guy who was barely a man was not.

"Did the two of you have a nice walk?" India asked us in the car.

"Yes. I want to travel like Deepak," I said.

"Don't drive her away from us," India said to Deepak.

When we reached the compound, the servant opened the gate and ran to the car. He opened the trunk and took the picnic basket inside. India and I got out.

"Let's leave by noon tomorrow," India said to them.

"Bye, Aunty." Arni waved from her seat.

When we were back in the bedroom and had taken off our shoes to relax, I said, "I am sorry about this morning."

"You've forgiven me for having had a puff of weed?" she said somewhat sarcastically.

I didn't want to fight again. Speaking to Deepak had made me feel as though the world was very big. My trials and tribulations of the moment seemed petty. In fact I was sure that at the end of my life even my current love affairs would seem of little significance. A single shower of rain out of seventy seasons of monsoons. A moment. I was sure it would be years before I met anyone who would be my partner in the world.

"I think it's your business if you want to escape now and then, that's all," I said amiably.

"I think we should go up to the terrace after our showers and check out the view," she said.

India decided to shower first. By the time I was changed and ready, she had left the room. I walked up the stairwell and stood at the top of the landing. India had her back to me. Her face was lifted a little. She was smoking a cigarette and looking out at the hills. She had wrapped a thin men's *dhoti* around her waist and was wearing a flowing white *kurta*. Her hair was loosely coiled in a bun. I thought of paintings and great books as I watched her. I knew then that I would always be in her grip, because like my other India, the greater India, she had a hundred different moods. She could surprise me when I least expected it and be many things all at the same time. I could imagine famous classical musicians from the old days composing *ragas* for her and kings asking her to be their queen. Simply standing on the terrace, striking her pose, she could transform into the whole history of art and inspiration, a nation, a land.

"You didn't go outside, *Babyji?*" the servant asked as he climbed the stairs with tea.

I walked out of the shadowy landing area and went to India. She greeted me without turning.

"What were you looking at?" she asked.

"Your clothes are so white, they make your arms and face look darker," I said.

"Do you think fair is lovely, just like everyone else?" she asked.

"No. I think you are as beautiful as our country itself," I said.

We sat on the terrace looking at the sky. I thought of the conversation with Deepak. I wondered how he had successfully settled with Arni after having sampled women from so many parts of the world. Did Arni rank the highest? For me it was as important to settle with the best person as it was to make the best of myself.

"You are very quiet," India said.

Was I with India because she was the best person? I had had so many bad thoughts about her, but now I felt different. It made me feel as if I'd betrayed her. My love could not exist in the world of flaws, fleas, inebriation, plumbing problems, and endless brain chemicals gushing out like streams because one ate chocolate.

"Love can only exist in perfection, and perfection is impossible," I said.

"There you go again. You're so abstract. What does that mean?"

"Do you love me the same way and as much all the time?" I felt presumptuous saying she loved me, but I couldn't come up with a more delicate formulation.

"No. Sometimes you're distant, and I love you less. But I really do try to see you for who you are and accept you for yourself. I wouldn't want you to force on an act when you're with me." Her voice had become very calm. It almost seemed like she was listening to herself articulate her thoughts. I felt enraptured. I felt as if she had a secret wisdom that was eluding me. She felt like India, a mysterious country thousands of years old. Books could be written about her, but under all the written text and the coats of paint, deep inside her womb was something no one had yet grasped. This was why the Moghuls and the English, the Portuguese, the Dutch, the French, Coke and Pepsi, Star TV, everyone came, conquered, camped. It wasn't the spices or the Koh-i-Noor or the cheap labor alone but a tantalizing and unreachable quality that you could always glimpse but never grasp.

When she spoke about love, it didn't seem like treason. For

me, love had to be total or it could not be. The affliction of binary love—maybe Mrs. Pillai could posit a solution.

"And your love, does it change?" she asked.

"It's absolute," I said. It was true because when it was less than absolute it turned into vapor and ceased to exist altogether.

After we finished our tea we went downstairs and watched the news. Schools in Delhi were still closed. North India burnt like a large funeral pyre. The smell of kerosene and young upper caste flesh invaded villages where the reservation policy made no difference because there were no schools, no colleges, no drinking water. I wanted to make the same kind of heroic statement. I wanted to burn, too. I wanted to sacrifice myself for the right thing, for justice, for my pure *brahmin* genes, and for India. It almost didn't matter what the cause was. Giving one's blood, sacrificing one's life, was what was important. The holy country bathed in the blood of a hundred races. Her rich soil absorbing the sap of her children. Her hills, valleys, and rivulets like the breasts of a mother.

We ate a quick dinner and retired to the bedroom. After the servant had cleaned up and turned off all the lights, we heard him leave from the back entrance. The house was ours. The translucent whiteness of India's cotton clothing and the smell of sandalwood soap on her skin filled my senses. The *dhoti* unraveled quicker than a sari. It took me to the universe of sensations and spontaneous living, driving out my doubts, at least for the moment.

x x i

Birds of Paradise

As we returned from the hills, the industrial towns on the outskirts of Delhi seemed more decrepit than before. India's house was on the way to mine, so Deepak dropped her off first. When he pulled up to my gate I invited him and Arni in for *chai*. Arni said she was tired, but then my mother came out and insisted they come in for tea and some *halwa* Rani had made.

"Thank you for taking Anamika to Kasauli," she said formally.

"Aunty, it was such a pleasure to talk to her," Deepak said.

"Yes, Aunty. She's so mature," Arni said.

As they were finishing up their tea my father arrived home from the office. He shook hands warmly with Deepak. My mother got into a conversation with Arni about whether Arni should have children right away or wait. They spoke in hushed tones. Deepak and my father started discussing some bureaucrat they both knew. Deepak handed my father his business card, the one that said "Managing Director."

"*Babyji*, you look happy," Rani said once they had left and I was back in my room. I wasn't sure if I was happy because I was back or because I had gone away. The intimacy with India had made me feel older. The conversation with Deepak had given me a concrete idea of all the things I wanted for my future: Florence, Rio, and the pay of a senior bureaucrat when I was still in my twenties.

The drive back had left me exhausted. I fell asleep without eating. When I awoke the next morning it was late. My parents had already left for work. I spent the day organizing myself and getting back into the rhythm of work.

At dinner my mother told me that Vidur and Sheela had both called in my absence. I decided to return their calls the next day when my parents were at work so that I could speak to them freely.

"Rani knows the alphabet up to *Q* now," my mother said proudly.

"Will you show me later?" I asked Rani. She nodded.

My father, who had not commented on our teaching Rani before, looked at her directly and told her to keep it up. She smiled with her head turned down.

"I think I should call my mathematics teacher. She said she would give me free tuition," I said to my parents. After dinner I nervously dialed Mrs. Pillai's number.

"Ma'am, this is Anamika. I am calling about tuition," I said.

"Sure, child."

"When can we do it, ma'am?"

"No one has called me for tuition, so I can come to your house," she said.

"That would be great, ma'am."

"I can come at eleven thirty tomorrow." I thanked her and hung up.

It was the first time I had spoken to a teacher on the phone. I told my parents and Rani that my teacher would be coming over. Rani asked me if she should make lunch for us.

"Just make us tea. But after that I think it's better if we are alone. Otherwise she may find it hard to teach," I said.

"Yes, Rani, why don't you go after that to the electricity office to check on the bill?" my mother suggested. Rani ran all our errands for us. I knew that now even my father would never want her to leave because she had taken over all the time-consuming chores.

I lingered in the drawing room longer than usual, eager to spend time with my parents. It was hard to believe that I had been gone only a few days. I wanted to tell them about the drugs, but I restrained myself. I talked about Arni and Deepak and told them that Deepak had an MBA from America. My parents said they would definitely invite the young couple to dinner soon.

When I finally got to bed I was exhausted. As soon as Rani joined me we turned off the light and bolted the door. I lay in her arms. She felt familiar, like my house and my mother's embrace. I had thought that it would be strange to be with her after having spent several nights with India. Their bodies were different except for the deep arch of their lower backs. Rani had downy hair all over her body, including her legs and under her arms. India waxed. I slept with my back to Rani, her belly and breasts pouring over my spine. She encircled my chest with her arm and put her hand in mine. I was carried into a fitful sleep.

A cacophony of real and imagined lovers filled my head. They were screaming, shouting, accusing me of treachery and betrayal, infidelity and disloyalty. India and Sheela, Rani and Adit, Vidur, Chakra Dev, my mother, Mrs. Pillai, and Deepak all grievously claimed injury and showed me the damage I had done. Love in my dream was not a many-shaded thing but a single blinding light. Everyone bathed in it together, without distinctions, all balanced precariously on the edge of an abyss. The compartments in my brain were erased, compassion and maternal affection paraded naked with desire, lust conjoined with admiration.

I awoke several times during the night, choking to the point of suffocation. Each time I woke up and realized I was in my own bed with only Rani beside me, there was a moment of respite. When I fell asleep again I saw amputated limbs, hearts outside their bodies, thighs cut open like meat, knees swinging out of their sockets, and eyes, disembodied and bleeding eyes, watching me from everywhere.

Upon waking in the morning, I felt guilty when I looked at Rani. When my mother brought me tea I felt I had betrayed her. Remorse that real life had failed to induce was pouring down over me like a torrential monsoon rain carried by the southwest wind of my dreams. As I took my bath I cursed everyone for the roles they had played in my nightmare. Beauty had become permanently tarnished with bitterness, and it was my own night chemicals that had masterminded the deceit.

Normally I would have been excited about Mrs. Pillai seeing me in civvies and made an effort to dress, but I didn't care too much anymore, so I chose the striped red shirt in which I had committed my violence against Sheela. I combed my hair and wet it so that the side parting would stay. I found some Old Spice aftershave in my parents' bathroom and splashed it on my face like the wind surfer in the TV commercial did. I set out my books in the living room for my lesson.

Mrs. Pillai arrived in a pale pink *salwar kameez*, her *chunni* wrapped around her neck several times. She was holding her helmet in her hand when I opened the door for her. Her helmet was one of the newer ones, a sleek red design with a dark visor. I wanted to see her in it.

"Good morning, ma'am," I said, bowing a little.

I asked Rani to get her some *nimbu pani*. Rani had squeezed one hundred limes and made several bottles of sugar syrup a few weeks ago, so all she had to do was mix the lime juice and the syrup with a little bit of water. After serving us she left for the electricity office, and we settled down to study. I had never got a private lesson before from a teacher. We were able to move rapidly ahead, and if I wanted to know something more than what was in the course syllabus, it was possible for Mrs. Pillai to answer. In class, whenever anyone asked a question beyond the syllabus, the teachers would say there was too much material to cover for our board exams and not enough time to deviate.

The phone rang at some point. I got up and lifted the receiver.

"Anamika, I got your letter this morning," Sheela said. My breath caught on hearing Sheela's voice.

"Hello, are you there?" she asked.

"I am so sorry," I whispered.

"When can I see you?" she asked.

"In an hour," I said.

I wanted the lesson to end so that I could bike to Sheela's house. I hadn't thought she would ever forgive me. When I had written the letter in Kasauli I had only hoped it would ease my conscience and allow me to sit in the same classroom with her again. But I had failed to address the matter of the episode between us. My honesty in the letter about my life had been a form of cowardice.

I returned to the table, aware that Mrs. Pillai had overheard the conversation and afraid she would guess everything from the tone of my voice.

"Child, you have turned scarlet," Mrs. Pillai said when I sat down.

I was embarrassed that something personal had come up in the short time Mrs. Pillai was with me. I stared furiously at the register and avoided direct eye contact with her. We returned to our chapter on differential calculus, but I found it hard to concentrate.

The phone rang again. This time it was Adit.

"Hi," he said.

"Hi," I answered tersely.

"When did you get back?" he said.

"A couple of days ago."

"Who did you go with?" he asked.

"India."

"The mysterious India again! Why didn't you call me earlier?" he demanded.

In the dream, Adit's role had been particularly gruesome. He had held up his castrated member to get Sheela's attention. Who did he think he was?

"My business," I said.

"Call me when you're in a better mood," he said and hung up.

"Lots of monosyllabic phone calls here," Mrs. Pillai said. Her voice had an edge to it. I was afraid she would never come back to teach me again. An hour was almost up. Mrs. Pillai picked up her purse to leave. I walked her out.

"Go in, child, it's hot," she said.

"I want to see you in your helmet," I said. I spoke in a tone that lacked all deference. I was in the doghouse with her anyway after the phone calls.

She laughed and said, "My kids say I look like an astronaut in it."

The last few words came out muffled because she put on the helmet as she spoke. Mrs. Pillai wrapped the *chunni* around her neck and moved the scooter from its stand. She kick-started it, but it failed to come to life. Through the delicate white straps of her sandals I could see her small feet tense up as she kicked the starter a second time. This time the engine roared. Mrs. Pillai got on the seat and waved as she zoomed off, the scooter kicking up dust behind it. I walked back to the house and slammed the door behind me. I gathered my books from the dining table and dumped them on my bed. I found the key to my bike and waited impatiently for Rani to return so that I could leave.

"But *Babyji*, it's too hot to cycle," she said when she got back.

"I have work," I said.

"Please ride in the shade or you'll get the *loo*," she said.

"You always worry too much about me," I said.

I rode to Sheela's house. It was so hot that my palms kept slipping off the handlebars. Sheela's servant opened the door and told me I could go up to her room, she was expecting me.

Sheela acted as though everything between us were normal. She kissed me on the cheek and hugged me. She asked about Kasauli and the colors of the sky I had described in my letter.

Sheela's servant had *nimbu pani* ready within minutes of my arrival. After he had left two glasses for us on the table, I wanted to shut the door and talk to her privately. But I was afraid she would take my shutting the door in the wrong way.

"Sheela, I need to talk to you," I said.

"Shh," she said, putting her finger to my lips. Then she whispered, "Let's just be quiet for a few minutes." She pulled me onto the bed. We stared at the ceiling and the pattern of light and dark cast by the metal grill on her windows. I became aware of soft music playing in the room. It was instrumental music, and I could not place it. We lay entirely still, our bodies close but not touching.

At first I found it hard to relax and just stare at the light pattern. But then I closed my eyes and drifted all the way to the moon. Mrs. Pillai was wearing her astronaut helmet and doing the moonwalk out of a Michael Jackson video. On the stark lunar landscape, Rani had found a corner arrangement of rocks where she was able to light a small fire and make *rotis* on the *chullah*. Sheela and I lay on our backs, staring at the blue green earth as it spun around the moon. We held hands and raised our arms up in the air. We found that they fell at a different speed than they would on earth. Sheela was very tickled by this. I explained how the gravitational force of the moon was different from that of the earth. India sat with her back to me, pretending not to listen to what I was saying to Sheela. She smoked a cigarette. The smoke rose high up and remained visible because there was very little atmosphere on the moon. I was sure that even people on earth could see the wisp of her cigarette. Every now and then she turned her head a little as she puffed and threw her head back as she exhaled. There were no men on the moon.

I felt movement and sudden moisture. It woke me up with a jerk. Sheela was staring at my face. There was drool on the pillow beside my head.

I slept with my mouth open, and my saliva flowed freely. I had to accept this about myself just the way a chemical like hydrogen sulfide, if it were a living thing, would have to accept that it stank. I remembered the letter I had written.

"What are you thinking?" Sheela asked.

"There is a notebook like this one," I said, picking up a copybook from her desk and flipping it open. The page had points on the properties of fold mountains from Mrs. Thaityallam's dictation. I pointed to the left side where Sheela had written "Fold Mountains" and said, "Anamika Sharma." Where she had written defining characteristics of the mountains, I pointed to the first point and said, "Sleeps with mouth open." Then to the second and said, "Dribbles." And then the third, "Rapes."

Sheela's forehead creased. She wiped the side of my mouth.

"Don't speak of yourself like that," she said. Then she got up from the bed and went to the door. She shut it and fastened the bolt on top. When she came back she sat by my head and pulled it onto her lap. I could see her nose and cheekbones, her long brown eyelashes, her palate when she opened her mouth to speak.

"I've reread your letter many times already. It's beautiful, Anamika," she said.

She stroked my forehead with her hand. I did not feel I was any younger than India or my mother or Rani. I closed my eyes so that I could listen to her with all my concentration and only the feeling of her hands on my forehead. They cooled my head and provided relief from the heat.

"You don't think I molested you that time?" I asked anxiously.

"I think I overreacted, Anamika. After you left I wished you had stayed longer. I wished we had continued," she said a little breathlessly. She seemed nervous.

"So you've forgiven me?" I asked.

"Yes. But we have to do it slowly," she said.

Her phone rang. I expected her to move away to get it, but she just let it ring.

"Aren't you going to answer?"

"No. It rings all the time. I've been getting blank calls."

"How often?"

"Sometimes twenty times a day, sometimes fifty," she said. I got up from her lap with a jerk.

"Do you think it's Chakra Dev?" I asked.

"Maybe. He called me once," she said, stroking my head as if she wanted me to stay calm.

"When?"

"The day you came over and we had the fight," she said. Did she really think of it as a fight?

"What did he say?"

"He wanted me to come to his house and meet his mother," she said.

"What?" I said, incredulous. Of all the things in the world I would have expected Chakra Dev to offer Sheela, an invitation to his house was not one of them.

"He said that his mother would like to meet me because he had told a lot about me."

"And what did you say?"

"Said I didn't believe him and he was a pig."

"And then?"

"He said I could talk to her myself and passed the phone to her."

"Did you talk to her?" I asked.

"I didn't have a choice."

"Well, what happened?" I asked impatiently.

"She said her son could be a real *badmash* sometimes but that he was good at heart. She said I should give him a chance."

"You mean she knew he liked you."

"She seemed simple and not very educated, actually. He had told her about me, and she had told him to be decent and invite me home instead of hassling me at school in the break."

"And then?"

"She told me not to turn him down since he had asked nicely," Sheela said.

"What a strategy! Did it work?"

"I told her I couldn't. I said my parents don't allow me to go to boys' houses."

"Otherwise you would have?" I asked, suspicious.

"No. You know I hate him. Though his mother wailed on about how falling for me had dampened his anger," she said.

"What is he angry about?"

"She said something about his father but I was trying to get off the phone."

So he was just like everyone else! He had a crush on Sheela. Hearing that Chakra Dev had a human side made me want to throw myself with him into a vat of the blackest material around, the ingredient that I had recently discovered constituted the dark side of the human soul—mine, his, India's, everyone's.

"Did Chakra Dev call you again after that?" I asked.

"No. But I started getting these crank calls," she said. Just then the phone rang. This time I lunged to pick it up.

"Hello," I said.

There was no sound from the other side. After a few "hellos" I put it down.

"What else happened while I was gone?" I asked, still digesting everything she had said.

"Vidur came over a few times."

"Does he know about Chakra Dev?" I asked.

"Yes, I told him. He said he was going to get some older boys he knew to beat him up."

"Did he?" I asked, a little alarmed.

"No. I told him that I wouldn't talk to him if he did."

"Does he like you?" I asked, knowing full well that he did.

"Only as a friend. He's my best friend," she said confidently. I felt strange. How could he be Sheela's best friend if he was mine?

"Did he say that to you?"

"No. He hasn't said anything. But I've told him he's my best friend. I can talk to him about anything. Even about you," she said.

"About me? What have you told him about me?" I asked.

"Not about that," she said, her eyes dropping to the floor.

"Then about what?"

"He knows I love you," she said.

"In what way?" I asked. She had not told me before that she loved me.

"Just that I am crazy about you and think the world of you," she said, looking shy.

"Why do you love me?" I asked. I couldn't help feeling Vidur deserved her no less than I did.

"Because you are good. Because you have always been good," she said.

"But I am not. What if you find out I am not?" I asked. I didn't want Sheela's love for me to turn weak and watery the way mine for India had.

"It's impossible," she said, bringing her face to mine and putting an end to our conversation.

On my bicycle ride back I thought about what she had told me about Chakra Dev. I considered calling his mother and telling her about the bomb. I also wondered about Vidur. It was strange to think he had been to her house and in her room. Where did they sit when he visited? I felt the need to know every detail about his visits, even if it was none of my business. I was glad for Rani and India, that they were not linked to my life at school.

Rani made me tea when I returned. As I sat sipping it I told her I had had nightmares about blood. I said that in my dream everyone I had loved had suffered, though it wasn't really true. They may have suffered, but it was really I who had suffered, and they had made me suffer by parading their innermost monsters to me. The dream had filled me with the foreboding that my own vivisection was imminent.

After tea I called India and told her about my nightmare.

"It sounds like something out of Hieronymous Bosch," she said.

"Who?"

"I'll show you next time. I have an art book you'll like."

Neither of us mentioned when the next time would be. We had only just returned, and I knew she wanted to spend time with Jeet. I also wanted time to think about the rise and fall of my feelings for her.

I called Adit and apologized for my abruptness on the phone earlier that day.

"How was Kasauli?" he asked.

"It was clean and pure."

"I went there for my honeymoon. Is it still a sleepy town, or is it overrun with tourists?"

"It's sleepy," I said. It was my heart that was overrun with tourists, I thought.

"Let me come and see you," he said.

"No. Rani's here," I said.

"Let's plan something together, all of us," he said.

"Who's all?"

"Vidur, Sheela, you, and me," he said.

"Have you met her?" I asked.

"I went to her house a few times to pick Vidur up. He's lost his head for her."

"What do you think of her?" I asked. I wanted Adit to be friends only with me.

"She's a sweet girl. Not the smartest, but cute. Bedable," he said, laughing.

"Hold your tongue," I said sharply.

"Where's your sense of humor?"

"Aren't you ashamed of thinking that about someone your son likes?" I asked.

"I'm joking. I can't joke with him about this, so I thought I'd joke with you," he said.

I didn't respond. The idea of Adit staring at Sheela's pouty pink lips or smelling her hair or touching her breasts made me want to heave. I couldn't stand the idea of anyone within two feet of Sheela's body.

"Don't speak to me about her like that again," I said.

"Why are you being so touchy?" he asked.

"I have to go, Adit," I said, hanging up.

Adit's words rankled me. I remained in a serious mood the rest of the evening. I thought about the dream from the night before.

I understood Chakra Dev and why he wanked seven times a day. Why he had set off the bomb in the watercooler, why I had withdrawn my bloodied finger from Sheela, feeling not horror but pride, why the Hindus and Muslims had killed with so much bloodthirst at Partition and left sacks of penises to be discovered: circumcised or not. The binary world with its simple classification system had so easily bisected every male genital into Hindu and Muslim. The world, into love and hate. India, into upper caste and lower.

In the world of zero and one, self-immolation was a simple act. Fire, a purifier. Violence, an unrefined response to the complex machinery inside the head that manufactured a thousand kinds of sordid poison—each corrupting and vilifying, dislocating, blaspheming, decapitating, and corroding the universe of feelings that arose in the human breast.

On the other hand, I had seen the range of my own desire, mutating from disgust to longing, love turning into viciousness, the warmth of Rani's skin kindling passion one night, vulnerability another, and ugliness, the third. I too wanted to embrace the simplicity of binaries, one large sun and another small, circling each other, smug in their combined sufficiency. A grand, utterly destructive gesture made more sense than repetitive small episodes of pain. I decided to call Chakra Dev.

I went through the papers on my desk till I found the cyclostyled sheet with the class phone numbers. I wanted to convince Chakra Dev to apologize before schools reopened. I thought I could approach him differently this time.

The phone rang a dozen times before a woman answered. I froze on the spot and replaced the handset. After a few seconds I dialed the number again. This time Chakra Dev answered.

"It's Anamika, the Head Prefect," I said.

"What do you want?" he said. He had not been expecting my call.

"Listen, I want to talk to you."

"Are you calling about the bomb again?"

"No," I said, deciding that he would just hang up on me if I said yes.

"Then?" he asked. I tried to think of what to say. There was no question of telling him what Sheela had told me about his dinner invitation, though I wished he knew that had he invited me, I would have accepted.

"I visited one of our classmates. Are you giving her blank calls?" I asked.

"It's none of your bloody business," he said.

"You shouldn't disturb other people," I said. My heart sank. It was the wrong thing to have said. He would think I was calling him to moralize.

"I decide what I should and shouldn't do," he barked.

"What have you decided you should do?" I asked, changing my strategy with him, my voice as soft as I could make it.

"Why? Will you help me do it?" he asked derisively.

"I'll try," I said, wondering if he would say something filthy about Sheela. How would I come up with a nonchalant reply?

"Get Sheela to talk to me," he said. He sighed, as if saying it had been too much of an effort. It seemed as if the thought of Sheela made him weak. It was time to strike, I thought to myself, remembering Deepak's advice from Kasauli.

"And what will I get in return?" I asked calmly.

"Huh! What do you want?" he asked, taken aback.

I knew I was supposed to ask him for an apology letter addressed to the principal, but what came out took me by surprise.

"A conversation with you," I blurted.

"Ha! Ha! You have a crush on me," he said, laughing. It was not a smart thing to lay oneself bare with a lout.

"I do not," I said sharply, mustering the full authority of my Head Prefectship.

"Then?" he said. He was still listening, open.

"I just want to improve you," I said, my strategy falling to pieces.

"Bitch," he said and hung up.

I sighed and went back to my room, Chakra Dev's parting words pumping in my blood. Despite the rejection I could not help thinking that somewhere deep down the bubblings of his soul were no different from mine.

As soon as I woke up the next morning I called Sheela and made plans to go to her house. Vidur had left another message for me the previous afternoon. I had no intention of talking to him as long as I could help it and left standing instructions with my mother and Rani to say I was not in or I was ill. They both asked me why, and I said we had had a fight. No one made further inquiries.

I did not discuss Chakra Dev or Vidur with Sheela. I knew

that I could only keep her by seeing her constantly and capturing as much of her imagination as I could, before Vidur or Chakra Dev or even Adit got to it. School remained closed the next week, and I saw her almost every day. We would lie down on her bed and stay like that for hours. Whenever she moved I would be intensely aware of the voluptuousness of her body and would wait patiently for her to make contact with me, the long, seemingly interminable wait heightening my senses. If she rubbed my forearm I would take it as a sign that I was allowed the same. I was careful not to go too far. Sometimes we would draw circles on each other's skin. If the phone rang she would ignore it, but hearing its sound tear through Sheela's room I would think of Chakra Dev, my heart and head both a little heavy at the thought that he was suffering. Sheela would pull the phone out from its socket, and I could not help but wonder if she had a soft corner for him as well. But I knew she would never admit it, even to herself.

"Will you be my mistress when we grow up?" I asked Sheela.

"Maybe," she replied. She had not taken me seriously.

"We'll have very little furniture and large windows," I said.

"I've always wanted thin red curtains," she said.

"Red, with a gold border. Like a sari," I said.

"We'll have *gadela*-type seating on the floor. We'll cover the living room mattresses with block-printed bedspreads and cushions with beads," she said dreamily.

I could visualize the room exactly, its panoply of riches. I wished we had it now.

"Our dining table will be quite low. And the chairs, too," I said.

"Can I have flowers?" she asked.

Roses were girlie. They didn't match what I had in mind for the interior of my house.

"You can have birds of paradise."

"I haven't seen them," she said. I had seen only a photograph in *Span* magazine.

"They are flat and orange with long green stalks. We'll have to import them," I said.

Money would be the key to my life with Sheela. If you had money you could be in control. Otherwise you'd have to compromise and do what everyone else was doing: conform.

After such conversations with her I would ride my bike home to spend a few hours reading before making a supplication of all my highest and lowest sentiments of the day at Rani's feet, mouth, belly, head, or ass depending on the sentiments, the day, the peace I had made or not made with my own self. For now she was my partner, the person with whom I let down my arms after battling with the world.

Hello, World!

One such night as I lay in bed, having made Rani the receptacle of all my passions and counterpassions, the phone pierced through the calm. It was late, past midnight. My first thought was of Chakra Dev. But as soon as I was fully awake I knew it had to be someone else; maybe India was finally missing me. I took the big risk of running out naked into the hallway, the bedsheet Rani and I used to cover ourselves wrapped around me.

"Listen, I need to talk to you," Vidur said. He sounded miserable.

"Talk," I said, awake and tense on hearing him.

"You've been avoiding me," he grumbled. I didn't respond.

"I need to meet you. Can I come tomorrow? My father will drop me. He's taking the morning off to see the dentist."

"Okay," I said, pushed to the corner and anxious to get back to my room before I was discovered.

When I was back in bed I said, "I can't sleep."

"Shhhhh," Rani whispered and pulled me close. She stroked my eyebrows till I drifted off.

The next morning the father and son showed up an hour after my parents had left for work. Rani came out to the living room.

"You're being a stranger," Adit said.

I kept quiet. Rani greeted Vidur and practically ignored Adit.

"It's unforgivable, you know. Ditching both your best friend and his old man," Adit said.

"I heard from someone that he has a new best friend," I said, laughing. I didn't want Adit to leave us. It was easier for me to be myself with him in the room.

"Have something to drink," I offered.

Rani went to the kitchen and came back with four *nimbu panis*. It was the first time she had brought a drink for herself without being asked. She sat herself down by my feet at the sofa, glaring at Adit.

"What have I done to you?" Adit asked in Hindi, looking at her.

Vidur's eyes bulged out in shock at his father's tone.

"Leave her alone," I said. I didn't care if Vidur was taken aback.

Rani maintained her silence and glared some more. Then she turned to Vidur and smiled. I laid my hand on her shoulder and let it stay there.

"The Mandal situation has calmed. I think you kids will soon have to go back to school," Adit said, finishing off his *nimbu pani*.

"I've forgotten what school is like," I said.

"You've forgotten me in my time of need," Vidur accused.

"I'll leave you two to talk," Adit said, getting up. I walked him to the door, but only after pressing my hand on Rani's shoulder to make it clear to her to stay put. I heard Rani start up a conversation with Vidur about having learned the alphabet. Her notebook was lying on the coffee table; she had picked it up to show him. Before leaving, Adit bent down and kissed me on the mouth without any warning.

After a few seconds I pulled myself away and whispered, "Leave." I lingered in the hallway after he had gone to wait for my heartbeat to slow down. Somehow the kiss had not come as a surprise. I had expected it since the day I had met Adit.

Back in the living room Rani and Vidur were laughing. When they saw me come in, Rani got up and said she would be on the veranda in the back washing clothes. As soon as she left Vidur got up from where he was sitting and chanted dramatically, "Sheela Sheela Sheela." With one hand he was pulling his thick hair. With the other he was nervously fiddling with the top button of his shirt. He paced like a maniac.

"So, you like her," I declared, getting ready for the discussion we could no longer put off.

"I've never loved anyone before," he said. I got angry. He was too immature to know love. He was naïve and inexperienced. He would have understood nothing about my dream.

"It's a crush," I said.

"I have had crushes before. She is different. This is different," he said, enunciating each word, almost shouting down the house. He'd never told me before that he had a crush on anyone.

"Please help me," he said, suddenly coming close to me and grabbing my hand between both of his.

"Help you?"

"Yes, only you can help me."

"How?"

"Tell her that I love her. Tell her that I am a good guy," he said avidly.

"Why don't you tell her?" I said.

"Every time I see her I try. I just can't do it."

I was quiet.

"So will you?" he asked.

"Shh!" I said to him, putting my finger on my lip. I couldn't think straight with his jumpy energy, his oscillating and noisy photons. I didn't know whether I should tell him about myself. Explaining why I wouldn't help would be difficult if I couldn't tell him the facts.

"So, are you going to help or what?" he asked again, irritated at my silence.

"Vidur," I said slowly.

"Yes?"

"Love is not that sort of thing. It happens between two people, and no power on earth can hinder or help it."

He shook his head violently. "I simply want you to act as a catalyst," he said.

"Only Hydrogen Sulfide can help you with catalysts," I said.

"Very funny," he said, sticking his tongue out at me.

His irritation helped me stay firm. "Vidur, it's complicated. My relationship with her is complicated. I can't act as a catalyst."

"Why is it complicated? She loves you, doesn't she? She told me she loves you."

"Precisely," I said.

"You don't think I'm good enough for her? Is that it?" he said, looking very upset.

"It's not that. Obviously it's not that. You're my best friend," I said.

"Then?"

"Well, if she fell for you because of me you wouldn't be able to stand it. You'd always wonder if she fell for you because of me or because of who you are." I was making things up. I didn't know if I really thought this way. I was just going to jump from one argument to another, simply countering his. That way I didn't have to think through a plan. I had always been good at arguing and could usually argue on any topic from both sides, irrespective of what I thought. The school counselor, Mrs. Shah, had given us all aptitude tests and told me that I should be a lawyer.

"I thought about that already. I won't wonder," he said.

Then his face took on an expression I had seen on Adit's face, an expression that spoke of elaborate explanations. He said, "You see, I don't think you can make something happen that isn't meant to happen. But your help could melt her inhibitions."

I was sure he had thought of that phrase "melt her inhibitions" many times before saying it to me. It distracted me; I saw Sheela's inhibitions melting away under my touch, the way Rani's had.

"Well, if it's meant to be it will be, even without my assistance," I said.

"I don't understand why you won't help me if you agree that we are best friends," he said.

"I can't, Vidur, it doesn't feel right. I'd feel I were manipulating her."

"It didn't even occur to me that you would say no, Anamika," Vidur said, shaking his head. He looked glum for a few seconds. He had sat back down, his crazy excited energy having discharged itself about the room. He idly picked up Rani's notebook and flipped through the pages.

"Okay, I have another idea," he said, brightening up.

"What?" I asked wearily. I felt exhausted by him.

"You can help me write a poem for her," he said.

"It's the same thing, Vidur."

"No, it isn't," he said, his face once again expressing an entire landscape of reasons. I sighed and sat back. This time I'd let him talk for as long as he wanted and only argue after he had finished.

"First of all, you'll just write it, you won't be speaking to her in person. Second, she'll never know you wrote it. Third, it would be my thoughts she would fall for because I would tell you what to write."

"You want to dictate a poem to me?"

"No, I want you to write it. The prime minister has speeches written for him. Come on, Anamika, you do that for everyone. You wrote that poem that I gave to my mother on Mother's Day. You don't have a problem with that. You even helped Ashima write that thing for that boy, and she's not even a good friend of yours. You know Sheela personally. It will be the best poem."

The boy, the boy Jay. I had fallen in love with him writing that poem. But it was different. I had willed myself into imagining him, young, strong, energetic, as Ashima had described him.

"Precisely because I know Sheela I can't write it," I said.

There was no way I was going to spend two days finding rhyming words in the dictionary only to have Vidur benefit from it. She really would fall for it, and I'd have to compete against my own poem. I could put up an honest fight against anyone else, but against myself I could only lose.

"You could try for my sake. That's all I'm asking," he said, begging me.

"I just know I can't do it."

Vidur picked up his *nimbu pani*. There was only a drop left in the glass. He tilted his head back at a hundred eighty degrees, waiting for the drop to trickle into his throat.

"I will write the poem," he said after he'd had the last drop.

"Good," I said. It was better to fight Vidur for first position than to fight myself.

"Do you have a piece of paper?"

"Now?"

"Yes, you can help me. I'll write it, and you'll just help me polish it," he said.

I was at a total loss. There was no excuse left. I resented Vidur for forcing me to do something I didn't want to do.

He flipped open Rani's notebook.

"Not that. I'll get you another," I said and went to my room. I wasn't going to help him. I could go the other way and make suggestions to ruin the poem, but then I would feel guilty. So I decided I would just nod and let it be exactly as he wrote it. He couldn't force me to suggest things. In my room I dawdled for an extra few minutes to put off facing him again.

When I returned to the living room, Vidur was pacing back and forth, looking distractedly at the cut-glass pieces in our cabinet. He grabbed the notebook from my hands and tore out two pages from the middle. I handed him a pen. He sat at my dining table with his head tilted to one side, supported by his hand. I couldn't think of what else to do, so I sat down next to him. He wrote something I couldn't see and scratched it out. He bit his lips. I wished he would get on with it. I wanted to see what he would write.

The phone rang and startled both of us.

As soon as I said "hello" Sheela asked, "Anamika, did you mean it about the birds of paradise?"

"Yes," I said. I had to be careful—I didn't want Vidur to know it was her.

"Can we meet? I can come over if it's difficult for you. *Bhaiyya* is going that side. He'll bring me," she said.

"Maybe," I said, not wanting to say too much.

"You don't want to see me?" she said.

"Of course I do," I said, alarmed.

"Then?"

"There's something else I have to do," I said.

"Are you seeing that India Aunty from your letter?" she asked. I couldn't tell if there was a sharpness in her voice, a hint of jealousy.

"No. Not at all," I said.

"Then?"

"Something else," I said.

"Why is it such a secret? Why won't you tell me?"

"My mother wanted me to take care of something," I said, relieved at having come up with a lie in the nick of time.

"When will you be free?" she asked.

"I'll call you," I said and hung up.

Rani had walked into the room on hearing the phone ring.

"Tell your *Babyji* to help me with Sheela," Vidur said to her in Hindi.

Rani looked at me questioningly, not sure whether she should make the request on Vidur's behalf. I could see she was happy that he had asked her.

"I am," I muttered to her and shrugged. I watched her as she left the room.

Vidur was gazing at the wall when I went back to the dining table. I peered at the paper. He had written, "You smell like a rose." I wanted to laugh. No one smelt like a rose. Not India, not Rani, not Sheela, not me, not my mother. Why couldn't he grow up?

"Do you think it's good?" he asked.

"You have to write the full thing," I said.

"I think we should just call Sheela," he said.

"What for?"

"Let's see if she's free. We can meet."

"I have to do some things. I can't meet her."

"Can I use your phone? She's not far from here. I can go meet her."

My heart sank. There was no way to refuse. And since I'd just turned her down she was sure to be free and say yes to him.

"Go ahead," I said, looking over at the phone and hoping that in the seconds it would take him to pick up the receiver the electricity generator in the DESU office would malfunction.

"Sheela, it's me, Vidur," he said. His eyes were animated, sparkling. He nervously tapped the phone table with his long fingers. I felt bad for him. For myself.

After a short silence from his side he nodded into the receiver and said, "I'll be there."

He replaced the handset and looked at me triumphantly.

"At least I can see her," he said enthusiastically, coming back to hug me.

I shrugged and moved away.

"I thought you were my friend," he said.

"I wanted her to be my mistress. I wanted a house with her," I blurted out.

"What do you mean?" he said, shaking his head. He sat down in front of the poem he had started.

"You know what I mean," I said.

"I thought you were a sweet girl," he said.

"I'm not sweet. In fact, I'm rather sour," I said, regaining my humor.

"I thought you were normal," he said.

"Fuck off with your normalcy," I said, getting irritated. He wasn't going to sit around in my house telling me I wasn't normal. No one was going to accuse me of being abnormal. Though abnormal I was, and not in the way he thought. I was abnormal because of that dream I had had and because Chakra Dev had successfully gotten under my skin. Vidur would have had a nervous breakdown if he had ever had a dream as abnormal as mine, and here I was going about my life, riding my bicycle, making love, eating, studying, and talking to my parents about politics as if I were normal.

"Okay, then I'll fuck off," he said, angrily marching toward the door. I followed close behind and heard it ring in my ears as he slammed it shut in my face. I went back to the drawing room and sat on the couch. I stared at the wall. A few minutes later Rani came in.

"Where did Vidur *baba* go?" she asked.

"I have to go somewhere," I said in response.

I walked out the front door, also slamming it shut. I walked in the middle of the street rather than in the shade, hoping that the burning sun would cause a fatality to end the corrosion of my insides. But no such thing happened. I found myself at India's door, ringing her bell.

"Hello, World," Jeet said as he opened the door. I was suddenly worried that he was an idiot child with a vocabulary of just those two words and no memory for human faces.

"Is your mother home?"

"Whoosh," he said, as if taking flight. He spread out his arms and ran inside the house, leaving me at the door.

India came out wearing her sheer nightie. She obviously liked to work in her nightclothes. My mother would have disapproved. I had been taught from the time I could use the bathroom on my own to brush my teeth, shower, and change into day clothes before starting my day.

"What a surprise!" she said.

"You shouldn't have let him answer. He just let me in."

"But he knows you," she said.

"What did he tell you?"

"He said it was the *Bhaiyya* who was a *Didi*."

"Great!" I said sardonically.

"What's the matter?" she said.

"Hello, World! Hello, World!" Jeet said, jumping up and down.

"Darling, go to your room and play. I have to talk to Anamika," India said.

"Whoosh! Whoosh! Whoosh!" he said, taking flight once more.

She led me to her bedroom and closed the door behind us.

"I wasn't expecting to see you so soon, especially after we talked on the phone the other day," she said.

"Why do you say that? Because I didn't say I'd come by?"

"I thought you might need some time after the trip. We had some tough moments."

I wondered if this meant she didn't want me there. I couldn't blame her. I had acted difficult and moody. Moreover, her time with Jeet was precious.

"I'm sorry. I should have called before coming," I said.

"You look so bare, so open," she said, embracing me. I felt the tension that had been pulsing in my body dissipate. For a second I had a desire to unburden myself to her about Vidur, Sheela, Chakra Dev, Adit, and Rani, but as she pushed me down onto her bed and unbuttoned my shirt, it gave way to the desire to live.

Since the very first time I had fumbled around with India I had become much surer of myself. I wondered if India knew that I had not learned all my lessons at her feet. The nights with Rani had made the world of sex familiar. I understood the grammar of its pauses, its punctuations. I could claim its language of transgressions as my own. Intimacy felt like a flight into an extraordinary world, and that morning, with India, entirely unexpected and spontaneous, it felt like a blessed escape. I walked home an hour later with no greater clarity about my imperiled friendship but with a distance from it that only the act of love could have provided.

"Will you eat lunch, *Babyji*?" Rani asked when I returned home. I could sense she had been waiting for me, but she didn't ask where I had gone.

"Sure," I said.

She told me that Sheela had called, saying it was urgent.

I called Sheela back immediately.

"Anamika, can you come over please?" She sounded terrible.

"What's the matter? Are you okay?"

"I need to see you. I can come if you can't."

It was out of the question for Sheela and me to sit in my room tracing circles on our bodies with Rani waiting outside. I went to the kitchen and apologized to Rani, who was humming away as she peeled potatoes. I told her I couldn't eat lunch. She looked highly upset.

"Make them for dinner," I said, walking out of the house once again, banging the door shut and suffocating from her unspoken claim on me. I knew I was hurting her, but I was unable to help myself. Easing my own life was my sole concern.

I wondered if Vidur had told Sheela that he had called her from my house. I wondered what he'd said or done that had got her so upset. Sheela opened the door for me, her male servant nowhere to be seen.

"Vidur's gone mad. You shouldn't have told him."

"What?"

"That you want me for a mistress."

"Did he tell you he's in love with you?"

"Of course not."

"He didn't?"

"I mean, he isn't. Why would he?"

I told her about the poem and Vidur's visit.

"Is he crazy? He comes here, and I talk my head off about you, telling him I love you."

"The poor fellow doesn't manage to get a word in with you," I said.

"Rubbish."

"Ask his father. Even he knows," I said.

"Adit Uncle knows that Vidur likes me?" Sheela said, her eyes widening. For a second she looked like Rani.

"He's probably told his mother, too."

"These boys . . ." she trailed off.

"Which boys?"

"I mean, Chakra Dev and Vidur can tell their parents they like girls, and their parents even try to help them. We can't tell our parents anything," Sheela said.

"What do your parents do?" I asked. I had never met them.

"They run a business. My mother didn't work till three years ago, but then she joined my father's business."

"Are they busy people?"

"Yes. I see them only at dinner and on the weekends. I have so much more freedom than when my mother used to sit at home."

"What did you say to Vidur?" I asked, remembering that I myself, his best friend, had told him to F-off. I could still hear my own door slamming in my face when he left.

"I told him not to worry about you, that we're too young to know what we want when we grow up," Sheela said. I realized she really believed it.

"So you think our interest in being together is just juvenile?" I asked. I closed my eyes for a second and thought of the morning with India. If she could take me seriously, why couldn't Sheela?

"No, but we're young. We don't know what's written in our futures," she said, looking at the lines on her palm. I frowned in response.

"Your future," she said flirtatiously, touching the lines on my forehead.

"We write it ourselves," I said.

"He writes it," she said, pointing her finger up to the ceiling, to heaven.

"He definitely wrote this down," I said, pressing my finger to her lips, which yielded to take it in.

After a few seconds she pulled away and said, "I think Vidur likes you."

"What rubbish!"

"When he visits he says the things I want to say about you. It's like having a release. All the things that are pent up in me come out of his mouth."

"What do you talk about?"

"Your Adam's apple, your smile, how you look when you are thinking and speaking, how cute you look when you stand on-stage and tell the whole school to line up, Miss Head Prefect."

Vidur liking me was much more disturbing than him liking Sheela. I felt confused and derailed. I could see Vidur and me spinning in a vortex.

"I need to make a call," I said. My head was pounding.

"Go ahead," she said, leaning forward to kiss me before releasing me to the phone.

"Can you leave and go to your room? Shut the door," I said.

"Okay. Will you call him?" she asked, her face innocent, trusting, as if I were incapable of hurting her or doing anything she would disapprove of.

"No, someone else. A friend," I said.

I waited till I heard her footsteps reach the top of the stairs and then the click of her door. I called Adit in his office.

"He's nuts. Your son, my best friend, he's nutty," I said, feeling hysterical, forgetting that Adit had kissed me in the morning, that he too was now a node, a part of the asymmetric geometric figure that was no longer a love triangle but a pentagon.

"Calm down, calm down," he said.

"I am calm."

"First things first. When can I see you next?"

"Never. Why didn't you tell me about Vidur?"

"Tell you what?"

"That he likes me."

"Of course he likes you."

"Do you think he is in love with me?"

"He's in love with Sheela," Adit said.

"She says he's in love with me."

"He probably doesn't know himself," Adit said, laughing.

"How can you laugh?"

"What do you want me to do?" Adit asked.

"I don't know. Make him read *Lolita*, tell him the world is disturbing and that human beings are not pure. Slap him till he wakes up. Make him say 'Hello, World,'" I yelled.

"Hello, World?"

"I mean hello to the world," I said.

"Just let him be for a few days, he'll be fine," Adit said coolly.

"You're his father. Don't you care?" I asked.

Adit sighed. "Listen, I can't do a thing. At his age all I wanted was sex. Wherever I could get it and whenever, for whatever price. This boy is like his mother. Always the good thing, the right thing. Always heavy and serious."

"What am I going to do?" I asked.

"I'll have a talk with him. Can I see you again?"

"No, *Uncleji*. No. Don't you get it, Colonel? Don't you understand NO? I don't want a hexagon, a heptagon, an octagon, a nonagon. I've had it," I shouted, then tensed up. I was afraid Sheela would hear me and come running down.

"Ha! Ha!" Adit laughed, then hung up.

I went to Sheela's kitchen and poured myself some water from the fridge. I imagined the shapes I had mentioned and thought about studying them with a cool head. The sum of the angles of each and the properties that might be used to determine their unknown angles. I chuckled.

I heard Sheela gingerly open her door and come down the steps.

"Are you okay?"

"I'm fine," I said.

"I heard you shouting. I had to turn up the music because I know you didn't want me to hear what you were saying."

"Let's go up to your room, mistress," I said.

Chemistry Lesson

After I got home from Sheela's I took a close look at the structure of the benzene ring and confirmed my detestation of chemistry. I was imprisoned in my own ring. My fantastic journey into freedom had turned out to be a fantasy, my acts of free will serving only to bind me.

At dinner I despondently mulled over everything. If only there were a way to sweep my brain like Rani swept the house. A thorough disinfecting, a dry-cleaning. And then I would fold everything properly and keep it pristine. I managed to avoid a conversation with my parents over dinner, pretending to read my chemistry book. Without having to pretend, I looked perplexed.

The phone rang after we had finished eating. My parents had retired to their bedroom, and Rani was cleaning up. It was Vidur.

"I am sorry," he said.

"For what?"

"For calling you abnormal." I didn't believe him.

"Did your father talk to you?" I asked. As soon as I had asked the question I recognized my folly. Vidur had no idea I spoke to Adit as often as I did.

"He did. How did you know?" he asked.

"Just a guess," I said as nonchalantly as possible.

"Smart guess. He's my best friend," Vidur said, as if officially declaring that I was no longer his best friend.

"I don't have one. You're lucky," I said.

"Listen, I don't want to fight," he said.

"Then don't."

"Did you know Chakra Dev gives Sheela blank calls?" he asked, changing the topic.

"Yes. So what?"

"I think you should speak to the principal about him when school reopens," Vidur said.

"I called Chakra Dev again," I said. Despite everything that had happened, I still felt open with Vidur. It felt natural to tell him the truth.

"What did you say to him?" he asked.

"I asked him what he wanted, and he said he wanted to have a conversation with Sheela."

"He's such a bastard."

"What's wrong with him wanting to talk to her? I'm going to try to convince her to talk to him once. Maybe he will improve," I said.

"Are you crazy? He's such a *cheapad*."

"Listen, he's a human being like us. He has crushes, just like you and I do. And on the same person, if I might point out," I said, whispering into the phone.

"I can't believe you're so mean," Vidur accused.

"Mean? It's only fair he should have a chance."

"A chance! I can't believe my ears, Anamika. You wouldn't help me write a poem for Sheela, but you want her to talk to Chakra Dev?" I let him rant. It was best he let off some steam.

"Vidur, I think she could make him turn over a new leaf," I said evenly.

"Is this some political statement?"

"What does politics have to do with Sheela?"

"Is this your *brahmin* guilt, trying to be nice to a *yadav*?"

"You know it isn't. He's just disturbed. I feel bad for him," I said.

"I'm disturbed, too," Vidur grumbled.

"Not the same way."

"Well, you were a nice best friend to have. I'd have done any-thing for you. I can't believe you favor Chakra Dev over me," he said, disappointed.

"Vidur, please, it's not that," I said, sighing. I regretted having told him about it.

"I knew I shouldn't have listened to my father and called you. He just thinks you're the cat's whiskers. But I should have known how selfish you are," he said bitterly, then hung up.

I went back to my room and feigned sleep. After having left for Sheela's house without eating lunch, I had stayed out of Rani's way upon my return. When Rani came into my room she whispered "*Babyji*" a few times. She stood by the bed waiting for a reaction. There was none forthcoming. I wondered if she would still get into bed with me. She chose the floor.

I waited till I heard her snoring lightly. I waited some more. Then I did the unthinkable and went to India's, leaving Rani alone in my room for the first time since she'd moved in. The conversation with Vidur had wiped out the last of my self-reliance. I had failed Vidur as a friend, failed to put his interests over mine or even on par with mine. I could not bear the thought of my problems growing exponentially and then disin-tegrating into thousands of smaller problems, each resembling the bigger one, each without a solution. I needed the comfort of India's wisdom.

After a few rings India came to the door. She was wearing a thin nightie.

"It's you," she said.

"Can I come in? Can I spend the night?"

She stepped aside to let me in. I walked to her room and sat on her bed.

"Anamika, what will happen if your parents find out?" she said.

"Or the servant," I said grimly.

"You can't do this," she said.

"I don't have a choice. I need you."

The door to Jeet's bedroom was open. In the light filtering through his window I saw him asleep. Maybe after school re-opened the headmistress would admit him into my school.

"You didn't get enough of me today already?" she asked, coming closer to me.

"I need to talk. I really need to talk," I said, clutching my head.

"I'll listen all night," she said.

"I can't stop thinking about that dream," I said. I was afraid to tell her about everything that had happened. I didn't want her to get upset with me about Sheela.

"You think too much," she said massaging my temples. Usually I would have countered that there was no such thing as thinking too much, but I knew she was right. I could think and think forever; it didn't mean I was moving forward. I was like a benzene ring locked into myself. A big fucking circle, a *gulla*, a zero.

"Did something happen?" she asked.

I shook my head, not wanting to spill my guts out. If she got upset it would just add to my problems. Even though I had questioned her actions in Kasauli, looking back on it now I realized I had come to know her for who she really was. After the initial shock of seeing her smoke and drink, I preferred knowing that she had been open with me. I felt as if I could reveal myself to her in ways that I couldn't to Sheela or Rani or my mother.

"Let me show you the Bosch paintings I had mentioned," she said.

I sat still on her bed as she got up and left the room. Soon she was back carrying an enormous coffee-table book. She showed me one painting after another of men turned into pigs and tables, holes in their guts, naked figures running everywhere, some calm, some not so calm.

"That's definitely the stuff in Chakra Dev's head," I said.

"He may not be as interesting as you think," India replied.

"Well, it's definitely the stuff in my head. Dreaming it is bad enough. Put it away," I said, my nerves frayed.

"Is there anything I can do?" she asked.

"Maybe you can actually teach me some orgo."

"Let's go," she said, getting up and holding out her hand. "My books are in the living room."

She retrieved her books from the wooden cabinets at the bottom of her living-room display case. We sat at her table for the next few hours, her love of elements and compounds and hydrocarbon derivatives leading her into an impassioned rendition of organic chemistry that drew me in, freeing me from my concerns. Studies were a wonderful distraction.

At three in the morning India insisted we sleep. She said she had not stayed up so late since the day she signed her divorce papers. That day, to celebrate, she had danced and smoked with her friends all night.

I slept deeply, waking up only at six. As soon as I saw the clock my heart started racing. I jumped out of bed and scrambled to put on my clothes. I ran out of her house, buttoning the last buttons of my shirt as I went, my shoelaces still untied. I hoped against hope that my mother and Rani had overslept. I ran past the *jhuggi* to the back street. Usually the entire *jhuggi* would be asleep when I went back in the morning, but today one or two men were awake, doing their daily constitution. I remembered the day I had seen Rani take a pee in the same area. I ran fast and heard the men laugh from a distance.

I arrived at my back door, panting. The door was closed the way I had left it. When I pushed it I realized it was locked, like the other back doors. My heart, which was already beating fast from running, started to pound. My lungs hurt, but I was afraid of breathing too loudly. What was I going to do? Obviously my parents knew I was not home. I had to go in through the front door. If they had just found out, they were probably frantic, trying to call the police. If they had found out during the night they would be worried to death by now. I tried to think of an excuse. On the one hand I wanted to go in immediately and relieve them of their worries, but I was terribly afraid that I wouldn't hear the end of it from my father. I might be grounded and locked up.

I thought fast. It was best to tell them that I had been with India. It was the truth. Moreover, they had already let me spend nights alone with her in Kasauli. Apart from being angry that I went without telling them and left the door unlocked, they couldn't really say much else. But what if they called India and she denied it because she wasn't sure what to do? It would be asinine if my parents thought I was having an affair with some local Romeo in the colony and gave me a thrashing. It would be way too ironic to be caught the one time I had actually spent the night studying instead of fornicating. I ran back to India's house. There was a piercing pain in my lungs and stomach as I ran. Passing the *jhuggi* section, I noticed the men had done their morning jobs and were walking back toward the hutments. They gave me peculiar looks as they saw me pass again. I got scared and ran faster. At India's house I rang the doorbell repeatedly, impatiently.

"What's the matter?" she said, coming to the door after an interminably long time. Her flimsy white nightie came all the way down to her ankles. Is this the way she opened her door for the man who came to collect her garbage in the mornings?

"The door's locked, they found out," I huffed.

"Damn! I just knew it. Now what are we going to do?" she asked, standing in the doorway. I brushed her aside and walked in.

"Tell them the truth, what else?" I said, going to her living room.

"They'll put me in jail for taking advantage of a minor," she said.

"Hello, World! You were actually teaching me last night," I said.

"No one will believe it," she said.

"Look, the books are still here," I said, pointing to her table. And in her handwriting, an explanation of everything including the benzene ring.

"It's statutory rape," she muttered.

"Not last night," I said.

"But yesterday morning was. I grabbed you as soon as you got here."

"Shut up!"

"Oh, God, what have I done?" she exclaimed with total alarm. I hadn't seen her like this.

"For God's sake, calm down!" I shouted. She sat still.

"I'll tell them I came here because I couldn't fall asleep. I had spoken to you yesterday. You'd offered to help me with chemistry. You were going to work all night anyway since you had a deadline, and I decided I would study here. I left the back door unlocked—my fault. I was going to call them as soon as they woke up. Not to worry. But I got engrossed in studies," I panted.

She was silent for a second. I waited, hoping she would agree to my story.

"Fine, let's do it," she said.

"Do what?"

"Call your parents and tell them you are here. Ask your father to pick you up. He can't get too mad if I am right here. He can see the books and notes for himself," she said.

"Okay," I said, getting up and walking to her phone. My heart was beating so fast I thought it was going to explode. My stomach and all my muscles felt tight. My hands and legs were unsteady. I dialed my number, my fingers shaking.

"Hello," my father said, immediately answering the phone.

"Papa, it's me," I said, trying my best to sound normal.

"Where are you?" he said softly, his voice full of love, fear, thankfulness. I felt wretched. He had probably imagined the worst.

"Papa, I am sorry, I was going to call earlier. I came to Mrs. Adhikari's house to study chemistry. I know you must be worried. I am sorry," I said, imploring him, afraid he was going to roar over the phone.

"I'll come and get you," he said, his tone hard all of a sudden. He hung up.

"So?" India asked.

"I'm in for it," I said.

"I'm in love with a minor," she said, starting up again.

"For God's sake, don't have a fit of conscience now," I said.

Jeet had woken up. We heard him say, "Maaammma!"

"Oh! Just great," India said with a frown, walking to get him.

Who was I to tell her not to have a fit of conscience? My conscience was practically epileptic. I was frothing at the mouth about my feelings, my thoughts, and even my dreams.

She came back to the living room with Jeet in her arms. He was pouting.

"Your father will hate me. Your mother will never talk to me again," India groaned.

"Listen," I said, shaking her by the shoulder, "change from this nightie, that's the first thing. Second, they must think you're entirely in the clear. We'll say that I told you it was no big deal. We'll say I never told you about the back door being left open. Now go and change fast. And give him to me," I said, taking Jeet in my arms. I had no idea if he had understood what I had said.

India's phone rang. I wondered if I should answer it. It rang a second time. I picked it up. It was my mother. Jeet shouted, "Hello, World!" into my free ear when I answered.

"I am so glad you are okay. Rani woke me when she found you missing and the back door unlocked. I almost died. She's been hysterical for an hour," she said.

"I am sorry. I am sorry. I just couldn't sleep, and I thought Mrs. Adhikari could help me with chemistry," I said, careful not to call her Tripta.

"Papa is livid."

"I am sorry, Mom."

"Why couldn't you have woken us up and gone through the front door?"

"Mom, I didn't want to wake you. It was the middle of the night," I said.

"If Papa says anything, don't answer him back."

"I won't," I said, hanging up. I could tell that my mother had already forgiven me. But I'd have to find a way to placate my father. I might have to ride it out for weeks.

India had changed into a modest-looking, dull green *salwar kameez* just in time to answer the doorbell.

"*Namaste, Madameji,*" my father said. He was already in his formal office clothes, but I could tell he had not shaved. He looked grim.

"Please come in. Would you like some tea or coffee?" she asked.

"Nothing," my father said. They were both in the drawing room now. My father looked at me. I could tell he was angry, but he didn't disbelieve the story.

"No, you have to have something. It's the first time you have visited. Even Narayani has not been to my place," India said with much charm. My father was left with no choice.

Jeet ran to my father and held his hand. He said, "Hello, World! Uncle."

"Hello, *Beta,* what is your name?" my father asked, lifting him up on his lap.

"Jeet," he said, kissing my father on the cheek. Jeet hadn't been as friendly with me the first time we'd met.

"So, coffee or tea?" India asked.

"A cup of coffee in that case," my father said.

India smiled and left the room. I looked at my father and said, "I'm sorry, Papa. I didn't think straight."

"Despite all your brains you have no common sense," my father said.

"Common sense so uncommon," Jeet chanted. Did he know what he was saying?

"Where did you learn that?" my father asked, laughing. Jeet was now holding my father's hand in his and comparing the sizes of their palms.

I shook my head morosely. It could have been so much worse. I wasn't sure how my mother had softened him so much.

"What did you learn from *Madameji*?" my father asked me.

"Well, these books that Aunty used in her M.Sc. course are much better than what we have now. I am going to borrow them," I said. The "Aunty" felt like a big stony lie in my mouth. I picked up the notes India had written in her own hand the previous night and held them up.

India came back to the room with three cups of coffee and some cake rusk on a tray. She got Jeet his milk in a plastic cup. We sat and dipped our rusks in the coffee and ate them since the coffee was still too hot.

"So, Sharma *Sahib*, which ministry do you work for?"

"Water Works," my father replied.

"My former husband used to work for Natural Resources and Minerals in the gems section, but then a private company hired him," India said.

"This coffee is very good. It's not instant," my father said.

"I get it from the Madrasi store in the market. They grind it fresh."

"Thank you for helping Anamika with her chemistry. She said your books are better," my father said, pointing to the massive nine-inch-thick textbooks sitting on the table.

"No problem at all. She can come anytime," India said.

"Can I borrow those two books?" I asked her.

"Sure, keep them as long as you like," she said.

"We should go," my father said, looking at me and getting up. Jeet clung to him.

I got up and closed India's books. They must have weighed a few kilos each. I had to hold them close to my chest to manage the weight.

"*Madameji*, thank you for the coffee," my father said, freeing his hand from Jeet and folding his hands in *namaste* to India. Jeet grabbed my father's leg and embraced it.

India said *namaste* to my father and then called Jeet back to her.

"Papa, will you please carry one of these?" I asked, giving him one of the books.

As we walked back I almost swerved in the direction of the *jhuggi* shortcut but stopped myself in time. When we got back, Rani and my mother were both at the door.

"Mrs. Adhikari gave us some coffee," my father said, then added, "excellent coffee."

"She's nice, isn't she?" my mother said.

"Yes. Very nice."

Rani just stood there, her eyes bloodshot and her nose still runny.

"There was nothing to worry about. I was just studying," I said to her in Hindi, pointing to the large load in my father's arms and mine.

After my parents had left for work I spent some time teaching Rani words in English and telling her about vowels and consonants. On the surface our interaction was normal, but there was an undercurrent of distance. I had failed to apologize for the previous day when I had left abruptly for Sheela's and had provided no reassurance for having left her at night. I couldn't get myself to. A while later the phone rang. Rani went to get it.

She came back and told me it was the *Memsahib*. I wondered if she thought anything of the night I had spent at India's.

"I wanted to make sure you didn't have any problems after you left," she said.

"All is fine."

"I am thinking of having a party, a real *dawat*, a feast," she said.

"Who will you invite?"

"Everyone I know. You'll call all the people from your dream. You'll see everything will resolve itself. You'll figure out how you feel," she said breezily. It sounded like a test by fire.

I was silent.

"You don't think it's a good idea?" she asked.

"No, it's not that."

"Then?"

"Will you dance to 'Dum Maro Dum' and do drugs?" I asked. I felt uneasy asking, but better that than to expose my parents to the other side of Mrs. Tripta Adhikari. They would like her less if they knew her better. Considerably less.

"Do you think I'm dumb?"

"Maybe in your social circle everyone does this sort of thing," I retorted.

"Come on! Only in front of Deepak and you. I'd never roll joints in front of anyone else in Delhi. This place is so backward," she said bitterly. I suddenly felt very backward for not accepting her. She accepted me, after all, my wretched mood swings and my carnal imagination in the space between my temples that reduced all love, friendship, and filial affections to an orgy in the gutter.

"Okay, have a *dawat*," I said.

"I want it to be a true *dawat* with excessively rich food. I have a caterer whose family used to serve the Nawab of Hyderabad for generations. There will be *naan* stuffed with nuts. There will be ground cashew nuts and almonds and rich spices in everything," she said dreamily.

"Christopher Columbus embarked on a dangerous voyage just for our spices," I said. I imagined him disembarking on India's shores. Her shores. I wished he'd made it.

"Can you invite your parents? And please invite some of your friends! Anamika, I want to meet your friends, the people who are important in your life," she said.

"When will you have it?"

"Saturday night. I already told Deepak and Arni. They said they miss you," she said.

I called Adit at work right away to invite him, his wife, and Vidur of course. I thought Vidur might not accept if I called him directly.

"Have you relented about me?" Adit asked.

"No. But Vidur is still angry with me."

"Is that why you're calling?"

"India wanted me to invite you to a party on Saturday. Can you please convince Vidur?"

"Ah! India, the sexy woman I could have an affair with if you continue to refuse me."

"Exactly," I said. I couldn't take all his jokes too personally.

"Let me come and see you," he said.

"You can't. I'm in turmoil," I said.

"Turmoil makes for hot bedfellows," he joked.

"No! I got caught today," I said, getting exasperated.

"Did your parents see you with the servant?" he said lightly.

"No, it was India," I said, hanging up. I hadn't explicitly told him about India, but I was pretty sure he knew. He was sitting on top of so much information about me, he could land me in a lot of trouble.

I made a cup of tea for myself instead of asking Rani. I felt guilty about how I had been treating her. I sat with a large sheet of paper and decided to list my problems. In the past twenty-four hours I had lost a best friend and hurt Rani—indeed, I continued to hurt Rani. I had almost been caught by my parents, and I had discovered that Sheela thought of our activities as some kind of experiment. My school life, which earlier had no connection to my home life, was now deeply implicated in it. India's *dawat* could be a grand confrontation; once I got through it I wouldn't have to worry about all my lives colliding. On the other hand, things were definitely coming to a head. I wanted to escape before there was a giant explosion.

I drew a line down the middle of the sheet with a ruler. There was something to be said about Mrs. Thaityallam's method of comparing things point by point, pro for con. I wrote America in one column and Delhi in another. In the America column I wrote freedom, money, independence, no social control, and washing dirty plates and bathrooms. In the Delhi column I wrote being dependent on my parents, going to *sagais* and social receptions, worrying what people would think, and being at the mercy of a backward society and its judgments. I could imagine Mrs. Thaityallam looking at the columns and objecting, "But *Beta*, America is a country, and Delhi is just a city." If I left Delhi and went to Benares or Powaii or Kharagpur to study at IIT, I could join a hostel and have more freedom. But even there I would have to follow rules, and I would be subjected to the tyranny of a hostel warden.

These were the wrong reasons for leaving my country, but the promise of escaping was incredibly tempting. I thought about my future career choices in India—engineering and law—and wondered about the abundance of options in the West. I searched for Deepak's card and found it in my desk drawer. I called his office. I felt as if I might be disturbing him, but he reassured me.

"I have all the time in the world for you," he said warmly.

"I have to go to the U.S. as soon as possible," I said.

"Let's go to USEFI to get the forms you need."

"That would be great," I said.

"I have a slow day in the office today. I can take you," he offered.

I debated calling my mother and telling her. If she put her foot down, what would I do? I didn't want to risk it. I told Rani that Deepak was taking me for some important work and that I would be back soon.

"Did you marry Arni because she was the best person you ever met? Is she better than your Polish girlfriend?" I asked Deepak in the car. It had been playing on my mind since our discussion in Kasauli about marriage.

"The best person? Come on, Anamika, you know better. Life is not like school with its grades and rankings."

It was and it wasn't. What I had meant was that the best person would always do the best things. The best person would be like India without the drugs or Adit without his constant passes at me.

"Do you love her more than anyone else?" I asked.

"Love is just raw material. To create something from it is what marriage is about. Arni is committed to making our marriage work. Agatha and I loved each other in a different way. As soon as our careers or futures were at stake we chose ourselves

over the relationship. Our relationship didn't outlive its conven-
ience."

"Is Arni the one who makes all the sacrifices in your marriage?" I asked.

"Do I look like such a typical male chauvinist pig to you?"
Deepak asked, laughing.

"No, but she's the one who stopped working after marriage."

"When I came back to India I really wanted to get a job in
Bombay. But Arni wanted to stay in Delhi because her parents
are here, as are mine. I took another job, one I wanted less."

We had reached the USEFI building. Deepak craned his neck
to look for a parking spot.

"There, to the left," I said, pointing to a free space.

As Deepak steered his car to squeeze it in, I said, "I hate com-
promises."

"At your age you should. This is the time for you to do something for yourself. Once you've achieved your goals you'll want
other things. You'll want to live for other people. A family,
maybe."

At USEFI the guard directed us to the second floor. A large
number of people were sitting in the room, filling out forms. I
went to the receptionist, who told me I had to fill out a preliminary questionnaire. I sat down and started filling it out. Deepak
walked around, looking at books they had on a shelf. He seemed
happy to be there, nostalgic as he leafed through college literature. He chuckled every now and then.

The questionnaire was five pages long and asked for my contact information, my parents' income, my marks on the last
board exam, class rank, extracurricular activities, and when I
intended to take the SAT. In the section that asked about my
future study plans, I checked off physics. I asked Deepak where
I should study. One could check up to five states.

"California, for sure," he said. I checked it off.

"New York, Massachusetts, Illinois," he said. I checked them
all off. Then he stared at the others. I was sure they were all the

same. I pointed to Wyoming. He shook his head. Texas. He shook his head again. Florida. He frowned slightly, undecided.

"Why not? It's warm," he finally said.

I signed the form and handed it back to the receptionist. She looked at a big register in front of her and told me when the counselor had a free slot for an appointment.

"Take these bulletins and read them," she said, handing some booklets to me. When we walked out Deepak handed me some things he had picked up from another section. They were about individual colleges and were glossier than what the lady had given me.

On the drive back I worried because I'd written my phone number on the form. If the USEFI called me at home, my parents would find out I had gone there. I asked Deepak his opinion.

"Let me talk to your parents. Are they coming to Aunty's party on Saturday?"

"Yes, we'll be there. But I am not sure they will listen to you," I said.

"Don't worry. It's normal for parents to be anxious about their kids leaving home. On top of it you are rather young, and you are a girl. They will feel reassured talking to someone who has been through the experience."

When we got home I invited Deepak in and asked him to eat lunch with us. Rani busied herself with lunch, happy that we had an unexpected guest. She made hot *chapatis* for him and insisted he eat a couple of extra ones. After lunch I went to wash my hands. I returned to find them in the middle of a conversation.

"We were all so worried, we had no idea where she had gone," Rani was saying.

"Is she talking about this morning?" I asked casually.

"Yes. No wonder your parents are worried about letting you go. You just leave the house, door wide open," he said.

"Not wide open. Just unlocked," I said.

"And all that for chemistry," he said with a chuckle, pointing to India's books, which my father had placed on the coffee table.

"Chemistry makes the world go round, even in your R & R world," I said, unable to resist.

"That's a different kind of chemistry. You are so studious, I'd be lucky if I had a daughter like you," Deepak said.

"You don't know what you'd be in for," I said.

He rose to leave. He thanked Rani for lunch. She smiled at him. She didn't seem shy at all. She had emerged from her servant mode in a way I had never seen. I suddenly felt close to her again.

"Rani, I am sorry for the way I've behaved. I had to go away at night. My studies were driving me crazy," I said.

"You are free to go and come as you like, *Babyji*. I'll never stop you," she said.

"Please forgive me," I said, pulling her hand and taking her into my room. We lay on my bed and chatted.

"Deepak *Sahib* is different," she said.

"In what way?"

"I don't know. He treated me like you treat me. Not like a servant."

"He lived in America," I said.

"In Amreeka?" she asked.

"Yes. They don't have servants there," I said.

"They don't?"

"No. Everyone is equal. There is no caste, either. Of course some people are rich and others are poor, but that's everywhere," I said.

"He told me you wanted to go away. Do you want to go to Amreeka?" she asked.

"Yes."

"But why, *Babyji*? You are a *brahmin*. You have it good here. Why would you like to be less, an equal?"

"I want to be free. I don't want society telling me what to do all the time," I said.

We fell asleep. After I woke up I spent the rest of the day

cooped up in my bedroom, taking the few abbreviated sample
tests in the bulletin and reading every word in every brochure.
The nightmare that had nearly brought me to ruin faded away.
Large libraries with Doric columns and cornices inscribed with
names like Herodotus and Socrates, Plato, Homer, Emerson,
and Galileo beckoned me to sample their wares.

Back to School Special

The morning news said that schools were likely to open in the next day or two if there were no further incidents. I dreaded the idea of going back. I had always enjoyed school, but nonetheless in the mornings I would often have a lingering feeling that I had not done my homework, a foreboding that I was going to be caught and punished for an omission or transgression I could not recall. I felt it strongest on the first day of school after the summer holidays. But I also felt it on Mondays and after long weekends and holidays. It had started in kindergarten as the dread of leaving my mother. Over the years it had come to exist seemingly without context or reason.

Could one have other feelings like this? Vestigial feelings that once had a cause but lingered on long after the cause was gone, a love without a basis? My mind told me there was a reason for everything, just as India's mind told her that everything was chemically induced and Sheela's that fate conceived our futures. Every now and then an editorial in the newspaper argued that money or economics was the reason for everything. It all seemed equally absurd.

Often when I thought about abstract things I would feel invincible. It was a little like the Star Trek trailer that showed the world first only from as far as the moon but then from Pluto and eventually from another galaxy. I felt as if I were at a great distance from daily life but still able to see clearly, nothing blurring my vision, everything just small.

"Rani made *puris* for you today. Will you come to breakfast?" my mother asked.

"Yes," I said, getting up.

My father was already at the table eating his toast and marmalade.

"I don't want to go to school tomorrow," I whined.

"You've had a big break. You need to start focusing on the IIT exams," my father said.

"Deepak suggested I study in America. I was thinking of finding out more."

"It's very costly," my mother said.

"Mom, I can get a scholarship. If I get a scholarship, will you let me go?"

"Depends on Papa," she said.

"The IITs are as good as anything in the world," my father said.

"You can go abroad after graduation. You're too young to go now," my mother said.

"Mom, it'll be too late after college. I will already have chosen a specialization."

"On the contrary, it's better. You'll know exactly what you want to do," my father said.

If I stayed in India I'd have to make a decision within the next year and be bound by it for the rest of my life. I didn't know about law or engineering or architecture or economics, and if I made the wrong choice I would suffer it with no escape. It was precisely because I needed help in deciding that I needed to go now. But I knew neither of them would buy this. The only way to convince my parents was to say I wanted to do something for which the facilities of the West were very important, something like computer science. This was going to be difficult because in school I had already chosen biology over computer science or mechanical drawing.

"The future is in computer science. And because I didn't take it after tenth, the only way I can do it in college is by going abroad because they don't require you to have studied it before."

"We'll see," my father said, putting an end to the discussion.

During the day I went to Sheela's house. I invited her to India's party. Both of us were very calm and didn't speak about Vidur. The afternoon news confirmed that schools would start the next day. I came home and packed my schoolbag. I called Adit at his office and told him about my decision to go abroad.

"I miss you already," he said.

"I may not get in," I said anxiously.

"You will, relax," he said.

"Can you come to India's party? Did Vidur agree?"

"We'll come. I wouldn't miss an opportunity to meet her after all I've heard," he said.

"I invited Sheela, too."

"Your rape victim," he said. He had put two and two together. I was afraid he knew too much.

"My friend. Vidur's friend," I said.

"Can I meet you before that?"

"No."

"You should be kinder to this old man," he said.

At dinner I told my parents India had invited us to the party. They both seemed happy and said we would go. It occurred to me that if India and Adit and Deepak all talked about studying in America, it would help my case. I would ask them to talk about it. That way my parents would see that other people thought it was a good idea, too.

At school the next morning, when I stood onstage during assembly, everything seemed silly and like a game. The real thing was going abroad. I couldn't take my life seriously anymore. I was sure I would meet kindred souls in college, people who had read the books I had read. Not eager to break out of my pleasant and faraway mood, I decided to head back directly to my classroom after assembly instead of joining my class line. Only Chakra Dev was in the classroom when I got there. I felt electrocuted at the sight of him. Did he go through people's schoolbags when no one else was there?

I sat down and pulled out a textbook, ignoring him. I behaved as if we hadn't talked about his suspension. He got up from his seat and came over to me.

"You don't have a crush on me anymore, huh?" he said, gloating.

I shrugged.

"Anyway, I'm sorry for calling you a bitch that day. And for the bomb," he said. From the way his mouth turned up at the corner I could tell that he relished saying "bitch" again. I was sure he was imagining the firecracker sending my skirt up in flames. I felt my pulse rise. I had been insane to ask the princi to forgive him. I had to tell the princi I had failed to elicit an apology from him.

"Why do you study so much?" he asked, looking derisively at my book and coming closer to my desk.

I shrugged again.

"So, are you arranging Sheela for me?"

My body recoiled when he took her name.

"Does she like me?" he asked, moving even closer.

"Why should I tell you?" I said.

"Stop being such a bitch," he said, moving yet closer. I could feel his breath on my face. I wished I had not come back to class alone. Where was everyone?

"Move back," I demanded, not making direct eye contact. I felt he was going to hit me any second. He was too close for comfort.

"Mooov back, mooov back," he driveled, moving closer.

I moved a few inches back in my seat and stood up. He was towering over me. As quickly and with as much force as possible I slapped his face. As he reeled backward, I got out from Vidur's side of the desk and made my way to the door. I heard him laugh.

"Why are you running away?" he called after me.

I turned back to look at him.

"You can slap me again if you like," he said, his hand moving toward his zip.

I went to the watercooler to have a drink and calm down. I reentered the classroom only after other students had arrived. When I walked in I caught Sheela's eye. She smiled at me. Then

I took my seat next to Vidur, the air between us heavier than a Dostoevsky novel.

Just before Mrs. T. walked in I said to Vidur, "Listen, I have to talk to you urgently. Can we go out in the break together?" He agreed.

I had no idea what I was going to say to him, but I couldn't go on the way things had become. I would talk to the princi about Chakra Dev after school ended; my friendship with Vidur was much more important.

The rest of the morning was awful. Paranoid, I couldn't help turning to look behind me. Each time Chakra Dev looked at me as if we had a big secret. His left hand was lodged in his pocket. I remembered the way the *cheapad* on the bus had been stroking himself. Vidur didn't seem to notice. I considered telling him about the incident but decided against it. I didn't want him to think I was always turning to him in my hour of need but ditching him when he needed me. He already thought that.

After Mrs. T. we had two classes with Mrs. Pillai. She was wearing a pale yellow sari with small flowers embroidered on the border. I was transfixed by the glide of her neck and the movement of the hollow space at the center of her collarbone when she spoke. Every time she said "probability," it looked as if a river were cascading along the inner surface of her neck.

When the break bell rang I grabbed Sheela and led her out of class. We went and stood in the shade of a large *gulmohar* tree.

"Why are we here?" Sheela asked.

"We are waiting for Vidur. We need to talk," I said.

"About what?"

"You'll see," I said mysteriously, though I had no plan.

We saw Vidur walking toward us across the PT field. The bright sun made him squint.

"What do you want?" he asked.

"I have decided to go to America," I said to them both.

"You have?" Sheela said, surprised.

"Yes, I made an appointment with the USEFI counselor."

"Why are you telling us this?" Vidur asked.

"You're my friends," I said, looking from Vidur to Sheela.

Vidur picked at the bark, getting dirt under his fingernails. He looked morose.

"Listen, Vidur, I need to make peace with you," I said.

"Why, because you are going away?" he asked.

"No, because this is silly," I said, pointing to Sheela and myself.

"We're all friends, isn't that what matters?" Sheela asked him.

"Well, the two of you seem to be more than that," he said.

"Come on, Vidur. At our age nothing is serious. It's not like we're doing anything together," Sheela said. She smiled her charming smile and looked at him without blinking. I wondered if she really believed it. Strictly speaking it was almost true; what happened alone between Sheela and me was nothing compared to what I did with India and Rani. I was almost convinced myself.

"Is that true?" Vidur asked, looking at me for corroboration.

"She told you," I said.

There was an immediate change in Vidur. He stopped playing with the bark of the tree and placed his hand on his hip. He relaxed.

"You'll leave India?" he asked, changing the topic.

I thought of India the woman and not the country. I would have to leave her if I went away.

"It's just four years. I'll come back after I finish my studies."

"My cousin said that, and now he's working in New York."

I didn't want Vidur to compare me to his cousin. Did his cousin love India as much as I did? Was he trying to score one on me with Sheela?

"I think you should come with me to the USEFI and apply abroad," I said to neither of them in particular.

"I'm not leaving," Sheela said immediately.

"I'm joining the army. I'm never going to leave India, either," Vidur said. I didn't want him to think I was a traitor through and through, betraying both him and the country.

"All our great leaders studied abroad—Gandhiji, Nehru, Subhash Chandra Bose, Ambedkar. If they hadn't maybe we would never have had the freedom movement or won our independence from the British," I said.

"But we're already independent," Sheela said.

"India needs us," Vidur said. I imagined India, her sheet wrapped around her body, and me knocking on her door in the middle of the night, needing her just as much as she needed me.

"He's right," Sheela said. For a second it felt as if they were a couple, like Arni and Deepak. The bell rang, and we trudged across the field in the heat.

Compared to the fierce summer light outside, the school building was as dark as a dungeon inside. We stopped for a second to let our eyes adjust. As we neared the classroom, Vidur and I veered toward the watercooler. Sheela saw Ashima and walked in her direction.

"Why does everyone think the West is better?" Vidur asked me.

"It isn't that. We are just bound by so many constraints here. Even in our choice of subjects, each decision restricts us further rather than setting us free. It's like marriage."

"You think it's different anywhere else? At least this is our own country."

We had reached the watercooler, and I bent down to drink. Then I wiped my mouth with my handkerchief as I waited for Vidur to have his drink.

"Anyway, I think you should study abroad just so that you can see for yourself how it is better and how it is worse. So that you can improve India later, after you come back," I said.

"If you go you won't come back. You'll change," he said.

"We'll see."

We entered our classroom just in time to hear a high-pitched scream. It was Sheela. Vidur and I ran to her desk. Ashima and a couple of boys were standing around her desk. She had her hands up to her ears, blocking them, and her eyes were shut. She screamed again. I was about to pull her hands away to ask what was going on when Vidur nudged my elbow and pointed to her

desk. There was a translucent rubbery thing on it. Ashima had a
look of total disgust on her face. I thought it was a condom but I
couldn't be sure. I had never seen one. I raised my eyebrow in a
question mark.

"Condom," Vidur muttered under his breath. How did he
know?

Mr. Garg had walked into class. I noticed that Chakra Dev
was back at his desk. The image of his hand in his pocket flashed
to my mind.

"Sir," I called out to Mr. Garg. Sheela died with embarrassment.
He came up to us and looked at Sheela's desk. His face turned
red like a chili.

"Who did that? Which bastard did that?" he roared.

"Chakra Dev," I said calmly. I had no doubt he had done
something fishy in the boys' room during the break.

There was a collective gasp. All eyes turned to him.

He got up from his seat, his usual haughty self, and looked at
everyone, his shoulders defiantly square and his head held high.
Mr. Garg walked toward him. I walked with Mr. Garg.

"Did you do it?" Mr. Garg yelled, moving closer to him.

"No, she's lying," he said. So cool and calm, even I could have
been taken.

"Anamika is the Head Prefect, she doesn't lie," Mr. Garg
shouted.

I was near Chakra Dev now. I raised my hand and brought it
squarely against his face with all my might. Slapping him on his
left cheek and then, before he or Mr. Garg or anyone else could
recover, I gave him an equally vicious one on the right.

Mr. Garg stood rooted to the spot. Chakra Dev had brought
both his hands protectively to his cheeks but a little late. His
nostrils were flaring. He was seething.

With no warning Chakra Dev cut the air with his hands and
brought them down on my neck with a snarl. I saw his teeth and
felt the pressure of his thumb on my neck. Mr. Garg, who had
remained entirely petrified till now, flew into his face. Vidur

jumped over my chair and started tearing Chakra's hands away. There was a collective outtake of breath when Mr. Garg and Vidur had him in their control.

"We need to take him to the principal. He's threatened me before," I said calmly. My heart was thumping in my chest, and my body felt very hot. But on the exterior I had already regained control.

"Let's go," Mr. Garg said, holding Chakra Dev by his collar.

"I'll come, too," Vidur said, leaving no room for argument. We all marched off. I heard the slow hum of voices start up behind us as soon as we left class.

Mr. Garg asked Vidur and me to wait outside the office while he took Chakra Dev in.

"You shouldn't have slapped him. Even teachers aren't allowed to," Vidur whispered.

"I slapped him this morning, too," I said.

"When?"

"Right after assembly. We were alone in class. He was acting badly, as usual."

"Why didn't you tell me earlier?" For a moment I felt that Vidur and I were best friends again.

I shrugged.

"Are you sure he was the one who left the condom?" Vidur asked.

"Yes."

"And you wanted Sheela to talk to him!" Vidur exclaimed, looking at me in disgust as if my suggestion had been as unclean and slimy as the condom.

I shrugged again, though I knew he was right from a rational point of view.

I knew that not a single other teacher, not even Mrs. Pillai, would have put up with my slapping another kid. Mr. Garg was possibly the only person in the school who would have stood by me. I was lucky it had happened in his period.

Mr. Garg came out and told Vidur to come back to class with him. The princi had asked to see me alone with Chakra Dev.

"I told him how you stuck out your neck for him just before schools closed. Does he have a written apology?" the princi asked.

I looked at Chakra Dev, who stared at the wall.

"No, he doesn't. I even called him when schools were closed, hoping to have a civil discussion," I said.

"Did she call you?" the princi asked. Not even the rowdiest boys had any nerve in front of him. His large frame commanded instant respect.

"Yes, sir," he said, then added, "she had a *Playboy*."

"She had what?" the princi asked.

"*Playboy* magazine, in German," Chakra Dev said imperiously. My heart was thudding in my chest. I would end up being suspended from school now. I was afraid my face was turning red and the principal would know it was true.

"Mr. Chakra Dev Yadav, what makes you think your word would hold up against the Head Prefect's?" the princi said, not even bothering to look at me. I was relieved. I had regained my calm.

"Ask her," Chakra stated confidently, looking me straight in the eye.

The princi swirled around to look at me.

"No, sir. It's an absurd allegation," I said without batting an eyelid. Did Chakra Dev think I was as self-destructive as he was? I rarely lied, but I had enough common sense to know that it was absolutely necessary in this case.

"I am going to suspend you," the princi said to him. I wondered how long it would take Chakra Dev to relent and grovel and apologize. There wasn't a whimper from him, but beads of sweat broke out on his face.

"Do you want to be suspended? I don't think your mother will like it," I said suddenly. It wasn't my turn to speak. Normally this would have been impermissible when the principal was meting out justice, but this was the boy for whom I'd stuck out my neck earlier.

He looked at me and then at the principal.

"No, sir, I'd rather not be suspended," he said, too boldly.

"Yadav," the princi roared, "you would have been suspended before the school closings had it not been for this lady's good offices."

"I am sorry, sir."

"Sir, can we give him another chance?" I hadn't planned on coming to his aid. I had opened my mouth, and the words had spilled out on their own.

"What?" the principal asked, looking at me incredulously. Even Chakra Dev looked shocked.

The principal stared hard at me and then at Chakra Dev.

"Go wait outside," he said, looking at Chakra Dev, who walked out of the office.

"What's this nonsense, Anamika?" the princi scolded when we were alone.

"Sir, I think he has family problems," I said, trying to come up with a good reason. I remembered that Sheela had mentioned his anger at his father.

The princi buzzed the school counselor on the intercom. "Mrs. Shah, do you have the files for Chakra Dev Yadav? He's caused trouble before."

While he waited for Mrs. Shah to get back to him, he put his hand on the mouthpiece and said to me, "Really, Anamika, I have to question your judgment on this one."

"Yes, Mrs. Shah," he said, removing his hand from the mouthpiece. I wondered if there was more to Chakra Dev than I knew.

"Both parents alive. No divorce. Anything else?" the princi asked and then hung up. "His problem is himself, Anamika," he said, looking up at me from behind his desk.

"Isn't that everyone's problem?" I asked boldly. My problem was definitely myself. If Chakra Dev's was himself then it explained the affinity I felt for him.

"What do you mean?"

"Sir, if he doesn't improve now it really will be too late," I said. I was convinced.

"The problem, Anamika, is that he has shown no signs of *wanting* to improve."

"Sir, please, for my sake. I've been in this school for twelve years. I've always had a good record. If you value me at all, please forgive him this time," I said. My words were rushed. Even as they came tumbling out, I saw the word "compromise" in my mind, its letters expanding and contracting like a rubber band.

"What are you trying to say, Anamika?"

"Sir, I'll have to resign my Head Prefectship if you don't forgive him," I said recklessly. Now I was sure I had blown it. The princi would see it as a threat and suspend not just Chakra Dev but me. As I spoke I felt my resolve get harder and harder. I would be stubborn and unbudging, like Mina who failed to trot in the horse riding ground even if Sameer *Bhaiyya* beat her with a stick.

"Mandal has driven you kids mad," the princi muttered.

I imagined giving up my badge and Prefect's tie. The whole school would be talking about it. After the excitement died down, I'd be just like any other student. All the enemies I'd made in the course of my duties would feel free to taunt me. In the end it wouldn't matter whether I had resigned of my own will or been divested. The only thing that would count would be that I had no more power.

"What is taking you down this road, Anamika?" he asked.

I stood in silence, trying to reflect, but I could not think at all. Images of Chakra Dev's hand in his pocket, his stranglehold on my neck, the condom on Sheela's desk kept coming to my mind. I saw the princi move some papers on his desk impatiently.

"I can't accept failure. I'm determined not to lose to his sort," I said. I was sure that, having known me for many years, the princi would buy this.

"I will let him go lightly this time. But there is a condition," he said and paused.

"What is the condition, sir?"

"You will have to resign if he misbehaves again," he said.

"Yes, sir."

"Do you understand why I am doing this? I can't let a rowdy student go unpunished just because the Head Prefect has a soft

corner for him. So as a true leader, if you take responsibility for
your troops, you have to fall with them when they fall," he said.

I nodded. In the years he had been the principal he had lec-
tured us every week on leadership, responsibility, moral duty,
becoming a better person. I knew exactly how he thought.

The princi buzzed for the *bahadur* and asked him to send
Chakra Dev back in. I stood in his office squeezing my palms
tighter and tighter. The full impact of the conversation hit me. I
was so used to the privilege of my position, the singularity it
afforded me in the school, that I knew I would feel stripped
without it. Humiliated, ashamed, powerless, and indeed naked.

Chakra Dev came in and stood at attention in front of the
princi.

"You are one lucky hoodlum, but I will leave it to Anamika to
tell you why," the principal said, handing a sheet of school letter-
head and a pen to Chakra Dev.

"Sit there and write an apology statement," he instructed,
pointing to the sofa for visitors, then added, "if you are rounded
up for causing trouble again you will be expelled from school
without any yellow cards or warning suspensions. I want you to
state that and acknowledge it in your apology. And return a copy
signed by your father to my office tomorrow."

"My father is not in the country, sir," Chakra Dev said.

"Then get your mother to sign it," the princi said.

"Anamika, I hope you have a lot of faith in him," the princi
said, rising from his seat. He walked to where I was standing,
touched my shoulder lightly, and whispered, "For your sake, I
hope it works."

I walked back to class thinking about what had happened.
Being named Head Prefect was a reward for all my years in the
school. The Prefectorial Ceremony was the biggest event in the
school each year. The Head's appointment was debated internally
by the teachers and the previous year's Prefects with great passion
for months. My parents had been incredibly proud when I was
invested with the position. Even my classmates had celebrated. I
would have a lot of explaining to do if I were forced to resign. No

one would believe I was doing it voluntarily for Chakra Dev. Rumors would start that I had done something wrong, like cheat or steal, and that to save face a resignation had been accepted in place of an impeachment. Staking my badge for Chakra Dev was like staking twelve years of my school life—my hard work, my grades, my extracurricular accomplishments. Was all of this worth it for a mere "soft corner," if indeed that was what it was for?

When I got back to class I discovered Sheela sitting next to Vidur, the offending piece of latex still on her desk, and the class, between copying physics formulae, turning around every so often to make sure it was still there. I had no option but to go and sit at Chakra Dev's desk. I casually turned to his schoolbag with the pretense of taking out his physics book and tried to see if it held any other clues to his soul.

Chakra Dev returned to class after Mr. Garg's period had ended. Hydrogen Sulfide was late as usual, so there was no teacher when he came to claim his desk.

Politely and softly, so that no one else could hear, I asked him to remove the condom and clean Sheela's desk. I gave him my handkerchief.

"You can toss the hanky once you're done," I said.

Without arguing or saying anything snide he walked over to Sheela's desk. Everyone was watching. The class had never been so silent in the absence of a teacher. He borrowed a piece of paper from someone and picked up the condom with it. Then he wiped the desk a few times with my hanky and put it in his pocket.

He walked back to my desk, where Sheela was still seated, and said to her, "I am sorry for doing that. Now you can go back."

Sheela was too taken aback to say anything. She lifted her books from my desk and left. The class started to murmur again as attention lifted from Chakra Dev.

"I took the liberty of taking out your physics book," I said.

"It's okay," he said. Then he put his hand in his pocket. I was terrified that he would produce the hanky. Despite all my prurient interest and my instincts for playing the devil, I did not want to touch it.

"Here," he said, giving me a folded sheet of paper. "It's a photocopy of what I wrote for the principal. He told me to give it to
you."

"I need to talk to you on the phone later today," I whispered.
He nodded in acknowledgment, equally discreetly.

The rest of the day dragged. I was distracted and nervous.
When I walked through the corridor I felt as if my badge had
already been taken away. It made me feel as if I were not wearing
my shirt and my nipples were visible.

On the bus ride home I read Chakra Dev's note. In a staccato
tone he owned up to the bomb as well as to having placed the
offensive item on Sheela's desk. He used the brand name Nirodh
instead of the word "condom." He apologized for having disre-
spected me on more than one occasion. The only point of interest in the letter was his confession that what he had placed on
Sheela's desk was a soiled prophylactic, one that he had personally used before. What had the principal thought? Had he even
read the note or just filed it away, telling Chakra Dev to present
me with a copy out of courtesy? Courtesy?

I slipped the letter in my bag. At home I tried to relax. I asked
Rani to lie down with me and told her about India's party.

"Deepak will be there with his wife," I said.

"Will Vidur *baba* come?" she asked.

"Yes, he is coming with my friend Sheela. He likes Sheela," I
told Rani.

In the evening when my mother and Rani got dinner ready I
tried to assess the school situation. Was I better off not telling
Chakra Dev about the deal I had struck with the princi? He
might decide to do something nasty again, just to spite me. I
decided not to call him at home. I would bide my time and see if
he returned the signed note to the princi.

I tried to convince myself that resigning my Head Prefectship
was of little consequence. I told myself there were bigger things
to think about, like my relationships with India and Rani. If I
were going to leave the country, everything with Rani would end
in less than a year, so I decided to make the most of it. The bliss

and sweetness of our time together heightened as the expiry date appeared in my mind's eye. We slept in a tight embrace, my chin on her shoulder and her hand holding my neck.

At school the next day Sheela materialized with light makeup on her eyes. She fluttered her eyes when I walked up to her. We set up a rendezvous for the break.

The first four periods flew by. I looked back at Chakra Dev a couple of times. He looked somber. I couldn't be sure he had really changed, but he didn't have the usual air of smugness.

In the break Chakra Dev came to my desk and said, "I got the note signed. I am taking it to the princi's office." He unfolded the letter as he spoke and showed me his mother's signature. She had signed in Hindi, which meant that she didn't know English. I was surprised but just nodded. I wondered if the princi was going to call his mother since she obviously would not have understood the letter.

After he left the class, Sheela and I went to the canteen and bought pineapple pastries. We went to the faraway rock to sit and eat them. I told her Vidur was coming to India's party with his parents.

"Can I invite Chakra Dev, too?" I asked.

"After what he did to me yesterday, how can you even think of it?" she asked, looking hurt. I wished he'd put the idiotic rubber on someone else's desk.

"He will have no choice but to behave himself with all the adults around," I said.

"I don't want to speak to him," she said.

"You don't have to. I'll tell him you won't speak to him," I said.

"Why do you want him there? He's dangerous," Sheela said. I was tempted to tell her how dangerous but then decided against it.

"Sheela, even a demon like Ravana had his good points. Lord Rama himself said that Ravana would be remembered for his good deeds, not just his bad ones. And he himself conducted Ravana's last rites," I said, taking recourse once more in the many shades of gray in Indian mythology.

"I don't like it when you talk about him," she said.

"What should we talk about?"

"If you're going to leave we should talk less and make better use of the time we have left," she said flirtatiously.

"You're right," I said. I moved closer to her and held her hand.

"I never thought I would have a girlfriend," Sheela said.

I had never thought of anyone as a girlfriend before. I thought of Rani and India as women and as lovers.

We spent the next twenty minutes of the break sharing our pastries and not saying very much. Life was adventurous and exciting. For once I felt I was living it instead of waiting for it to happen.

Mrs. Pillai's class was after break. When it ended I went up to her and invited her to India's party. I referred to India as a family friend.

"I'll check with my husband. If we are free we'll come," she said.

In the afternoon India called and said, "I need you all day tomorrow. I want to rearrange the house. You and Deepak need to come in the morning to help me."

"Will you buy olives and lemon rind for martinis?" I asked, remembering the definition of martini I had read in the dictionary.

"Yes, I will. What will you wear?" she asked.

"I am not sure," I said.

"You look good in blue. I think you should wear a blue shirt. What should I wear?"

"I don't know," I said.

"I was thinking of wearing the *choli* I wore in Kasauli."

I remembered Deepak taking every opportunity to touch her spine as he herded her into and out of his car. Adit would probably want to touch her. And all the other men.

"Do you remember that rowdy boy Chakra Dev I told you about? He put a condom on my friend Sheela's desk," I said.

"What happened?" she asked.

"The princi was going to suspend him, but I begged for one last chance."

"What are you going to do?" she asked.

"I thought of inviting him to your party, but my friends don't like him," I said.

"Do you think he would come?" she said.

"He might. Sheela says he's dangerous. What if he breaks your things?"

"Nonsense. We don't need to worry about some school kid with Deepak here. He's a black belt in karate," India said.

"And Vidur's father, Adit, is a colonel in the army," I said.

"There you go, it'll be fine."

"I'm afraid Vidur and Sheela will boycott me if he comes. What should I do?"

"That's for you to decide. If you're ready to risk their friendship and really want this guy to come, then call him. But don't worry about the *badmash*, worry about going against your friends' wishes."

"I'm going to change him. Everyone will agree I did the right thing when it works," I said.

I had already risked my badge, my parents' pride, and my teachers' faith. I would put my friendships on the line as well. I would perish or flourish with Chakra Dev or not at all. If I didn't want to commit *sati*, I would have to win.

The Beast

The next morning I called Sheela as soon as I woke up. I was determined to keep my other relationships intact even if I was playing dangerously with Chakra Dev. I wanted Sheela to feel that her opinion was important even though I had already decided to invite him to the party.

"I asked India. She said the grown-ups can handle Chakra Dev," I said.

"Anamika, don't tell me I didn't warn you," Sheela said, sighing.

"Will you still come?" I asked.

"Yes. But I'm going to stick to Vidur all night," she said. My stomach tightened. I wondered if she had said it to make me jealous.

"How did your parents agree to let you come to the party?" I asked.

"Adit Uncle came over to pick up Vidur yesterday, and he convinced my mother," she said.

"What happened with Vidur?" I asked.

"Nothing. We played Scrabble," she said.

I hung up on Sheela and called Vidur. India's warning about my friends had seemed ominous.

"It's out of the question," he said.

"Vidur, we have nothing to fear. Your father will be there. My father will be there," I said.

"Anamika, don't you see you are sanctioning his behavior if you reward him with an invitation to a party?" he said. I felt for a second it was Adit speaking.

"He knows I am sanctioning nothing. He was almost suspended by the princi," I said.

"What will he think, then, when you invite him?" Vidur asked.

"He already thinks I have a crush on him," I said.

"Yuck! Anyway, for Sheela's sake you shouldn't," he said.

"I asked her permission. She says she's going to stick to you the whole evening," I said, knowing he would relish the idea.

"If he misbehaves I'm going to beat him to pulp," Vidur said, his voice full of violence.

"You should thank me for this. I'm being a true catalyst, bringing Sheela closer to you."

"But you're doing it for Chakra Dev, not for me," he said.

"Even I don't know why I'm doing it," I said. All I knew was that I was playing with fire. And deep within it felt right.

Having spoken to them both I decided to hold off calling Chakra Dev till later in the day. A last-minute invitation was best. He'd have little time to find a way to make trouble.

Rani and I got ready and went to India's house to help. Deepak was already there. He was wearing a T-shirt, his muscles bulging as he moved India's sofa and shifted her dining table. India gave him instructions and touched his arm more often than necessary.

"Where is Jeet?" I asked.

"I sent him off to his father's. He's too much to handle when there are a lot of people around."

"Did you speak to our headmistress?"

"Yes. She said they'll make a decision on Monday. She said it looked hopeful."

Deepak was sweating profusely moving the side tables. I gave him a hand, talking all the while about everything I had learned from the brochures and asking him questions before he could fully answer the ones I had already posed. India said we had to go to the market.

"I'm ready, Aunty," Deepak said, fishing his car keys out of his pocket. Rani was going to stay back and clean.

"Where to, Aunty?" Deepak asked, turning on the ignition once we were in the car.

"The local market first, then Diplomatic Enclave," she said.

Deepak drove us to the local shopping center, where we went to the general store. India loaded Deepak's car with snacks and fruit juices and then took us to a shop where she bought booze. I didn't want to go inside a liquor store, so I went to a stationery shop. One corner was piled with children's books. I found one that had pictures and simple words like cat, mat, and bat. I bought it for Rani since I had some pocket money with me. Then I went and stood by the car in the heat, waiting for them to return with crates of alcohol.

We drove in silence for a little while. I loved Lutyens' Delhi, the wide roads of Shantipath where all the embassies had their offices. Large, well-trimmed gardens lined every side. Since my parents didn't have a car we didn't come here often.

We soon pulled up in front of a large bakery called Bread Box. It was a corner shop with huge windows that displayed an enormous selection of pastries and breads. The people behind the counter all wore long white paper hats. On one side there was a sitting area with tables.

"I should feed you both for your efforts," India said.

I chose a cheese sandwich with tomatoes.

"Choose a pastry, too, and then why don't you get a table for us," India suggested.

I pointed to the Black Forest and went and sat at a round table for three. There were people, mostly foreigners, at other tables having coffee or soup. At the next table a small unattended child was in a pram. He had blue eyes and fine blond hair. I played with him, making faces. He stared as if he could not see me, but when I brought my glasses down to my nose, raised my eyebrows, and shook my finger like a retired headmistress, he broke into a large smile.

"The lemon for me," I heard an American voice say. I turned in the direction of the voice and saw two tall men bending in front of the pastry counter, looking at the lowest shelf. They were standing very close to each other. I followed my gaze from their shoulders down to see if their bodies were touching. Their hands were interlocked. Not in the usual way that people may casually hold hands, but with each finger interlaced. My heart started to beat fast, as if I were watching a suspense movie. I thought of Rock Hudson. They were both wearing shorts and had strong, muscular legs. I could see one of them in profile; the hair around his temples was graying, and his eyes were blue. He was terribly handsome.

"Ga ga ga," the baby in the pram gurgled at me.

India and Deepak came toward our table, carrying two trays. Deepak had my sandwich on his tray and placed the tray in the middle so that we could eat.

"I better check on him," the handsome man told the other guy, pointing to the baby. The other man had straightened up; I could see that he was younger. He didn't have any gray hair. The older man walked past our table, saw me look at the baby, and said, "Hi."

I smiled at him. India saw the baby and smiled, too.

"Should I buy a few cakes or not?" India asked Deepak.

"Are the caterers making *kheer*?" he asked.

"Yes, and also *khurbani*. But it's nice to have some cakes, don't you think?" India asked, looking at me.

"I don't know," I said. I had never organized a party. My mother managed everything at the dull gatherings in our house. But India's party would be different. All kinds of ad people and freelancers would be there.

"We'll buy some cakes," India said.

The other man came toward our table. He was carrying a tray with three pastries. He was also very good-looking.

"I got everything," he said to the older man. His tray had a lemon tart, a slice of chocolate cake, and another huge pastry with cream oozing from every side.

"Hello," the younger man said, looking at the baby and touching his cheek.

I wanted to look at the two men. I wanted to be invisible and watch them. The younger one was sitting so close to my chair I could feel his body heat, but I could see only the older one.

I turned around to face them and asked, "Are you from America?"

The younger man turned fully to face me and said, "Yes. Have you been there?"

"No. But I want to. I hear it's free," I said.

The older man laughed. The younger one touched my hand and smiled.

I turned back to face India and Deepak. Behind me I heard the soft sound of lips touching.

"I love you, Nathan," I heard the guy near me whisper to the older man.

India brought her hand in front of her mouth so that only Deepak and I could read her lips.

"They are gay," she mouthed.

The younger one got up and pushed his chair into Deepak's in the process. He turned around to look at us. "I'm sorry," he said as he walked in the direction of the men's room.

"No worries," Deepak said, smiling at him.

"How are those pastries?" India asked the older man.

"They're great," he said.

I took a bite of my Black Forest. Deepak had finished his food and was eyeing my cake.

"Can I have a bite?" he asked me.

"Only if you tell me why you called her a 'corrupter of youth,'" I said, pointing to India.

India chuckled.

I had wondered since the dinner in Kasauli if India had been responsible only for Deepak's first drink or for other things as well.

"When I had a crush on the school bimbo, Aunty told me to ask her out. When I wanted to go out late with this girl, Aunty convinced my parents to agree. When I wanted to drink, she got me the booze. When I wanted a cigarette, she lit my first one. The list is endless," he said.

"We should get home and finish up," India said.

"So if you turned out okay in the end it's no thanks to her," I said jokingly.

"On the contrary. I see all these things as part of growing up."

Deepak picked up both the trays and took them away. India went back to the pastry counter. I went over and bent down by the pram.

"It's a boy, right?" I asked.

"Camille's a boy, all right," the older man said.

I wanted to invite them to India's party and ask them a thousand questions about where and how they lived, who took care of the baby, and what they had studied in college. India had paid for the cakes, and Deepak was carrying everything in three large packages. I said bye and ran after Deepak to take one of the packages from him as we headed back to the car.

The sun on the drive back made my eyes spin. Hot-air mirages rose from everywhere, and the road glinted with blinding silver flashes. India pulled out a pair of dark glasses and put them on. By the time we got back to her house it was three. Deepak and I made a beeline for the couch and fell into it. Rani was dusting the living room. India said she would make tea for us.

Deepak and I started talking about America. Rani dusted India's glass cabinets as words like Amherst, Wellesley, Tufts, and Stanford came tumbling out of Deepak's mouth. India came out with a tray that had four cups of tea. I was surprised she had used the same cup for Rani as for us. Before Rani could sit down on the floor with her tea I asked her to sit on the sofa beside me. India didn't show any surprise.

After tea, Rani and I helped India put flowers around the room, and Deepak set up a bar by one corner. Then Rani and I left to go home and freshen up.

I called Chakra Dev as soon as we reached home and invited him to the party.

"Obviously after what you did the other day you can't expect Sheela to talk to you," I said.

"She'll be there?" he asked. I could hear the anticipation in his voice.

A sense of great peril overtook me. Without the risk of injury to myself it would be impossible to know if I was going to end up like a diamond or like a piece of charcoal. When I faced the bathroom mirror while changing, I felt more responsible for the things that were going to happen to me than ever before.

"What are you wearing?" I asked Rani after I had changed.

"One of my two saris," she said simply. I suddenly wanted her to be the most beautiful woman in the room. More beautiful even than India or Mrs. Pillai. I went to my mother.

"Mom, can you give Rani an old sari you don't wear?" I asked. My mother's face looked imposing. I didn't think she was going to say yes. In fact, she looked poised to ask me several questions. But "why?" is all she said.

"I'm tired of her looking like a servant and being treated like a servant. I feel almost as if she is a member of the household. I want her to dress better," I said. After I had spoken I was sure my mother would say with irrefutable logic that Rani was a servant.

My mother opened her cupboard and asked me to choose something. She didn't look too happy, so I couldn't understand why she was doing it.

"Just give her something that's old, that you don't wear," I said.

My mother pulled out a green sari with a golden border. She also took out the matching blouse and petticoat. When Rani wore it I asked her to pull it down and wear it lower on her waist.

"*Memsahib* won't like that," she said, refusing to pull it down.

My parents led the way to India's house, with Rani and me following a few steps behind. We had circumvented the shortcut through the *jhuggi* but had to walk past a small section of it. There was a sudden barbaric sound like the bleating of a dying pig. Before I could recover a man was hissing at Rani and me, his teeth exposed. Rani let out a sharp cry, equally primal. The acrid smell of fear enveloped us. My parents had turned around.

"*Rundee*," he was shouting. The crude Hindi word for whore, just sharper, more derogatory.

clasped his hands in between hers and brought her forehead down to touch them. I was afraid she would fall at his feet.

"Let's go, we are late," my father said, reddening. He nudged my elbow and gestured to me to go ahead.

Rani and I now walked ahead of my parents. I grabbed her hand and held it all the way to India's house, aware my parents were watching, scared I might be suspected, but utterly unable to let go after what had just happened. The streets seemed new, as if I had never walked on them.

Dawat

When we reached India's house and I rang the bell, it sounded louder and more menacing than at any other time. As we waited for someone to open the door I imagined that people were dancing to "Dum Maro Dum" and partaking of chemical substances. Arni answered the door, her bright voice putting aside any misgivings I might have had about the party.

"Hello, Aunty. Hello, Uncle. Hi, Anamika," she beamed.

My parents and Arni immediately started chatting. I left them and walked into the drawing room. Deepak was off to the side, taking everything in. The bar took up a prominent spot. Bottles of booze were lined up neatly in a row, and an ice bucket sat on one edge. I watched my parents from the corner of my eye to gauge their reaction. I thought I detected disapproval on my father's face, but he did not say anything or make it obvious. Deepak walked over to shake his hand.

I suddenly became very anxious about Adit's arrival. I was as tense about my father seeing through him as I was impatient to see him myself.

India came into the room a few minutes later. She was wearing her backless *choli*. It sheathed her bust and torso from the front and left nothing dorsal to the imagination. Anyone who saw it could only want to tear it off. A jet of poison shot into my blood with such unbelievable force I could feel my face and entire body get hot.

"You're looking fantastic, Tripta," my mother said immediately.

"*Namasteji,*" my father said formally.

I knew India had discerned how upset I was—she had read my expression. I wished I could hide my feelings better. She hugged me somewhat coldly. The doorbell rang. I felt great relief. I wanted more people to come into the room. Seeing India half naked like that, the thin bones of her neck exposed and her lower back on display, filled me with shame, desire, violence, jealousy, and distaste. I was glad Rani was mine to own.

Some of India's friends had arrived. The men kissed her on the cheek and touched her back in different spots when they spoke to her. I felt powerless, almost cuckolded. One woman lit a cigarette as soon as she came into the living room. She was even more glamorous than India and regal in her bearing. My father glanced up at her. So did my mother. Rani, who had brought in glasses to place on the bar, also looked at her. As she took her first puff of smoke, her eyes met mine. I thought I saw a smirk on the corner of her lips. I decided to ignore her for as long as I could.

India introduced my parents to some of her friends. I joined the group. Two of them worked at India's old ad agency and were very funny. They told my father about a government contract they had once had and the bureaucratic rigmarole they had to go through for each version of their ad to get approval.

The doorbell rang again. This time Mrs. Pillai and her husband stood in the doorway. "Good evening, ma'am," I said.

"Hello, child. This is my husband, Kotak," she said. I shook his hand.

"This is Tripta Adhikari," I said, introducing India. I took them to my mother and introduced them to everyone in the circle. The bell rang again and more people came in, filling the room. The place felt crowded. One of India's friends was behind the bar, shaking what could only be a martini in a steel glass. He poured it into a long-stemmed glass and handed it to the glamour queen.

I went to the bar and asked him for a Coke. When I turned around I saw that Adit and the family had arrived with Sheela.

They were walking toward my parents. I felt immediate disappointment at seeing Mrs. American Express and her rotund
behind. I had imagined Adit's wife looking like the glamour
queen. I joined my parents, and Adit introduced her to all of
us. Vidur and Sheela were laughing. Sheela had worn a cobalt
blue blouse that lit up her light skin. Her hair tossed about her
shoulders.

Mrs. Pillai and my mother were already involved in their own
separate conversation and returned to it after this new round of
introductions. I watched Vidur's mother for a few seconds. She
was tall for an Indian woman but rather ordinary looking. She
carried herself with a sense of importance. I was sure she had a
lot more power over people with her international banking job
than my parents did in the government or even Deepak did as a
managing director in a small firm. But she lacked the sophistication and urban edge that India and the glamour queen seemed to
possess so naturally.

"Should I get you a scotch?" Adit asked his wife.

"Yes," she said.

Then he looked at my father and asked, "Mr. Sharma, what
would you like?"

"Nothing, thank you," my father said.

I followed Adit back to the bar. On the way Adit saw the
glamour queen. They looked at each other. I told Adit in a whisper about the two foreigners in the pastry shop with the baby.

"They're making a huge mistake. You need a woman to raise
a child."

"Stop being so narrow-minded," I said.

The man behind the bar chatted with Adit as he poured two
glasses. Adit rested his hand lightly on my shoulder, and I saw
the glamour queen look in our direction. We went back to Adit's
wife so that he could give her the scotch. Then Adit said, "Let's
find ourselves a spot."

We walked away from everyone else and stood in the corner.

"Who is Vidur talking to?" Adit asked.

"Mrs. Pillai, our mathematics teacher."

"She's hot."

"And that other woman is even more hot," I said, referring to the glamour queen.

"Way too hot," he said.

"Don't even try."

"I can't. The boss is here," Adit said, looking in his wife's direction.

India walked over to Adit and me.

"I'm Tripta," she said, putting her hand forward.

"Adit," he said, gripping it.

"Are you Vidur's father?" she asked.

"Yes. And you are India herself?" he said. India looked taken aback. I had told her only once about the name I used for her. I wondered if she would be angry that I had told Adit, but she didn't show it.

Deepak saw us talking and came to join us. He was holding Arni's hand. Sheela was now talking to my father. I could tell he liked her. I noticed there were even more people in the room now. India slipped away to greet them. I followed her. From where I was I could see the glamour queen move away from the men she was talking to and walk toward India. I let my hand rest on India's lower back, my thumb pushing inside the edge of her sari.

"This is a great party, Tripta," the glamour queen said.

"I thought it was time," India said. They seemed very comfortable with each other. I could tell they were good friends. But India had never mentioned her to me.

"By the way, I'm Maya," she said, turning to me and offering her hand. I shook it.

"You haven't met? This is Anamika," India said, touching my cheek.

"Nice to meet you," Maya said.

"Want to get a smoke?" India asked Maya.

"I was smoking here," Maya said.

"Let's go to the back veranda. It'll get too smoky inside," India said.

"Coming?" Maya asked me.

"Later," I said. If I disappeared with two women who smoked, my parents would think I smoked, too. I walked over to Mrs. Pillai and my mother, who were talking to the ad agency guys. Vidur had moved to my father and Sheela. I could tell he was not going to leave her side the entire evening. Mr. Pillai had walked over to Adit and Deepak, but Arni was holding court. The men stood quietly listening to her.

"I need some fresh air," Mrs. Pillai said when I reached her.

"We can go to the veranda, ma'am," I said. I led the way. We passed the kitchen on the way. I saw Rani working with someone from the catering company, filling bowls with soup.

On the veranda India and Maya were staring at the sky and smoking. India was standing in the middle of the veranda, and Maya was sitting on a wicker chair. Mrs. Pillai walked to another corner and stared at the stars, too. I didn't know where to stand. I didn't want to breathe in the smoke, but I didn't want to ignore India or the glamour queen or Mrs. Pillai.

"It's a full moon," India said to no one.

"The full moon makes me go mad," the glamour queen said.

"It makes me sad," Mrs. Pillai said. I was surprised she had joined the conversation.

"And you, Anamika?" the glamour queen asked me.

I always imagined walking on the moon or living there, but it had nothing to do with whether the moon was full or not. I didn't respond.

"Mrs. Adhikari, do you have some pills for a headache?" Mrs. Pillai said.

"Sure, but please call me Tripta." She walked back into the house, Mrs. Pillai close on her heels.

I was standing two feet away from the queen and felt incredibly stiff. I was aware of her movements but did not look at her. She threw her cigarette by my foot. I stamped on it with gusto.

"Come here," she said.

I walked to the chair beside hers but remained standing and looked down.

"So, what's your story?" she said.

Who did she think she was, asking me so presumptuously? I just shrugged. We stood for a few seconds in a vastly uncomfortable silence.

"Talk to me. I am so curious about you," she said.

I couldn't tell if she was drunk. I looked into her eyes. They didn't seem unfocused.

"Why are you curious?"

"Tripta told me about your affair," she said. I couldn't blame India for telling her. She must have wanted to tell someone. But I felt ill that this woman saw me as a curiosity, as if I were a monkey on display at the zoo. I wanted to go back inside, but it would seem rude.

"When did she tell you?"

"Just last week, when you almost got caught." It was when I had told Adit as well. I grunted. "I'm sorry, maybe I shouldn't have mentioned it," she said. I kept silent. She seemed uneasy now that she had upset me. "When Tripta told me about you, I really couldn't understand how she could like someone so young. But as soon as I saw you I knew it was you and could see why it had happened," she said. She was speaking rapidly, as if she were trying to sweep away the earlier awkwardness.

"I guess that's a compliment," I said, lightening up.

India came back on the veranda. There was no one else with her. She came to where I was standing and immediately took my hand.

"I don't want Maya to charm you away from me," she said, squeezing my hand. I kissed India on the cheek. I heard a footstep on the veranda. It was Chakra Dev. I had never seen him out of school uniform. He was wearing pleated pants and a shirt almost the same shade of blue as my own. He had even worn a tie in the stifling heat. He looked like any other person. Almost like one of the young *ad wallas*.

"Hi," I said and proffered my hand. He came closer and shook it. I smelt Old Spice.

I introduced him to India, calling her the host.

Then India introduced him to the glamour queen. "This is my friend Maya."

"Hi, Chakra," Maya said with a smile, unaware of all the shenanigans I had gone through to get him here.

"Hello," he said. I noticed he hadn't called her "Aunty."

"So are you one of Anamika's school friends?" Maya asked.

"Yes," he replied, smiling. He had a dimple when he smiled. I hadn't noticed it in all our years in school. I smiled myself, amused that we were suddenly having to say we were friends.

"Did you meet the others yet?" I asked, looking at Chakra.

"No. I came straight to the veranda since the servant said you were here," he said.

"Do you want something to drink?" I asked him. I wanted him to be nice to me.

"If you go back in, can you get me another martini?" Maya asked Chakra.

"Sure," he said. I went into the house, and Chakra followed me. I wondered if he knew what a martini was. When we passed the kitchen Rani saw us and stared at him for a second.

In the living room I saw Adit and walked over to him.

"Adit, this is Chakra Dev Yadav. He's in our class," I said. Chakra Dev looked surprised at hearing me address Adit by name.

"Hello, Uncle," Chakra said, shaking his hand.

"Oh, yes! I've heard about you from my son," Adit said.

"He's Vidur's father," I explained.

Chakra looked away for a second. Sheela and Vidur were in a corner with Mrs. Pillai, their backs turned to us. They had not seen him yet.

"India's friend Maya wants another martini," I said to Adit.

"Let me make her one," Adit said, touching Chakra Dev's back in a friendly gesture. As they walked toward the bar, I went over to where Vidur and Sheela were talking with Mrs. Pillai.

"He's here. He's behaving," I whispered, coming up to them. Sheela peeked over Mrs. Pillai's shoulder to see for herself while Mrs. Pillai rolled her eyes heavenward. It was a miracle that Sheela was standing so peacefully beside Mrs. Pillai.

"I told Dad about him," Vidur said to us.

"I know. Your father knew exactly how to handle him."

"Will you protect me?" Sheela asked Vidur. She suddenly seemed older than her years.

"Yes," he said, reddening. Sheela looked embarrassed, seeing him blush.

"If the princi knew you were in cahoots with the school *goonda* he'd never have rooted for you to be Head Prefect," Mrs. Pillai said to me lightly.

I wondered if the princi had already told the teachers about our discussion. Maybe all the teachers were watching for Chakra Dev to slip up.

"I thought it was you who rooted for me," I said to Mrs. Pillai, my tone flirtatious.

"I was kidding," she said.

"Anyway, a true leader leads even the blackest sheep," I said, putting my arm on Sheela. Mrs. Pillai and Vidur laughed. Sheela didn't.

I was watching Adit and Chakra Dev from the corner of my eye. Chakra was leaving the bar with two identical glasses in his hands. He walked out of the living room without glancing at us.

"I'll leave Sheela in your able hands, then," I said to Vidur as I made my way to Deepak, who was standing alone. Rani and a butler from the catering company brought in soup on trays.

"Deepak *Bhaiyya*, soup," Rani said to him, handing him a bowl. I had not heard Rani use any term other than *Sahib* or *Memsahib*.

As we drank our soups Adit joined us. "Please convince my parents to let me go abroad," I said to them both.

"I can convince them," Deepak said confidently.

"Can you convince Vidur to do the same while you're at it?" Adit asked Deepak.

"What does he want to do?" Deepak asked.

"*Fauj*. Like me," Adit said.

"I think you're in a better position than I am to dissuade him about the *fauj*," Deepak said.

Adit's wife joined us as well. "Our son is adamant about the army," she said to Deepak.

An *ad walla* came into our circle, though none of us knew him. Adit and Deepak inclined their heads a little to acknowledge his presence. Taking their cue, I did the same.

"I'm working on a multinational bank's account. I heard your wife works for Amex," the *ad walla* said. He had addressed Adit but was looking at Adit's wife.

"I do," she said before Adit could respond.

"Which division?"

"Retail marketing," she said.

"She's always talking shop," Adit muttered to Deepak.

The *ad walla* and Mrs. American Express had launched into a conversation that I could barely follow. India announced that dinner was served, and people made their way to the table to help themselves. I excused myself and walked to the kitchen. Rani was alone. I walked in and grabbed her waist from behind.

"*Babyji*, you scared me," she said.

"I haven't seen you all evening," I said.

She smiled.

"You look happy," she said.

"I am," I said.

"Who was that boy with you?" she asked.

"Chakra Dev."

She gasped. "You didn't tell me you were going to invite him," she said.

"We are in the same class. I decided to make peace," I said.

"I tried it with my husband again and again but he always preferred war," she said.

"Oh! He's fine," I said, leaving the kitchen. Instead of rejoining the party I went out on the veranda to see what Maya and Chakra Dev were up to. They were sitting in adjacent chairs, smoking and looking at the moon.

"I didn't know you smoked, Chakra," I said.

"Now I do," he said, pointing his cigarette in Maya's direction. He sounded a bit drunk.

"I'm going to go and get some food," Maya said, getting up.

"Hey, sit down," Chakra Dev said, pointing to the chair Maya had just left.

I sat down, wishing I had a drink with me and unsure of what to do with my hands. My throat was parched and I felt like having another Coke.

"This party is pretty good. How do you know everyone?" he said, his words unclear.

"I'm friends with Tripta Adhikari," I said.

"You or your parents?" he asked.

"They met her through me."

"I used to think you were stuck up, but you're not," he said.

"No, I'm not."

"I'll forget about Sheela," he said, putting his hand on my knee. Even through my pants they were warm and clammy.

I felt paralyzed. But if I didn't stop him I was afraid he would do something else. I eyed his hand as if it were a snake and slowly moved my hand to his, watching it carefully lest it move. I held his hand by the wrist and gently placed it back on his knee. I didn't make eye contact with him.

"No, I'm serious, I'll forget about Sheela," he said, placing his hand right back on my knee. It felt heavier now.

I was afraid to say anything. He would misinterpret my words exactly as he pleased. I tried moving his hand again. This time he leaned forward. The glass he was holding tipped, and a little spilled on my pants. He noticed.

"I'm sorry," he said, placing the glass on the floor. Clumsily he tried to shake off a few droplets of martini that were visible on my pants. Then he let his hands rest there. I wasn't sure he knew what he was doing and hoped no one came out to the veranda. If Vidur or Sheela or my parents saw this, there could only be terrible consequences. I gripped both of his wrists as firmly as I could. He moved even closer into my space, his face dangerously close to mine, his breath smelling of alcohol, his lips wet.

I moved my head farther back in the chair. His head was hanging low, and his hair brushed across my cheek. I could smell his scalp; he had applied some kind of oil to his hair. I was wondering what to say. I was afraid how my voice would sound.

"Is it true you'll have to resign next time I do something?" he asked.

"Yes," I said. I looked him straight in the eye when I said it because I knew he would not believe me otherwise. I felt I was in greater proximity to him than I had ever been to India or Rani. The smell of liquor mixed with that of Old Spice and his sweat.

"Come closer," he said, his head swaying midair as he looked at me.

"Chakra Dev, take control of yourself," I whispered urgently.

"I won't tell anyone," he whispered back, raising his head a little to look at me. I pulled my head away from him.

"Oh!" I heard a woman say from the doorway. Chakra turned his head.

"I don't want to disturb you two lovebirds," Maya said, emerging onto the veranda.

"You're not disturbing us at all," I said. I hoped my voice didn't sound too desperate.

"Did you get your food?" Chakra asked her.

"Yes," she replied.

"Why don't you sit down?" I suggested, getting up from the chair.

"No, no, don't worry," she said.

"No, really, I have to go inside," I said firmly. Before Chakra Dev or Maya could say anything to stop me, I was striding back into the house. I went straight to the bathroom and locked the door. I convinced myself that Chakra Dev had moved that close to me only because he was drunk. I decided it was best to make my way to the drawing room and simply avoid him for the rest of the night. Thanks to Maya I had gotten out of the situation without a scene. One had to be careful with the words one used with him or he would explode. I was afraid of him.

I washed my face in the sink and dried it with India's towel. Then, having regained my composure, I stepped out into the darkened bedroom.

"I thought you'd be here," he whispered. I could make out his faint shape as my eyes got used to the darkness. He moved closer and clasped my hand in his. I jerked my hand away from him with much greater force than I needed because I thought he was going to tighten his grip. My hand hit the wall behind me. I shook it out.

"Why are you running away?" he asked. He sounded dazed, hurt.

I wasn't quite sure what to say.

"Chakra Dev, you've drunk too much," I finally said.

"You should have some, too. That martini was good."

"Please don't misbehave here. Don't cut my nose in front of everyone," I said in Hindi.

"Why are you so worried? Don't you trust me?" He spoke slowly.

He took my hand in his tenderly and looked at it. "Does it hurt?"

This time I didn't pull it back. His palms were still a little clammy, but they were soft.

He turned his body in slow motion to face me. I gradually tried to reduce the contact between his hand and mine, moving mine out of his an inch at a time. When I had just about freed it I pulled my hand down, accidentally brushing it against the front of his pants. I felt the sudden shock of something rigid. I froze. His eyes closed for just a second, and he smiled. Then he seemed to recover himself and shifted in embarrassment.

"I have to go," I said brusquely and sought to leave the room before he could say anything. It was dark and I walked the few steps to the corridor so quickly that the edge of my glasses collided with the wall. I could feel the crunch of my frames on my temples.

I stood in the corridor, back in the light, readjusting my spectacles. "Are you all right?" I heard Adit's voice boom from behind me. He was walking back to the living room from the veranda. He must have gone looking for me.

"Yes, I'm fine," I said, moving away from him. I didn't want to talk to Adit in front of the bedroom where he would notice Chakra Dev lingering in the dark.

As I passed the kitchen I saw Rani tending a large kettle of tea. The party was going on as if everything were normal. I went to the bar and got a glass of water to calm myself down.

"Your parents told me about Rani's husband. Were you scared?" Adit asked, catching up with me.

It took a second for me to realize what he was talking about.

"Oh yeah, I was knocked out of my wits," I said. I felt knocked out of my wits now.

I saw my parents engaged in a discussion with Vidur and Sheela and Deepak.

"Let's go to them," I said.

Everyone was eating and talking. The sight and smell of the rich food on their plates made me ill. The room was filled with too many sensations. It was the opposite of what it had been like in the dark with Chakra Dev. Against my will I remembered what my hand had touched.

Deepak looked at Adit and put his hand on his shoulder, saying, "Colonel, I think I'll eventually convince your son."

"You will? How?" Adit asked.

My father chimed in, "Deepak has been saying that it doesn't matter where great discoveries are made. They benefit all of humanity in the end."

"Hence, country of origin and country of discovery are not important," Vidur said.

"And all mankind is one," Deepak said.

"I think our kids should be studying wherever they can best achieve their full potential," Adit said, looking at my father. On the surface they were joined by their concern for their children, for Vidur and me. But I wondered if this fraternity of fathers was real for Adit.

Chakra Dev walked into the drawing room. His face had a freshly washed look. He stood in the doorway for a second and looked around. He took a plate from one of the waiters as his eyes panned the room, eventually coming to rest on our group. To my absolute horror he started walking toward us. I dreaded his every step. I was sure my father and everyone else would smell the alcohol on his breath. Sheela and Vidur would give me a superior look to let me know they had been right. I prayed fervently that he wouldn't make an ass of himself.

"Can I join in?" Chakra Dev asked. I looked at someone else when he spoke. His words didn't sound as slow as they had in the bedroom. I felt my stomach relax a little after he had spoken.

"Yes, of course," my father said, stepping back a little to enlarge the circle.

"I was just trying to convince your classmates that they should go abroad to study," Deepak said to Chakra Dev. I didn't want to see Vidur's or Sheela's reaction to his joining the group. Or his face. Or anyone else's.

"I don't think it's the same whether you invent something in your country or in a foreign country," my mother said.

"I agree with Aunty. The Japanese make cars and cameras, and it's their country that benefits," Sheela said. I was surprised to hear her speak in front of adults. Everyone turned to look at her, including Chakra Dev, who was stuffing a *naan* in his mouth. I looked away.

"I'm going to go to New York. My father is there," Chakra Dev said, almost quarreling, his mouth full of *naan*.

"What does he do, *Beta*?" my father asked him. My hand was sweating. I dried my palm on my pants.

"We just got a letter from him saying he has a deli. What's a deli?" Chakra Dev asked.

"A delicatessen. It's a store that sells everything from bread and cheese to essentials, like a corner shop," Deepak explained.

"My father says I can study at a community college," Chakra Dev said. He was talking much more than I would have expected him to. He seemed comfortable talking to adults.

"How is the food? You're the only one not eating, Anamika?" India said, coming to our group with Maya.

"The food is great, thank you," Adit said.

"Let me get something," I said, deciding it was a good way to escape. I pulled Sheela away with me.

Maya threw a knowing glance at Chakra Dev and me as I left.

I put a *naan* on my plate and ate it standing in a corner with Sheela. It was stuffed with ground almonds and raisins.

"He's actually behaved better today than he ever has at school," Sheela said.

I nodded even though at that very moment I had been debating whether I should tell Sheela that Chakra was drunk and that she shouldn't talk to him alone if he tried to.

Maya separated from the group and came to us. "Why don't you like me, Anamika?" the glamour queen asked. Sheela had her arm around me and was listening to us, but Maya was talking as if Sheela were just a kid and didn't understand. I felt Sheela's arm stiffen when Maya spoke.

"I don't dislike you," I said.

"I think you're scared of me," she said with a condescending smile.

"Anamika's not scared of anyone, and she's a great lover, too," Sheela said, walking away from us both toward Vidur. As she left I remembered the glamour that had first attracted me to her. She still had it and knew how to wield it at the right time.

Maya had opened her mouth to say something, but no words came out.

I looked around to check that no one had been within earshot.

"I hope you don't believe I'm scared of you, Maya," I said, looking directly in her eyes.

"No," she said, recovering. With a look in India's direction she added, "But maybe Tripta should be. You're a real Romeo."

"She doesn't need to be. I love her," I said.

Deepak and Arni walked up to us. Deepak said, "I think we'll leave soon. I offered to drop your friend home. He lives really far, and I don't think a bus at this time of the night is a good idea."

I nodded, the word "friend" gluing Chakra Dev to me.

"Let's take our leave," Deepak said to Arni.

They walked toward India. Adit's wife was saying bye to some *ad wallas* who seemed to be taking off. Chakra Dev came up to Maya and me and fidgeted with his tie, but I continued looking elsewhere. From the corner of my eye I saw her put a hand on his shoulder and then run it through his curly hair. I looked at his face directly for the first time since that moment. I wanted to see how he would react to Maya. I even looked down at the zip of his pants. He did not react to her at all.

"*Beta*, take care of yourself," she said to him. I couldn't help feeling that she was warning him about me. She had misunderstood what had happened out on the veranda.

Deepak came up to us and patted my head in a good-bye gesture.

Arni said, "See you soon, Anamika."

Chakra Dev waved as he walked away. He looked at me till he had stepped out of the main door without so much as a glance in anyone else's direction.

"You are wrong about what you saw outside," I whispered to Maya.

"I was? You're really with Sheela, not with him?" she said sharply. What was her problem? India had told me herself not to get too attached. She had inspired me to freelance.

I grabbed a Coke from a waiter who was walking by with a tray of drinks and took a sip.

"You know, I don't need to explain any of my friendships to anybody. Least of all to you," I said. I was fed up with Maya. I took another sip of my Coke, expecting her to leave in a huff. To my amazement, she smiled.

"You're right."

"As long as I can put up with the consequences of what I am doing, I don't see how it matters," I said.

"Yes, yes. It's just that sometimes the consequences are different from what one expects." She spoke as if from personal experience. I didn't feel it was a reproach for what I had said. "I need to smoke a cigarette. Will you come out on the veranda with me?"

"Sure." As we walked away from the living room, I suddenly wasn't worried anymore if my parents thought anything of my going to the veranda with a smoker.

Maya sat down on the chair she had previously been sitting on. I took the one that Chakra Dev had used. The strong smell of him from earlier had dulled and was now a mere fragrance of suspended Old Spice particles. The entire evening diffused within me.

Maya threw her head back and exhaled. It reminded me of India on the terrace in Kasauli. I followed the smoke from Maya's cigarette and thought I could see it rise almost all the way to the moon. The Delhi sky was glittering with stars, the galaxies dancing in clusters. I felt relaxed for the first time that evening, in fact for the first time since all the tension in school had started with Chakra Dev.

The greatest danger was not that I would have to resign or that I would fail to change Chakra Dev but that he would take me down with him heedlessly. Like the moon pulling at the ocean he pulled my feelings in low tide and high.

I remembered what Maya had said about consequences and realized I agreed with her. "Life isn't like a play or a movie, you can never map the consequences in advance," I said, breaking the silence.

"Yes, but it's hard to live with uncertainty."

I thought of Heisenberg's uncertainty principle. Just as one could never be certain of one's exact position given one's momentum at any instant, I could never be certain of the exact consequences given the impulses of my heart at any instant. And to know my heart with unfailing accuracy was crucial if I was going to be true to myself.

"Isn't uncertainty the price you pay for following your truth, for facing your darkness and fighting it?" I asked.

"I remember thinking like you."

"And?" I prompted her. Had she tried and lost? India had not spoken to me about these things, nor had Adit.

"Your darkness could get the better of you."

Maybe she was right. But I could not imagine losing either to myself or to Chakra Dev. I was sure of my strength. I admired Adit because he had stood in the battlefield and taken a bullet without running away. My battlefield was in my breast. Going to a new country like America where no one from my family had ever set foot seemed like child's play compared to stepping into the vast landscape that had just opened up within me.

I got up from my chair and reached out to kiss Maya's forehead. "I'm glad I met you," I said.

"So am I. You're somehow different than earlier in the evening."

"I feel lighter and clearer. Though Tripta would say I just had a surge of some new chemicals."

Maya chuckled. "I would say I've just managed to charm you."

"Should we go in? Everyone is probably getting ready to leave."

In the living room my father, Adit, and Mrs. Pillai's husband were all shaking hands. Vidur had become comfortable with India over the course of the evening and said, "It was very nice to meet you, Aunty."

I gave India, Sheela, and Maya kisses on the cheek when I said good-bye. My parents and I saw Adit and the Pillais to their cars before we walked back to our house with Rani.

"Your classmates are nice," my father said on the way back.

"Even the so-called *goonda*," my mother added. Obviously Mrs. Pillai or Vidur or Sheela had told my mother quite a lot about Chakra Dev.

Rolle's Theorem

was fast asleep when I felt Rani get up. It seemed the phone had been ringing. I followed her into the drawing room, wondering who was calling.

"Haloo," she said. She turned to me and said, "*Babyji*, for you."

"*Babyji, Babyji, Bitchyji*," he said. It was Chakra Dev. I couldn't tell from his voice if he was joking or serious.

"What do you want?" I said.

"I paid her seventy rupees, and I had thought of you that time." His voice was thick. I could tell that he had drunk a good deal more.

I was silent.

"Say something. I am confessing," he said suddenly, as if we had actually been having a conversation.

"*Chutiya yadav*," I said, slamming down the phone. My hands were shaking.

I felt Rani's arm around my shoulder and realized that she had been standing beside me.

"Are you okay, *Babyji*?" she asked.

"Let's go," I said, holding her hand as we walked back to my room.

Rani and I had been so tired after the party, we had got into bed without changing our clothes. When we were back in the room we took off our clothes.

"It was Chakra Dev, wasn't it?" she asked when we were finally in bed together.

"Yes."

"All *yadavs* are not *chutiyas*, *Babyji*," she said.

"I know that," I said.

"*Yadavs* and my family are the same caste," she whispered.

My anger at Chakra Dev had made me lose my senses. I hadn't even thought for one second that my comment would have hurt Rani.

"I didn't know. But my fight with him was really about something else," I said.

"I understand," she said.

"You believe me, don't you? It's just that he keeps calling me a *brahmin chutiya*. I just got angry with him this time," I explained, feeling bad at having hurt her.

"Are you all right?" she asked.

"Yes. I just need you," I said, hugging her tightly.

"I am always here," she said, the love of her "always" plugging the holes in my heart.

I spent Sunday trying to study for the Monday tests in mathematics and physics and anxiously anticipating the meeting with the counselor at USEFI in the afternoon.

Between my chapters and sums my mind would flash to Chakra Dev. It was impossible not to remain preoccupied with what he had said about the seventy-rupee woman. Had he really thought of me? The information filled me with distaste, but after all my affairs what right did I have to be sanctimonious about Chakra Dev's personal life? The drink with Maya had probably given him the courage to approach me on India's veranda. He had made the mistake of phoning and confessing in a weak moment in the middle of the night. He had made himself vulnerable to me in a way I had never done to my lovers.

As I sat in my room thinking about him, Rani came to inform me that there was a phone call for me.

"Hello," I said into the receiver.

"It's Chakra," he said.

I remained silent. I wanted him to realize I was angry.

"It's me," he repeated.

"I knew you would call," I finally said.

"You did?"

"I know you better than you think."

"Anamika, I have an urgent question. Did I call you last night?"

"Yes." As soon as I had spoken I wanted to kick myself for having replied so swiftly. He was like a wild animal. If I observed him long enough I would learn to communicate with him in a language that he understood.

"I am so so sorry," he said. He sounded as though he meant it.

"Are you?" I asked.

"Listen, please forget last night. Please forget whatever I said."

"Was it true?" I asked.

He was silent.

"Was it true?" I repeated. This time my tone was the same one I used in assembly.

After a moment of silence he quietly said, "Yes."

"God damn you," I said.

"I'm going to fail the test tomorrow," he said, changing the conversation.

I was silent. I decided it best to let him steer the conversation for the moment.

"Anamika?"

"Just study Rolle's theorem and you'll get passing marks. Do you need me to explain it?"

"Is this your *brahmin* idea?" he said, turning irritable. He had hesitated a second before *brahmin* as if he had stopped to eat the word *chutiya* that would have naturally followed.

"What are you talking about?" I asked.

"To stake your badge for me, invite me to the party, help me with the test?"

"All my ideas are *chutiya brahmin* ideas by definition, aren't they?" I asked grimly.

"Huh?"

"Do you want me to explain Rolle's theorem or not?" I asked, my impatience now obvious.

He sighed. "Yes, wait, let me get my book." Whenever I got irritated with Chakra Dev and was ready to walk away, he relented.

I waited for Chakra Dev to bring his book. I explained whatever I could by looking at my notes from Mrs. Pillai's class. At the end, it was like having explained something to Sheela—I didn't know if Chakra Dev had really understood anything.

"I am going to USEFI tomorrow. Do you want to come? If you want to go to the U.S., you will have to take some exams and apply to colleges months in advance," I said.

"I can't come tomorrow," he said.

"Why? Are you busy with the seventy-rupee woman?" I asked, unable to help myself.

"Anamika, I'm sorry about it. Please," he said.

"I'll bring information for you," I said, relenting. "Okay, bye," I added, wanting to end the conversation before it took another turn for the worse.

"Anamika," he said, and then paused.

"What?"

"Thank you for inviting me to the party. I really enjoyed it. I'm sorry I drank." I detected none of the derision I had come to expect from him.

"I want to be able to trust you," I found myself saying. Like in all of my conversations with him, we maintained an elliptical orbit around each other. Only time would tell if I was right or wrong about him. After all, life itself—its environment and reproducing mechanisms and all of mankind—had arisen from the complete disorder that followed the Big Bang, a moment when the universe was smaller than a nut and infinitely hot. Even I could emerge calmer, more functional, a better human being from the anarchy of Chakra Dev's world.

The next day in class, as I sat through the test, I cast a backward glance at Chakra Dev to see how he was doing. I had guessed correctly, and the main question for ten marks was on Rolle's theorem. I saw him write for a while and then stop. It seemed like he didn't know any other application of differential calculus.

In the break, Vidur and Sheela and I went to the canteen. They said they had enjoyed the party. Vidur said he was trying to convince his mother to let him have a big party at home one night for the class. He said his father was all for it but his mother was afraid we would leave the house a mess. Vidur said he had almost been taken in by Deepak's arguments for going abroad, which made me think my parents would eventually come around to the idea.

"So, will you go to America, too?" I asked. I was sure we would become best friends again if we both went abroad.

"No. But I'll come with you today. I promised my dad," he said.

"Why don't you come, too?" I asked Sheela.

"You're both traitors," Sheela said. I could see guilt release its colors on Vidur's face.

"He's not going to apply. He's just coming along," I said, defending him.

"We should go to support Anamika," Vidur said. "Deepak *Bhaiyya* is fun. We can get ice cream later," he pleaded.

In the afternoon, when Deepak came to pick us up from school, we all packed into his car. I asked Vidur to sit in the front seat so Sheela and I could sit in the back.

"I have good news for you," Deepak said.

"What is it?"

"Tripta Aunty just called my office. Jeet has been admitted into your school," he said.

"I'm happy," I said. At least one positive thing had happened while I was Head Prefect. If Chakra Dev made me lose face in front of the entire school, then maybe in the future Jeet would make up for it.

At USEFI I waited anxiously for the counselor to call me in while Vidur and Sheela played a word game, oblivious of my nervousness. I looked over Deepak's shoulder as he flipped through assorted glossy material on various universities. The brochures each had a letter of introduction from the dean, a few pages on student life, information on courses, and colorful pictures. Everything was highly professional; even most Indian corporations didn't have this kind of material.

A bookshelf in the waiting room was filled with large folders arranged alphabetically. I walked up to the shelf and pulled out a folder marked "H." There were hundreds of universities listed under *H* alone. The number of students, degrees granted, and other statistics appeared on each page. Harvey Mudd was known for its sciences, a true science university. How could a country with a quarter of India's population have so many more institutions of higher learning? Deepak had warned me that there was too much choice and that I should apply only to the best. By their fact sheets and brochures, they all looked like the best. How would I choose?

"Anamika," a woman called, popping her head out from the counselor's office. A boy walked out from her office carrying a folder. She saw him out and said, "Good luck."

I walked to her office.

"Shut the door behind you," she said. She was good-looking and very young. I was expecting someone like Mr. Garg, not someone wearing jeans and a red top and sporting short hair like mine. She smiled.

"I'm Sim," she said.

"Hi," I said nervously.

"Your profile is very interesting. It's very good," she said.

"Thank you," I said, staring at her desk. It was neat and clean, free of clutter.

"What do you want to study in college?" she asked.

"I am not sure," I said. I suddenly wanted to tell the truth. I didn't want to end up going to a place like Harvey Mudd and doing only physics or mathematics. I wanted to keep my options open.

"You should definitely go to a liberal arts school. You can try different things, then. I would suggest you apply to a few Ivy Leagues and then some second-tier schools."

I nodded. Deepak had told me about Ivy Leagues. The dictionary had yielded a definition about social prestige and scholastic achievements.

"How many should I apply to?" I asked.

"Six to be safe, I think. Three Ivies and three others." She explained the application procedure to me and told me the tests I had to take.

"I kept some college materials for you. I think you're the best candidate from Delhi who has walked through the door this year," she said, pointing to her office door.

"Thanks," I said.

"There are others with the same grades, but you have the best extracurriculars."

I smiled sheepishly. I could suddenly think of no extracurriculars except Sheela and India and Rani. I felt hot in the face.

She had brought out a massive folder that was pleated like an accordion. She opened its big flap and pulled out a glossy brochure. She turned to the first page and pointed to the table of contents to show me how the information was organized and what was worth reading. I saw the back of the brochure. There was a crest in crimson, and below it "Veritas."

"Meritas," I thought to myself.

Acknowledgments

For his support of this novel at a critical stage, I would like to remember the late Giles Gordon, unforgettable and sorely missed.

For support in the form of grant money, I am grateful to the New York Foundation for the Arts. Many heartfelt thanks to Claudette Buelow and Robert Steward for immensely useful criticisms of multiple versions of this book. For their valuable comments on my first draft, I thank: Ashwini Sukthankar, Devika Daulat-Singh, Krzysztof Owerkowicz, and Plamen Russev. For their hospitality during my itinerant months spent working on this novel, I am indebted to Yasmin Boyce, Beti Cung, Margarita Michail and Raoul Kantouras, Sabita Uthaya and Trishul Mandana, Brent Isaacs, Freyan Panthaki, and Priti and Ravi Aisola.

To everyone at Curtis Brown in London and Anchor Books in New York involved with this book at various stages, thank you for your dedication. I am, above all, grateful to my editor, John Siciliano, for his belief in *Babyji* and his painstaking thoroughness in getting it to its current form.

The unflinching support and undiluted love of my mother, my father, and my aunt have sustained me. Without them, nothing would be possible.